The Iskander

Prophecy

One king to rule them all

Richard Westover

The Peter Leroux series

The Rand Conspiracy

The Iskander Prophecy

ABOUT THE AUTHOR

Richard Westover was born in 1967 and lives with his wife and family in London.

DEDICATION

for

my daughters

May 1453, Constantinople

Swim like a dog! A crossbow bolt whirred in the still air, skipping like a stone beyond him. *Paddle faster!* He flinched at the close harsher shouts, flaming torches flickering through the trees, paws scrabbling on the foreshore. Pain seared through his shoulder as the next bolt scoured through wet skin. He gasped and let himself sink, hiding in the inky womb until his lungs screamed. The current would carry him. He drifted to the surface. The hounds still snarled but only tussling over his kaftan on the rocks, the voices fainter now and uncertain. *You were tested Alexander, keep the faith.*

He rolled onto his back and lay still, his breath rasping in his head as he calmed, and he prayed that the silence would fox his pursuers. The stars were familiar friends and the current pushed him the right way. *God favours you, Alexander.* He smiled as the seawater stung the welts that striped his wrists, a fresh reminder of his freedom. Three years a slave since he had been captured on a pilgrimage to the imperial city and had chosen conversion to Islam over the sword. How he had dreamed of seeing the Church of Holy Wisdom in all its glory and now he was within sight of the city walls, the walls that had never fallen. God willing, the intelligence he carried would keep it that way. And he could study to be a monk again. He just needed to round the headland and cross the harbour.

1

That was far further than he had ever swum, but the work of carving stone balls for the soldiers' bombards had calloused his ink-stained hands and made him strong. And he had learnt much about their strategy too, which filled his heart with hope.

Lights beckoned on the distant ramparts. The current would tug him back when he reached the turning point. He had to keep right or be sucked into the Sea of Marmara, where his corpse might even pass as far as the Hellespont. He concentrated on his breathing, his stroke, blocking out the pain in his shoulder, the current pulling against him now. Acrid smoke drifted by, and the tang of gunpowder stung his nostrils. He choked on a gulp of water and faltered, clawing at the sea, and he clenched his teeth against their chatter. *Don't let my strength fail me now.* The call of the muezzin reached out to him over the sea, a cold hand on his shoulder weighing him down as the companions he had left behind were summoned to evening prayers. *You could not have risked freeing them, the information you carry is too important.*

Something loomed ahead, and he thought he heard the clank of iron. The fabled chain across the Golden Horn! Great timbers fastened together with iron plates made a platform, about twenty paces long. Sheer-sided at first, above it receded like a pyramid. An enormous chain hung from the top, curving down through the stars in the direction of the city. The outline of another pontoon bobbed dimly against the backdrop of walls and towers. He flailed in vain for purchase on the slimy wood as the water swirled, sucking and slapping. A thinner chain descended to the depths to his right. He lunged at it, but a swell knocked him against the side and pulled him down. The shivers had got him. He thrashed and

2

kicked, just breaking the surface, and screamed to the heavens, 'Do not forsake me!'

'Oi!' A lantern swung over the guard rail.

'The Turks are attacking!'

'Nah. Looks like someone drowning. Who goes there?'

'Help me!'

An end of rope splashed by the novice. He grabbed it and held it as close as a splinter from the true cross while they hauled him over the side and onto the deck.

'Who are you, laddie?'

'They call me Iskander.'

20th July 1896, The High Court of Justice, London

Peter Leroux slunk into a seat at the back of the courtroom as the three presiding judges conferred on the bench. He gripped the smoothed woodgrain of the seat edge, the scent of varnish mingling with the musky anticipation of his neighbours. A trial at bar was reserved for the most important of cases. In the matter of "R. vs Jameson, Willoughby and others," the first named defendant walked in alone. The Queen had made Dr Leander Starr Jameson a Companion of the Order of the Bath just two years before but now she was R, or Regina. The prosecutor. A high colour burned across Jameson's wide forehead as he traversed the room. A man of giant reputation, he scarcely stood level with the chin of his counsel. He shrank into his seat, crossing his sinewy limbs.

It was the first time Leroux had set eyes on Dr Jameson, although he felt partly responsible for the man's predicament. Dr Jameson, under the orders of Cape Colony prime minister Cecil Rhodes, had led a private army in a reckless attempt to overthrow President Kruger of the Boer Republic. It was a daring plan to gain the immense gold resources of the Witwatersrand for the British Empire, but it had been a fiasco. Leroux had been there, a junior journalist on an assignment for Rhodes. And he had made a decision, a decision to prevent a war engulfing his homeland, a decision that doomed Rhodes's plan to failure.

Jameson bowed his head and gazed absently at the floor. His heavy eyelids drooped, unflinching as the bang of the senior judge's gavel echoed around the chamber and the last few places filled in silence. Timing is everything, as every lion and springbuck knew. Jameson had pounced too early, before the miners of Johannesburg had risen in rebellion. He had crossed the border as an invader, not a saviour, and the Colonial Office had been obliged to denounce the raiders, killing the rebellion in its crib. Rhodes had resigned in disgrace and refused to produce the cablegrams between himself and the Colonial Office, ensuring that the buck passed no higher. The blame would fall to Jameson. His dark frockcoat, spotless white necktie, and pale grey gloves invoked the family physician he had once been, rather than the buccaneer he had become. But the attire of an English gentleman would not help him here or in Holloway.

The barristers' wigs bobbed and nodded out of earshot, as they passed papers between them. Not one of Jameson's defence team caught Leroux's eye. Why had they not called him as a witness? No attempt had been made to contact him. It was as though he did not exist. Probably for the best. His testimony might incriminate the Colonial Office, but it would not show Jameson in a good light. The prosecution would not call him, for they wanted to sweep the government's involvement under the carpet. And Leroux was not in a hurry to offer his testimony. He had cabled the Colonial Office when Jameson crossed the border. But he had not told Rhodes the whole story, because he had also alerted President Kruger, who captured the raiders before they could start a war and handed them over to the British as prisoners for punishment. Now they were back in Britain to face trial.

Rhodes had been pleased enough with Leroux's work to recommend him to Whitehall as a man of useful talents. Better to let sleeping dogs lie. The lancet windows of the High Court would shed no more light on the matter, and Leroux slipped outside and donned his battered slouch hat.

July 1896, Ottoman Armenia

'Do they know what they have done?' Zeki Pasha said, squinting against the sun. He brushed his hand over the silver decoration on his breast and whispered the words inscribed on the back, 'Medal for those that have shown exceptional loyalty and bravery for the Ottoman Empire.' He remembered the day the Sultan had bestowed the Imtiyaz upon him as though it were yesterday but prayed that he would be able to forget this day. His scarlet fez tapered in the style favoured by the Sultan and its lustrous black tassel swung lazily across the back of his neck at the proscribed length. His horse whickered and swished its tail, while next to him a man looking uncommonly large astride a hardy mountain pony sighed and pulled out his pocket watch, flipped open the cover, and raised his spyglass.

Down in the valley, a village nestled by the broken water of a stream. Neat, white stone houses gleamed in the sun under terracotta roofs. They dotted the path from the church, which stood proudly below a conical steeple reminiscent of Mount Ararat. Sheep grazed in the blossoming meadows and an occasional scream of delight carried up the slopes from a group of children playing by the water.

'These people?' the man said, 'No, but they will serve their purpose, nonetheless.'

The Pasha suppressed a pang of conscience and followed the cast of the man's spyglass. Could he trust him? They conversed in French, the

7

language of diplomacy at the Sublime Porte, the seat of the Sultan's government. 'Your information is sound?'

'The name I gave you is an Armenian revolutionary,' the man said keeping his eye to the glass, 'It is you who said that he comes from here.'

The Pasha had not expected a straight answer. They were not friends but for now they shared a common interest, although they could never let it be known. His hopes that the Sultan would become a liberal reformer had withered. The Sultan had dissolved parliament and hoarded power in his own hands, dismissing many of the modernisers. But one day the Sultan would make a mistake, and the Young Ottomans would be ready.

'It is nearly time,' the Pasha said, surveying the road which led down from the settlement and curved around the bulwarks of the mountain. The church bell rang once, and he signalled to his attendant, who barked out a command. A large red banner unfurled and snapped in the wind gusting over the ridge. Below, a troop of light cavalry trotted up the road towards the village. The commanders and most of the men wore bright blue tunics edged in gold that reached down to their calves, while the rest rode in sheepskin vests and loose striped broadcloths bound by sashes. Curved swords glinted in their hands. The Pasha looked to the far end of the village where another squadron formed astride the road to the mountain pass. He was the Sultan's commander in these provinces and was pleased to see the soldiers putting on a disciplined display in front of the foreigner.

'So, they are the Hamidiye?' the man said and collapsed his glass, tucking it into his jacket. 'You can rely on these men? They are Kurds, are they not?'

'Yes, Kurds. Once they ruled this land and the Christians here, but we broke their castles and they became brigands, proud and cruel. Their hatred of us is surpassed only by their jealousy and contempt for the Christians who now prosper. They will do as commanded.'

'Will they talk?'

The Pasha held the man's stare. 'No. They face no retribution from the law as long as they follow the Sultan's orders. And here, my orders are the Sultan's orders.'

'Ha! For doing your dirty work,' the foreigner said.

'For protecting our eastern provinces from traitors,' the Pasha said.

'Touché,' the foreigner said, but there was no curve in his mouth.

Across the stream, on the far slope, horsemen nudged their mounts forward and picked their way down between the rocks, dislodging one which tumbled down towards the churning water, clacking as it smashed into ancient boulders strewn over the ground.

A villager stopped and turned. He shielded his eyes, shouted out in alarm, and the church bell rang again and again. Children ran, summoned up from the stream by the desperate clanging, and elders emerged from the modest dwellings to gather them in. Curls of smoke rose where the horseman lit torches and trotted down to the village, corralling the few villagers that ran in their direction. One stood his ground, a man thin with age, in a loose shirt. A scimitar flashed in the sunlight as it arced down, and the man collapsed in a spray of scarlet and disappeared under thundering hooves.

'It begins,' murmured the Pasha as the villagers scrambled into the church seeking shelter.

'How they bleat as they flock to the slaughterhouse. Why won't they fight? Do they not want to die with honour?' the man said.

The Pasha fingered the medal again. 'I suppose there is someone more odious than the executioner. The victim.'

'Ha!' the foreigner grunted, 'Very good. How long?'

'Until the bell rings three.'

'Who will ring the bell?'

The Pasha snorted. 'A good question. We will see to it after lunch.' He dismounted, handing the reigns to a valet, and sat at a trestle table where his attendant had laid out the meal. The foreigner joined him, and they ate to the sound of screams.

'The Sultan is surrounded by jackals,' the Pasha said. Had that sounded convincing? His guest looked up from his plate, unsure whether the Ottoman commander was addressing him. The Pasha continued, needing to talk over the pitiful cries for mercy.

'It is all he can do to cling on. If he agrees to the demands of the Armenians, each of our provinces will demand their independence, and what remains of the Empire will fall apart and be devoured by the Great Powers. And if he gives in to the demands of the Europeans, the Christians will enjoy more rights than us Turks, and his own people will turn on him. It is better to make the problem go away.'

Did that sound too forced? The Armenians were traitors. They had supported the Russians in the last war, welcoming their armies. If the Young Ottomans were to succeed in re-establishing parliament, inshallah, they would need a period of stability. They would have no time for rebellions or wars. What we do here is wise, necessary. And let someone

10

else take the blame. That was the point, of course. The Sultan would be blamed. He ran a finger around his collar and swallowed.

The foreigner spat an olive stone to the ground. 'If accounts of today get out, the European politicians will be forced by their own subjects to demand more protections for the Christians. It is the sickness of democracy. The less they know the better.'

For now, thought the Pasha, nodding and turning to the valley as flames took hold of the church roof. But soon they would be ready to tell the world and the Great Powers would do the Young Ottoman's work for them. His chewing slowed to a halt. He lowered his head. 'Why can they not accept their place in the Caliphate? Nowhere are they better treated!'

'That is why they must be crushed,' the foreigner said, captivated by the slaughter below.

The Pasha grimaced. What was the foreigner's game? There was no point asking him. He raised his voice, 'The Sultan does not like to hear bad news.'

The man turned to face him and drummed his fingers on the tabletop. 'Then don't give him any. How will you report it?'

The Pasha smiled to himself, for he had already written it. 'Not finding any rebellion, we cleared the country so none should occur in the future.'

'Good. The less the Sultan knows of the details the better. It will only make it harder for him to deny it.'

'The Sultan has spies everywhere.'

'And you have been truthful, loyal, and performed a challenging task with admirable efficiency. You spared him the unpleasant details. But if the worst happens, we will take care of you.'

The Pasha looked down to the village again. "Take care of," did not sound appealing. When the killing died down, the looting began, and they rose from the table and with loose reins let their horses pick their way down before splashing through the chill water to the village. The foreigner drew his sabre and held it low as the Hamidiye commander approached and saluted.

'It is done, but the men are uneasy, my Lord.'

The Pasha raised an eyebrow. 'No witnesses?'

'None.' The Kurd lowered his gaze and patted his mount. 'My father was a bandit, as was his father and his father before him. We have taken tribute from these people for as long as we remember. They may be cowardly dogs, but they are hard workers, and recover quickly to pay again. To kill them all is bad business.' He held a bulging coin pouch out to the Pasha, who sat motionless while his attendant hurried forward to take it.

'It was important to send a message. The Sultan wished it,' the Pasha said.

The message. Total annihilation. This was not punishing revolutionaries from a village or the bandits helping themselves because the Armenians owned all the bakeries. This could not be ignored. Not by the Armenians. In the face of annihilation what could they do except rebel? And hopefully distract the Sultan's forces. Nor could the Great Powers ignore it. The newspapers would fan outrage, riling the people, and their rulers would lose confidence in the Sultan's ability to protect the Christians of the Ottoman Empire and demand change. The Young

Ottomans would be waiting. The Grand Vizier himself had assured him. When the time was right, they would make their move.

The Hamidiye leader surveyed the smoking ruins and wondered who would take the message. He swallowed hard at the sight of the villagers prostrated over the blood-soaked ground and bowed his head.

'As you command,' he said and wheeled his horse to join the stream of men heading to the high pass, hauling wagons loaded with sacks of grain and the meagre valuables of a village and driving cattle and sheep before them.

The foreigner rode through the village, bending occasionally to prod a corpse with his sword. The sun beat on his back, but the vacant doorways sent a shiver down his spine. He looked up at the church bell. There was no need to ring it. The flames licked higher, embers swirled upwards as timbers cracked and popped. Behind him a roof crashed down, and he turned to see dust and smoke billow from the ruins of a cottage. A roasting blast of air peppered him with cinders. He raised his arm to protect his face and saw the flames reflected on the running wolf engraved on his blade. His mount shied, and he fought to control it. As the horse settled, he felt haunted by something, but through the shimmering air nothing stirred bar the flies that already bothered the fresh corpses.

21st July 1896, Vienna

The stuccoed Italianate facades of Metternichgasse glowed in the afternoon sun as Theodor Herzl hurried to what he hoped was his fate. His representations to the British government had not elicited a single response. The greatest project of the age, his all-consuming dream, and not even an acknowledgement. And then, out of the blue, a scrawled note came from Reverend William Hechler requesting an urgent meeting. Herzl's long stride brought him a few minutes early to the entrance of Number 6, set back into the rusticated masonry and he leant against the warm stone to recover his breath.

Herzl placed his card on the reception desk and turned it so that the clerk could easily read, "Neue Freie Press, Paris Correspondent." It was not the clerk's place to wonder what Herzl's business was in Vienna, but these days people were often suspicious.

'Reverend William Hechler. He is expecting me.'

The clerk blinked, carefully consulted his appointment book, and rose lethargically to escort Herzl, who had become accustomed to the everyday slights that were ever more frequent and pointed. Herzl turned to the grand staircase and wrought iron balustrade that wound up to the main floor, where the high double doors of staterooms looked down. The gilded panelling, picked out in greens and greys, the ornamented cornices, and the crystal chandeliers commanded respect. Perhaps, finally, there was to be official recognition of his mission. That is what he craved. It would confer legitimacy to his dream and elevate his status, perhaps even make him the unofficial leader of his people. But the clerk headed past the staircase, through a discreet door and into a dingy corridor that led to the rear of the building. Herzl followed, his heart sinking as they passed each anonymous doorway, until the clerk knocked on the last, paused a moment, and opened it.

'Mr ... Herzl for you, Reverend.'

Herzl squeezed past the clerk into a cramped room, the air fuggy for want of windows. Bookshelves covered every wall, and in the middle a pint-sized man in plain black clothes sat behind a small desk. His head seemed upside down, bald on top with a prophet's beard that may or may not have concealed a clerical collar. The Reverend beamed and his pate flushed as he rose to greet his guest.

'You came! We have so much to discuss!'

Herzl extracted himself from his frockcoat and tugged at his wing collar. The man must be nearly fifty and still languishing in this... this storeroom. The Reverend rubbed his hands and reached for a book on his desk, already opened to a marked page. He beckoned Herzl closer and put his finger to the text. 'It is written in Luke XXI:24 that "Jerusalem shall be trodden down until the time of the Gentiles be fulfilled." Do you understand what that means?'

Herzl knew enough scripture to recognise the significance. The Reverend's eyes widened, and Herzl felt them searching for his reaction. What did he want from him? Herzl cursed himself. He had worked himself to the bone to promote his dream, but supporters had been hard to find. Even his best hope, the Rothschilds, had turned him down. He had chased every lead, but now he was reduced to this, travelling half-way across Europe in the hope that this meeting signalled official support for his cause. But this man was not a diplomat, nor, apparently, in full command of his faculties. Well, at least he could pay a visit to his wife. 'I think so, go on.'

'Yes, I knew you would see. I have made all the calculations,' the Reverend said and patted a folder on his desk. 'The end of the time of the Gentiles will be Easter of 1898. When I read your book, I realised that you were the one.'

'You've read Der Judenstaat?'

'Yes, don't you see? Your plan for a Jewish state will be the catalyst. You have raised the banner for your people, and they will follow you to Palestine. The foreordained moment is upon us. The prophecy is nigh!'

'But—'

The Reverend flipped the pages of the Bible. 'And ye shall know that I am the Lord, when I shall bring you into the land of Israel, into the country which I gave to your fathers.'

Herzl stammered. He knew the stories, although it had been many years since he had attended synagogue.

'You will lead your people back to Israel and bring about the End of Times. Jesus Christ, our Lord and Saviour, will rise again!' Beads of perspiration glistened on the Reverend's forehead, his eyes staring past Herzl. 'Blessed are the servants whom the Lord shall find watching when he cometh.'

The Reverend's smile stretched wide, and he cupped his hands to Herzl's face.

16

'But I don't—'

'Do not be hesitant. There is no time to lose, Easter of ninety-eight will be upon us. If you disagree, your quarrel is with the words of scripture not with me. You will need to persuade the Sultan to accommodate you. And I think I can help…'

23rd July 1896, 10 Downing Street, London

'I've just come back from the Palace,' Lord Salisbury barked. He manoeuvred stiffly, a vein throbbing at his temple. 'The only thing Her Majesty wants to discuss is the Armenians!' He muttered something unintelligible through his wiry beard and tossed a folded copy of The Times on the table.

The man sitting there pushed on his palms and rose. 'Prime Minister.'

'Sit, Beaumont, sit.'

The Director of Naval Intelligence, Rear Admiral Lewis Beaumont, eased back into the seat which creaked like a mooring line under strain. His tanned face contrasted the white whiskers that sprouted from his jawline, cut square in the current fashion. He glanced at the newspaper.

'You wanted to discuss the Eastern Question?'

Salisbury grunted. 'What are these rumours of a massacre in Armenia?'

'Reports from missionaries. The Sultan has strenuously denied them to the Ambassador.'

'The Liberals are playing it up. Got their eye on the by-election. Taking the moral-bloody-high ground. I must govern, and they're trying to skewer me with principles!'

Salisbury paced the room shooting his arm about like a conductor. 'They know I can't push the Sultan too far. What if he takes up with the Tsar? He'll have his paws on Suez and what then for India? I won't be the Prime Minister who buggers that up. And that shit Roseberry knows it, he's talking about tabling a motion in the House for an investigation. And what does Her Majesty care about Gregory the Illuminator anyway? Are they even real Christians?' Salisbury reached the window and spun around, scarlet at the collar. 'We don't even know if there's any truth to these rumours!'

'The missionaries have local expertise and no reason to lie.'

'You can't trust experts. If you believe doctors, nothing is wholesome. If you believe the theologians, nothing is innocent and if you believe soldiers nothing is safe.' Salisbury slumped onto a leather couch and nursed his forehead. Beaumont reached for a manila folder and opened it, sifting one of the pages out.

'The Liberals have been manipulated before to drive a wedge between us and the Sultan. By the Russians.'

Salisbury opened an eye. 'You mean Madame de Novikoff?'

'I do.'

A smile quivered over Salisbury's lips. 'Damn nearly brought Gladstone down. No fool like an old fool!' The smile became more of a leer. 'Does she still keep a salon at Claridge's?'

'Symond's now. Apparently.'

'Well, if Roseberry wants an investigation,' he chuckled, stroking his beard, 'Let's give him one! There might be more to this Armenian situation than meets the eye.'

Beaumont coughed. 'The Sultan will be insulted if we doubt his word, or at least pretend to be for some advantage. Perhaps, if Rosebery agreed to a more discreet approach, we could gain first-hand knowledge of the situation on the ground. If it's unofficial, then the Sultan cannot blame us. If he finds out, we can always deny it.'

Salisbury sat up. 'Go on…'

'It can't be anyone from the embassy. The Sultan has spies everywhere. They would be recognised, defeat the whole purpose of the thing. It must be someone not connected to the government, but with a reason to go there.'

'You have someone in mind?'

Beaumont pulled another sheet from his file and slid it over the French polish. Salisbury ran a stubby finger down the sheet, grunting.

'A Boer?'

'Half. His mother is English, but he was raised in the Transvaal.'

'Young, isn't he? The Sublime Porte is, well, Byzantine. I doubt he has the experience to deal with their guile.'

'Rhodes recommended him. He unmasked a German agent in Johannesburg. As luck would have it, he is a journalist, which will serve as a cover. He's in London now.'

Alarm flickered across Salisbury's eyes. 'Will the Sultan let a journalist travel to Armenia?'

Beaumont leaned back in his chair. 'It will look suspicious if he doesn't. I'd expect him to insist on an escort to ensure that he never got to see anything incriminating.'

'Dangerous for him if he were caught.' Salisbury tapped the table. 'That German agent was tied up with the Jameson debacle, wasn't he? A parliamentary enquiry is inevitable after the criminal case. Jameson and

Rhodes will take most of the blame of course, but how much higher will it go? It could bring down the Government.'

Beaumont nodded. Salisbury had veered off in a direction he had not anticipated. The grandfather clock chimed.

'They'll want to question this Leroux fellow,' Salisbury continued, 'It ... might be useful if he wasn't in London for a while. An excellent suggestion, Beaumont. See to it.'

'Of course, my Lord. But there's no point doing this unless Rosebery will be satisfied.'

'Don't worry about that. I'll speak to Rosebery this evening at my club. That will be all. Oh, and look into Madame de Novikoff.'

'Sir, there is one other thing, related in a way. A Reverend Hechler from the Vienna embassy has been badgering us about some journalist he's met, convinced that this man is going to lead the Jews back to Zion, fulfil a prophecy and bring about the Second Coming of Christ. Wants us to back his petition to the Sultan to provide a homeland for the Jewish people in Palestine. And then this fellow will persuade them all to go there. Hechler says he has the proofs of the prophecy if we have any doubts. I can't think of anything that would upset the Sultan more.'

'Good God! This is all we need. Who is this chap?'

'Hechler? Something of an eccentric, an evangelical and devoted to the idea of restoring the Jews to Palestine—'

'No, no, the other fellow.'

Beaumont consulted his notes. 'Theodor Herzl? Jewish, Austro-Hungarian, well-to-do. Journalist with the Vienna paper, the Neue Freie

Press, somewhat recently been agitating for an independent Jewish state. Wrote a book about it.'

'Never heard of him. A far-fetched prophecy and an obscure activist. Hechler can't seriously think we can promote this to the Sultan?'

'The thing is, if we don't humour him, he'll pass it up the holy chain of command to the Defender of the Faith, and you'll have Her Majesty bending your ear again.'

Salisbury snorted and stomped back to the window. 'Well tell him that we will take it up with the upmost urgency. Then get your man Leroux to pick up the dossier on his way to Constantinople, before this Reverend does anything else with it. Then give it to Ambassador Currie. He'll know what to do with it. Carry on.'

'Yes, sir.' Beaumont retrieved the sheet of paper with Leroux's scanty credentials. He had done surprisingly well in Johannesburg, but that was his home, he knew his way around. The Prime Minister seemed unperturbed by the low chances of success. Beaumont snapped the folder shut and rose. If Leroux was to have any chance in Constantinople, he would need more than fair winds and following seas.

24th *July 1896, London*

The horse tossed its head at Leroux, its glossy dun coat shining beneath the harness. A well-groomed animal and a good cab usually went together.

'Take you anywhere, sir?' the driver said from his perch at the rear of the Hansom.

'Not today.' Leroux caressed the mare's muzzle. It had been too long since he had been in the saddle.

'Cor, blimey!' the cabbie said, looking over Leroux's shoulder. A man approached at a slow march, waving a red flag. Behind him, at the steering wheel of a motor car, a portly fellow bellowed, 'Don't dawdle man!'

The flag bearer increased his pace and the driver fiddled with a lever, accompanied by the obligatory mechanic. The motor car lurched forward and then emitted a bang and ground to a halt. The horse shied, unbalancing the cabbie, and Leroux caught the traces to stop it bolting.

'Don't reckon you have much to fear there,' Leroux said patting the horse's neck.

The driver winked. 'Tied 'em up in regulations 'ain't we,' he cackled, 'Two miles an hour!' Leroux had been in London long enough to know better than to cross the Hackney coachmen. Too long.

'Leroux! Hold the cab!'

A lady bustled out from the Doric columns guarding the entrance to offices of The Times, her spectacles swinging from a neck chain. Leroux

23

doffed his hat to his boss, the colonial editor Flora Shaw, and an elderly woman, who followed in her wake. Leroux opened the cab door as Flora ushered her friend forward, but her companion waited awkwardly. It was unlike Miss Shaw not to introduce an acquaintance and she had always been more than generous with her time since taking him on. Leroux smiled and bowed his head.

'Mr Leroux, a humble reporter at your service.'

'Madame de Novikoff,' the woman said with a half-smile of allure. Her face was hollowed with age, but it only accentuated the beauty of her bone structure and perhaps he imagined a twinkle in her watery eyes. She turned to Miss Shaw, cocking her head.

'Leroux works for me on the foreign desk. Made a name for himself in Johannesburg. Something of a conundrum. Deeply cynical, judging by his writing - I throw most of it away. Funny, I'd always thought adventurers would be optimists.'

'Johannesburg?'

'We must get on, Olga.'

Miss Shaw hustled her in, avoiding eye contact, a blush on her cheek the first crack Leroux had seen in the steely determination she had forged writing under a male by-line.

The cab pulled away, leaving a steaming heap of manure. Leroux loosened his tie. An ally of Rhodes in his empire building and implicated in the Jameson affair, Miss Shaw was scrambling to save her reputation, but if that was *the* Olga de Novikoff, she might be in even deeper trouble. Leroux was damn glad he didn't get involved in politics and retreated to the cool of the building.

A day's worth of reports crowded his desk, but he reached for the envelope perched on top and ran his thumb over the embossed admiralty stamp. Miss Shaw had been right about his writing. Neither the readers nor the editors, especially the editors, were interested in the tragedy of conflict when there was jingoism to sell. Nor would discarded articles dispel his nightmares. They were as useless as spears against the Maxim guns that had slaughtered Chief Malaboch's warriors. Leroux inserted a paper knife and sliced the envelope open. It almost felt like action. Surely this was the summons that Rhodes had intimated, the reason he had travelled to London. If he couldn't make a difference as a war correspondent, he could try from the inside. And there was something else. He felt the sun on his face streaming through the window, taking him back to the tree that looked over the river, where he had fallen in love, this Christmas past. A tear rolled down his cheek. Lara was her name. She had known the danger but did it anyway. It was part of why he had loved her. Like Leroux, she had been a waif and stray swept up into Rhodes' schemes. But she had paid the ultimate price and Leroux blamed himself. The hope of crossing paths again with her killer lay in his hands, a smooth and stiff card. He was to present himself at the office of the Director of Naval Intelligence, The Admiralty, at 4pm. Today. Just half a day to kill.

Beaumont set his cup of tea and saucer down with care, as though they might slide away in a rough sea. He wiped away an invisible speck of dust from his Regency desk.

'Sit.'

Leroux perched on the edge of a deep armchair, cradling his slouch hat between his knees, and discretely wiped the sweat from his palms. The mantlepiece groaned with invitations, and above a single lonely ship lay at anchor, its masts as bare as the bleak arctic seascape.

'First time at the Admiralty?'

Leroux nodded and bit his cheeks to summon some saliva.

'You come highly recommended - a man of interesting talents, according to Rhodes.'

'Thank you, sir.'

'Don't thank me, thank him.'

'Yes sir.'

Beaumont massaged the thumb joint of one meaty hand with the other. 'Well, wait and see. You might not want to thank him, either.' A chuckle resonated deep in Beaumont's throat, and Leroux eased back on the smooth leather, forcing a smile.

'You still harbour ambitions to be a journalist – a war correspondent if I'm not mistaken?' Beaumont said, taking a few sheets of foolscap from the sole manila folder on his desk.

'I don't think it's for me. I doubt Rhodes recommended my writing.' And if he carried on writing what he thought, he'd be out on his ear soon enough.

'No,' Beaumont coughed, 'but that might not be a problem.' He picked up his pen and made a tick-mark. 'You work for Miss Shaw, don't you? What do you make of her?'

Leroux hesitated at the turn of conversation. It sounded like politics.

He leaned forward but had to squint, caught in a slant of sunlight.

'I see little of her, but she's been very good to me.'

Beaumont harrumphed. 'Under a bit of a cloud,' he muttered.

'I guess so.'

'You do?' Beaumont latched onto his comment. 'Why?'

'I saw her today in interesting company.'

Beaumont arched an eyebrow. 'Go on.'

Leroux's cheek prickled in the heat as Beaumont's impassive stare warned against flim-flam.

'Madame de Novikoff. I met her this morning at The Times.'

'You met Olga de Novikoff?'

'Yes. She was on her way out with Miss Shaw.'

'On her way out with Miss Shaw?' Beaumont's piercing eyes were at odds with his dumb repetition of news that seemed to undermine his assumptions.

'Yes.'

'Ha!' Beaumont emitted a short laugh which turned into a small coughing fit, until he slapped his hand down on the table. 'I bet she took a shine to you! Well, well, well. That's the second time today her name's come up. Madame de Novikoff showing her face again, no doubt dripping nectar into eager ears and gold into willing palms. It's been a while since she lured Gladstone into spreading Russian propaganda. How he survived that I'll never know…the M.P. for Russia, what?'

'Pardon?'

'Disraeli. Called her the M.P. for Russia. Very drole. What does this portend I wonder?' He stared darkly at the window for an answer, nursing his top lip with a finger, before abruptly returning to his notes.

'You speak French?'

'Fluent, sir. My father was half French.'

'That could be useful. And you served in a Boer commando unit? – I assume that means you're comfortable on long treks in the wilderness?'

'Rarely happier, sir.'

Beaumont's pen twitched again over the paper.

'And you can't return home?'

'There are some people who would be disappointed to see me again.'

Beaumont's face creased and the ice-blue eyes glinted. He must know that Leroux would be arrested on sight were he to return.

'You've heard of the Eastern Question?'

The papers were full of it. Should the Great Powers prop up the ailing Ottoman Empire or carve it up between themselves? The only thing that saved the Sultan was that nobody could agree on how to share the spoils and didn't want to fight over them, at least not yet.

'Yes, sir.'

'Well, for the moment we're backing the Sultan. Suez, route to India, jewel of the Empire and all that. But there is a fly in the ointment. The Sultan has a nasty habit of massacring Christians. He promised to stop and introduce reforms safeguarding the Armenians - they're the Christians - but apparently, he's at it again.'

'I've read a little about it, but nothing like the coverage last year.'

'Reports are mixed. We need someone to confirm them unofficially one way or the other. My idea is for someone – you – to go to Constantinople and seek permission to travel to Armenia as a journalist. We will arrange an interview with a bishop there as a cover. On the way, see some of the missionaries, find out what they know, and if you can, reconnoitre the area. I don't suppose you know any Arabic or Turkish?'

Leroux shook his head.

'I expect you'll pick up a few words quick enough if you managed to learn Zulu.'

Beaumont drew his papers together, aligning them with a tap on the table. 'Apart from a lack of knowledge of the area, the people and the language, you do seem perfect.' A smile.

'Thank you, sir.'

'Your French will come in useful. The bureaucrats of the Sublime Porte all parlez-vous.'

Beaumont ran his hand down the dark blue tunic that restrained his stomach and looked too hot for a blazing day like this.

'I'm sure you will manage, it's not as if I'm asking you to go to the Arctic.' His eyes wandered to the window again, and he shivered.

'Will I have a contact at the embassy?'

'Not officially. We can't be seen to be helping you. The fewer people aware of your mission the better, but there is one person there I can vouch for. Not the most practical man, but trustworthy, a nephew of mine. A young fellow called Randolph Simpkins. I will contact him privately. He will meet you at the station, Sirkeci, I believe it's called, and help you with the travel permits. You will not be able to lodge at the embassy, but Simpkins will arrange an alternative. Oh, and there's a package I need you to pick up in Vienna on the way. My secretary will fill you in on the details.'

Leroux stood to leave, and Beaumont steepled his fingers.

'You dealt well with a tricky situation in Johannesburg. But Constantinople is a whole different matter. They've played power games for a thousand years and more. Spies spying on spies. Hard to know who to trust...' Beaumont lowered his hands. 'Even on your own side.'

26th July 1896, British Embassy, Vienna

'Do you get many visitors?' Leroux asked cheerily as the clerk guided him down a dimly lit corridor.

'Not here. Mind your step.' The clerk kicked over an upturned corner of the runner carpet and knocked on the final door. A lean man with dark deep-set eyes and a bushy beard looked down at the visitors. Behind in a book-lined room, an older, smaller man dressed in black, rose from a desk and extended his hand.

'Ah, Leroux! We've been expecting you,' Reverend Hechler said. 'This is Theodor Herzl, author of Der Judenstaat.'

Herzl barely raised a smile next to the beaming Reverend.

'You are rather young for a diplomat, aren't you?' Herzl said.

'I'm more of a courier. Here to pick up a package.'

'A courier?'

'We have a lot to discuss,' the Reverend interjected. 'How much did Beaumont tell you?'

'Just that Mr Herzl has plans for a Jewish homeland and that you have documents supporting the importance of Britain aiding his mission, which I am to take to Constantinople.'

Herzl propped himself against a bookcase and crossed his arms, toying with a pair of leather gloves as the Reverend beckoned Leroux.

'Yes, yes. But it is so much more than that. When Mr Herzl leads his people back to Palestine, the prophecy will be fulfilled. With the Jews restored to Zion, the necessary conditions for the Second Coming of our Saviour will be in place, and He will come as foretold. In Easter of '98 if I'm not mistaken.' The Reverend held his hands aloft, but Herzl chewed his lip and bowed his head, either in prayer or, perhaps, to avoid eye contact.

'Beaumont was most anxious to present your evidence to the Ambassador. If you have it ready, the express train leaves tonight.'

'I have it here,' the Reverend said, patting a folder on the desk, 'but first things first. Mr Herzl will travel with you, should the Ambassador have any questions. I am given to believe that Mr Herzl already has an audience with the Sultan in the works. Support for his mission is growing throughout the courts of Europe. Mr Herzl has just arrived back from an introduction I made to the Grand Duke of Baden, who is most sympathetic. I tutored his children you see, and we can expect him to recommend the project to his nephew, the Kaiser. Careful where you step!'

Covering the floor in front of Leroux were two overlapping military staff maps.

'We have prepared the ground for you,' the Reverend said to Herzl and knelt gingerly, pointing over the maps. 'According to my calculations this is where the new Temple should be located, here at Bethel, at the centre of the country. Did you know Bethel means House of God? Of course, you did. It is first mentioned in Genesis, where Abram pitched his tent. It is where Jacob dreamt of a ladder stretching between Heaven and Earth, thronged with Angels. God stands at the top of the ladder and promises Jacob the land of Canaan.' The Reverend's hand swept to a shelf and a scale model of an ancient temple, whittled in wood.

Herzl clasped the Reverend's arm, helping him up, and then buttoned his frock coat. 'Your support will not be forgotten.'

'But I have Sachertorte!' the Reverend said and released the sweet aroma of apricot and chocolate as he lifted a cloche on his desk. 'We must celebrate!'

'If I am to make the evening train, I must gather my things and meet Count Nevlinski.' Herzl straightened to his full height, extended a firm grip to Leroux, and hurried out.

'Are you a Christian, Mr Leroux?' the Reverend said, offering a slice of cake.

'I was raised in the tradition, a church school in a small farming community.'

The Reverend clasped his hands in prayer and reached for the folder.

'I have detailed the calculations of the prophecy and the verses that support it. It requires some explanation. In Revelations XI:2, we read that the Gentiles shall tread underfoot the holy city for forty-two months. At thirty days to the month, we have 1,260 days or, as we say in prophetic terms, 1,260 years.'

The Reverend faced up to one of the shelves and pulled down a tomb, Gibbon's "Rise and Fall of the Roman Empire." Leroux's jaw slackened as he took in the rows of books, mostly versions of the Bible or ecclesiastical texts of one type or another.

'Gibbon tells us that the Saracens took possession of Jerusalem in the autumn of 637, so when we add 1,260 to that year, we have September

1897 as the end of the subjugation of Jerusalem! Well, give or take six months, because our years have been adjusted by Acts of Parliament. The best way of dealing with that is by spheroid measurement.' The Reverend scanned the books, but not immediately able to locate the compendium he sought, continued, 'We then get the true end of the Gentile times as Easter 1898.'

'That is excellent news,' Leroux said, wiping his hands and checking his watch. 'I really must be going.'

'Wait! I realise that the Sultan will not support this, so this proposal is not for his ears. I am not even sure that Herzl believes me - I understand Herzl and Count Nevlinski have a more ... commercial ... proposition for the Sultan. But the Ambassador must understand the importance - for every Christian - that the chosen people return to Palestine, so that he can support Herzl in whatever way he can. The time is nigh. The stars are aligning.'

'Who is Count Nevlinski?' Leroux asked as he took the folder.

The Reverend wrung his hands. 'He has attached himself to Mr Herzl. He is, I hear, an impoverished Polish aristocrat and operates as a freelance diplomatist. He lacks gravity and has the whiff of a charlatan, but Herzl seems taken by him.'

'Freelance? Who else does Nevlinski work for?'

'Herzl suspects that the Count works, at least in part, for the Sultan. It doesn't seem to bother him, even welcomes it, as the Count has made some useful suggestions about how to get the Sultan interested.'

'Like what?'

'That he didn't say.' The Reverend squeezed Leroux's hands. 'The important thing is that we all help Herzl to reach his destiny. Remember my son, blessed are the servants whom the Lord shall find watching when he cometh.'

The minute hand of the station clock clicked to vertical, and the shrill whistle of the guard drowned out the rattle of the compartment door as Leroux slid it open. Slumped against the window, a nondescript man acknowledged him from under his homburg hat with a grunt. Leroux stowed his bag and knobkerrie, a Zulu fighting stick that could pass for a cane, on the rack above. The clock slipped from view as the Orient Express eased out from the platform, and Leroux lowered the brim of his slouch hat to cover his eyes. Everything was new to Leroux. His first time in Europe and, in a few days, he would be in Constantinople, the gateway to Asia. After months of drifting, he finally had a sense of purpose and a task that he could throw himself into. Perhaps he could make a difference and even help prevent further atrocities. And maybe then the nightmares would ease. He ran his hand down the varnished panel under the window – he could still smell the wood smouldering from the heat of his old rifle barrel. Leroux shifted in his seat. A worrying thought pulled him from his memories. If the Sultan knew everything that went on, could his chances of travelling to Armenia be endangered by his association with Herzl?

The man opposite snuffled and clucked his tongue in a way that felt deliberately annoying. By the time a light tap on the door announced Herzl, the man had started snoring. Herzl rolled his eyes. 'Nevlinski's gone to the dining car, but we can talk in my compartment if you prefer.'

35

Relieved, Leroux slipped out.

'First of all, I apologise for my earlier coldness,' Herzl said. 'I had expected a diplomat and was taken by surprise. But that's no excuse. It was difficult to speak openly in front the Reverend, he is not enamoured with my advisor.'

'How long have you known the Count?' Leroux said, nodding in what he thought was the direction of the dining car.

'Not long.' Herzl smoothed the seat and dropped onto it with a wheezy exhalation. 'He picked up a rumour at the Sublime Porte that I sought an introduction to the Sultan. I have been making no secret of it.'

'The Reverend seems genuine enough. He is the reason I was sent, to take his proposal to the Ambassador, although his connection with the Kaiser seems more promising.'

Herzl wrinkled his nose. 'I am not so naïve as to believe the Kaiser concerns himself with our welfare or our goal of an independent state. Or that he believes in the End of Times.' The dark eyes twinkled, and his face widened. 'Why would a temporal King welcome that?'

'You don't think he will support you?'

'Maybe he will. The Kaiser desires influence in the Ottoman Empire and putting Jewish migration under his protection furthers that goal. If Germany has nationals there, he will claim the right to protect them, increasing his authority in Ottoman lands. All part of the games the Great Powers play, in which we are just pawns. I have little enough help, so I must take it where I can.'

'Do you believe in the End of Times?'

Herzl raised his eyes to the luggage rack, or perhaps to heaven.

'I am not a religious man, Mr Leroux. Does that surprise you?'

'A little. I assumed it would be necessary to lead your people.'

'I have my dream. I give everything to it, there is no room for anything else.'

'Does Reverend Hechler know?'

Herzl grimaced and pushed his hands down his thighs. 'I didn't mention it. He may have leapt to conclusions, but what matters to him is that we are restored to Zion. And that is my goal too. We just have different reasons.'

'It's an incredible project. What inspired you?'

'Are you familiar with the Dreyfuss affair?' Herzl's eyes darkened to coals.

Leroux nodded. 'The French captain accused of spying for the Germans.'

'The Jewish French captain.' Herzl coughed and paused as he recovered his breath. 'He was not guilty. The trial was conducted in a closed military court to hide the paucity of their evidence. But he was an ideal culprit. I covered it for the paper last year. Afterwards at the ceremony of degradation they stripped him of his badges and stripes. The crowd didn't chant "Traitor." They chanted "Death to the Jews." The final straw for me.' Herzl turned to the window and his eyes flicked back and forth as the trees and telegraph poles flashed by. 'I'm told you're a Boer. You must know something of being an outsider.'

Leroux laughed. 'It's worse than that. The Boers considered us outsiders. My father was only half-Dutch and wasn't a farmer, he worked in the mines with all the other foreigners.'

'You don't have a people or a home?'

'Yes and no.' The smallholding up on the veld where his mother had raised him was a world away, where right and wrong were as clear as the thin air. It was the only home he knew. 'I got caught up in a game between the Great Powers. I did what I thought was right, but there are powerful people there who do not want to see me again. The Boers stumbled upon something far too valuable and became pawns themselves. Their fate is inevitable. You'd better hope Palestine doesn't sit on a mountain of gold!'

'Help me and there will always be a home for you in Palestine.'

'I have orders to help you, as far as they go.' It was an exaggeration, but Leroux meant it. It was hard not to warm to Herzl, like a David taking on Goliath.

'I am under no illusions how tough it will be. How I tried to be accepted, but no matter how hard we work, how successful we are, or how much we contribute, our loyalty will always be questioned. That is why I wrote the book. I finally understood that the only way is to have our own homeland.'

'And you're already making progress.'

Herzl tugged at a shirt cuff. 'I have yet to convince my own people, let alone get a homeland. The Rabbis are not sure what to make of me. In the West we have flourished, in business at least. They do not take these prophecies literally and fear they risk everything if we claim to be a separate nation. How could we be treated as loyal citizens then? In the East, our people are more devout and lead simpler lives. They believe in the prophecies, but the Rabbis call me a heretic. They say I am presumptuous, for it is the prerogative of the Messiah and no one else to lead us back to the land of our fathers.'

The challenges Herzl faced practically singlehanded were daunting and his dedication had come at a price. Flecks of grey highlighted Herzl's jet-black hair brushed back from his broad square forehead, and darker skin circled the deep-set eyes.

'If you show them the way, it will be there for those that want it.'

'That is my hope. Every step I take, every breath I draw, I work towards that. The Reverend told me you were a journalist like me, but you also seem to work for the government?'

'That's the long and the short of it. When the government heard that I was travelling to Constantinople, they asked me to collect the Reverend's folder on the way.'

'So, why are you going there?'

'I'm a war correspondent. After Constantinople, I hope to travel to interview an Armenian bishop about the rumours of persecution. I try to condemn war rather than glorify it, but my editor prefers a more jingoistic slant.' There was enough truth in that for it to roll off the tongue easily.

Herzl chortled and coughed at once. 'Your career will be short and not very sweet.'

Leroux didn't doubt it, but Herzl's plan was not without flaws either.

'I got the impression from the Reverend that the Sultan would not look favourably on the contents of the folder, that they should be kept from him, and you will need to persuade him with other arguments.'

The train lurched over a set of points, and someone stumbled in the corridor, bumping the compartment wall. Herzl tilted his head for a few moments while the train settled back into its rhythm.

'He would of course be reluctant to help fulfil a Christian prophecy. But the Sultan has few friends and many enemies and is running out of funds to defend himself. Count Nevlinski feels that may be an opportunity. He has arranged for me to meet the Grand Vizier and if that goes well, perhaps even the Sultan himself.'

The door slid half open and sharp eyes darted over the compartment.

'The very man himself! Your ears must be burning,' Herzl said and introduced Nevlinski, a Count, but not above eavesdropping.

Nevlinski frowned and took a seat next to Herzl. 'So, you are the journalist-courier? I have not read any of your articles.'

'I'm new to The Times, I worked in South Africa before.'

'Ah yes. I have done some journalism in my time. All journalists together, how nice. What exactly are you hoping to achieve in Constantinople? Perhaps I can be of assistance?'

Was Nevlinski pitching for work or fishing for information? Herzl picked at a fingernail, seemingly annoyed. They made an odd couple. Both attired in the frockcoats of gentlemen, but there the similarity ended. Herzl's clothes were fresh from the tailor. A man of independent means, for no journalist could dress or travel as he did. Groomed, confident and determined, but with a sallow tinge to his skin. Nevlinski perched small and round next to him. Clean shaven like Leroux, but pudgy, and his clothes on the edge of threadbare, tailored for a slighter man, and in need of a press. Nevlinski proffered his tobacco and smoked a cigarette with courtly flourishes, but his restless eyes negated any attempt at nonchalance.

'I'm going to Erzurum to interview the bishop,' Leroux said, 'if I can get permission from the Sublime Porte.'

'There I can help you,' Nevlinski said rubbing his hands.

'The Times has already made arrangements for someone to help.'

Nevlinski sniffed and flicked his cravat. 'Who?'

Leroux shrugged. The man was irritatingly persistent. 'I'm expecting a message at the hotel. It was all a bit last minute.'

Nevlinski's eyes narrowed. 'Seems odd to have a journalist run an errand like this, and doubly odd to send an inexperienced writer to interview the bishop at such a sensitive time. Am I missing something?'

'It's rough country. Perhaps they felt the time I spent with a Boer commando would come in useful?' Leroux hoped Nevlinski might be intimidated and button up.

'You were a soldier?'

'Back on the veld everyone is called up when there's a tribal war. I worked for the Cape Argus after that.'

Nevlinski seemed satisfied with the answer, but Herzl leaned forward clasping his knees. 'Why is The Times of London so interested in the Armenians, all of a sudden?'

'A worrying report came back from a missionary that set the cat amongst the pigeons. It's become a political problem.'

Nevlinski yawned. 'If you need my help, I will be staying at the Hotel Pera Palace.'

'As am I,' Leroux said. Was it a coincidence?

41

'You have quite the expense account for a journalist,' Nevlinski said.

'Haven't we all,' Herzl said, eyeing Nevlinski.

The train shuddered and screeched to a halt, Nevlinski tumbling into Leroux's lap. The lights flickered and the brakes hissed as Leroux helped Nevlinski to his feet. He rubbed condensation from the window and peered into the darkness. A door slammed further up the carriage. There was a stagecoach on the tracks, stopped in the middle of a level crossing. At the front the driver stood swinging a lantern. The horses were skittish, and the driver set the lantern down and shook the reigns. The coach rolled off the crossing. A figure moved away from the train towards the coach. Leroux leapt up, pushing Nevlinski aside. He raced along the corridor to his compartment. The door gaped wide open. The snoring man had gone. And so had Leroux's bag. He grabbed his knobkerrie and scrambled to the end of the carriage, bumping past the conductor. Leroux jumped off, tripped, and rolled on the stony ground.

The silhouetted figure reached the coach and threw something in it. He clambered onto the elevated seat at the front as Leroux sprinted along the train, three carriages away from the crossing. The driver cracked the whip. The stagecoach surged forward, and the man fell back into the seat next to the driver. Two carriages to go, still gaining. The driver whipped harder. The other man turned to face Leroux, the unmistakable shape of a pistol in his hand, his arm braced over the stagecoach roof. Leroux sprinted onto the road, a clear line of sight. The man fired. Not even close. Firing from a moving platform at a running target in the dark. Not impossible, but hard.

A whistle blew behind him. Leroux pounded on. Another muzzle flash and the crack of the gunshot. Nearer, dirt sprayed off the road just in front of him. The driver thrashed the horses, pulling ahead now. The couplings of the carriages clanked under strain as the train chugged into motion. Leroux drew his arm back and flung the knobkerrie. End over end it flew, towards the lantern and the driver's seat. The driver ducked sharply, or had he hit him? The coach swerved right, and the other man reached across. Leroux ran on. The coach straightened on the verge of the road, its left side wheels off the ground, tilting alarmingly. The chuffing quickened and deepened as the train gathered pace. The drivers head re-appeared again, and the coach regained the middle of the road, accelerating away.

Leroux turned. He would never catch them. And now he was going to miss the train as well. He raced back down the road and cut across a field, to try and meet the end of the last car. He stumbled, diving to get a handhold on the guard rail. He clung on, his hands slipping on the cold iron, his feet skimming the ground, finally getting a foot onto one of the buffers. He hung there a moment, catching his breath. The light of the lantern crested a shallow rise and then disappeared. Leroux hauled himself onto the narrow viewing platform. The sleepers flew past beneath him, disappearing as fast as his pride. He had been caught off guard on the first watch. Only a handful of people knew of his mission, and someone had gone to considerable lengths to find out what it was. The wind whipped through his hair as he was swept along by the iron horse, the tracks straight and narrow, fleeing from his grasp but confining him. What was he caught up in? The carriage door opened behind him. Leroux spun.

43

Nevlinski. Alone. No one to see them. But he carried no weapon, and the pear-shaped outline presented no threat.

'Everything alright Leroux? What on earth were you doing?'

Wednesday, 29th July, The Ottoman Empire

The azure waters of the Sea of Marmara shimmered as the train wound around the approaches to Constantinople. Leroux pushed his plate away. The fillet of beef with chateau potatoes was cold now and the little he had managed left a sour taste in his mouth. The food was not the problem. What had Beaumont meant when he warned him about trusting those on his own side? Did he have someone specific in mind, like the Ambassador, or just a general concern that the Sultan's agents were adept at infiltrating British intelligence or the embassy? He had been caught out before he had even arrived in Constantinople. And he didn't know why.

Tramp steamers belched towards the harbour punctuated by the occasional sailing ship tilting away from the breeze, as though to remind visitors that here ancient mixed with modern as East met West and prophecies from the past collided with the ambitions of empires.

Leroux pulled out his notes and ran through them again. Could he remember anything else of the Reverend's papers? It was a small offering to deliver. He had let Beaumont and Herzl down, despite the warning. The waiter cleared the plates, a furrow in his young brow, and poured coffee. Leroux toyed with the spoon. How could he make amends? Nevlinski had harped on about Leroux's naivety and shut down any attempt by Herzl to discuss the dossier or potential negotiations with the Sultan, not that Leroux was able to promise anything. Herzl, to Leroux's relief, had not been too concerned with the loss of the Reverend's proposal. He had not expected the Ambassador to take it to the Sultan, in fact he was nervous that all the talk of prophecies and 'End of Times' would make any discussion over settlement in Palestine impossible. He did however want Britain's support, but Nevlinski made it clear that Leroux had already bungled one mission and on no account should such a junior and hapless emissary be entrusted with details of the proposal they were working on. He suggested that Britain was a fair-weather friend at best and their respect for the project could be divined from the lowly level of staff assigned to it. Not even a proper Government employee.

Leroux had kept to himself after that, but as the journey neared its end, he felt compelled to atone for his mistake before they parted ways. He didn't need to know what Herzl's real plans were, but he did want to pass on Beaumont's warning, even if it would just confirm Nevlinski's suggestion that Britain was an unreliable ally. The coffee had done its job and as he made his way back to his compartment, Nevlinski shuffled down the companionway to the water closet. Leroux looked in on Herzl to clear the air.

'If the thief was working for the Sultan, they could think that the dossier represents the real motive behind your proposal.'

Herzl nodded. 'It's a risk.'

'And if the Sultan suspects that it is a Christian plot to herald the End of Times, he will never allow it.'

'Doubly bad then,' Herzl said, 'Do you believe in the prophecy?'

'No, or at least not literally.'

'I doubt the Ambassador does, and I have the impression that he would not act on it anyway. It risks Britain's relationship with the Sultan and interests in Suez.'

Herzl was unperturbed, confident in his own judgement.

'Does Nevlinski know about the Reverend's theories.'

'I mentioned them.'

'Valuable information to the Sultan. Outside of British Intelligence, only myself, the Reverend, you and Nevlinski know. And I've heard that the Count is close to the Sultan.'

'Don't worry, I treat Nevlinski with caution. You think he instigated the theft? What makes you think the thief was after the Reverend's dossier? That isn't the main purpose of your journey.'

'There was nothing else in the case.'

Herzl smiled. 'Who knew that?'

Herzl had a point. This could be nothing to do with the Reverend or Herzl. 'I'm concerned my mistake has threatened your plans.'

'I don't think so. But I need British support. Can you do anything there?'

'As Nevlinski said, I am very junior. And now I've blotted my copybook, I doubt I can be of any use to you. For what it's worth I think you're right about the Ambassador. Suez will dominate his thinking. There's a chance though, if the rumours from Armenia are true, that public pressure will leave the Government no choice but to take issue with the Sultan. I'm not sure how that helps you though.'

Herzl plucked a piece of lint from his trouser leg. 'I suppose one must be careful what one wishes for. But the more pressure there is on the

Sultan, the more he will take friends where he can find them. Do what you can to find out what's really happening out there.'

Leroux stretched back in his seat. Herzl had a keen sense for opportunity and a gracious way of soliciting help to his cause. As far as Leroux was concerned, he owed Herzl and couldn't see any conflict with his assignment. 'I can promise you that.'

Herzl took out his pocket-watch and nodded to the door. 'The Ambassador will not be pleased. Mend yourself first, before worrying about me.'

'Why don't we meet after I've seen him?'

'I'll leave a message at your hotel where you can find me,' Herzl said warmly.

They shook hands and Leroux returned to his compartment as the blue coaches rolled past the walls of Topkapi Palace, the seat of the Sultans until it was deemed too vulnerable to naval gunfire, and coasted into Sirkeci station. The platform porters hustled to greet the best dressed passengers and set to work on the luggage vans at the front and back of the train. Leroux took his knobkerrie, knapsack, and hat and with a rueful look at the luggage rack, filed down the empty corridor to the top of the carriage steps. He waited, admiring the marble, brick, iron, and wood of the station that combined to great effect, flowing lines of Art Nouveau embracing Oriental arches. Nevlinski fussed around Herzl, ushering him into the tide that flowed down the platform, and berating a porter to keep up.

Leroux had only to let Simpkins pick him out. To the side of the entrance under a circular stained-glass window a swarthy middle-aged man casually read a newspaper in a plain white shirt that bulged out from black trousers, topped off with a scarlet fez. He cast his eye over the passengers each time he turned a page and his moustache twitched into a smile when a young man in a white safari suit struggled past against the stream of people and possessions. His unruly mop of ginger hair and enthusiastic perspiration marked him as indisputably English as a toffee apple. Even at a distance, Leroux was sure it was Beaumont's nephew, and from his perch he followed Simpkins' bobbing progress as he looked left and right with increasing frequency as the stream of departing passengers thinned. Leroux removed his battered slouch hat, jumped off the steps and proffered his hand.

'Simpkins?'

'Why yes, how did you… Mr Leroux?' the man said, eager as a puppy. He was unmistakably Beaumont's kin, with the glint in the eye and the wide curve of his mouth, despite his cherubic appearance with skin a world away from weather-beaten and no signs of whiskers to match his hair. 'I hear it's all hush-hush. Unofficial,' Simpkins said, looking behind Leroux and then quizzically up at him.

'I'm travelling light. I'll explain later.' Leroux chewed his lip. At some point he would have to confess that he was travelling a bit lighter than he had intended. Probably better to tell the Ambassador directly, or he might not even make it that far. 'Did Beaumont tell you what I need?'

'It all sounded a bit haphazard. I suppose mostly hazard. I'm to show you around Constantinople and get you a travel permit.'

The man behind Simpkins continued reading the newspaper although the remaining passengers had dispersed. He glanced up at Simpkins and his moustache twitched again. His gaze slid over to Leroux for a knowing second, his eyes dull, before returning to the paper.

'The less attention I attract the better, but I think we're already being watched.'

'The man in fez reading a paper?

'Yes, how…?'

'That's Abdul. He follows me everywhere. If I tried to shake him off, it would only make him more suspicious. Pretend to be an old friend. The Ambassador is expecting you, unofficially. He'll be at the embassy tomorrow morning. Meet me there and then we'll go on to the Sublime Porte to see about the papers.'

Leroux hefted his knapsack and headed for the entrance. Simpkins followed and the watcher turned a page, shook the newspaper, and nodded to Simpkins. They spilled out of the domed concourse and were enveloped by a riot of noise, smells, heat, and gesticulating hawkers. A cab swung out of the confusion. Simpkins turned his back to the driver to open the door for Leroux, brushing a finger against his lips, before climbing in. 'Pera Palace Hotel!'

A light swish of the driver's whip tickled the horse and Leroux jolted back in his seat and basked in the late afternoon sun, the gentle breeze with a tang of salt, and the rumble of cobblestones. Simpkins cleared his throat and spoke with exaggerated clarity.

'As a personal favour, I have requested an audience with the Grand Vizier's assistant in the morning. Please tell your editor at The Times that there has been some very irresponsible reporting based on little more than hearsay. This does nothing to help the situation. On the contrary it simply inflames passions on both sides and so I really do hope that if you are permitted to travel as you request that you use this opportunity to establish the facts and put these reckless rumours to rest.'

Leroux waited as the carriage trundled over the ancient planks of the Galata Bridge. 'My editor wouldn't dream of embarrassing you, and neither would I.'

'First time here, you must try the Turkish delight,' Simpkins gestured at a stall, 'it's an institution.' As Leroux craned his neck to the stall, a wailing pierced the street din.

'Call to prayer. You'll get used to it. Dawn, midday, afternoon, sunset, and night-time.'

A group of men funnelled out of a large stone building in the direction of the summons. Simpkins leaned over. 'That's a hammam, a wash house. Wonderful places, could do with some in London.' At the next corner a huge block of brand-new cream stone, seven stories high, striped with wrought iron balconies towered over them. The driver turned round and flashed his teeth. 'Hotel!'

'You must be exhausted after your journey, and I have an embassy function to attend,' Simpkins said as Leroux hopped down. 'See you in the morning. Come to the embassy at ten.'

Leroux stifled a yawn. Porters swarmed around him, helping themselves to his few possessions, and as he followed one to the reception he felt in his pocket and pulled out a scrap of paper. On it, Simpkins had scrawled, 'Your room is not secure, guard the dossier. We will meet the Ambassador in secret.'

Leroux dropped onto plump pillows and a mattress that yielded just enough. His eye toured the lamps, the paintings, the rosewater bowl, struggling to stay open. Did they conceal some spyhole or listening device? Well, the dossier was already gone. He stretched out, sliding over the cool linen and fell into a fitful sleep. He woke with a start, the nape of his neck sticky with sweat. The room had slipped into twilight and Leroux reached for a glass of water on the bedstand to rinse his mouth. What had woken him? The babble from the street wafted in and the hotel pipework clanked and gurgled. A few of the faithful hurried past below his balcony and he supposed it had been a call to prayer that had stirred him. The bathroom tap squeaked as he turned the handle, and he waited for it to run warm to splash his face. The Pera really did have running hot water. That was something for the next letter to his mother. But what would he say to the Ambassador? He adjusted the shaving mirror. The stubble had to go. He fished Simpkins's note out from his pocket and put a match to a corner. Would the Ambassador even let him continue after such an inauspicious start? Leroux felt his prospects withering as the scrap of paper shrivelled and died, until a curl of ash rose from the plate and spiralled to the ceiling. It took him back to a campfire on the veld, sparks reaching for the stars. Nothing he could do about the Ambassador. Dawn would come with or without the rooster.

Thursday, 30th July, Constantinople

A thick fog cloaked the city, courtesy of a star-filled night. Leroux stretched on the balcony, tuning into the sounds of dawn. The dull tap of a nightwatchman's stick kept time and the moan of a foghorn rose from the harbour. He sensed the sun pressing through and one by one the tips of the tallest minarets on the far side of the Golden Horn emerged from the mist, and then in a rush the curved outlines of stately mosques and dark cypresses broke through. Windows caught the sun with a hazy shimmer while down in the harbour a forest of masts appeared, then funnels and finally the low-lying Turkish ironclads at anchor like leviathans of the deep.

Would the city reveal its secrets so readily? Why had someone stolen his bag? It only made him keener to head for open country and Armenia. The Ambassador would have buried Hechler's proposal and for a moment he considered passing his notes off as the Reverend's to avoid the Ambassador's ire. In some way, the fact that someone had gone to such lengths to steal Leroux's bag was more important than the proposal itself. Beaumont and the Ambassador would want to know who was so interested and why.

Leroux made a point of asking the receptionist for directions to the embassy and dropping his need for a travel permit into the conversation along with his work for The Times. The staff at the hotel favoured by foreigners surely reported to the Sultan's agents. Act normal, don't arouse suspicion. He donned his slouch hat and turned up the hill, each step bringing him closer to a dressing down from the Ambassador. The embassy was a huge square monolith exactly as you might find on Pall Mall but set behind the walls of a courtyard, an oasis surrounded by lawns. A light breeze flicked at the Union Jack hanging above the entrance and the guard straightened with the easy creak of leather, his upper lip stiffened by the mandatory moustache.

The guard eyed Leroux's knobkerrie but let him pass and the marble lobby echoed to his boots, quiet of official business at this hour. A soft-shoed cleaner busied himself behind the receptionist.

'Mr Leroux? Someone will collect you from the waiting room,' the man said indicating across the hall. Heavy oil portraits peered down, but it was the attention of the cleaner that had followed him when he turned to close the waiting room door. A light lemony scent of verbena wafted in from the walled garden dispelling any aura of a London drawing room, even as Her Majesty gazed severely down from above the mantlepiece. Leroux reclined in an armchair and pulled out his notes just as sharp footsteps clicked up to the door and snatched it open. Simpkins closed it firmly, crossed to the window, and pulled that shut too. He pulled on a lever concealed in the bookcase and one of the sections swung open. The Ambassador glided into the room. Sir Philip Currie was tall, lean of limb and with the gait of a peacock. He sported a Van Dyke beard, a wide full moustache above a pointed goatee.

Leroux pushed himself up, but the Ambassador chopped his hand, signalling to stay where he was. He glanced at the window and then stood to the side of it, back to the wall, glowering in silence. Simpkins returned to the door and positioned himself in front of the keyhole.

'Speak softly but clearly,' the Ambassador said.

'Rear Admiral Beaumont ordered me to deliver a dossier from Reverend Hechler. I regret to say—'

'I know. What was in it?'

How on earth did the Ambassador know? Leroux had not even told Simpkins.

'Don't gawp! I know because it's my business to know what goes on here. It was your business to safeguard the dossier.'

Leroux stammered and raised his notes. 'I made these from what I could recall. In short, Reverend Hechler believes that Theodor Herzl will lead the Jews back to Palestine, fulfilling the prophecy from the Book of Revelations and heralding the second coming of Christ.'

'Is that all? Let's hope we get a second chance at the second coming!' The Ambassador shot a look at Simpkins who stood rigid, thumbs jammed down his trouser seams, freckles hidden by his high colour.

'Mr Herzl is not concerned with the prophecies, that is the Reverend's motivation. Herzl wants statehood for his people and is seeking permission from the Sultan for largescale emigration to Palestine, perhaps even some form of sovereignty and requests our help.'

'Beaumont supports this?' Currie barked.

Leroux shifted in the leather armchair which grumbled in embarrassment. 'He didn't say one way or the other. I was just the ...' He couldn't bring himself to finish the sentence and Currie let it die, hanging in silence. He ran his hand down his face and groaned.

'Good God, the Reverend's stark raving mad! And what does Beaumont expect me to do? Go to the Sultan and say sorry chap the stars have aligned, and you need to give up Jerusalem. Our man upstairs is in charge now. The Sultan will chop my head off and then launch a Jihad. That'll be India and Suez up the spout. And if the Sultan sees fit to return my head, Her Majesty will stick it on a pike!'

'I don't think Beaumont knew exactly what was in the package,' Simpkins sputtered.

'I don't doubt it. The intelligence service they call themselves – what?'

'He said you would know what to do,' Leroux said.

'Yes, well.' His eyes wandered over to the unmade fireplace and he took the notes from Leroux, glancing through them.

'You say Herzl is not a religious man?'

'No, he feels culturally rejected, treated as second class citizen. He wants the Jews to have their own state where they can be equals. It is not a religious quest, for him at least.'

'Whatever the motivation, the Sultan will not agree to it. Jerusalem is a holy site for Islam as well, and I very much doubt he wants to be known as the Caliph who lost Jerusalem. What makes Herzl think that the Sultan will agree?'

'I'm not sure. He solicits support from anyone he can. Whether it's Hechler and his prophecies, or through him the Kaiser, who may have an interest in being the protector of Jews in the Holy Land. There is also Count Nevlinski - I got the impression he thinks a deal can be made.'

'Nevlinski?' Currie sneered, struck a match, and set it to the first page, dropping it into the grate. One by one he lit the notes, occasionally glancing at the window. 'Not another word about this. We cannot put it to the Sultan or even be associated with it. There is Suez to consider and the Muslim population of India. And waiting to pounce on any mistake is Russia. They would dearly love for us to burn our bridges with the Sultan. Simpkins, you will write to Hechler and tell him that it is being taken care of. We'll just have to string him along.'

'Yes, sir.'

'And Leroux, forget about this religious nonsense. Remember you're only here because of over-sentimental Liberal politicians who think that with a bit of amateur detective work they can fix a game that has been playing out for hundreds of years. I have already pushed the Sultan to protect the Armenians as far as I can. We cannot allow a wedge to be driven between us and the Sultan. The Russians will surely exploit it. Simpkins will take you to the Sublime Porte this morning to apply for your papers, and then I don't expect to see or hear from you again. Submit your report to Beaumont if you must. Understood?'

Leroux rose. At least he was still going to Armenia. 'Yes, sir.'

The Ambassador grabbed a poker from the fireplace and pointed it at Leroux.

'I shouldn't need to remind you that the national interest is at stake, but you aren't exactly English, are you?'

'Understood, Sir.'

'No more mistakes.'

Leroux mechanically stood to attention, more from muscle memory than respect as the Ambassador prodded the ashes in the hearth and left by the secret entrance. Just as it clicked shut, Simpkins opened the door to the lobby, where the cleaner polished on his knees just paces away, and ushered Leroux out. They were two minnows in a shark pool. Back in Cape Town great whites circled in Table Bay at the meeting of two oceans. What predators lurked here at the gateway between two continents? They walked in glum silence to the head of a short queue of cabs.

'Currie is an old friend of Salisbury,' Simpkins finally said. 'I'm afraid he sees your mission as a Liberal inspired venture and wants nothing to do with it. Why didn't you tell me about the dossier?'

'Sorry. I should have. I don't know who's behind it and I wanted to keep the knowledge close, hoping that someone might reveal their guilt. How did Currie learn of it?'

'I don't know.'

Their cab climbed steadily along the forested road to Yildiz, the Sultan's palace. Atop a hill and behind a forest as well as a wall it was far better protected from the sea than Topkapi, although the guns of modern dreadnoughts would not be too inconvenienced. They swept through the gate and wound up through the gardens and fragrant woods and past ornate bungalows known as kiosks. Arriving at the main courtyard, the driver ignored the Sultan's residence and reined the horses in by the entrance to the adjoining Government building. A single soldier in a simple blue uniform stepped aside to admit them into a cool atrium where a courtier approached and referred to his appointments book. He beckoned another official and murmured into his ear as though reluctant to disturb the peace of the sanctuary.

'Could be hours,' Simpkins said, settling down on a divan. There was no set time for the appointment, and Simpkins was not sure who would receive them. The other seats filled with petitioners in robes, kaftans, and western style suits and discreet asides between them slowly built into a hubbub of different tongues. Simpkins occasionally greeted a familiar official, all attired in collarless frock coats called a stambouline, and briefed Leroux. The empire encompassed a wide variety of peoples which the Sultans saw as a strength, recruiting the business expertise of the Greeks and Armenians to the top of the Government while the ferocious Albanians went to the army. Nearly half of the representatives of the old Parliament had been non-Muslim, but the loss of the Christian provinces in the Balkans had concentrated the Muslim majority and the pressure to rule in their favour.

Leroux wandered to a window, stretching his legs. Waiting was a bureaucratic skill he had yet to master. A small man in the black stambouline of the palace administrators entered causing a flurry of pocketed papers and straightened robes. He approached Simpkins, who waved urgently at Leroux. The administrator pointed at several other visitors and led the small group to double doors leading to the heart of the Palace. Simpkins shrugged his shoulders, and they turned down a long corridor, the floor made of imperial porphyry, the red quartz of the polished stone glistening beneath walls decorated with gilded mirrors and slim tables dressed with delicate Dresden porcelain. Simpkins tugged a handkerchief from his breast pocket and mopped his brow. 'This is the way to the Hall of Audience. Most unusual.'

Two tall soldiers heaved open the doors to the great chamber. Simpkins rummaged through his pockets and turned up a pen but no writing material. 'I should get a message to the Ambassador. I thought we were seeing the assistant to the Minister.'

'Who are we seeing?'

'Looks like the Grand Vizier.'

Leroux straightened his tie and smoothed down his hair. Simpkins bent to retie a shoelace. They were corralled in front of a raised dais with an armchair so wide it was practically a sofa. Gilded woodwork framed green silk cushions, and a soldier guarded each armrest tilting a gold tipped flagpole forward so that the tassel-edged red silk banners hung to clearly display the gold crescent and star. Another petitioner shuffled in front of them, his thin frame merely a hanger for his kaftan. Even under a thick beard, his left cheek was swollen by a growth. His hands rubbed together with a papery rustle as he bowed his head. To their side a small wiry man in a white linen shirt and the double-breasted crimson vest of the Balkans chatted with a well-to-do Egyptian in a long-sleeved tunic that reached below his knees.

A dozen musicians lined the window wall, one with a kos, like a giant kettle drum, three with double-headed davul drums slung around their necks, and the rest with trumpets that Simpkins called borus. They struck up an urgent, but odd, rhythm overlain by a mystical wailing that harked back to the days of the Janissaries.

'If it wasn't for this lot, we wouldn't have the Band of the Grenadier Guards. The original marching band they are,' Simpkins said, wincing. The far doors swung open and a gaggle of advisors in navy blue jackets overloaded with gold embroidery spilt in and split into two groups facing each other in front of the raised seat.

Leroux inclined towards Simpkins and whispered, "They sound a bit stuck in time. Does this always happen?'

'No.' A dozen more soldiers filed in and formed a corridor from the entrance towards the sofa. Simpkins blew his nose and swallowed. 'I don't think we're seeing the Grand Vizier.'

The music stopped with a final boom of the huge kos.

'May you walk with fortune!' the soldiers exclaimed.

Leroux craned his neck to see if anyone had entered.

'Sultan Abdul Hamid Han!' the soldiers chorused.

Leroux imagined a splendid figure in a turban with egret feathers and a lavish satin coat, straight out of his childhood memories of reading 1,001 Nights.

'Always the victorious!' the soldiers chanted in unison.

A red fez moved between the heads of the guards.

'May Allah bless your way!'

From the soldier's tunnel a man emerged in the same simple black uniform of the palace, swinging a slim cane. A red sash across his starched white shirt and a silver brooch on his chest were the only embellishments. Under the neat brim of his fez, the eyes were the most notable feature. Alert, questing, they scoured the petitioners as he crossed the parquet floor and perched on the edge of the chair. It would be easy to see this figure, dwarfed by his guards, as a manifestation of the decline of the great Sultans, but his gaze was calm and intense. Portrayed in the press as saturnine, Leroux found his features more delicate than forbidding.

A firm tap of his cane commanded utter silence. An advisor stepped forward, bowed to the nearest red banner, and kissed the fringe, before lifting it to brush his forehead.

'Great Sultan, we are ready to receive your wisdom.'

The Sultan's stambouline splayed out, and he sat upright, his feet planted squarely in front of him, the fingers of one hand thrumming his cane. Simpkins discreetly identified the Grand Vizier, and the captain of the Sultan's bodyguard, who sported a moustache that one of Napoleon's Imperial Guard would have been proud of, although he lacked their imposing height. Simpkins hushed as the Sultan stared directly at him. Without breaking eye contact, the Sultan summoned the Grand Vizier closer and muttered something. The Grand Vizier bowed and turned.

'The Sultan requests that you send for the Ambassador. He wishes to be assured that what you say here today is vouched for.'

Simpkins stammered, 'At once, your Majesty,' and stumbled as he backed away, at once bowing and feeling his pockets again for his pen. Leroux felt the weight of the Sultan's gaze shift to him, followed by the curiosity of the advisors and the petitioners as the slap of Simpkins boots diminished. Leroux steadied himself, tightening to his best parade ground posture. Was he expected to say something? Before he could blurt anything, the Grand Vizier's assistant called out a name. Leroux's ears burned so hard he didn't catch it.

The Balkan man shuffled forward, and a torrent of words sprang forth. His hands flew about before clasping together at his breast as he ran out of breath and sobbed. An official stepped forward and summarized his complaint in French for the benefit of the foreigners. The man was from Bosnia, a simple Muslim trying his best to live under Austro-Hungarian rule. But Christians had beaten him, burnt his shop and forced his family to flee, and here they were, destitute.

The Sultan pursed his lips and closed his eyes. When they opened, they fixed straight on Leroux, before sweeping back to the Bosnian who sank to his knees and prostrated himself. The Sultan spoke gently to the man, who wept, rocking on his knees, scraping the ground. The translator announced that the Sultan had provided the man with a job in the palace gardens. The Sultan tapped his cane and two attendants sprung forward and helped the man to his feet and led him away. As he exited through the double doors, Simpkins slipped back into the hall. The next petitioner summoned was the Egyptian, who presented a sheaf of papers. He complained of the corruption of the British officials that ran Egypt and cited copious examples. Midway through his pleas a herald announced Ambassador Currie, who scuttled alongside Simpkins and muttered, 'Damn unorthodox,' and cast about the room, nodding at some of the advisors. When the Egyptian had finished, the Grand Vizier conferred with the Sultan and turned to Currie. 'The Sultan invites you to answer the accusation.'

The Ambassador clasped a wrist in front of him, cleared his throat, and rose on the balls of his feet before sinking back. 'I have heard but one side of the story, your Majesty. I do not claim our administration in Egypt is perfect, but this is the first I have heard of this. If you will allow me to coordinate with your scribe, I will see that the complaint is referred to the appropriate authority and I will personally follow it through.'

The Sultan nodded, and the Egyptian was escorted away. All eyes turned to the old man with the cancerous tumour on his jaw.

'Who is he?' Leroux said.

Simpkins shook his head. 'The white band on his turban signifies a cleric.'

The Sultan stood to welcome the man and they began a discussion on Islam, the cleric arguing for a return to the original ideals to foster greater unity among the faithful. That this would empower the brotherhood of Islam, the Ummah, to regain its former strength against the Infidels. A shorter quiet exchange followed that was not translated and the man thanked the Sultan, who gently cupped the old man's elbow preventing him from sinking to his knees.

'Let everyone know,' the Sultan announced. 'Jamal al-Din al-Afghani is under my protection.'

Two soldiers strode forward to offer their arms to the cleric and helped him to the door. No other petitioners remained.

'And what do you want?' The Sultan addressed the Ambassador. Leroux swallowed. Why was the Sultan dealing personally with his request and why had he summoned the Ambassador?

The Ambassador flashed a sideways glare at Leroux and Simmonds.

'I understand from my attaché that Mr Leroux, a representative of The Times, requests permission to travel to Erzurum to interview the bishop.'

'You wish to stir up more trouble in the Armenian provinces! I know what your papers say – I read them! "The Bloody Sultan." That's what you call me!' The hollow thud of his cane striking the dais echoed across the room. 'What you do not understand is that your intervention in our affairs only riles the masses and fuels their grievances against Christians. I am not persecuting them. Yes, there are local disturbances, but I am trying to restrain my people. All races are welcomed here, but your missionaries stir them up. It was you in the West who gave the world the Spanish Inquisition, the conquistadors, Cesar Borgia, the Puritans, not to mention General Booth and his Salvation Army! Look at the Congo, the Philippines… yet you want to lecture me about the Armenians?'

Currie inclined his head. 'I would not dream –'

'Who is that?' The Sultan threw out an arm in the direction of an advisor, short and round but rigidly at attention. The Ambassador wrung his hands behind his back. 'Mikael Portukal Pasha, your Majesty.'

'The Minister of the Privy Treasury and an Armenian.'

The minister stood straight, chest out, clear eyed, his badge of office prominently displayed, his cheeks tinged with the fuss.

'Do you know why?' The Sultan continued. 'Because they are the best. You see one Greek may be able to cheat two Jews, but one Armenian can cheat two Greeks!' He clapped his hands together and all the advisors chortled in unison. 'Perhaps you should question your Egyptian administrators before promoting an investigation into the treatment of my own subjects? Is this any way to treat an ally?'

The Sultan looked between Leroux and the Ambassador. Had he detected the coldness between them?

'Mr Leroux's assignment is nothing to do with me,' the Ambassador spluttered. 'As I understand, it is merely a request to interview the bishop of Erzurum.' A bead of sweat ran from the Ambassador's temple, as his hands clenched and unclenched, and he looked to Leroux.

'The Ambassador wishes you to say something,' the Sultan said.

'Your Majesty,' Leroux said meeting his glare, 'You are right that I have been sent to report on rumours from Armenia. Our Christian readership is concerned to learn of the fate of their brothers. There are conflicting reports and no doubt some people are trying to make mischief out of it, but I have been sent to report faithfully on what I see, with your permission. I expect the bishop will have a balanced view.'

'What is the latest news from Armenia?' the Sultan asked the Grand Vizier, who snatched his hand away from his beard.

'I received a report from Zeki Pasha only yesterday. There are some minor disturbances. The missionaries cause unrest. It is regrettable, but under control. There are of course some disagreements between the Kurds and the Armenians,' he spread his hands open, 'ancient blood feuds...'

'It has always been so,' the Sultan said, 'We cannot interfere in matters of honour.'

'Quite so. Most wise, your Majesty,' the Grand Vizier said, 'This proposed trip will only stir up trouble.'

The Sultan bent forward and crooked a finger at Leroux. The Ambassador sucked his teeth and rocked on his heels.

'Come forward,' said the Grand Vizier.

Leroux approached the platform and genuflected as best he knew.

'Your paper should do more to portray me in a fair light,' the Sultan said evenly. 'False news travels fast for fools are so willing to hear it. The truth requires a bit more effort. You must see both sides of the curtain.

The Grand Vizier will arrange for you to visit the Kum Kapu hospital, which treats victims of the violence. They are Muslim, are they not?'

'Nearly all, your Majesty.'

'And the captain of my guard will see to the travel permit and escort you personally through the Armenian territories. It is bandit country, and it wouldn't do for The Times to accuse me of killing journalists as well.'

The captain snapped to attention, face front, but his eyes swivelled to Leroux. The Grand Vizier kissed the tassels again and resumed his station.

The Sultan rose and strode through a ripple of bowing heads, the captain and the guard following in his wake, as the hall resonated to their lock step.

'I hope you're satisfied,' the Ambassador said, loosening his collar as the midday sun beat down on the flagstones of the palace courtyard.

'I've never had an audience with the Sultan before,' Simpkins said turning to see who was in earshot.

'What did you learn?'

'Learn, sir?'

'Why was I summoned?'

Simpkins coughed into his fist. 'He wanted us to show us that he knows Leroux does not just represent The Times. He's on official business.'

'Exactly. And?'

'And he will hold us responsible for his report.'

'Precisely. Got that Leroux?'

'The petitioners were to send us a message,' Simpkins said.

'It was quite a performance,' Leroux said. 'Before you arrived a Bosnian complained of persecution by the Christians.'

'A charge of hypocrisy,' said Simpkins. 'To show us that Christians persecute Musselmen even as we accuse them.'

'And he threatened you with the Egyptian,' Leroux said. 'The administration is seen as corrupt. The people await only a word to rise.'

'And Al-Baghdadi is the worst of all,' the Ambassador muttered darkly. 'He was behind the assassination of the Shah earlier this year. Claimed he was too subservient to the wishes of foreigners, specifically the British. He is well-connected in India, where I fear there is more support for the Caliph than the Queen.'

'He wants us to know that if we don't accept his friendship, he can be a bad enemy,' Simpkins said.

Leroux kicked at the ground. This was the message that the Ambassador was reinforcing, that he wanted Leroux to remember and that he should bear in mind when he reported on the Armenian situation. This was worse than having an editor.

'Are we boring you Leroux?'

'No, sir. I was just thinking about the one thing the Sultan didn't mention.'

'What thing?'

'He made a point of demanding your presence to make it clear that he knew about our relationship and that I was travelling to Armenia for the government.'

'Yes, so?'

'And he went to great lengths to detail every perceived slight.'

'And?'

'He didn't mention or even allude to the Reverend's prophecy or Herzl's agenda. Seems odd. That was what we were most frightened of.'

The Ambassador chuntered.

'He's right, sir,' said Simpkins.

The Ambassador turned back to the palace and the long line of windows looking down on them. 'The Sultan is wily enough not to tip his hand. I wouldn't read anything into that.' He checked his timepiece and grunted. 'What we do know is that we are on thin ice with the Sultan. No more mistakes. Collect your travel papers. Stick to the conditions, meticulously, and remember the national interest is at stake.'

Leroux gritted his teeth. 'Are you telling me to only report what the Sultan would want?' A roll of flesh bulged over Simpkins's collar as his neck recoiled.

'Of course not!' The Ambassador's cheeks reddened, and he slapped his gloves against his cane. 'Just make sure that what you discover is relayed through, and only through, the proper channels.' The Ambassador stalked off to find a cab on his own. No doubt Currie would see to it that Flora Shaw only printed an approved account.

Simpkins stared after the Ambassador, biting his lip.

'Torn between your uncle and your boss?'

'I think my uncle's right. We need to know what's really going on. Turning a blind eye to mollify the Sultan will only encourage him. And as you say something else is going on. If I've learnt one thing in Constantinople, it's that no news is rarely good news.'

A young lad in a ragged oversized shirt sat on his haunches in the shade to the side of the hotel entrance. He winked as Leroux crossed the road and jumped up. 'Laruu?' It was the only word he had, but he reached out and touched the slouch hat. Leroux nodded and the lad produced a cream envelope sealed with scarlet wax from under his top, handling it with great care. Leroux swapped it for a coin and received a bright smile in gratitude. The boy skipped off into the street before the doorman could shoo him away and a skinny dog followed, running around his legs, and pawing him. Leroux returned to his room. The letter showed no sign of tampering. Back in Johannesburg even sealed messages were vulnerable, such was the desire for advance knowledge of test results from a mine. Tweezers could be inserted where the flap was not secured by the wax seal and the letter rolled up and slid out. It left a tell-tale curl in the note, but none was apparent here.

It was from Herzl. He was wise not to trust the clerk at the front desk and the fewer that knew of their association the better. He wanted to meet at the Café Anglaise, Grande Rue de Pera, at 8 p.m. and asked Leroux to take care not to be followed. Leroux gripped his balcony rail. Below the bustle of the Grande Rue wound down the hill to the thin haze above the coal fired steamers that crammed the quays. He couldn't pick out the Café, but slender kayiks scurried between the shores, their oars dipping in unison. A passenger vessel, its two funnels raked back and pumping out billows of steam, picked up speed and turned into the Bosporus heading to the Black Sea. Perhaps it was heading for Trebizond, the gateway to Armenia.

The thin news Leroux had for Herzl was that the trip to Armenia was proceeding, he doubted that the Sultan was behind the theft of the dossier, and the prospect of receiving help from the embassy for either of them was slim. Perhaps Herzl had learnt something about the dossier. His caution was reassuring, but how to give the Sultan's agents the slip? As the sun sank, Leroux left his slouch hat behind and walked toward the café, bartering awkwardly in shops, just one of the many Franks that thronged the streets around Pera. He bought a three-yard-long strip of indigo cloth in one shop, wrapping it around his waist and buttoning his jacket before leaving. In another he selected the flimsiest pair of leather sandals, tucking one each into his two inside jacket pockets and finally he chose a selection of baklava in a small box. As he left each shop, Leroux checked for the incurious dawdler, or a man who had suddenly become captivated in the contents of a haberdashery shop window, but none stood out. Carrying the pastries, he walked past the Café Anglaise and continued retracing the route he had taken in the cab from Sirkeci Station until he saw the stone building that he was looking for.

Two Turks emerged chatting amiably, fresh faced and glowing, their hair glistening and Leroux inhaled the humid jasmine air as he paid the hammam attendant in the marbled reception. A door opened and a man emerged, adjusting his belt, and looking curiously at Leroux as he passed. Leroux found a free space half-way down the changing room next to the largest kaftan he could see. When the chubby man at the far end disappeared through an archway into the billowing steam, Leroux turned his trousers up to show his ankles, pocketed his socks, tied his boots together by the laces and hung them from his neck, and pulled on the sandals. He unwound the material from his waist and slipped the kaftan over his head. It reached well below his knees and was capacious enough to allow him to squeeze his boots between his arms and ribs. Tying a slipknot about a yard into the cloth he placed it at the back of his head and pulled the rest forward over his scalp, twisted it and wound it three times around his head, tucking the end in to form a turban. He released the knot and pulled the yard of cloth forward around his face, draping it over his shoulder in the manner of a desert tribesman. Leroux left the baklava next to the peg where the kaftan had been and walked out into the hall and towards the exit. This was the first test. The disguise was far from perfect, but enough to fool someone either not paying attention or looking for something completely different. The attendant didn't even glance up. Leroux pulled the cloth tighter against his face, waddled down the steps feeling his hip, and headed back towards the Café Anglaise. He ignored odd looks from two waiters skilled at sizing up their customers, and threaded through crowded tables to the back, catching snatches of French, German, and English. The sprinkling of Ottoman businessmen took no notice of him, deep in frantic gestures and negotiations. Nevlinski brooded at a small corner table deep inside the café, his back against the wall. A newspaper, folded to an article, occupied one hand, but his eyes roamed. Leroux edged past him and through a beaded archway, past the kitchens to the toilet. He removed his turban and wrapped up the kaftan with it. As he left the toilet, a waiter emerged from the kitchen with a platter of drinks held aloft, and Leroux waited while he served a table of Europeans. When he returned, Leroux paid him to run the parcel back to the hammam and leave it next to the box of baklava. Leroux followed him out and rested his hand lightly on Nevlinski's shoulder.

The Pole snatched his newspaper to his chest. 'What the …. Leroux? Where did you come from?'

'I received a message from Herzl to meet here.' Leroux slid around the table and along the banquet next to Nevlinski. No one in the café paid them any attention, not even the waiters.

'I hear you were at the Palace earlier, caused quite a stir,' Nevlinski said sulkily. 'I could have arranged for a travel permit with much less fuss.' His stubby fingers fluttered over his cravat and then snapped in the direction of a waiter. 'Still, Herzl has taken quite a liking to you and asked me to help.'

'Hopefully, the permit is in the bag. Does your source know who took my dossier?'

'That we should talk about some more….' Nevlinski said, smoothing the table linen. The waiter arrived and took the coffee order, and Herzl appeared behind him.

'Were you followed?'

'I don't think so,' Leroux replied.

Herzl grinned. 'You are gaining a reputation. I'm not sure it's wise to associate with you.'

Nevlinski smirked as Herzl pulled a chair out. 'But you're not doing too badly. You saw the Sultan. I am yet to have my audience.'

'Patience, my dear Theodor,' Nevlinski protested. 'The ground must be prepared. We wait for the most opportune moment.'

Herzl sighed. 'I am a wealthy man, but this is an expensive business. I think I prefer Leroux's approach! Scatter the pidgeons!'

'I'm afraid my news is mixed at best,' Leroux said.

'Your Ambassador has cold feet about the Reverend's proposal?' Herzl said lightly.

'And he's less than enthusiastic about my trip to Armenia.'

'I didn't think he would want to rock the boat.'

Nevlinski leant forward. 'But you're still going?'

'Yes.'

'Then the Ambassador can't feel that strongly about it. You asked who stole your dossier. I can look into it. My fees are reasonable. I imagine the Ambassador would want to know too. He can pay. Ask him.'

Leroux sat back as the waiter arrived with the coffee. A thin stream of dark liquid poured from a copper pot which the waiter undulated high above the porcelain cups, encouraging frothy heads on the brew. Leroux's shoulders eased down as he breathed in the earthy aroma. Nevlinski knew more than he let on but wouldn't waste information on Leroux if he thought he wasn't going to get anything in return. No point revealing that the Ambassador had sent Leroux packing, Nevlinski would just clam up and he had a few questions to answer. He had the mottled complexion of a drinker. Maybe it was time to see how he took it.

Nevlinski scowled at the lack of a response, excused himself and pushed through the beads as the waiter finished arranging glasses of water and pink squares of Turkish delight.

'Cat got your tongue?' Herzl smiled.

'Between us, I don't think the Sultan was behind the theft of the dossier.'

Herzl tilted his coffee cup, examining the dregs. 'A guess?'

'Just a guess.'

Nevlinski clapped Leroux on the shoulder as he thudded back down and lit a cigarette.

'The Ambassador respects my advice, don't be afraid to ask him.'

'Who else do you work for?'

'I can wear more than one hat. I will let you know if there is a conflict of interest.'

'I have to trust you on that?'

'Of course. I have my reputation to consider, I would not get far without that.'

'All I know is that you used to work for the Austro-Hungarians.'

Herzl winced.

'That was a misunderstanding. Herzl vouches for me. And to prove my bona fides, I will take you to an establishment tonight where you will hear the real gossip of Constantinople. We can toast our new friendship. Unless of course you have a better offer?'

'That's very generous of you,' Leroux said, although he suspected he would be footing the bill. Herzl eyelids drooped and he leant on the table to rise. 'Enjoy tonight, gentlemen. Leroux, I wish you luck in your mission. Us journalists should stick together.'

'I'm going to the Kum Kapu hospital tomorrow morning. It's a condition of the permit that I see the other side of the story first.'

'Don't let Nevlinski lead you astray.' Herzl coughed, loose and phlegmy, and rubbed his chest. A waiter grabbed a glass of water for him, but Herzl declined and walked straight-backed out of the coffee house.

'Herzl understands that it is hard to reach the bottom of a matter here and that you need a guide like me.'

'You can really discover who took the dossier, the truth?'

Nevlinski chuckled. 'Truth? What on earth are you going to do with that? As for giving it to voters, heaven forbid! Stupid enough to give them a vote. No, I can help you get what you want, but only if I know what it is that you really want. Why has your government really sent you here?'

'You already know all there is to know. Drink?'

Nevlinski snapped his fingers at the waiter again. 'Look at it from the Sultan's point of view. You might be here to sensationalise the unrest for The Times. You could be here to liaise with Armenian revolutionaries on behalf of your government. Or there's the Reverend's proposal. That might be popular with British voters, but it would infuriate the Turks. If I knew a bit more, it would help me learn who took the dossier. Information is currency, as they say.'

Leroux shrugged. 'I've already told you everything.' Nevlinski sunk his chin into his chest and brooded until a waiter set two chilled glasses of white wine on the table, condensation running down the sides.

Nevlinski raised his glass to Leroux. 'Have it your way. But by inflaming the Armenian situation you are also giving the Tsar the opportunity, the right, the duty even, to intervene. The Tsar is the head of the Orthodox Church, appointed by God, and responsible for the protection of the Armenian Christians here. If you provoke trouble, you might mess everything up for all of us.'

Leroux topped up Nevlinski's glass whenever it reached low tide and the Pole dropped ever weightier and doubtless distantly connected names. 'Have I told you about the Kaiser's interest in Islam?' Nevlinski spluttered, putting a sweaty palm on Leroux, and leering up.

'Now we go to Theodora's,' he said and sauntered into the street leaving Leroux to pay. Nevlinski walked steadily, with not even a slur as they strolled under the streetlights to the harbour accompanied only by the dogs that ventured out at night to pick the roads clean. One mangy mongrel sniffed Leroux with a sweeping wag of its tail, but Nevlinski batted it away with his cane. If the Sultan's agents were following them, they were either so good Leroux hadn't spotted them or so bad they hadn't picked him up again. Unless of course, Nevlinski was the Sultan's agent.

They turned into a side street and the character dropped quicker than a sailor's trousers on payday. The wooden houses crowded over, almost touching at the top and the air had a foetid tinge. A ponytailed doorman, his arms folded to highlight the bulge of his biceps, marked the entrance under a dim oil lamp. He greeted Nevlinski with a bellow over the muffled strains of music, swinging the plain door open and pressed his hands in prayer, bowing with a wink, as Leroux followed Nevlinski in.

The Count acknowledged the maître d' and made straight for an alcove at the back, where the pink satin seats had lost their shine. The clientele was rougher than Leroux had expected, although gossip needed no carriage as Byron had warned. A waiter sporting tails and a powdered wig seemed to anticipate Nevlinski's order and served a bottle of whisky and a magnum of Champagne. Nevlinski poured the whisky overfull.

'They say that when a man goes to Pera, you know what he is going for - Ivresse et plaisir!' Nevlinski exclaimed, raising a toast to intoxication and pleasure.

A passing pair of Greek dancing boys left nothing to the imagination as they performed to a lute and castanets. Nevlinski waved them away and lectured Leroux on the attraction of the Hejazi women with their hooked noses and blue lips, and the pretty but badly behaved Armenians, before declaring that the Circassians were beyond compare. His hands rose up in delight as the maître d' ushered over a quartet of dancers and unhooked the ropes that pinned back the velvet curtains, as red as the carmine on the ladies' lips. Nevlinski clapped, assuring Leroux they were Circassian with their dark blond tresses and startling blue-green eyes. The gold chains that hung at their hips rattled and the sheer muslin dresses sighed with their gyrations, the patches of intricate beading struggling to hide their modesty. Nevlinski refilled the whiskeys, mesmerized by the rippling flesh and clapped to welcome two of the dancers either side of him. The others pulled Leroux around to sit with his back to the curtains, drawing their chairs up close, helping themselves to champagne. Leroux lowered his hand under the table to tip away his drink, but long fingernails caught his wrist and guided the glass to his lips, stroking his cheek. Nevlinski refilled the glasses and reclined spreadeagled opposite him, damp patches at his armpits. A dancer thrust another drink into Leroux's hand and bought it to his mouth pressing her body against him, the stale smell of sweat swimming up. Leroux was losing his contest with Nevlinski and pushed forward, elbows on the table.

'Have you travelled in the country?' he shouted.

Nevlinski leaned in, cocking his ear, and topped up the drinks again.

'God no. It is very poor. Impossible to get a decent room, except perhaps with the missionaries or the Governor's house. And the food...' He had a decent grimace on him. Leroux blew his cheeks out, as the Circassians caressed his arms.

'So, you will be at the hospital tomorrow morning?' Nevlinski said.

'Yes. And if I do not get the permit tomorrow, I'll reconsider your offer.'

'You know, a bit of baksheesh will get you a long way,' Nevlinski winked, as a waiter arrived with another magnum and Nevlinski produced a small pocketbook and paid him. It was the first time Leroux had seen the Count pay for anything. Nevlinski refilled everyone's glasses and raised a toast.

'Na Zdrowie!' Nevlinski drained his glass and looked expectantly at Leroux.

'Bajabule!' The liquid burned and had a bitter after taste.

'What?'

'Good health in Zulu.'

The lady on Nevlinski's right flourished her fingers, her sharp nails drawing down his cheek, and a lithe arm curled around Leroux's neck, tilting his glass to his lips. Another dancer draped over Leroux, her jewellery pressing into his shirt, pinning his arm, sweet perfume strong but not strong enough, and he struggled to focus. Nevlinski poured from the bottle and a dancer helped, laughing. Nevlinski grinned maniacally, slapping his thigh. 'You are seeing the real Constantinople now!'

The dancer put the bottle down, said something to the Count and purred.

'These ladies know everything. Ask anything you want.' Nevlinski said something in Turkish to them and they batted their eyelashes.

'Who's your best customer?'

They stroked Leroux's chest, feeling around his waist. 'Unfortunately,' Nevlinski said, 'they don't speak English or French. You need me.' He raised his drink and clinked Leroux's glass. One of the ladies bent down in front of him, her necklaces swayed and tickled his thigh. Her mouth was alive, but he understood not a word, her eyes duller than a quagmire. Leroux rocked back, giddy. His hands felt strangely limp. The woman opposite crossed her legs and he tried to follow the movement, but his head spun, and he slumped into the dancer at his side. She pushed him up and he struggled to raise his head, only to see Nevlinski's ferrety eyes fixed on him. Someone stroked his cheek, and Leroux mumbled through her hand.

'What?' Nevlinski said.

'How do you think you will be able to persuade you-know-who to agree to Herzl's plans?'

Leroux reached for the bottle as something to focus on. Nevlinski must be loosening up a little by now. How much can he tuck away? As Leroux reached to top up Nevlinski's drink, the girls pulled him back, smothering him, seeing to the drinks themselves.

Nevlinski fondled one who playfully slapped him. 'With you-know-what!' He rubbed his thumb into his fingers.

'Is that all?'

Nevlinski tapped his nose. 'More drinks!' A girl filled the glasses and held one below Leroux's nose, the smell sickening. She caressed his chin, slipping a finger into his mouth, probing, tipping the liquid in, giggling.

The Count's head swayed from side to side as Leroux tried to follow the blur of his lips. He took a deep breath, but the air was musty and did nothing to dispel his dizziness. The dancers gyrated, light flashed and swirled blending into one and he felt a soft hand supporting his cheek. He rested against the warm flesh, but it was gone, and he jerked straight again. Nevlinski's face closed in, his hand waving back and forth and then he felt a grip on the back of his neck, holding him in place. The hand wasn't soft, the fingers weren't delicate, the nails not long. They squeezed and curled around his throat. Firm fingertips dug into his collar bone. The ladies' hands swept up his thighs and pushed his arms behind his back, their faces swimming into view with Nevlinski's. Where was his strength? A length of silk ran over his wrists and tightened. The bristle of a beard scratched his neck, and a hot breath entered his ear.

'Who are you working for?' Leroux's stomach churned. The voice was guttural and spoke in heavily accented German but from which part he knew not. He couldn't think straight, however many times the question came. Did he know what he was doing or why? His eyelids drooped. The more he tried to think the heavier they became. The man shook him. 'Who?'

Leroux's jaw hung slackly. He wanted to say something. What? He mumbled, 'The Times.'

A hand slapped him. His face moved but there was no pain. Nevlinski's face loomed in, peering into his eyes. He grasped Leroux's cheeks, forcing flesh between his molars with his thumb and forefinger, prising his mouth open.

'Give him more.'

A girl tipped a drink in and Nevlinski released his grip and moved his hand under his chin, forcing his head back. Leroux choked, the liquid burned, his eyes watered and then the pain melted.

'Ja, The Times, who else?'

Leroux clenched his teeth, who else? The Government. He was working for them. They weren't asking him to do anything more than The Times. His head jolted. Or were they instructing The Times? It was so confusing.

'Are you working for the British government?'

Yes, that was it. He nodded, grinning. 'Yes.' He licked his lips, a thirst now raging.

'What do they want you to do?'

'The same. Same thing.'

'Same as what?'

'The Times.'

'And what does The Times want you to find out?'

Leroux giggled. The British government wasn't interested in finding out about the Armenians or whatever else these people were trying to hide. They were going through the motions. The sweaty hand smacked him again, a salty tang kissing his lips, but only numbness in his face.

'The Armenians. What's happening to them.'

'What else?' The hands at his neck tightened. 'What else?'

Nevlinski's nose seemed to touch his, white-headed pores and bloodshot eyes.

'Why are you working with Herzl?' the guttural voice demanded.

That was it, Herzl, End of Times. 'Prophecy.'

Another voice, Nevlinski. 'The crackpot Reverend I told you about, the British aren't interested in it, they don't know anything.' The fingers tightened.

Friday 31st July, Constantinople

He woke to the taste. Sour like a rancid pear. His tongue unstuck from the roof of his mouth. His head pounded and his cheek rested on something hard and rough. A groan. Not his. He shifted and his joints complained. Leroux opened an eye to threadbare carpet. He propped himself up on his elbows and dry retched, wincing as his head pounded. He was next to a bed. Someone was in it, and behind them light filtered through thin curtains. Another groan and the shape under the blanket squirmed, followed by a girlish squeal. Leroux jumped up and a hairy face popped out from the covers.

'Merhaba!'

'Sorry!' No time for introductions. Leroux stumbled through the door into a gloomy corridor. His heart raced and he felt an overwhelming urge to swallow but couldn't. He bent over and his head hammered in protest. He sipped breath in and wiped a sheen of sweat from his brow, paint flaking from the wall when he put his hand out to steady himself. He staggered to the end of the corridor and a bolted door. The metal squealed painfully as he drew the fastening open, and he fell through the door into the harsh light of day. Leroux covered his eyes and hung his head, sweat running through his hair, prickling his scalp. He panted and bile dribbled from the corner of his mouth. Where in the hell was he? And what had happened? He braced his hands on his knees and leant back against the wall. The palpitations receded. He focussed on his breathing. A man hurried past keeping as far away as he could in the narrow alley.

What time was it? Leroux headed towards the noisy, nearer end of the alley, rubbing his wrists. It was a back street, but he was right next to the entrance to Theodora's, sad and seedy in the daylight, its shutters barred, and lantern doused. He made his way to the main road, where the sun was already punishingly high. A memory pierced the fog. The appointment at the hospital! He had to be there at ten! He jumped back, startled by the trampling of hooves and blare of a horn, as a large omnibus trundled by on iron rails that had seemingly come from nowhere. The uniformed conductor raised his white gloved hand in exasperation.

Leroux approached the first European he saw, a thick set man chomping on a breakfast cigar, and asked him the time. 'A quarter of ten, sonny, and whaddayaknow?' he said, distracted by a Numidian Ottoman officer riding past, followed by white attendants on foot. Leroux's hopes of a travel pass hung on reaching the hospital in time. He smoothed his hair and tucked his shirt, and hoped his eyes weren't too bloodshot as he hailed a cab. The driver seemed to know the hospital, but as they pulled out into the traffic, Leroux knew that he would be late. He hunched over and cradled his bristly cheeks, rummaging through his memory. He had a score to settle with Nevlinski. He had been played, again. He thought he could drink Nevlinski under the table, but all the time he was being set up. By whom? The man spoke German, but not any kind of German he had heard. Not a native. A deception of some kind, but they knew he spoke the language. He checked his pockets and came up short. Not a lira, not even a piastre. Bastard. And what the hell had they given him to drink, his head felt like a blacksmith's anvil and his stomach sloshed around like the bilges of a steamship after a storm. The driver shouted something as they swung through the hospital gates and lurched to a halt. Simpkins glanced to the dignitaries at his side and hurried over like a startled deer.

'Leroux, what –?'

'Can you pay the driver?'

'For heaven's sake, look at the—'

Leroux doubled over the side of the cab and retched. The driver shouted what must have been obscenities in Turkish, and Leroux staggered down, careful to avoid the puddle of vomit and wiped his sleeve across his mouth, feeling a tad better.

Simpkins calmed the driver with a dose of lira and grabbed Leroux under the arm, marching him towards the entrance.

'The Ambassador is livid!'

'The Ambassador?' Leroux said checking the faces of the two officials waiting by the door. The one in uniform looked familiar, but he couldn't place him. The other in a white shirt and waistcoat, presumably a doctor.

'Nevlinski came to the embassy first thing, furious.'

'Nevlinski, but he—'

'Told the Ambassador you were an embarrassment to your country, a disgrace to the British intelligence service and had jeopardised Nevlinski's own negotiations with the Sultan.'

'What?'

'Told him what you were up to last night. In your cups, carousing with courtesans, telling anyone who would listen how you were going to save the Armenians and liberate Jerusalem.'

'But—,' Simpkins cut him short with a hiss.

'I stood up for you yesterday, after you left. If Beaumont sent you, I said, I would stake my reputation.'

Leroux's head pounded harder, and he put his palm on Simpkins shoulder to steady himself.

'Nevlinski's lying.'

'Too late now,' Simpkins stammered. 'The Ambassador's ordered me to put you on the next boat home.'

The doctor approached, neat of hair and hands, calm of voice. 'Is this Mr Leroux?'

Simpkins looked at the ground and nodded curtly.

'Please come with me. You are…' he paused for a brief examination, 'late. I think you may already have met Captain Emre of the Sultan's bodyguard. Come this way.'

Leroux squeezed Simpkins' shoulder. 'Trust me, I'll explain later.'

Simpkins blinked and Captain Emre shook Leroux's hand with the grip of a galley slave.

'I'm delighted you could make it,' the captain said, but his eyes were as hard as his handshake. 'Perhaps the doctor can prepare a tonic after the tour.'

They followed the doctor on his round through the high-ceilinged wards, a gentle draft flowing in through tall windows. The patients, all men, were victims of violence, rather than disease or infirmity.

The doctor felt the brow of the first invalid and checked his pulse. The man barely stirred. He was either heavily sedated or the wound under the dressing wrapped around his head had rendered him senseless. The doctor turned to Leroux. 'This man was beaten trying to protect his family during the riots in Sasun. The story that is not told is that the revolutionaries often use their demonstrations to settle old scores.'

'He is a Muslim?' Simpkins asked.

The doctor lowered his head in affirmation.

The next patient was swathed in bandages around his chest, oozing blood and pus. He seemed to suffer from burns and grabbed the doctor's arm, babbling in his own tongue, with his eyes darting about, until they fixed on the captain, and he screamed. The doctor pushed him back speaking firmly. Leroux covered his nose with his arm and turned away.

'The man is afraid of any strangers now, fearing what they may do,' the captain said. They reached the end of the ward, and the doctor led them to the next.

'Are Christians kept in a separate ward?' Leroux asked.

'That is not necessary, and there are no Christians here now. The victims of the violence in many places are Muslim.'

The captain washed his hands in a basin and dried them, and Leroux followed rinsing his mouth and splashing his face.

'That is what the Sultan wished you to see,' the captain said, and they entered a second ward, fresh with the tarry smell of carbolic soap. Two nurses hurried to the doctor. One had the same dark blonde hair, green eyes, and erect posture of the Circassian dancers. Leroux shut the thought out. The other nurse was African, but from further north than the people

88

Leroux could talk with. She gestured at the first patient and spoke in Arabic. The doctor and the captain went to either side of the patient's bed, who sat upright, lank dark hair matted against his sallow sweaty skin.

'It sounds like the patient is refusing his medicine,' Simpkins said.

The doctor held out his hand and the green-eyed nurse passed him a tincture bottle. The patient shook his head and, as the doctor bent in, shrugged him off with his arm. The doctor cursed and the captain lunged at the patient, who bucked and thrashed. Leroux backed away, stumbling into the bed behind him and reached out to catch himself. A cold clammy hand grabbed his wrist and tugged him further back. An elderly man lifted his head, his dark eyes full of pain, imploring Leroux. His other hand delved under the sheet for something. Leroux stooped and the man pulled himself up to Leroux's ear. 'Englishman? Do not believe them,' he lisped through his missing front teeth. He pressed something metallic with a chain into Leroux's palm. 'Take this to my people. Tell them what happened at Akrag.'

'What—'

'What's going on here?' The doctor said.

The old man's eyelids closed over the pinpricks of his pupils, and he sank into the thin mattress, a peaceful smile on his lips.

'I think he was asking for more medicine.' Leroux closed his fist around the object, the imprint of a cross digging into his palm. The old man's grip fell away, and Leroux turned to the window. The sun was at its zenith, the scent of orange blossom wafted in, and the siren call of the muezzin began. When he turned back the man's hand hung limp over the edge of the bedframe.

'The tour is finished,' the captain said. 'The Sultan has instructed me to escort you to Armenia. We leave on this evening's ship for Trebizond.' The captain fished a folded paper from his breast pocket and handed it to Leroux. 'Do not be late.'

In the slim shade of a cypress tree Simpkins shrugged off his jacket, and threw it to the ground, and loosened the top buttons of his shirt.

'Damn it, Leroux. What am I supposed to do?'

'They were lying.' Leroux sat back against the tree, his legs like jelly, trying to block out the despairing eyes of the old man. He looked away from the haunting windows of the hospital.

Simpkins hung his head. 'I know. I've only a few words of Turkish, but when the patient ranted at the doctor, the captain's translation was wrong.'

Leroux opened his palm. The cross was intricately worked in silver, and the bars ended in flared points each worked into three petals. 'The man who died slipped this to me.'

'That's an Armenian cross. No mistaking that. And that patient with the doctor, whatever he was saying, he was terrified of the captain, as a soldier, not a stranger. I don't think they were all Muslim.'

'Were any of them? No-one reacted to the call to prayer.'

'They were so sedated, most were asleep. A kind of opiate, I think.'

'Maybe. The old man mentioned a place called Akrag. Does it mean anything to you?'

Simpkins shook his head.

'He said "Tell my people what happened at Akrag."'

'What happened?'

'We were interrupted before he could say anything. And then … Can you check the embassy reports and see if that village is mentioned in connection with any of the disturbances?'

Simpkins kicked a stone and his ginger mop flopped down over his eyes. 'You know I can't. I've orders to put you on the next steamer home.'

'After what we've just seen? That's even more reason to follow up the reports from Armenia.'

'The Ambassador is getting someone else to do that.'

'But Nevlinski was lying about last night. He drugged me. Someone else was there, not Herzl. They interrogated me.'

'Interrogated you?'

Simpkins had acquired Beaumont's habit of repeating Leroux's words.

'I don't know what's going on,' Leroux said, 'but if I go back now, I go home in disgrace, because of that liar Nevlinski. And whatever is going on is not good for the Ambassador either.'

'Nevlinski even asked Currie to pay him for the information...' Simpkins shuffled with his hands in his pockets. 'Even though Currie holds a low opinion of Nevlinski, he is a Count. He will be believed.'

'That's why I must go to Armenia. Amidst all the lies, this is real.' Leroux held out the cross, swinging from his ring finger. 'Don't try and stop me.' He tried to give his voice a hard edge, but he felt no anger towards Simpkins.

'I told Currie it didn't sound like you.'

'Say that you waited for me. I didn't show. You went to the hotel to look for me. When you came back to the hospital, I had gone, but the captain made it clear that it was the Sultan's wish that I travelled to Armenia.' Leroux unfolded the travel papers. 'That's nearly all true.'

Simpkins' head waggled, half-way between nodding and shaking, caught between duty and desire to do the right thing, and God bless him, the right thing was winning.

'The ship for Trebizond leaves at eight tonight, tell him after that.'

Simpkins reached for his jacket and dusted it down. 'I'll check the reports and cablegram Beaumont.'

'I'll search for Nevlinski. He's got some questions to answer. Something's wrong. The man he was with disguised himself with an odd German accent. He seemed to fear that I knew about his plans and knew that I spoke German. Whoever they are, they're not on our side. I thought he was going to kill me. Maybe they got interrupted and when I woke someone had untied me.'

Leroux suggested walking back, partly to clear his head, but mostly to help Simpkins keep his nerve. One foot in front of the other. Whatever that bastard poured down his throat had given him a worse hangover than the filthy Cape Smoke moonshine that rotted the miners' guts in Johannesburg. What was Nevlinski after? Should he really head off into bandit country against the orders of the British Ambassador in the hope of finding out? With somebody stalking his every move, taking the dossier, and drugging him? He had no idea what he was getting into, just the way his childhood friend Tom liked it. Leroux closed his eyes, feeling the sun on his face. Tom stood in the long grass of the veld where they ran wild growing up. Leroux could hear him saying the old Zulu proverb, 'Almost doesn't fill a bowl.' You either do it, or you don't. No half-ways. Tom usually said it just before doing something crazy. Tom was right. Leroux couldn't go back to Beaumont in shame.

Simpkins tapped Leroux's shoulder. To their right on the brow of one of the seven hills of Constantinople the mighty presence of the Hagia Sophia loomed over them. 'Akukho mango ongenaliba,' Leroux murmured. That was another saw.

'What?' Simpkins said, shielding his eyes from the sun, high behind the colossal dome.

'There is no hillside without a grave.'

'That's a bit bleak. You're looking at the finest church, well mosque, in the world,' Simpkins said with a renewed cheeriness.

'Not bleak for a believer. Death is inevitable. Don't fear it.'

'Are you telling me there's death in my future?'

'I'm trying to reassure myself about the trip.'

'This,' Simpkins said, splaying his arms to embrace the scene, 'I find reassuring, somehow. The history of Christianity runs through this building. I like to think it's simply waiting for the next chapter.' The sun glinted on the few remaining marble panels standing proud from the crumbling yellow and red stucco. What had once been renowned as a shining beacon of beauty was now more arresting for its decrepitude. Yet Leroux felt himself drawn in by the sheer mass of the Hagia Sophia. Simpkins stopped by the foot of one its minarets, a thin tower of bright white limestone with a small doorway that admitted the muezzin for the long climb to proclaim the call to prayer. 'The stories this place could tell,' Simpkins said, squinting as he looked up to the vast dome.

'Don't tell me, there's a prophecy?'

'Many. The first emperor, Constantine the Great, who built this city in Rome's image, saw a snake come out of its nest and an eagle swooped down to capture it. As the emperor and the citizens watched, the eagle flew away with it. But the snake wrapped itself around the eagle and they fell back to the ground. The citizens rushed to kill the snake and free the eagle.'

'And?'

'The eagle is Christianity, the snake Islam. People now say that it foretold the rise of Islam, and that one day, Constantinople will be reclaimed for Christianity.'

'Sounds like clutching at straws.'

'There's more. Constantine XI, the last emperor, is believed to lie beneath the Golden Gate waiting to rise from the dead and lead an army to reclaim Saint Sophia for the Orthodox faith.'

Leroux sat down on a low wall, facing the mosque, basking in its presence.

'What is he waiting for?'

'Mehmet II beat him to it,' Simpkins laughed. 'He bricked up the Golden Gate so that Constantine couldn't get out! And there are other prophecies. In the last days of the siege of Constantinople, the sky lit up. The citizens gathered here at the Church of Wisdom and a flame issued forth from the uppermost windows and grew and swirled around the dome until it gathered into a shaft of light of indescribable brilliance that rose to the sky. The gates of heaven themselves opened to receive it.'

The sun beat down from the perfect sky above. 'And?'

'The gates closed. They said the Holy Spirit had left Constantinople. The city fell.' Simpkins scratched his chin. 'Beaumont thinks it was St Elmo's fire. You see it at sea sometimes on the spars of ships in certain atmospheric conditions.'

'What do you think?'

'This place holds a lot of power for many people. For a thousand years it was the largest cathedral. As Rome fell, Constantinople became the seat of the Empire, and when the disputes with the bishops of the Vatican became too much, the Church split into the Eastern Orthodox and Roman Catholic rites. This is the Holiest place for the Orthodox Church, and you can still see the Christian mosaics through the whitewash, as though they are struggling to come back. It's where Olga, the Grand Princess of Kiev came to convert to Christianity and spread it among the Rus. She became Saint Olga of Kiev, named equal to the Apostles.'

'I met an Olga…' Leroux doubted she was a saint. 'Let's get going.'

Down the hill to the Galata Bridge a pack of dogs snoozed in the shadows and a man in a loose white kaftan tossed them a scrap of bread to tussle over.

'How do you know so much about its history?' Leroux said.

Simpkins said nothing for a while and then sighed. 'I was supposed to go into the clergy. But that didn't …work out, so I was encouraged to take a foreign posting.'

'Encouraged?'

'I wanted to be a vicar. From a young age I knew that was my path and I enjoyed the study.'

'What happened?'

Simpkins's face flushed and then he frowned, as if frustrated with his display of emotion. 'I developed a friendship with the vicar's daughter....'

'Ah.'

'It looked much worse than it was. We were caught in a compromising situation... but nothing actually happened.'

'But it would have done, if you weren't caught?' Leroux teased.

Simpkins's ears reddened. 'I still think about her. You're right. But we, or at least I, had no idea what I was doing,' Simpkins shoved his hands deeper in his pockets. 'Still don't.'

Leroux remembered the stern lectures the old Boers gave and their Old Testament ways. They would have given Simpkins a good thrashing with the hard rhinoceros skin of a sjambok whip, but that would have been the end it. They wouldn't have ruined the boy's life for one mistake.

'Your parents sent you away for that?'

Simpkins nodded. 'In disgrace. My uncle, Beaumont, helped me. He thought it was hilarious, never did get on with my father. He got me posted here, and said he wished he had been sent here at my age rather than shipped off to sea.'

'Any scrapes to write to him about yet?'

Simpkins shook his head. That might change if he got caught helping Leroux.

'I'll start looking for Nevlinski at the hotel,' Leroux said.

'I could go to Theodora's. Perhaps someone there will corroborate your story?'

Leroux sucked his teeth. 'Nevlinski got me in an alcove, behind a curtain. I doubt anyone saw anything, apart from the dancers, and Nevlinski seemed on good terms with them and the maître d'. Still, you could always say someone corroborated my story...'

'Do I have your word? That's what happened.'

'On my life.'

They hailed a cab back to Pera, past the stock exchange and the banks, and up the steep hill dominated by the crumbling Galata tower. Built to watch out for fires, it had lost its roof many years ago to a storm.

'I don't know how long I will be in Armenia,' Leroux said. 'Find Theodor Herzl for me. Tell him what happened and that he shouldn't trust Nevlinski. If Beaumont comes back with anything, send a telegram to the post office at Erzurum.'

'Currie will be incandescent. He's terribly proud and cannot abide insubordination. It's his wife. Violet Fane...you may have heard of her, the ... poet? We had better turn up something worthwhile.'

Leroux slapped the cab farewell and skipped up the hotel steps, across the polished marble and slid to a halt in front of the startled concierge.

'Surprised to see me?'

'Non, monsieur! The housekeeper said your bed had not been slept in. But you know,' he said shrugging his shoulders, 'in Pera, one knows not to ask what a gentleman does in the night.'

'Have you seen my friend Count Nevlinski?'

The man pressed his lips together and put his hand on the counter. Leroux slid a little baksheesh over.

'He came in very late.'

Leroux pushed another coin across.

'He left early.'

'Where?'

'I don't know. Truthfully.'

'Checked-out?'

'No.'

He was probably lying low until Leroux left town and Nevlinski knew the lay of the land too well for Leroux to find him. As long as Simpkins kept his word, Leroux didn't need to worry about the Ambassador, at least not until after the voyage. He got directions to a cartographer and sat with the man examining maps of Armenia until he was sure he had identified where Akrag was. There was only one village that sounded close to what he had heard. The cartographer showed him the likely route from Trebizond to Erzurum up in the mountains, a seven or eight-day ride. The village lay a good two or three hours from their path over a mountain pass.

Leroux returned to the hotel with two maps and half a plan, and the lock of his door turned smoothly with a solid thunk. The room looked the same. Just the five of us in here, as Beaumont had warned him. You and the four walls. Leroux spread the first map out on his desk. It showed all of Anatolia. The port of Trebizond towards the east end of the Ottoman Black Sea coast. The mountainous hinterland, the roads up to the main

Armenian towns, Erzurum, Van, and Yerevan. He took a pencil and circled the port. Then he marked Erzurum. What the hell, if someone was going to search though his belongings, he'd better circle Constantinople too. Leroux studied the names and got a feel for the orientation. There was Sasun, site of the rebellion last year. He folded the map and put it in his knapsack. The second map was larger scale, showing only the area inland from Trebizond. He found the turning to Akrag and traced a square around the route from the main road and cut it out, folded it small, and concealed it in his hat's inner band. Leroux disposed of the rest of the map in the fireplace and flopped on the bed, pulling his hat over his eyes.

They say everyone who comes to Constantinople passes over the Galata Bridge, and Leroux now recognised many of them. The Arabs with their long cloaks of coarse wool and keffiyehs. The Albanians in white breeches and orange sashes, usually bulging with pistols. The Greeks in their flared white kilts and Kurds in their embroidered waistcoats. A brown jacketed porter, a hamal, carried an impossible load lightly on his back as drays and cabs rumbled past over the ancient planks, and Leroux followed him down the steps to a pontoon.

The steamer was moored at the far end. Brown streaks ran from the seams of the funnel and the hawse hole where the anchor ran out, her best days behind her. He stood aside as four men bent under several hundredweight of hogsheads slung between stout poles squeezed past. Leroux swung on to the narrow gangway, running his hand up the iron railing, loosening flakes of rust and paint, feeling freer with every step he climbed. Had the Ambassador heard about the travel papers? Hopefully, he would be too distracted by weightier matters to try and stop him.

Polished leather boots waited at the top of the ramp. Above them, a gleaming scabbard and the hard stare of Captain Emre, one hand resting on the hilt of his sword. His dark blue uniform was adorned with a minimum of gold braid and fastened with a white pipeclayed belt and he turned stiffly to escort Leroux to his cabin.

'Make yourself comfortable. The passage is two days, and the food is terrible, even the pilaf.'

Captain Emre disappeared without further conversation and Leroux stowed his belongings and returned to the deck. A dozen more passengers scaled the gangway accompanied by hamals humping their possessions at the hot end of the day. In the harbour, a kayik arrowed towards them, shedding molten waves with each heave of the oars, and bearing a double headed eagle high on the prow, the mark of Imperial Russia which had adopted the emblem of Byzantium. It glided under the bridge, the sun-burnished oarsmen immaculate in white robes and scarlet fezes and they backed their blades to stop alongside. In the stern, the helmsman was dwarfed by a man lounging in front of him, resting his leather cavalry boots on yellow cushions. He scanned the ship while sailors lowered a gangway for him, and then levered himself to his feet and sidled forward, untroubled by the rocking of his slender launch.

'We have a late arrival,' Captain Emre said, appearing at Leroux's side.

'You know him?'

'Maximoff, the Russian Dragoman.'

'Travelling to Armenia too?'

'With us. A last-minute decision.'

The captain flinched as the ship's whistle blasted a long note, prompting deckhands to recover the gangways and release mooring lines. Maximoff strode past, greeting the captain in Turkish.

The deck shuddered, water churned from the stern, and the steamer eased away from the dock, under a flock of ravens, which cawed and kraaed before settling in a grove of cypress trees. The houses of Constantinople faded into the twilight as the gas lamps were lit in the streets and the howls of dog packs reached over the water. Five soldiers gathered on deck to smoke but kept out of earshot of their captain and the foreigner.

'Do you mind if I practice my German?' the captain said.

'Not at all.'

'The army is modernising, and all the new trainers are German…'

It wasn't the German accent he had heard at Theodora's. Far from it.

'How did you know I spoke German?'

The captain stroked his luxuriant moustache and planted his hands on the guardrail. 'I know many things about you. It is my job to keep an eye out. It is better that you are aware – so there are no misunderstandings.' He patted his gun and looked steadily at Leroux, but not with malice. 'The Kaiser is a friend to the Sultan. I was here when he arrived in the year of '89. They even say he is secretly a Muslim! He is at least prepared to help train the army and supply us with modern equipment.' The captain patted his sidearm again. He was clearly proud of it, with its odd broomstick shaped handle protruding from the leather casing.

'You have not seen one before?' The captain grinned and drew it. 'A Mauser, the new model we are testing.' He trained the long barrel on a passing vessel, and curled his finger around the trigger, which had a box in front of it instead of a cylinder above.

'No. An unusual magazine?'

'Semi-automatic. Ten rounds, long range.' He paused and drew his eyebrows together. 'The Boers are also armed by the Germans, perhaps you will get to use one?'

'Or we could practice in the hills?'

The captain waggled the gun. 'No hunting. We stick to the road always. The mountains are bandit country, so you must not leave the party unguarded. It would be embarrassing for the Sultan were anything to happen to you…'

Leroux pushed his hat down against a gust of wind and the vessel pitched gently among the masthead lights of a score of ships plying the narrow strait to the Black Sea. The captain smiled. 'So many. Allah has blessed us with the Bosporus. Every ship that passes pays gold and every year more ships come and soon many more. They say the black earth of the land to the north can grow enough wheat for all and the riches of Siberia will come on the new railroad the Russians are building.'

'Is that the business Maximoff is on?'

'No, no. They claim the right of protection over the Armenians. He heard about your trip and insisted on coming.'

'You dislike him?'

'The Sultan is wise. He does not trust any of the Great Powers. Queen Victoria, the Tsar married to her granddaughter, her grandson the Kaiser, her cousin King Leopold. In the end blood is thicker than water and stronger than any treaties.'

'Yet the Sultan seems to manage relations to his advantage, playing one off against another.'

'For now. But each year you chip away, little by little, undermining him. Your commissioners wander the lands collecting taxes to repay your loans. Missionaries roam unchecked stirring up trouble. You force the Sultan to share the sovereignty of his own lands. He is Caliph of all Muslims, yet you humiliate him! Now his own people make mischief and the greatest danger to the Sultans has always been from within.'

'If this trip puts an end to the ugly rumours, surely that would help?'

The captain muttered in his own language and a burst of spray doused them as the ship punched through the building sea. He wiped his eyes and retreated through a hatchway, scowling at a lady who tumbled past him and against the rail. Her scarf, wrapped around her bonnet, whipped in the wind and made her look top heavy and in danger of falling overboard.

'Madam, can I help you?'

'Quite alright young man, just a little queasy.'

She spoke with a soft American accent, but from where in that vast country he couldn't decipher.

'Watch the horizon, or one of the other ships. Looking down will just make it worse.'

She rested her hand on his forearm. 'Mrs. Willis of the Episcopal Church. And where are you headed?'

Leroux leant closer as they both turned their faces away from the wind. 'Erzurum. And you?'

'Bayburt, to a mission school nearby. I'm to replace the headmaster there.'

Leroux saw himself back in the classroom with Tom, swapping notes. His mother writing on the chalkboard in the small mission outside of Krugersdorp.

'That's on the way to Erzurum, isn't it? How are you travelling?'

'I will arrange something in Trebizond.'

'The Sultan lets you travel unguarded?'

'He would not be unhappy if the bandits got me.' Crow's feet spread from the corners of her bright eyes as she held her bonnet down.

'Then you must travel with our party. We have six of the Sultan's soldiers and a Russian diplomat. If that isn't safe, nothing will be.'

'Why that's very generous, Mr Leroux. I hope one day I can repay the kindness. Tell me, what brings you here?'

'An interview with the bishop. I'm with The Times, covering the Armenian disturbances.'

'I see.' Her gaze turned to the soldiers. 'Don't mention me to the bishop, he dislikes missionaries.'

'He does?'

'We offer schooling with our faith. The Muslims shun us. Leaving Islam is punishable by death, or at least banishment, but Armenians come to the schools, and some adopt our faith.'

'Have you heard the rumours?'

She glanced over to the doorway and lowered her head. 'I was told there had been more killings, but that I was not to spread gossip.'

Her strong jaw set against the elements as the wind drew a tiny tear from the corner of her eye. What brought her to this place?

'You think I've lost my mind? I did for a while. I lost my husband and children five years ago, crossing the Atlantic. Our ship sank. Somehow, I survived, but I had no reason to live. Eventually, I found solace and purpose in my local church, and now each and every day I work towards preparing the way for Him and when I can see my little angels again.'

Leroux's thoughts turned to Lara, the angel he had lost in Johannesburg, murdered by a German spy for helping Leroux. One day their paths would cross again. He wiped his forearm across his face. 'I'm sure they are waiting for you. I travelled to Constantinople with a gentleman who hopes to return the Jews to Zion and herald the End of Times.'

Her eyes blazed with fervent desire. 'Then there is no time to lose,' she said. 'I must redouble my efforts so that He is met by as many true believers as possible.' She clasped her hands at her breast. 'You know the scripture?'

'A little. Blessed are the servants whom the Lord shall find watching when he cometh.'

Her knuckles whitened on the rail, and she closed her eyes for a moment as the sea hissed past.

'Thank you, Mr Leroux. I'm feeling quite revived now.' She refastened her scarf and squeezed his hand as Leroux opened the door for her. He returned to the rail and the salt air. The straits widened a little, and the steamer kept to the right shore where the outline of a fort squatted on a promontory, guarding the approaches to Constantinople from the north. Occasional lights flickered from the garrison.

The motion of the vessel changed, rolling now, leaving the short chop of the Bosporus behind and corkscrewing through the swell of the open sea. He had spent so much of his childhood in the back of a wagon or on a horse that he found the motion comforting, a gentle reminder of the power of nature. And in a few days, he would be in the saddle again.

'Homesick?' Leroux turned to the gravelly voice of Maximoff staring down at him, his long dark curls streaming across his face and his extravagant beard lending a piratical air.

'A late night.'

'Not good to over-indulge before a voyage.'

'Not good to go drinking with Count Nevlinski.'

The rail shook as Maximoff slapped his hand. 'That old rogue! What did he want with you?'

'Curious about my trip. Too curious.'

'He's harmless. Peddles in information. As you must know, there have been some disturbing rumours coming from the Armenian provinces.'

'I hear we're travelling together.'

'Everyone wants to keep an eye on you, Mr Leroux!' Maximoff said and a meaty hand patted his back.

'You make yourself sound like a spy.'

Maximoff laughed. 'Aren't we all? No, it is simply my duty to protect the Armenians,' he leant down and lowered his voice, 'without upsetting the Sultan of course. What did the missionary want?'

'Nothing. She's travelling on her own, I suggested she come with us.'

'You haven't been in Constantinople very long, have you?'

It felt like weeks. 'I arrived the day before yesterday.'

'Befriending missionaries in front of the Sultan's personal guard? No, no,' Maximoff wagged his finger. 'Your Ambassador would be disappointed. You don't seem like the usual Britishers I meet.'

'I grew up in South Africa.'

Maximoff nodded as if that explained everything. 'I have been a diplomat in Constantinople for ten years.'

'They call you Dragoman?'

'It means translator. I know the languages and can deal directly with the Ottomans.' He shook his head. 'You get used to the constant spying and intrigue. Diplomacy is a long game. See that?' Maximoff stretched out his hand towards the light that flickered faintly over the luminescence of the ship's wake.

'The fort?'

'More of a ruin now. But the forts in the Dardanelles that guard the southerly approaches from the Mediterranean? The walls have recently been reinforced and the latest Krupp naval guns installed. The Royal Navy won't get through there! You should have seen Ambassador Currie's face! Never stops complaining about the dilapidated state of this fort, guarding the Straits from Russia! Cigar?'

Leroux declined and Maximoff pulled out the lapel of his coat to shelter the strike of a match. A glowing ring formed as he turned the cigar in his mouth, and he held it out to the breeze to brighten a little before taking a deep draw.

'You are a journalist, aren't you?'

'Not a well-known one.'

Maximoff smiled and fastened another button as a large vessel ploughed through the waves towards them, lying perilously low in the water with one huge smokestack at the rear. As it passed close by, Leroux made out the Union Jack on the ensign and "Murex" in large white letters in the pall of the stern light.

'What's that?'

'One of yours. Oil tanker going to China. They can't get enough of our kerosene for their lanterns.'

'Strange name.'

'Latin for a type of shell. There's a fleet of them, clam, turbo, conch. All to serve the oil fields of Baku. We produce nearly as much of the stuff as America now. And there's a liquid we used to pour away in the river after producing kerosene – gasoline. People buy that now too, for motor vehicles.' He tapped a cavalry boot against the guard rail stanchion. 'Good luck with that if the roads are like the Russian ones!'

'You don't worry that Currie will be whispering into the ear of the Sultan about the forts while you're away?'

Ash from Maximoff's cigar flicked past as he pointed out to sea. 'This waterway carries much of our trade, and as you see it is growing. The Sultan makes money from every ship, why would he threaten that? Most of it goes to your financiers, of course. I think it's reasonable that he should be allowed some protection against bankers, don't you think? Although I'm sure they will find a way around a fort quick enough!'

Leroux thrust his hands deeper into his pockets as scraps of cloud scudded past the sliver of a crescent moon. 'I almost feel sorry for the

Sultan. If he's not being pressed for repayment or his forts or control of his trade routes, they want him to fulfill prophecies.'

Maximoff sucked on his cigar. 'You believe in prophecies?'

'Everyone seems to have one. They can't all come true. Are they really anything more than wishful thinking or chance?'

'Let me tell you about Oleg the Prophet, who conquered Kiev and founded the Rus, forefathers to the Tsars. The pagan priests foretold that he would be killed by his favourite horse, so Oleg sent the stallion away. Many years later he wondered what had become of it and was taken to where its remains were buried. He uncovered the horse's skull and when he touched it with his boot a snake slithered from within and bit him. He died, fulfilling the prophecy. Don't tell me that's chance.'

Was Maximoff mocking him? Leroux scratched his chin and looked north. 'If you cannot defy a prophecy, does that also mean you cannot help fulfill it?'

'You have a particular one in mind?' Maximoff bent close with warm tobacco breath.

Would it matter to Herzl if he reminded Maximoff of the prophecy? It was well known among Christians and Herzl was hardly keeping his ambitions secret, seeking help wherever he could get it.

'The evangelists believe that if the Jews return to Zion, Jesus will rise from the dead.'

'Yes, I have heard of this one,' Maximoff laughed. 'That would upset a lot of people's plans! I have another prediction ...'

'What?'

109

Maximoff's arm swung around Leroux swallowing him in a hug. 'You and I will work together! You are a good man, I think, concerned for the fate of the Armenians. They are under the protection of the Orthodox church, and it is my duty to ensure that they receive it. We may be on different sides of the Great Game, but for this expedition our interests are the same. Something tells me you are more than just a journalist. We are both Christians are we not?'

Maximoff tossed the stub of his cigar out to sea, and it spiralled away, tumbling, suddenly extinguished in the inky blackness. 'Time for a nap and to check those Turks haven't taken anything from my cabin. Don't look surprised! They will have searched yours too.'

Leroux remained on deck with his thoughts. A couple of the soldiers braved the night, sharing another cigarette, eying him with contempt. The gale built to a full-blown storm, the ship shuddering as it battered through the waves. Leroux returned to his cabin, cold dribbling down his back, shook off his jacket and tossed his dripping slouch hat onto the upper bunk. Trodden into one of the floorboards was a soggy shred of paper. Leroux scraped it up and examined it on his fingertip, then pulled the map out of his knapsack and unfolded it carefully over the lower bunk. The scrap he had inserted into one of the folds had gone. Maximoff was right. Leroux lay down on a thin mattress and studied the slats of the vacant top bunk as the iron bolts of the hull groaned and the light flickered, the ship fighting its way forward. There seemed little doubt that he would find unrest in Armenia, but in an ancient world riven by blood feuds, who was to say where it started? And how could he evade the captain and find the village? Could or would Maximoff really help and risk

110

his relationship with the Sultan? Even if he unearthed evidence of an atrocity, what would Currie or Beaumont do with it, given the stakes? He followed the trace of a bead of water down a bulwark. He knew he was being followed, watched, searched, but why? It wasn't just his interest in the Armenian disturbances. The interrogation in Theodora's had made that clear. There was something else. Something he knew, or they thought he knew, that someone felt threatened by. The only other connection was Herzl, his project for a Jewish state, hoping to fulfil the prophecy. Herzl and Nevlinski seemed optimistic of reaching an agreement, but the Sultan's more devout advisors would surely be outraged if the arrangement ceded authority over the holy site where Mohammed had ascended to heaven. And what was Nevlinski's game? Who was he really working for? The grip around his throat last night was strong, stronger than Herzl's hands. Was it one of the Sultan's men? Was he here? Did the Sultan suspect that the British Government was behind Herzl's project? That it was some crusader trick to regain Jerusalem and Leroux was part of the scheme? None of it made sense.

Monday, 3rd August, Trebizond

A splash of relief washed over the passengers as the anchor plunged down to the depths of Trebizond harbour. Lighters swarmed out to ferry them ashore where, after three long days, they took their first unsteady steps in the shadow of rocky green mountains stacked one after the other into the distance. A Greek trader scrambled up the quay in a crumpled suit, salty and damp, and sat on his trunk turning his face to the clear morning sky. A local man, whose craggy face bore lines to mark every one of his three score of years, approached Captain Emre, bowing and touching his forehead, and led him past the camels and donkeys to his train of pack horses, where they nibbled at coarse tufts of grass that grew from cracks in the road. The captain's choice of horses suggested urgency, but the porters ambled forward just the same to collect the baggage. They collected canvas bags too, stuffed with provisions, and tightened the strappings and cinches as if they had all eternity in front of them.

Leroux introduced himself to his mount, a mare no more than thirteen hands high, but with a long and muscular neck.

'Khalila,' the guide said.

'Good friend,' Maximoff said. 'The name of your horse is good friend.'

Leroux asked Maximoff to negotiate with the guide an extra mount and pack animal for Mrs Willis, a task Maximoff felt required him to remove his smoked glasses to get the best price. The captain refused to acknowledge the missionary or discuss her arrangements, but he stopped short of banning her from the party.

The guide flicked his reins and his horse plodded onto the stony road leading up the hill, summoning the others into motion. Leroux rode his gelding next to the captain, the soldiers muttering amongst themselves, until the captain called back to them, and they broke out in laughter. Maximoff joined in the merriment doffing his straw boater. 'Keep it up, Leroux, making my life easy.'

The eyes of the whole troop looked expectantly at Leroux.

'The men think you bring bad luck. The storm. The missionary. It comes in threes, and they worry what will be next. I told them if you don't behave, I'll sacrifice you to the bandits.'

The road climbed through the old town, where the ruins of ancient villas abutted newer dwellings of cruder architecture. Crumbling stone walls and broken towers clad in ivy marked the town's edge and still the road climbed. Pastures of sheep and cattle gave way to forest, and occasional blue curls of smoke rising from some hidden farmhouse. Torrents of meltwater gushed over white rock riverbeds and although it was hardly possible, the roads got worse. Built by the Romans, no one had seen fit to maintain them, leaving hard rock and rubble, satisfying Leroux's curiosity as to why so few bothered with carts. High above the ravine vultures circled, and in the shade the soldiers turned up their collars. It was seven or eight days to Erzurum, through the mountains of Lazistan, four to Bayburt near where the track to the village turned off. The days passed slowly, with meagre meals, unrelenting stony paths, and cold nights.

The fourth day dawned clear and bright, the green slopes sparkling as the night dew burned off, leaving faint white mists in the dips and hollows. They traversed a well-watered valley, groaning with orchards full of ripening apples and plums and fragrant vineyards. The mountain breeze tempered the heat of the sun, and as the day wore on the valley narrowed, and up on the ridges lone riders appeared, stood watch, and disappeared. Leroux reached down and felt for his knobkerrie. The smooth hardwood shaft ending in a solid bulb was reassuring in his palm. It was no match for a handgun but, in the right hands, was a useful weapon and could be thrown, end over end, to bring down small game. The terrain was made for bandits, but the captain left Leroux in no doubt that if he departed from the captain's view and protection, it was the captain he needed to worry about.

The road zigzagged still higher, each turn revealing a new and more breathtaking view. Leroux eased out of the saddle and rested on a sun-warmed rock. Mountains peaks serrated the skyline as far as the eye reached and he raised his field glasses following the spiral of a vulture, sensing the captain's gaze on him. He saw no bandits and when they started again, he walked Khalila by the halter, dropping back to talk to Mrs Willis, giving his pony as much rest as could. Khalila would need it. Akrag was close, and tonight was the night. Somehow, he had to slip out and find the village. And he needed the little horse as fresh and alert as possible for the precipitous tracks in the dark.

Mrs Willis draped a blanket over her shoulders and cocked her head as the sun dropped behind a peak. A low tinkle of cow bells mixed with the higher notes of teacup bells that shepherds used to ward off predators and steadily built, until after a few minutes a camel padded around the bend ahead, filling the narrow path cut into the rock face. More camels and mules followed until the road was alive with the encouragement of drivers and muleteers.

The captain ordered everyone to hug the rockface, forcing the traders to take the outside. One by one they passed, some with harnesses that seemed as ancient as the land, patched a hundred times over so they consisted more of stringy rope than leather. The last camel took offense from Mrs Willis's horse and dug its feet in, backing away. The driver, perched on the hump, swayed precariously over the edge, but put his faith in Allah and whipped the beast. The camel grunted and its cheeks bulged. Leroux knew what was coming and leapt down. He scrambled alongside Mrs Willis as the camel spat a gob of vomit in front of her horse, which reared, whinnying and striking out. Leroux lunged for the reins with one hand and held Mrs Willis with the other, while pressing towards the rockface. Her horse strained to land a blow on the camel, which, satisfied with itself, plodded forward.

Mrs Willis clutched her chest and swooned into Leroux's arms. A soldier rushed to take the bridle as Leroux set her down.

'What's going on?' the captain asked.

'Mrs. Willis fainted.'

'We must make the next village by nightfall. The roads are too treacherous in the dark.' The captain unscrewed his water bottle and shook it over Mrs Willis, who spluttered to her senses.

'Leroux, stay at the front with me.'

The track descended now widening into a valley and further down, just beyond a crossroads, a hamlet hugged the banks of a stream. Leroux squeezed the top of his hat, reassured by the patch of stiffness where he had tucked the little square of map. The smaller trail on the left headed east over a mountain pass to the next valley and would take him to the village the old man had named. Leroux touched the cross hidden under his shirt. The larger path on the right led to the town of Bayburt. Leroux raised his field glasses to the upper slopes to familiarise himself with the terrain.

'Are there bandits here?' Leroux said. 'I thought I saw movement up on the ridge,' he lied.

'There are bandits everywhere,' the captain said. 'You don't need to worry about them, they won't trouble us in daylight.'

Leroux lowered the glasses. The map showed the distance to be only three miles as the crow flies, but over the rough terrain it would be nearer nine. He would have to make good time to get there and back before dawn.

'I was concerned for Mrs Willis. She is leaving us tomorrow to take the road to Bayburt.'

The captain twisted in his saddle, as Mrs Willis bought up the rear, straight in the back, neck long, without a care.

'She has made her choice. Her God will protect her.'

Leroux would miss Mrs Willis. She led a simple life, with a simple goal, full of hope and love. She felt the animosity of the captain but did not return it or try to convince him otherwise. She wanted only to teach children, honour God, and somehow make sense of the tragedy in her

116

life. The times when they broke bread together, when she asked him about the missionary school in the Transvaal, Leroux dropped his guard and spoke about his mother and his late friend Tom. She had heard the rumours of killings but wouldn't indulge in gossip. She promised though, that if she saw for herself, she would tell him. And Leroux had to confess that a letter addressed to him, care of the embassy, was not a good idea. And she was sad that he had no forwarding address to give and admonished him for it. You need roots to flourish, or you will wither, she had said.

They slid aching from their saddles, as the rosy mountaintops glowed in the last rays of the day. The village was barely a handful of dwellings, simple stone and mud constructions with holes for windows that emitted the acrid stench of burnt cow dung. The door of the largest house creaked open, and an old man appeared, who could have passed for the guide's brother. He bent low in front of the captain pointing to his feet, showing his willingness to be of service. He put his hand on his heart as a sign of trust and welcome and finally touched his forehead, promising diligence.

The captain raised him up gently and billeted the soldiers in one barn, the horses in the other. Mrs Willis was to stay with a widow who had lost her teeth as well as her husband. Maximoff, Leroux and the captain would be guests of the headman. Leroux led his horse to the barn, its hooves striking the ground evenly, showing no sign of discomfort. He hung the saddle inside on the tie ring nearest to the door and dropped his panniers to stake his claim to the patch. Khalila drunk from the trough, her back glistening but free of sores. Leroux ran his hands down the horse's legs and felt around the hooves, massaging the rough pads to check for hotspots. The horse nuzzled Leroux and breathed easily, and Leroux let her finish her drink in peace and eat some grass while he found some grain to give her later. He waved at the captain, chatting on the doorstep of the house with the headman, as he returned and led Khalila inside, stabling her right by the door. The soldiers ignored Leroux, much more interested in a large bronze vessel they had found that stood about a foot high on its legs and they called out to their captain causing the headman to go inside and return with a sack. The captain grinned and hauled it over to his men. Charcoal rattled into the vessel and Maximoff strode over and rubbed his hands.

'A mangal! Tonight, we feast. At bloody last.' Maximoff haggled with the headman who gesticulated animatedly before disappearing around the side of his house. The soldiers gathered around the stove and built a fire, grins flickering at the bleats and scuffles that emanated from the backyard. The headman returned dragging a bloodied lamb and threw it in front of the men who drew their knives and set to work. Leroux held a pouch of coins between his fingers. The headman's eyes glittered.

'Maximoff, tell the headman that I would like to contribute. That incident with the caravan scared me witless. What can we get to drink here?'

'Raki.'

The headman darted inside, as the captain called sharply after him.

'We'll have to make do with two bottles then,' Maximoff said. 'Just as well, its filthy stuff.'

The headman scurried back with a flask in each hand, sniffed one appreciatively and shoved it under Leroux's nose. Christ, that should do it. Leroux thanked him and pressed his palms together at his breast.

The fatty aroma of the meat lifted the soldiers' spirits, and they admitted Leroux to their circle as he refilled tin goblets and offered a flask of water which the men added in small quantities. The clear liquid turned cloudy and, after the burning sensation had faded, left a hint of aniseed.

Leroux tipped the empty water flask end up and ducked into the house, following the earthy scent of turmeric to the kitchen where two women chopped currants and dried apricots and a young girl stirred a steaming pan of rice. They backed away, clutching their skirts as Leroux held a hand up with a coin and put the empty flask of water down. The older of the women, with a headscarf of dark green and scarlet, warily accepted the coin and dunked the flask in a bucket. Leroux placed a gold coin on the table and pushed it over the rough woodgrain. The woman's eyes widened, and she shook her head and stepped between Leroux and the young girl. Leroux held up the raki flask and three fingers and the woman smiled, raising her eyes, and bustled into the store, returning with the bottles.

The soldiers turned the cuts of meat, and the flames lit their grins and toasts to good fortune. The captain sat apart with Maximoff, the headman and the guide. 'Leroux,' Maximoff called, 'You leave those women alone, the chief here will cut your balls off!'

'Just checking on the horses,' Leroux said, concealing the flasks. He skirted around the soldiers and entered the stable. Khalila whickered and Leroux filled a nosebag with grain. The other horses munched away at their grassy hay, but Khalila would need extra energy tonight. Leroux whispered in her ear, patting her neck. The horse seemed to trust him, and Leroux crept out of the barn, easing the door shut and backing along the wall until the group of soldiers blocked the captain's line of sight. From there he made a beeline to the men and slipped the three bottles of raki to the nearest with a wink and then retreated to the barn door. He slammed the bolt home, dusted off his hands and marched over to the captain.

'Food looks ready.'

'We'll eat inside,' the captain said draining his cup.

Maximoff stooped into the main room, furnished with rugs and a fireplace in the corner and the women brought plates of pilaf and hunks of roast lamb. The guide circulated the raki and, when the attention passed him, Leroux tipped his portion away and refilled his goblet with water.

'You like?' the captain raised his goblet to Leroux, 'We call it lion's milk.'

'I like,' Leroux said, draining his cup.

The headman lit the fire, and despite the rank fumes of the cow dung, it was the best meal of the journey, by far. The women came in with seconds and the raki went round again and the headman appeared with a hunk of cheese the shape of a cannonball. And the raki continued to flow until nothing was left but greasy smears on the plates. Leroux stretched and stifled a yawn.

'Mountain air,' Maximoff said, rubbing his tummy.

'Another three days to Erzurum,' the captain said.

'I'm turning in,' Leroux said, and the others rose to join him, the laughter and chatter undiminished outside around the mangal.

'The first time I've seen them enjoy themselves,' Leroux said to the captain.

'They've earned it, they're good lads,' the captain said, his left eyelid drooping. 'But I'll tell them to keep it down.'

'Not on my account. I sleep like a log. I was a soldier once. Let them be.'

The captain grunted and swung the door open, hollering out to them. 'Just reminding them to set the guard.'

Leroux's room was past the kitchen, and he staggered for it, bouncing off the wall. 'G'night, captain.' It was the young girl's room judging by the embroidered cushion on the straw mattress and the sweet smell of dried poppies. She would be in her parents' room. Leroux stared at the ceiling, not trusting himself to doze as the babble outside died down with the embers of the fire and the last door creaked shut. All he could hear was his breath and the first wolf howl.

He pulled his boots on and stole out of the back door under the tiniest sliver of waning crescent. He padded around to the front. Rasping snores guarded the entrance, where the youngest guard cradled a rifle. Leroux lifted the man's lantern by its base, not trusting the rusty handle, and tip-toed over to the soldiers' barn. He opened his jacket and tested the lamp's mechanism, pressing a small lever which opened the shutter, and a beam of light lit the lining of his coat. The door stood ajar, but he could not see how many beds of straw there were or how many were occupied in the blackness. About a whole regiment judging by the snuffles, sighs, snorts, and wheezes, but he needed a gun. He felt his way forward and crouched by the wall. One of the men woke with a gasp and smacked his lips. Leroux held his breath until the man turned in the hay and returned to his slumber. He opened the lamp shutter a fraction. To his side, two rifles were propped along the wall and a few yards ahead of him a pistol holster hung on a chair. He crawled in the dust and grit until his hair brushed against the strap and he eased it down and backed up to the door. The snores kept their cadence and Leroux eased the door shut.

The gun had a familiar weight in his hand, the faint gleam of the barrel in the starlight confirmed it was the cavalry model of the Reichsrevolver. He'd used one serving with a Boer commando, much handier than a rifle in this light. He ducked over to the corner of the stable and froze at the faint crunch of footsteps. They faded. He peeked around the corner. The barn door was unlatched. Had the guard walked away to the edge of the hamlet or gone in? A glimmer from the far end of the frontage answered his question. The footsteps came back, the beam of the lantern swinging wildly until it was set down by the door. The guard pushed the door to and slid the bar across, before carrying on past Leroux, weaving a crazy lightshow back to his comrades.

The captain was no fool, even if his soldiers were drunk. Two of the five soldiers were on watch. The captain was on his guard for something. Did he know about Akrag? Or suspect that Leroux would try to go there? Leroux had got this far. He knew where the village was, and he had the means of getting there. He wasn't turning back. Tom would approve. Almost doesn't fill a bowl, he reminded himself.

Leroux saddled Khalila and led her out, stroking her muzzle. They kept to the back of the houses until they were clear of the village and rejoined the track. Without all the extra baggage, Khalila had a quick ambling gait and Leroux let her take her own surefooted pace down to the crossroads where they headed east up to the mountain pass. Leroux wrapped a blanket around his shoulders and tucked his chin down. The Garden of Eden was supposedly hereabouts, but Eve would surely have needed more than a fig leaf.

The track climbed up and reached a fork and Khalila's ears twitched as high-pitched yelps trailed off into a mournful howl. Should have bought some of those damn bells. Leroux sniffed the dry air. He reckoned wolves were smart enough to associate those bells with food rather than fear them. He opened the little map, but the side-paths now were too small to be marked. The stars above were not the familiar carpet he had grown up with, but he found the plough easily enough and followed the transit to the pole star. He kept to the bigger track, but even that soon deteriorated to a stony trail. Leroux let Khalila pick her way, with her natural night vision and ears that now flicked at unheard sounds in the darkness. Leroux halted and listened, the hairs on the back of his neck rising. He had the uncomfortable feeling of being watched and pulled the revolver from its holster. Nothing ahead or behind moved, and he dare not risk the lantern. To his left was the void. A precipice down to the susurration of a stream far below. Above, the slope was scarcely climbable, bar the odd goat track.

Leroux released a chink of light from the lantern and checked the map again and his timepiece. Nearly 1 o'clock already. He had to push on to

123

have any chance of returning before daybreak. The path descended now to where the village lay at the foot of the mountain. But all he could see was blackness, not a flicker of light nor a sniff of smoke. Not even the tiniest whiff of that wretched cow dung. The roar of the stream grew as it tumbled over some unseen waterfall and the dark ridge of the mountaintop loomed high above.

When they reached the bottom, Khalila pawed at the water's edge and shivered. Across the stream dim shapes of buildings squatted, somehow jagged and disordered, odd patches of wall reflecting the pale wash of moonlight. He prodded Khalila forward, but the horse shied to the side, forcing Leroux to take a firm hand. They splashed across the stream and the walls revealed themselves to be soot stained, the roofs broken and the timbers ashes. But Khalila would go no further, pulling up at the top of the bank, blowing and trembling between Leroux's thighs as the odour of rotting flesh and the first squeak of a rat met them. He dismounted, leaving Khalila to drink at the stream, and walked through the ruins, his lantern casting eerie shadows through empty doorways. The wolves, vultures and rats had done their work, and Leroux tied a neckerchief over his nose and mouth. The homes were bare of possessions and barren of life, but full of picked clean bones. Leroux stumbled into the street and retched. What bastards would do this?

The church tower scratched the sky, splintered and cracked. They'd even taken the bell. He pushed open the empty iron frame of the door, charred remnants of timber crumbling to the ground. A rat scurried away, evading the lamplight. Ashes and dirt and rain had created a carpet of filth, but amongst the animal spoors there were the prints of a child on tiptoe. The stench of death was stronger, and Leroux closed his eyes to his memories back on the veld of the heap of warriors before the wagons, shredded, bloated and flyblown. Inside the doors, bones were strewn all around. The villagers must have sought refuge here. Some burned to death trying to get out, crowded by the vestry door. Some would have suffocated from the smoke, some crushed by the falling timbers and joists of the roof. He followed the little footprints, a fresh trail, and they brought him to the altar. A cloth had been draped over it. Recently, judging by its cleanliness, and it covered most of the carved stone block. Leroux raised the fabric, revealing an intricately sculpted motif of a cross, like the one that hung from his neck, surmounting a solar disc in the form of an elaborate rosette, all within a rectangular border of flowers and leaves interlaced with a mesmerising geometric pattern. He ran his hand along the back of the altar where scrape marks ran up to the bottom of the cloth and lifted it, revealing a charred wooden chest on its side that blocked access to a recess behind.

'Hello?'

Leroux aimed the beam into the gaps and then turned it on himself. He took a crust of bread from his pocket and slid it over the top of the chest.

'Merhaba?' he said, the only greeting he knew.

A pair of eyes stared from the hole, infinitely sad, the deepest brown. They blinked once and a hand trembled over the chest and pulled the bread back. A tear ran between matted strands of hair. It was a girl. Her jaw worked fast as she crammed the crust in. Leroux held his cross up and extended his hand, palm up on the top of the chest. She swallowed. And a

125

finger crept out and touched his and Leroux wept. She reached her hand out further. Leroux levered the chest out, and she curled into his embrace, hugging herself, heaving, grabbing breaths between sobs. She was painfully thin, but more than a child, her dress filthy and ragged. They sat there rocking gently, Leroux silently promising the stars through the broken roof that he would make someone pay.

He checked his pocket watch and lifted the girl to her feet.

'Peter,' he said touching his chest.

Her mouth opened, but no words came. Leroux helped her into his jacket, only her fingertips showing at the cuffs as he led her outside. Had the old man in the hospital seen this or just heard of it? This girl might be the only remaining witness to what happened in this godforsaken place. He had to take her away, somewhere she would be protected, but where? The captain did not seem to be a cruel man, but if the Sultan was responsible for this, she would not be safe with him or his men. She weighed nothing in his arms as he scooped her onto Khalila. He passed her the blanket, and she reached around him, clinging tight as he pressed the rest of the bread into her hand. Had she ever left this village? There was nothing here for her now and Khalila needed no encouragement to cross back over the stream and make the climb back up to the pass.

The girl's soft hair rubbed gently on Leroux's back and her grip loosened as Khalila's steady rhythm lulled her to sleep and Leroux held her hands to his stomach. Would the guards have discovered that he had gone? The bunched-up clothes and embroidered cushion stuffed under

126

the blanket would fool only the most cursory inspection. Would the guard check the stables again and notice Khalila's absence? Maybe he should have stabled her at the back and risked disturbing the others as they left. And what to do with the girl? The first light of dawn was only three hours away now, and he had no time to lose. Khalila whickered and Leroux prodded her on as they approached the narrowest, highest stretch of the pass. The gorge yawned below and above the scree rose steeply out of sight to where it merged into a vertiginous rock face. Leroux had studied it from the crossroads earlier and the field glasses had told him there was nothing other than a goatherders track above.

Khalila's ears stiffened, and Leroux stroked her and checked his revolver, cursing himself. Too late now, only three cartridges. Shining the lantern would ward off a wolf, but his real concern was the soldiers. If his absence had been detected, they'd come looking for him, and the captain probably had a good idea where he had gone. A stone rolled from above, clacking in the darkness before disappearing into the void. Something flared up there. Leroux twisted to face the danger, peering up at the brooding mass of rock and the firmament behind. A shooting star? He squeezed the girl's hand, and she nestled into him.

Khalila snorted and skittered. Leroux dug his heels in, but Khalila planted her feet, flared her nostrils, and reared. Leroux slid off with the girl just as a blinding flash and the crash of an explosion erupted above, the thunderous noise echoing across the canyon. Khalila bolted, her hoofbeats drowned by the growing tumult of tumbling rocks.

Leroux swung the girl over the edge of the track. Her feet scrabbled to find purchase on the cliff face, her eyes bright with terror, and Leroux clamped her fingers down on a handhold. A boulder hurtled past, and Leroux scrambled along to find another place to shelter. He instinctively raised an arm, fending off a stone from striking his head, but another rock smashed into his ribs, knocking him sideways. He reached out desperately to grab something, anything, but caught only the darkness. He toppled, treading air, twisting to look for the girl, but he was plunging, flailing, now thrashed, slapped and scratched, and finally thumped in the midriff harder than he had ever been hit. But he had stopped. He gasped for breath, his diaphragm in spasm. Relief washed through him as he clung onto the tree. Boulders rained overhead, snapping branches away, stones and gravel showering over him.

Leroux spat out pine needles and grit and let his belly sag, trying to draw breath in. A sip at first, then gradually more. Sweat ran over his lip and salted his tongue, and he shivered. Was the girl still there? The tiniest of whimpers above to his left lifted his heart, and he thanked God for his mercy. He screwed his eyes shut to recover his night vision. The cascade slowed, with only the occasional rock whipping through the leaves and clattering down to stream far below. He hauled himself up through the branches. Somehow the tree had taken root on this ledge but climbing higher took him further from the rockface. He could just make out the girl, not far. He rustled a branch and her face, pale in the moonlight, appeared over her shoulder. Leroux waved and hoped she would understand the universal hushing gesture.

The rockslide was meant for them. Whoever was up there would be checking for survivors, ready to finish them off. The girl clung too close to the rockface. She wouldn't last long like that, too much effort for the

128

arms trying to pull in and up. She needed to relax, ease her arms, and take the load through her feet, angled into the foothold. But he had no way to tell her, and she was probably as scared of heights as he was. Even the stars seemed to weigh on his shoulders and a shiver ran down his spine. Something lurked above. How much longer could the girl hang on? Careful, deliberate footsteps receded along the track and Leroux shimmied down the tree to the ledge and felt for handholds. The first few came easily, protrusions he could get most of his hand round. He reached up. Nothing, but got a toehold and tested higher, just reaching a crease in the rock he could crimp his fingers over. No choice. The moment of no return. He pushed up, risking losing the hold before finding another. He ran his palm out to the side and got a grip on the underside of crevice. He paused and listened, his heart beating in his ears. Something or someone was scrabbling further up, beyond the path.

A scream, a death scream if ever he had heard one, and its ghastly echo fled down the ravine. Then nothing. Leroux waited, and then waited some more. He prayed the girl could hold on. Not a sound came from her. Brave girl. Bit by bit he inched up, the sickening pull of gravity in his belly, struggling to swallow and sweating like malaria. He drew level with her trembling fingernails. Leroux worked two fingers into a crack and heaved himself up, his feet searching for purchase, but he got a hand, then an elbow onto the ledge. He squirmed over, reached down, and clasped the girl's forearm. His rough gritty hand was a match for the sheen on her skin and he rolled and dragged her over the ledge and onto him. They clung to each other, Leroux listening above the thump of their hearts, drenched in sweat as the adrenaline still flooded through their veins, and Leroux thanked God for the small moon that had hid them and the dizzying drop.

'I bloody hate heights,' he whispered hoarsely. Her head shifted on his chest, and she tilted her face to his and raised a thin finger. She understood. Her eyes wandered warily up the slope. And then it struck him – she hadn't made a sound since they met. What she had seen, been through, she must be in shock. He held her close. 'Wait here,' he whispered, and her eyes seemed to know. Leroux crept up the slope as she hugged her knees in, her chin resting on top, her eyes fixed unblinking on him. He followed the trail of debris, clambering up. Something was wrong. The unnatural outline of the rock above. No rock was shaped like that, like a branch sticking out, but too bare to be a branch. He crawled up. The end of the branch was a hand. The arm extended awkwardly out from the body, flat on its back on top of a boulder, a bloody mess of hair at the back of the skull. The eyes of one of the captain's soldiers stared up at the heavens. Leroux had not learnt his name. The man had never spoken to him. Had he now tried to kill him? The sharp sulphurous scent of dynamite lingered in the air. Leroux searched the man's pockets. How had he lit the fuse? Had he dropped the matches, or did he have a companion? Leroux drew his gun and climbed until he found the crater. The scream had been minutes after the rockslide. Had the soldier lost his footing and fallen? Was he alone? Had another soldier left them all for dead? Or lost his nerve and gone for reinforcements?

Leroux muffled the revolver as he cocked it and stole back down to the girl. Why would the soldier try to kill him and why make it look like a landslide? Was it because he had seen the village? Or had the girl been seen and recognised as a witness? Sending one man to kill Leroux if he discovered the village was foolish, and the captain was no fool. If another soldier had already returned, they would come looking. Could Leroux sneak back to the village, play innocent and hide the girl? What choice did he have? He could leave now with her and try to make it back to Constantinople, but there were hundreds of miles of bandit country to cross. Even if they evaded the search parties, the Ambassador would not welcome him. He had broken the terms of his permit, and how could he prove what occurred at the village with a mute witness? And it was probably the last thing the Ambassador wanted to hear. It would just heap pressure on him, and proving the massacre happened meant nothing on its own. Who was to say who did it? Leroux needed to find out who was after him and why. He pulled the girl to her bare feet, and a soft neigh in the darkness lifted his spirits. Khalila had returned. He cradled the horse's head, whispering in her ear. You are a good friend. Is the path clear?

They walked down to the crossroads, not risking the lantern, not wanting to catch anyone up. The valley opened wider, and a light bobbed in the distance, approaching them. He led Khalila off the path behind a boulder. He went to Khalila's shoulder and cradled her head, easing it down, tapping her belly and the back of her leg, hoping she understood. Khalila shuffled her back legs in and sank down, just like a good Boer horse. Leroux peered around the edge of the boulder - it might just cover them. The light wobbled closer, the tight beam of the guard's lantern swaying as the horse ambled along, almost alongside them when it stopped. The horse tossed its head and whinnied. The damn thing was calling out to Khalila! The wash of light swept along the far side of the track, the guard muttering darkly to himself. Leroux flinched at a rustle behind him, and the girl's eyes met his as she lay across Khalila's neck. The light swung to their side now, slowly, inexorably, closing in. It reached a jumble of rocks not ten yards away. A sudden beating of wings startled the soldier as the beam scared up a bird and aimed drunkenly as the feathered friend fluttered into the night. The soldier cursed, hung the lantern from his saddle and spurred his horse on up into the pass.

Not a flicker of light pierced the dark where the village slept, and no beat of hooves broke the silence. They carried straight on past the crossing, down the road to Bayburt. Had another soldier seen them up there on the pass? Without that, the captain had no direct proof of anything, even if he was caught returning to the village. As much as the captain might suspect what Leroux had been up to, with Maximoff present, there was a limit to what punishment Leroux could receive. Probably, he would be sent back to the British embassy in disgrace. But the girl was a different matter. Once she was out of Leroux's sight, there was no knowing what might become of her.

After five minutes, when they were well out of view of the crossroads, they left the path by a bush, a shrine decorated with a hundred or more scraps of material fluttering from its branches, each one a prayer to Allah. They stopped by a distinctive stand of grey barked pine. The girl slipped into his arms, and he set her down at the foot of a tree. The first hint of grey showed in the east as he took his jacket back and wrapped her in the blanket, handing her his water bottle and the few scraps of food he could find in his saddlebag. He told her everything would be all right and what his plan was, not that she might understand, but to delay the moment he would have to leave. He could disappear now with her. Nobody would miss him. But he had promised the old man, and Beaumont had trusted him and given him a chance, a chance to prove himself. Leroux set the lantern on the ground and took her hand, guiding it onto the lever, showing her how it worked, hoping she knew what to do if a wolf came. He doffed his battered hat and presented the square of map to the girl. It was no use now, only incriminating evidence on him, but it showed where she was from and might help reunite her with her people. A confidant hand reached out from the blanket, past the map to his collar and fished out the cross. She knelt forward and kissed it, her hair brushing over Leroux's chin. She secreted the map inside her dress, pulling the blanket tighter around her, bunching it in her elfin fists, her eyes knowing this was goodbye. Leroux held her gaze as he returned to the track, the thought of turning his head unbearable until she faded into the wolf light.

Friday, 7th August, Armenia

Leroux swept the dirt for a jagged little stone, pocketed one, and led Khalila back to the village. The stars had faded in the east and the smoke of the first breakfast fire announced the village before the simple houses emerged from the indigo skyline. No challenge call greeted Leroux and the face of the man in the hospital came to him as he fastened Khalila's reins to a post behind the first house. *If you're up there, old man, watch over the girl.* He tethered Khalila and whispered in her ear, thanking her on behalf of the old man too, and ran his hand down her foreleg, lifting her hoof. 'Sorry girl,' he murmured as he wedged the sharp stone under the iron shoe. Khalila snorted and Leroux cradled her head, but she pushed against Leroux as if to say, 'no time to lose.'

He crept along, keeping close to the walls, until he reached the entrance to the widow's house, one of the few that had a second floor. Leroux tested the latch and the door opened with a low creak onto a small courtyard. Steps led up from the far corner between a well and a row of clay jars. Two doors led from a narrow landing. The widow would be in one, Mrs Willis, presumably, in the other. Leroux took a jug of oil from a lampstand and lit the wick, just as the Romans of Constantinople might have done a thousand years before and inched open the first door. A wheezy breath rasped under a heap of blankets. Leroux turned to the second door. Mrs Willis's habit hung on the end of the bed. Leroux perched on the edge of it and reached a hand over her mouth.

Mrs Willis's eyes bulged open in alarm.

'Don't make a sound,' Leroux whispered, withdrawing his hand. 'Sorry, but it's urgent. I've just come back from Akrag, an Armenian village in the next valley. I had been told there was trouble there,' Leroux looked to the door, trying to blot out the memory of the church. 'It's worse than you can imagine.'

Mrs Willis propped herself up, drawing the bedcover around her neck.

'What happened to your face?'

Leroux felt his cheek, scraped raw from the fall.

'There was a girl there, and I think she witnessed it. On the way back, someone triggered a landslide, trying to kill us. One of the guards died.'

Mrs Willis looked behind Leroux. 'Where is she?'

'I can't bring her back here.' Leroux stroked his chin. 'I have a favour to ask.'

The missionary reached out and touched Leroux's forearm. 'Tell me.'

'If they hear about her, she will be in danger. Can you take her with you and return her to her people? Maybe they can learn what she saw?'

Mrs Willis nodded. 'Where will I find her?'

'A few minutes down the turning to Bayburt, in a clump of trees behind one of those bushes people go to instead of a doctor. You won't miss it.'

Leroux turned to the window and the lightening sky.

'Won't it be dangerous for you to stay here?'

'They can't prove anything. And it would be dangerous for them to mistreat me in front of Maximoff.'

'I can say I'm not feeling well and wait until you go before setting off.'

'Good. There is one thing. The girl hasn't uttered a word. I think she must be in shock.'

'I'll take care of her,' she said, patting Leroux's arm, her eyes glistening.

'If she says anything, can you send a message to Randolph Simpkins at the British embassy in Constantinople.' Leroux pulled out the chain from his shirt.

'That's an Armenian cross,' Mrs Willis said, cupping it in her hand.

'A man in Constantinople gave it to me. He told me the name of the village before he died. Let her people know what happened at Akrag. Everyone was slaughtered. The village raised to the ground.'

Mrs Willis's lip whitened as she bit on it. 'What will you do?'

'Carry on and interview the bishop. Tell him what I've seen. Try and discover who was responsible. Then I'll send a report to the British embassy and The Times.'

She let the cross fall. 'Godspeed.'

Leroux blew out the candle and tiptoed to the street. One guard was dead in the landslide. Another had passed him on the road east. That left three and the captain, but not a sign of them. The one slumbering in the doorway had gone. Leroux scurried low to the mangal, the white ashes long cold, dropped the revolver, and returned to Khalila. Leroux led her, limping, towards the stable and he kicked a pail clattering into the trough. He walked her in a circle out front, where fresh tracks led in and out. One set turned right to Erzurum. The rest, at least three including his own, went back to the crossroads. The headman's door creaked behind him.

Leroux bent to lift Khalila's hoof. He drew his knife and prised the stone free from under the shoe.

'Good morning, Mr Leroux,' the captain called out from the entrance. 'What time are we off?'

The captain sidled over, unbuttoning his holster.

'We've been looking for you.'

Leroux took his hat off and ran his fingers through his hair, flushing out stray pine needles, and yawned.

'You have?'

The captain stopped inches from Leroux, looking from one eye to the other. 'Where have you been?' His breath was foul from the night before.

'I'm sorry. I couldn't get off to sleep.'

The captain sniffed. 'Not enough raki?'

'The men were enjoying themselves, and then the wolves started howling. I went to check on the stable.'

'And?'

'My horse was nearest the door, fretting, I thought she was going to start kicking out. I tried to calm her and took her out to walk it off, but she spooked and ran.'

The captain sucked his moustache. 'When that dozy cur Emin woke and found your horse missing, he raised the alarm.'

'I chased after her. But every time I got near, she just bolted further on, back the way we came.'

'That's the way you went?'

'Lord knows how far. Eventually I stopped chasing, otherwise we would have ended up back in Trebizond, then the horse went down to the river.'

'I sent men in all directions.'

'After a while I followed her down. The horse had calmed and let me take her.'

'Emin headed east, to the pass. He hasn't returned.' The captain's eyes bored into him.

'I heard a noise from that direction. A bang and a rumble.'

'Yes, so did some of the men. I sent one back out after Emin.'

Leroux looked up at the mountain tops, catching the first rays of the sun. 'What do you think they are doing?'

'What happened to your face?'

'I was riding back, and the horse went lame and threw me. Luckily, I landed in a bush.'

'Let us hope Emin has had such luck.' The captain ran his hand down Khalila's flank.

'The horse seems comfortable enough in your company now.'

'It was only a stone in her hoof.'

'In case I did not make myself completely clear before,' the captain said, closing his holster, 'you do not leave my sight for any reason without my express permission.'

The captain headed to the house, picking up the pistol by the mangal, and looked back as Leroux led Khalila to the stable. What would the captain do? He scarcely hid his suspicion that Leroux was lying but could he prove it? It was odd that he sent men in all directions, if he suspected

Leroux would go to the east. If the captain had intended Emin to kill him, why send him alone? Or was that a lie to put Leroux at ease until another opportunity to strike arose? Did the captain know he had seen the village and found a witness? Was he just waiting to see if the girl would appear?

Maximoff clattering out of the house, complaining that no-one had woken him and that they were late setting off. The captain replied that one of the guards and two of the horses had gone missing and we would all wait until the search was completed. Why were two horses missing? Had Emin taken a remount? Maximoff snorted and returned to bed, and it was not until the last of the breakfast dishes were scraped that a soldier returned, leading another horse with Emin's body draped over the saddle. The back of his head was a bloody mess of hair, already caked dry. The soldiers and the captain gathered around in silence and carried the body into the headman's courtyard to prepare it for burial. They were tired, hung over and cast dark looks at Leroux. Maximoff made a point of standing next to Leroux, he was a hand taller than any of the Turks and wore his Cossack sword.

'The captain was asking me about you,' Maximoff said.

'What did he want to know?'

'Whether you were trustworthy.' Maximoff could barely suppress a grin.

Leroux avoided Maximoff's gaze, pondering whether to tell Maximoff about the village.

'I said yes, of course.'

'Why?'

Maximoff shrugged. 'A favour. The men want you punished.' Maximoff strolled into the barn to check on his horse and chuckled. 'You went to the village, didn't you?'

Leroux followed him in. Maximoff's horse was the largest in the party with a glossy coat and clear eyes and looked well rested. Even so, Maximoff was huge, and Leroux pitied the poor beast that had to carry him through the mountains. 'You know about the village?'

'Everyone knows. The missionaries, the Armenians, the captain. You can't keep something like that secret. But no one can prove who did it.'

The girl could, and Maximoff didn't know about her. Not much escaped Maximoff, and it was the one card Leroux had. He would wait before playing it. If nothing else good came of this, at least she was safe, for now.

'Is that why you're here?'

Maximoff slipped a blanket over his horse and checked the barn door. 'You could say that.'

'Do you know who did it?'

Maximoff smiled. 'Most suspect the Sultan. Whether he ordered it directly, or turned a blind eye, I don't know.'

'That would explain why the captain is so keen to prevent foreigners seeing it.' Leroux's chest heaved at the memory. 'It was terrible.'

Maximoff stroked his beard and frowned. 'The captain knows where you went. I'm surprised he hasn't arranged for you to be sent back already.'

'If he thinks I killed Emin, he may have other plans.'

'He won't take the law into his own hands with me around.'

What did Maximoff want? 'You'd help me?'

Maximoff clapped Leroux on the back. 'Of course. The British Empire is already in the Sultan's bad books. And now they send you! You're making my life too easy!'

'And you support the Sultan, knowing what you know?'

Maximoff pursed his lips. 'Don't be too quick to judge. It is a delicate balance. The Armenians work hard and value education, and they end up with the biggest businesses, the best property, and the prize jobs. The Turks become jealous. And when the Armenians claim independence or demand special protections, the Turks feel like second class citizens in their own land and become enraged.'

'You think the Sultan let it happen?'

'Perhaps. But he has enemies within his own court too, who would be happy to discredit him. Modernisers who wish to reinstate the parliament, the Young Ottomans. If the reprisals go too far, you British, the French, and even the Tsar, will not be able to turn a blind eye, and will insist on replacing the Sultan with someone who can keep order and protect the Christians.'

'Is that what you want?'

Maximoff shook his head. 'Russia supports the status quo. A friendly Sultan, who will ensure the security of our access to the Mediterranean.'

'What about the Armenians?'

'We will protect them too,' Maximoff stretched up to his full height and flexed his back, 'High morals are not much use to a diplomat! It is wiser to have a foot in both camps, in case the Sultan should forget who his friends are.'

Leroux imagined Currie, beavering to ingratiate himself with the Sultan. Was he a step ahead of Maximoff? Or a step behind? Had Leroux wrecked his carefully laid plans?

Maximoff put a hand on Leroux's shoulder. 'I know you're angry about the village. But flying off the handle in a fit of rage will not accomplish anything and only serve to put the Sultan, or whoever is responsible, on guard. It is in hand, and in the right hands.'

'Your hands?'

'Yes. Don't interfere. Come, let us put on a united front for the captain.'

Leroux closed the stable door as the soldiers filed out of the courtyard carrying Emin, wrapped in a white shroud. The captain marched over to Leroux.

'We leave in one hour.'

Maximoff pulled out his timepiece. 'Where is the missionary?'

The captain glared at Leroux, spun, and stalked over to rap on the widow's door.

'You don't seem in imminent danger,' Maximoff said and went to finish saddling his horse. The captain remonstrated with the widow in her doorway who threw up her hands, retreated inside and then returned shaking her head. The captain braced a hand on the sundried bricks, towering over the little old lady, but she just shook her head more strenuously and slammed the door. A stone skittered across the street, where the captain had kicked it, and he marched back over to Leroux.

'Why are you really here?'

It was a good question and Leroux wasn't sure he could answer it. He had hoped it might ease the memories that haunted his dreams and Beaumont had believed in him. But now he felt he was doing it more for the old man who, with his dying breath, had entrusted him with a secret. And he felt sure that the trail would lead to whatever Nevlinski, or his accomplice, was up to. If he could solve that, he might be able to return to Beaumont with head held high, rather than in disgrace.

'I'm sorry about Emin, but it was nothing to do with me.'

'You think I am a fool? I know the rumours of the village. I know you went that way. And now my man is dead. I have my orders, but you try my patience and…' he looked over at the huddle of soldiers, '…that of my men.' They had started digging the grave and cast bitter looks at Leroux as they turned out each spadeful of dark soil to the side.

'I swear, I did not kill Emin. On my honour.'

'Your honour!' The captain spat at the ground. 'You! Poking around with your ratty straight nose. And what's that witch up to? Going off to spread her poison and your lies?'

'What do you mean?'

'Don't pretend you don't know. She's going to Bayburt. Says she's ill. But I,' the captain said tapping his temple, 'don't believe in coincidences.' Leroux's heart skipped a beat, and he grasped the captain's arm. And gambled.

'You must provide a guard for her. You cannot let her go alone on the road. I saw a bandit on the ridge yesterday.'

143

The captain's eyes narrowed, and he shook Leroux's grip off, looking up at the peaks. 'We will see what Allah wills. She will have to take her chances.'

'Then I must go with her, at least,' Leroux said as earnestly as he could.

'You,' the captain jabbed his finger into Leroux breast, 'are staying with me.'

Leroux lowered his eyes. The captain had taken the bluff and walked down to the graveside to take part in the simple service. Maximoff was right. Leroux was embarrassing the British Ambassador. Currie was going to be livid. Dealing with the news that the massacre was real was one thing. The Sultan would deny it and the Ambassador could pretend to believe him. But Leroux was accused of breaking the terms of his permit, personally approved by the Sultan, and suspected of murdering one of his soldiers. The Ambassador would not be able to deny that so easily. Leroux consoled himself by preparing Mrs Willis's mount but stayed away from her to avoid raising any further suspicion. She did not fear fate and had been prepared to travel on her own from Trebizond. Bayburt was only a handful of miles away. And the girl had a sixth sense for danger. A survivor.

Saturday, 8th August, Armenia

The men sagged in the saddle, hungover and sullen under a high sun. Mrs Willis had played her part well. No doubt she was reluctant to lie to the captain's face, so she just refused to come out of her room, pleading sickness. Leroux gave thanks for little miracles, or at least the missionary's fast recovery, and was relieved that she was leaving them, even if meant forgoing the protection of the guards. Trouble was following Leroux and he had not found out what the root of it was. Better that Mrs Willis and the girl stayed well away.

'What are you smiling about?' the captain said.

'Glad to be on the move again.'

'The Ambassador didn't want you here. Why is that?' the captain said.

'He thought I risked alienating the Sultan, just for a newspaper story.'

'The papers write bad things about the Sultan anyway. And the Sultan permitted this trip, he wants you to see the whole story. Last year, we caught two Armenian revolutionaries red-handed. At the insistence of your embassy the death sentence was commuted to expulsion. And now these men parade around London preaching war against the Sultan, accusing us of unspeakable cruelties. Where does lenience get us?'

Maximoff rode up the line to join them. 'You two seem to be getting on better. Why isn't the missionary here?'

'She's going to Bayburt,' Leroux said.

'Good riddance,' Maximoff said.

'You don't like her?'

'She will only try to turn good Christians to her heresy. The true Church has been here for over a thousand years, but the Americans think they know better, exporting their culture where it does not belong. They encourage these people to rise and spread their rebellion under the guise of God. Memories are long enough in this part of the world, without adding fuel to the fire. The missionaries have no right to interfere here, they are no better than the popish crusader thugs who pillaged San Sophia. The Americans should stick to slaughter on their own land. I hear they are quite successful when the enemy is armed only with bows and arrows.'

Leroux tried to reconcile Maximoff's depiction of missionaries with the selfless kindness he had seen in Mrs Willis. There was no guile in her, she spoke her purpose plainly and would be horrified by the accusations cast at her. It was a side of Maximoff he had not seen before or perhaps it was just a show for the captain.

Horsemen appeared more frequently on the ridges, watching their progress. Leroux rode alone, enjoying the solitude, the verdant mountain meadows splashed with pink, purple, and cream knapweeds and salsifies, while the thin air reminded him of the veld and home.

They stopped for the night at a small village just as a troop of cavalry clattered down the street to a halt, the horses blowing, the men a mix of light blue uniforms and mountain brigand. The captain approached the commanding officer as he loosened the girth on his mount. They seemed well acquainted, if not particularly friendly.

'Who is that?' Leroux said.

'Zeki Pasha,' Maximoff said. 'He is the commander of the Sultan's troops in this province, but it is strange to see him in a backwater like this. I wonder what brings him out this way?'

The captain had turned and was pointing to them. Zeki Pasha lifted his kepi and inclined his head. He had the eyes of a hawk and a beak nose. Maximoff and Leroux doffed their hats.

'It's been a long day, I'm turning in,' Maximoff said. 'Send my apologies to the captain, I shan't be joining you for dinner.'

The captain beckoned Leroux and followed Zeki Pasha into a house.

'I have heard there was trouble near Bayburt, what is going on?' Zeki said to the captain. 'I thought I'd put an end to trouble in this area, but there was a disturbance last night.'

'Quite minor,' the captain said. 'It is all under control.'

'You lost a man?'

'Yes.' The captain's cheeks coloured, and he folded his arms.

'You have caught the offender?'

'No. There were no witnesses. And bandits were seen in the area.'

The Pasha looked to Leroux. 'Your men suspect the foreigner.'

The captain stiffened. 'There is no proof,' he growled. 'And my orders from the Sultan are clear. Take Mr Leroux to the bishop in Erzurum.'

Zeki Pasha slammed his hand on the table. 'Why does the Sultan tolerate the insolence of the Europeans? Who are they to wander our lands, criticising our governance?'

'It is not our place to ask why!'

Zeki Pasha got to his feet, pushing the table loudly away. 'No good will come of this. I expect a full report of the incident first thing in the morning. Goodnight.' He stomped out of the house.

'Thank you.' Leroux said.

The captain stroked his moustache and got up. 'I don't need your thanks.'

Leroux remained alone at the table, finishing off a hunk of bread and cheese, chewing over the events of the day and hoping that Mrs Willis had found the girl and made it safely to Bayburt. He found himself doing a lot of praying these days. Perhaps it was something in the water of these ancient lands. The captain was no friend but had been fair and even defended him in front of the Pasha. The commander seemed to think Leroux's presence symbolised all that was wrong with the Ottoman Empire and had little doubt about his guilt. Leroux went to find his billet and passed a pair of the Pasha's soldiers patrolling the street, in their blue knee length tunics and black Astrakhan hats. Their moustaches too, twisted into points that stuck out like handlebars, seemed to form part of the uniform. Hamidiye, the captain had told him, recruited largely from the Muslim Kurds to enforce the law, or their version of it.

The room allotted to Leroux was in an abandoned house Leroux turned up his collar and followed the directions, the way lit by stars in a clear sky and disturbed only by the hoot of a lonely owl. He hadn't asked what happened to the unfortunate owner, although he suspected it had once been an Armenian dwelling. The main bedroom was taken by the captain and two of the soldiers shared the other. Leroux was assigned a storeroom that led off from the courtyard, with an internal door to the

148

kitchen. A stuffed straw mattress lay where a servant would have slept, and the room seemed not to have been swept since the owner had departed. The latch on the door hung askew from splintered wood, and the shelves were bare. Rat droppings littered the floor, and the flickering light of his candle revealed soil marks on the mattress. A flea jumped from it. Leroux took his bedroll and went into the kitchen, wiped down the table next to the smoking hearth, and laid his bedding out. He had slept on harder ground than this and he had been up for forty hours. He bunched up his coat as a pillow and stretched out, his ribs protesting, reminding him of the blow that knocked him from the path and the tree that broke his fall. He twirled his knobkerrie in his hands, throwing shadows on the ceiling. For a moment he was a child again, and then he leaned over and blew on the wick.

Leroux woke, clammy with sweat. The usual nightmare. The dead eyes staring up at the sun in front of his rifle sight. Had he heard something? Probably just a rat. Then a grunt came from his right and the umph of impact. Leroux swung his legs off the table just as the door from the storeroom swung open and a shape filled the doorway, glistening whites of eyes searching and then fixing on Leroux. They launched at each other, but the intruder had the advantage of starting from a standing position, and they fell back clutching each other, against the table. It skidded, scraping, jolting to a halt before the hearth. Leroux had a handful of bicep and slipped his grip down to the forearm, sensing the tip of a dagger homing in on its target. Bristles snarled in Leroux's face, he couldn't reach his knobkerrie, but he got his other hand under the man's chin and pushed it away as they rolled back on the tabletop, while the man's fingertips clawed towards his eyes. Leroux arched back, stretching his head away and then released his hand from the man's chin and whipped his own head up, butting him hard, the satisfying crunch of nose gristle stunning the man. Leroux wrestled him to the side as a second man roared, rushing on in the dim glow of the embers. Leroux instinctively lunged towards him, throwing up an arm and blocking the strike, the knife slicing along his back. The first man scrabbled on the floor and Leroux shoved towards the sound, until the man in his grasp stumbled onto him, toppling back until they all landed thrashing in a heap. A crack of light shone as a door began to open, illuminating the snarling face of the Hamidiye trooper on top of him. He bellowed and the gleam of his dagger arrowed towards Leroux just as a lantern lit the room and the flash and blast of gunfire crashed out, splinters and dirt showering down from the roof.

'Dur!'

The point of the dagger pricked in Leroux's throat, trembling as Leroux desperately pushed it off, and then the arm sagged, and the dagger dropped. Leroux twisted to the light. The captain stood in the doorway in his nightshirt, glaring down the sight of his Mauser pistol. He twitched the barrel, telling them to get up. The three men untangled themselves warily and Leroux backed towards the captain.

'Get my breeches and boots.'

Leroux left the room as the captain dressed the men down. He was still shouting when Leroux returned and didn't stop as he pulled his trousers on with one hand, the braces hanging down to his knees. The two Hamidiye stood to attention, their daggers on the table, fear in their eyes.

'Stay here,' the captain ordered Leroux and marched the men out at gun point, leaving Leroux none the wiser as to the men's motives. They had come in through the storeroom, presumably expecting Leroux to be on the mattress. Straw spilled out from two deep gouges in the bedding and Leroux grabbed a couple of handfuls to restart the fire in the hearth.

The captain returned after half an hour, slamming the storeroom door, and pulling the mattress across to serve as a crude barrier.

'Please accept my apologies.' The captain dragged over a chair and slumped down.

'You have nothing to apologise for and thank you for stepping in.'

The captain nodded, lost in thought.

'Why did they attack me?'

'Because of Emin.'

Leroux raised an eyebrow.

'The taller one claimed to be a friend of his.'

'Unlikely, isn't it?'

'Very. Emin was from the coast near Constantinople. I knew his parents,' the captain said and toyed with one of the Hamidiye's daggers. 'But I can hardly ask Emin.'

'It's a cover. Someone told him to say that. Whoever told him to attack me.'

'That's obvious,' the captain said. 'But I cannot question them any further, the matter is under the jurisdiction of Zeki Pasha. I will take it up with him in the morning.' He spun the dagger on the table as Leroux

151

removed his nightshirt and turned to wash the wound on his back, feeling for the warm wet blood where the knife had sliced his skin open. He put a dressing there and fixed it in place with a bandage wrapped around his ribs. The captain spun the knife again. Leroux turned back, wincing as he tightened the bandage. The dagger pointed at him.

'Where did you get that?' The captain indicated to his chest and Leroux realised that the cross hung free around his neck, and the captain's gaze had hardened. 'An Armenian friend gave it to me. I thought it might help when I see the bishop.' That was the truth, Leroux thought, or at least part of it.

The captain stared impassively, neither accepting nor rejecting the explanation. 'Make sure the men don't see it. There's been enough trouble for one night.' He took the knives and went to order one of his soldiers to sleep in the storeroom as a precaution, although it was probably as much to keep Leroux in as to keep intruders out. He lay gingerly back down on the table, pulling the blanket around him, and fell asleep to the crackle of the fire.

Sunday, 9ᵗʰ August, Armenia

Leroux rolled off the table, stiff and sore. The guard had left and the Hamidiye troop formed up in the street. Leroux slung his knapsack over his shoulder and headed for the stable. Maximoff was shaking out his blanket in the doorway and bounced over to Leroux, peering over his smoked glasses.

'What happened?'

Leroux touched his brow and felt the slight swelling, laughing. 'Something went bump in the night. I'll tell you later.'

Zeki Pasha mounted and wheeled the horse to inspect his troops. The captain approached him, handing him a paper and pointing over to Leroux. Maximoff took his arm, 'Come on, I want to hear this.'

Zeki Pasha raised his voice.

'He's saying his men are angry with you…

… the captain wants to question them…

… the Pasha says the matter is under his jurisdiction…

… and what are you doing about the foreigner killing your soldier…

…something to do with a knife and your testicles…

… the captain says you are under the Sultan's protection…'

'I get the picture,' Leroux said as the troop moved out in the direction of Trebizond, or more likely Akrag, and the captain irritably roused his men. The ill-will between the captain and Zeki Pasha and his men had infected the soldiers in their party, who seemed to sympathise with the

Hamidiye soldiers' attack on Leroux. The captain rode at the front with the guide and Maximoff, while Leroux trailed uncomfortably near the back, feeling the eyes of the soldier at the rear between his shoulder blades. The weather turned in the afternoon and fat raindrops made the track slick and treacherous, forcing them to dismount and walk the horses and they arrived for their last night before Erzurum drenched to the skin. Water streamed off the earthen roofs, and a muddy torrent gushed down the narrow street. The barn assigned for the mounts leaked, but Leroux found Khalila a dry spot and brushed her down until he found himself alone. Maximoff stepped in and shook off his cape.

'May I,' Maximoff said and sat down on a bale of hay.

'Be my guest. No one else wants to talk to me.'

'You owe me a favour.'

'I do?' Leroux patted Khalila and hung the brush from a nail.

'Did you think that guard on the mountain died of natural causes?'

'Unlucky to fall like that,' Leroux said.

'He didn't fall.'

'You were there?' Leroux said and pulled the barn door to as a gust of wind buffeted the walls, hoping Maximoff did not know about the girl. Maximoff nodded. 'I woke in the night. Two of the guards were bickering just outside the door. One had noticed that your horse had gone and was reprimanding the other. He must have fallen asleep. One of them went to follow you. He seemed to know where you would go.' He paused, watching for Leroux's reaction.

'Go on,' Leroux said.

'I waited and soon enough the guard fell asleep again and I followed you.'

'Your horse was not ridden that night,' Leroux said. He had checked.

'I didn't take my horse. The last thing I want is for the captain to bad mouth me to the Sultan.'

It could be true. Another horse had been taken.

'Was that the horse that carried Emin back?'

Maximoff clicked his tongue, pleased with himself. 'I let it loose just before I got back. The one who went to look for Emin must have found it.' He stretched his legs out leaning back on the bale.

'So, what happened to Emin?'

'He was a way ahead, but it was easy enough to follow his lantern.'

Leroux had not noticed a lantern behind him, but that meant nothing with all the bends in the mountain path.

'When he approached the top of the pass, he doused his light. I followed cautiously. I wasn't sure where he had gone, but I heard a noise above, scrabbling in the stones. It was so dark, but I found a little path up. You must have been coming back by then.' Maximoff looked for confirmation.

Leroux cocked his head trying to piece that awful night back together. 'I didn't hear anything. It took me by surprise.'

'I thought Emin was trying to stay out of your way, just observe you, so I kept my distance.'

'Was there a spark? Something caught my eye.'

155

'Then you must have been close, but I didn't see you. He lit something, some type of grenade, and placed it among a heap of boulders.'

'Yes.' Leroux closed his eyes. He had thought it was a shooting star, but the gap between that and the explosion was short, about right for a fuse. 'I was there.'

'He scrambled away,' Maximoff said, 'and hid behind a rock. I ducked down too, and then...'

The blinding flash. The avalanche of rocks. 'What then?'

'I heard a shout, and saw someone, which must have been you, tumble over the edge. Emin went down to look for you.'

'I fell into a tree.'

'Emin climbed back up. He can't have seen you. I'm sorry, I thought you were gone too.'

'So did I.'

'Emin stumbled upon me. He went for his pistol, and I shoved him as hard as I could.'

No contest in a shoving match between Emin and Maximoff.

'I heard the scream.'

'He died from the fall. I checked. I should have checked for you again.'

'I didn't know what was happening and stayed hidden. I should have called out. Don't blame yourself.'

They sat in silence for a moment, reflecting on how it might have been worse.

Maximoff hadn't mentioned the girl. Just about everything had gone wrong for Leroux since Beaumont had offered him this chance. Everyone was always a step ahead of him. But that was one little thing he could hold onto, where he knew he wasn't in the dark. He didn't know how it might help him, but he did know that disclosing her existence to anyone might endanger her.

'I'm glad you made it back,' Maximoff said in his gravelly voice and cackled. 'That guard was asleep again when I got back. I wondered why you were passing around so much raki.'

'The captain is convinced I killed Emin.'

'I know,' Maximoff laughed and slapped Leroux on the back. 'Oh well. I'm happy to let you take the blame for that. Can't let you get me in the Sultan's bad books. Never mind, you live to fight another day.' Maximoff got to his feet and stretched, still chortling to himself. 'And remember, you owe me one!'

'Why did you wait until now to tell me?'

'I like you Leroux. But we are not on the same side. I wanted to feel sure you won't tell the captain.'

'I won't.'

'Have you ever been interrogated?'

Yes, thought Leroux. Back in Johannesburg, but it was more of a beating than an interrogation.

'No.'

'The Sultan's interrogators are experts. No one can keep their silence.'

'So why tell me now?'

The corners of Maximoff's eyes creased and he sniffed in satisfaction.

'Now he won't believe you. If you wanted to – how do you say – save your gammon, you would have told him straight away. Why would you wait? Why would you cover up for a Russian? Now it will just look like an act of desperation. Their memories are solidifying around the story they already believe.'

Maximoff was a shrewd man, playing his hand with practiced ease.

'What do you want from me?'

'I didn't say I wanted anything. I might be able to help you more, and we should think about how we can help each other.' Maximoff struck a match and lit his lamp, hunching over it, casting a huge shadow on the barn door.

'How?'

'Do you know who he is trying to kill you?'

Leroux stared into the flame. Emin, the Hamidiye soldier. Before that perhaps the person in Theodora's. 'Not who's behind it, no.'

'No idea?'

'I don't even know why.'

'You can do better that that.'

At first it seemed related to Herzl's plan. Now it appeared to do with his prying into the Armenian rumours. What was the connection? Leroux stared into the flame as it hovered above the wick, bending to a slight draught.

'Have you heard of Theodor Herzl?'

Maximoff chewed a thumbnail. 'Yes. He's been telling Russian Jews to be ready to leave for Zion. I don't think they're so keen. Why?'

'My trouble started when I got involved in that. And then, when I go to see the Armenian village, Emin tried to kill me. The Hamidiye soldiers?

158

They weren't trying to avenge Emin - they were following the same orders. But from who?'

Maximoff offered Leroux a cigar and they lit them over the flame of the lamp.

'You're saying there's a connection?' Maximoff said.

Leroux put his feet up and blew a smoke ring that rolled over his boots. At last, he felt there was a light at the end of the tunnel.

'It's only an instinct, but if I can find what links Herzl's plan for Jerusalem and the massacre at that village, then I'll know who has been trying to kill me.'

'You might make a spy after all,' Maximoff said and pushed himself up to rummage out a bottle of vodka and a couple of small tumblers from his bag. 'This is all I've got until we get back to Constantinople.' He poured a couple of shots. 'Vashe zrodovye.'

Monday, 10th August, Armenia

The captain washed his face at the well and buttoned up his tunic as his soldiers prepared for the day's ride with quiet efficiency. The sour faces had gone, and they were looking forward to idle days in Erzurum, with nothing but the occasional guard duty to interrupt the endless games of dama, a type of checkers where the pieces jumped forwards or sideways to take an opponent's piece. Maximoff played enthusiastically and Leroux suspected that he let the soldiers win. The board had been Emin's and Leroux had never been invited to play, despite the opportunity to relieve him of the considerable amount of money the soldier's suspected all foreigners possessed.

As the day wore on, they joined a wider and dustier road where a carriage could easily pass and traders with handcarts or overburdened mules hauled their produce to market under a cloudless sky. The captain slowed to bargain with one, whose handcart creaked under a pile of watermelons. The man's thin arms engaged in the elaborate dance of haggling, until he sucked on a lonely tooth and passed a couple of the plumper specimens up to the captain, who cleaved them into quarters with his sword, tossing them in turn to the soldiers, Maximoff, the guide and Leroux. There was one quarter left, the one that would have been for Emin, which he gave back to the trader, compliments of the Sultan. The soldiers spat the seeds out with great accuracy and wiped the juice from their chins.

'Curious don't you think?' Maximoff said.

'The change in the men's mood?'

'That your own Ambassador is so displeased with you, but the Sultan seems determined for you to fulfill your mission.'

It was no surprise that Maximoff knew of the Ambassador's displeasure. With his years of service at the Sublime Court, he was well-tuned in to gossip, and for all his charm, Maximoff played his cards close to his chest.

'It is,' Leroux said. 'Unless the Sultan believes the rumours of the massacre are overblown.'

Maximoff snorted. 'You think there's a chance of that? With all his spies?'

'Or maybe he knows what happened but is not to blame for it and is trying to find out who is.'

Maximoff raised an eyebrow and shook his head like a weary schoolmaster. They had finished the bottle of vodka the previous night, exchanging war stories and the merits of life in the saddle. Maximoff had been to Erzurum before, as a young man with the conquering Russian army in '78. Leroux took little joy from describing the victory over Chief Malaboch in the Transvaal, a slaughter rather than a battle. Maximoff had never stalked a lion and Leroux had never fought a bear, but Maximoff was careful not to disclose anything that might be of use diplomatically. Leroux revealed little, not, he thought, because his stomach for vodka was as strong as Maximoff's, or his loyalty or guile, but because he had nothing to disclose, apart from the existence of the girl and he held that close. If she had witnessed what happened, maybe, just maybe, she might hold a clue to the riddle. But what knowledge was dangerous enough for someone to try to kill Leroux? Maximoff said that those who had heard the rumours already suspected the Sultan. Was it something that the girl could know, that was so important? But that couldn't be it. His troubles had started before then, when he was with Herzl and carrying the proposal for Palestine. Were the two connected? And was the connection the threat?

Erzurum lay in a bowl surrounded by mountains, commanding the trade route to Persia. The city sprawled out beyond the medieval walls, the skyline pierced by the minarets of mosques, the conical towers of Armenian churches and by the citadel squatting on a hill in the middle. The captain slowed to ride alongside Leroux.

'My first time in Erzurum,' the captain said, sitting back in the saddle and they plodded down a gentle incline.

'I'm not surprised,' Leroux said stretching his back, 'with a seven-day ride from the nearest port.'

The captain looked across, ignoring the attempted humour.

'Zeki Pasha could be back here at any moment. See the bishop, then we go. Understand?'

Leroux nodded. The soldiers would not be happy, but there was nothing he could do about that.

'I don't believe you are telling me the truth about the night Emin died, even if you didn't kill him yourself.'

'I did go to the village.'

The captain didn't react. The fall of hooves on the road seemed louder and Leroux swatted a fly away. 'I should have told you before.'

'The Sultan ordered me to take you to the bishop. You put me in a very difficult position. Do I follow my orders and deliver you to the church, knowing that you work against us, or do I torture you until you tell me the whole truth.' He spat on the ground and cursed and then looked to the heavens as if for inspiration. 'It seems I face the same dilemma as my Sultan. Should he go along with the demands of the Great Powers knowing that they wish us Turks ill, or should he deal with the traitors who undermine the country as they deserve?'

'I admit, I am trying to find out what happened at Akrag. Does it not bother you?' Leroux said.

'There are rumours. There are also bandits.'

'It does not mean that I am working against you. Someone, and I don't think it was you, has tried to kill me on this journey. Twice. And I don't know why.'

'Twice?'

'When I came back from the village there was an explosion above the path and the landslide nearly killed me. I believe it was intended to, and that Emin set it off.' Leroux let that sink in as he wrestled with how to leave Maximoff out of the tale.

'Emin?' The captain's voice was ripe with suspicion.

'The scratches on my face? I was knocked off the path and landed in a tree. I heard a scream but by the time I climbed up, Emin was dead. I found him on his back. It looked as though he had fallen in the dark and struck his head on a rock.'

The captain chewed the bottom of his moustache and muttered under his breath.

'You think he slipped?'

'I didn't see anyone else.'

'If you had told me that before I would have shot you on the spot,' he said shaking his head. 'But I saw with my own eyes the Hamidiye soldiers attack you. And I know they are lying.' The captain took a swig from his water bottle and offered it to Leroux.

'What's happened to yours?'

'I lost it in the landslide.'

The captain took the bottle back, screwing the cap on. 'I'm not sure why, but I believe your story.'

'If I am under your protection, whoever instructed those soldiers to attack me is working against the Sultan's wishes.'

'There is nothing I can do, for now,' the captain sighed. 'But when we get back to Constantinople…there is something I want you to do.'

'What?'

'You saw the village?'

'Yes. Massacred. Just bones and ashes.'

'Do you know who did it?'

'No.'

'Make sure your doubts are reported too because otherwise everyone will conclude that the Sultan is to blame.'

'I will.'

'The Europeans force the Sultan to give privileges to the Christians. This causes great resentment among our people and that pressure must go somewhere. Inevitably it falls on the weakest and the easiest to blame. And the Sultan is surrounded by serpents who each have their own agenda and use any discontent to their advantage. So, when you write your article, remember he is usually the one trying to restrain this violence.' The captain continued in silence satisfied he had made his point.

They entered the city by an Armenian quarter. The women hurried by or huddled in doorways, their eyes cast down through intricate braided hair, decorated with tiny silver balls. They dressed in long swinging one-piece dresses of white cotton and red aprons, richly embroidered with geometric patterns in the colours of earth, air, fire, and water, most with yellow shoes and red felt caps and scarves. The men shuffled sullenly, their eyes defiant, in long shirts of woollen multi-coloured threads and over-wide pants tucked into knitted socks. Leroux sensed the tension in the troop and the captain picked up the pace.

Rising above the houses ahead were two tall towers like Greek columns. As they got nearer, women were scarcer and the clothing changed to navy, sky blue, green, grey, and black. The men strode boldly, greeting the soldiers, but Leroux was fascinated by the columns that were twin brick minarets, decorated in glorious blue tiles, mounted on the upper corners of a huge rectangular limestone and marble façade. In the centre was a pointed arch with intricate floral carvings.

'The twin minaret madrasa,' the captain sighed. 'I wish I had seen it before the Russians looted everything.' The captain looked across to Leroux and down at his chest where the cross hung beneath his shirt. 'For centuries the crusaders have tried to tear us down, but it will never happen. Allah has decreed it.'

'Are you about to tell me a prophecy?'

The captain's eyes shone. 'The prophecy. The hadiths foretell a cataclysmic battle between the faithful and the forces of the Antichrist. Then the Mahdi, the Awaited One, will reign on earth as the final and greatest Caliph until the final judgement, when Allah will punish the sinners and bless the faithfull.'

'Who will be the Mahdi?'

'All the Great Powers attack the Sultan like jackals, yet he manages to fend them off by playing one against the other. Perhaps he can be the Mahdi, the final and greatest Caliph, and fulfill a great destiny. The forces of the Antichrist will make one last attack on Jerusalem, but they will fail and be destroyed. He will reign there as the greatest Caliph until the final judgement.'

'There are Christians who believe that the time of the gentiles is coming to an end in Jerusalem and that Jesus will soon return,' Leroux said.

'It is written,' the captain said, 'Jesus will descend to earth in advance of the Mahdi. He will encourage the faithful, show the Christians and Jews they have erred, and kill ad-Dajjal – the Antichrist.'

The captain fell silent, staring into the distance. Leroux had exhausted his theological knowledge and doubted that the captain would share his view that people just saw what they wanted to see in the writings. But how could the Sultan, as Caliph, possibly contemplate surrendering

166

Jerusalem? Did Nevlinski have some angle or was he just telling Herzl what he wanted to hear?

'The Sultan is fortunate to have such a loyal bodyguard,' Leroux said.

'He does not see the greatness in himself, but he will prevail, and the crusaders will fail again and for the last time.'

'Maximoff likes a good prophecy.'

The captain sneered. 'He is a snake. Whatever he promises the Sultan, he is only here to cause trouble.'

They turned onto an avenue heading away from the citadel. At the end, a pointed hat of tiles capped a tower poking up from a clump of trees. The road led into parkland and through a cemetery filled with crooked gravestones so old and covered in lichen that they resembled rotten teeth. Maximoff's horse broke into a trot. 'The Church of the Holy Mother of God! At last, we are here.' He pulled up under the bell tower that sheltered the western door. They slid wearily from their saddles, walking tenderly. Even for experienced cavalrymen, seven straight and long days on the road had left them sore and stiff. A young altar boy emerged alone and greeted them, and the heavy door screeched close behind him with a clang. He spoke with the captain and scurried away past the high pointed windows recessed in the side wall and disappeared into the adjacent building. The boy returned shortly, with halting steps alongside an old man limping with the aid of a staff, the polished silver top gleaming even in the dim light of dusk. His head was covered by the hood of a black cloak and rested on a bushy white beard. As he neared, eyes like currants glittered behind red cheeks and a bulbous nose. The bishop, cheery but curious, directed Leroux to a room in his house to refresh before dinner.

Leroux settled at the wooden desk by his bed to write. He had already admitted to the captain that he had seen the village, so there was no danger in putting his report on paper. He could send it tomorrow, perhaps even by telegraph. Simpkins would forward it to Beaumont, and then at least he would have accomplished something. The Ambassador could not deny that Leroux had fulfilled his task, and with luck Beaumont would hear a balanced version of events from Simpkins. What had happened was not in doubt. Who and why was a different matter. If he learnt anything new tonight from the bishop, he could add it. He would leave the girl out, in case his room was searched again, or the telegram was read. If she could reveal anything, Mrs Willis would get the information to Simpkins. And he would not mention Maximoff's involvement either, just report what he saw with his own eyes. Maximoff had told him about the guard in confidence, and writing it down here was as good as accusing Maximoff to the captain's face. His quill hovered above the sheet of paper as the scrape of a stool outside his door reminded him of the guard's presence. He reached forward and shut the window. Across the yard, the church door, closed and illuminated by lamps, took him back to the horror of Akrag and the bones that told of the desperate attempts of the villagers to escape the inferno. He included the landslide and the discovery of the dead guard as well as the assault by the two Hamidiye soldiers, before setting the quill down and blotting his name at the bottom.

A faint tap at the door announced the altar boy, who guided Leroux to the bishop's dining room, the guard following like a shadow. Maximoff joined them and dismissed the guard in Turkish. The guard protested, according to Leroux's smattering of vocabulary, but he reluctantly waited outside.

'I told him that he didn't guard your room from the inside,' Maximoff said. 'I doubt he speaks French, but why take the chance?'

The bishop's eyes disappeared behind his cheeks as he smiled, and a serving girl entered with a steaming dish of stew.

'Fasulya!' The bishop waved his hands encouraging the girl to load everyone's bowls with the concoction of tomato, green beans, and mutton.

'I have known Bishop Malachia since the war of '78,' Maximoff said, 'and we remained in touch. I hope you don't mind me intruding on your interview?'

'There is nothing,' the bishop interjected, 'that I would say that I would not be happy for Maximoff to hear.'

Maximoff crossed himself. 'O Christ God, bless the food and drink of Thy servants, for holy art Thou, always, now and ever, and unto the ages of ages. Amen.'

The bishop nodded in solemn approval of the grace. 'So, what news my old friend?'

Maximoff puffed his cheek. 'I can confirm the rumours of a massacre are true. The village of Akrag. The Sultan has been using irregular troops, Kurds mostly, some Circassians, to do his dirty work. You know their grudges against your people, and they need little encouragement to take revenge and loot.'

'I have heard this too,' the bishop brooded. 'And they are beyond the reach of the law. What will you do?'

Maximoff steepled his fingers. A curl of hair fell forward as he contemplated. 'The Tsar takes his obligation to protect you as a sacred duty. We do not forget that.' Maximoff cast a glance at Leroux and continued. 'But we must protect our access to the Straits. The British do not let us act decisively against the Sultan, so we must work from the inside and ally with him. Of course, the British endeavour to undermine our position with the Sultan. We must work together to maintain our relationship with the Sultan and urge restraint.' Maximoff turned to Leroux. 'You don't know, do you? The games your government plays?'

Leroux lowered his eyes. What could he say?

'Your capitalists lent the Turks money to fight us,' Maximoff said, 'and secured their loans against the Egyptian revenue. You cannot lose. The Ottomans are forever in your debt as you suck the marrow from her bones.'

'The more you squeeze,' the bishop said, his fist clenching as he brandished the spoon, 'the more they take out their anger on us!'

'It is the British and French,' Maximoff said, 'who prevent us from protecting you. The hypocrisy! The balance of power, they say! It must not be upset! France takes Algeria from Turkey, and Britain annexes principalities in India, yet according to the British, this does not disturb the balance of power. The British declare war on the Chinese, who have, it seems, offended them, and this is allowed. But Russia demands a treaty to protect millions of Christians, and that is deemed to strengthen its position at the expense of your precious balance of power. We can expect nothing from the West but blind hatred and malice.'

The bishop blew on a spoonful of stew and chewed thoughtfully.

'The revolutionaries get restless,' the bishop said at last. 'And they are young and reckless. They have no memories, no knowledge of the cruelty of war and see only victory. But the acts they plan will only bring more suffering down on us. What do they hope to achieve? Even in our heartland we are in a minority.'

'It is important,' Maximoff said, 'that their efforts are … coordinated. To act otherwise means certain defeat. The revolutionaries must wait for the right moment, the right opportunity.'

The bishop tilted the bowl to scoop up the last of the gravy and smacked his lips.

'Will you keep your promise this time?' The bishop's spoon hit the table with a thud.

'That was regrettable.' Maximoff turned to Leroux again. 'The British forced us to end the war. The Royal Navy threatened our supply lines as we approached Constantinople, we had no choice.'

'What choice did we have?' the bishop said. 'We rose up to support you, but your soldiers marched home and left us to our fate.' The bishop prodded the table. 'And you,' the bishop said to Leroux, 'Are no better. How many times does the Sultan have to call your bluff?'

Leroux offered no defence. Despite public support for the Armenians, the government always prioritised Suez and admonished the Sultan just enough to placate the voters.

'Our cause is hopeless,' the bishop said, 'not even a majority of Armenians desire independence. Many flourish under the Ottoman. We are being used again - I know the feeling well enough.' The bishop looked from Maximoff to Leroux and back. 'We are a cause that is picked up when it suits and dropped just as quickly. But we are the only ones who get hurt by the fall. We are merely a pawn in the Great Game. But for us it is a rigged game. There is no way to win, only new ways to lose.'

'Nevertheless,' Maximoff said getting to his feet, and towering over the bishop, 'the Tsar has sworn to protect you. Now, I have some business in town.'

The guard looked in as Maximoff left, and the bishop shut the door firmly in his face and dropped into his chair with a sigh. 'Our choice is between living under the Sultan or living under the Tsar. Not much of a choice, is it?'

Leroux was familiar with the plight of the underdog. Tom's people had faced a similar choice between the British and the Boers. Chief Malaboch had fought, and Leroux had witnessed his fate.

'I'm here to find out the truth behind the rumours.'

'Will the papers accuse the Sultan? Will your government do more than denounce him?'

'I don't know. We have no proof.'

The bishop's shoulders slumped. 'An honest answer, at least. We must be careful what we wish for. More publicity may bring more protection from the Great Powers. But more privileges only increase the resentment of our Muslim neighbours.'

'There is something you should know about.'

The bishop held his hand up while the serving girl cleared the dishes, and the door latch clicked down.

'I went to Akrag.'

'The soldiers let you go there?'

'No, I slipped out at night.'

'So, it was you that went there? Maximoff made it sound as though he had seen it.'

Leroux pulled the cross over his head and poured it into the bishop's hand. 'This was given to me by a man in Constantinople, dying from his wounds. He told me the name of the village and asked me to tell his people of its fate. Maximoff is the only other person I have told.'

'Was it as bad as they say?'

Leroux nodded grimly, knowing he had to risk the girl's life. The bishop's connections might hold the answers. 'There is something else. Another survivor. A witness.'

The bishop pulled his chair closer. 'Who?'

'A girl. I don't know her name, she couldn't speak.'

The bishop crossed himself. 'Poor child.'

'I left her with a missionary near Bayburt. She should be back with her people by now.'

The bishop's nose wrinkled. 'Missionary?'

'She is a good woman.'

'No one else survived?'

'Not that I saw.'

The bishop stroked his beard. 'It's not like those Kurdish bandits to kill everyone.'

'I cannot say who did it or why. It was dark and I had little time. I found no evidence to suggest who did it.'

'Maximoff said it was the Hamidiye. They serve the Sultan,' the bishop said.

'That is the most likely explanation. Do you know Zeki Pasha?'

'Of course.'

'Two of his men tried to kill me. I think he is involved.'

'He takes his orders from the Sultan. What difference does that make?'

'Maybe none. But the Sultan agreed to my request to travel here, to talk to you. I saw that with my own eyes. I think he wants me to get a fair impression. He may have me guarded and restricts where I can go, but I wonder if the Sultan knows the full story himself?'

'That's possible. He has enemies,' the bishop said, 'even within his own court. Reformers. Young Ottomans they call themselves, those that want to restore the old parliament.'

'Is Zeki Pasha a reformer?'

'I don't know. They are very secretive…. the Sultan's spies are everywhere.'

'You think they could be responsible for Akrag? Why?'

'The same reason any of his enemies would. To embarrass him in the eyes of the Great Powers. Make them lose confidence in him. Make him easier to replace.'

Leroux turned to a light tap on the door and a foot pushed it open, the serving girl edging in balancing a tray and two cups, the guard leering from behind.

'Ah, soorj,' the bishop said scooping the smoky aroma of coffee to his nose, and Leroux drifted for a second to the Magaliesburg mountains and the heady brew of home. The bishop sipped, deep in thought.

'It must be difficult to live in a land surrounded by enemies,' Leroux said.

The bishop raised his eyes, still gripping the cross.

'We were here first.'

'And the first Christian country?'

'Yes. And here we must stay. When Jesus was entombed, angels conveyed his body to Mount Ararat and lay him next to the remains of Noah's Ark. After he revealed himself to his disciples and ascended to Heaven, there he returned, to rest uncorrupted, awaiting his second coming.'

The cross hung from the bishop's hand, and he kissed it.

'I have heard the prophecy that Christians will once again rule in Constantinople, the eagle overcoming the snake.'

'It's from a book I have. You know the writings of Nestor Iskander?'

Leroux shook his head. 'Just that story.'

'They are known in the Orthodox Church, but seldom outside it. Maximoff will be impressed. Iskander's "The Tale of the Taking of Tsargrad" is gaining popularity again.'

'Tsargrad?'

'An old Russian name for Constantinople.'

'On my way here, I met a man determined to fulfill a prophecy, to return the Jewish people to Jerusalem and herald the Second Coming. At every turn I have been attacked or met with some misfortune. And I can't escape the feeling that the prophecy is in the background, somehow connected with what is happening here.'

'Then you should know all the prophecies.' The bishop drained his cup and stood stiffly. 'There's something you should see.'

The bishop led Leroux outside, shuffling to the church door, and heaved it open.

'We pray. You wait,' the bishop said to the guard, who looked suspiciously into the cavernous building until the door slammed shut with a dull echo. The bishop lit candles, revealing row upon row of stuccoed columns, and held his lamp up to paintings and icons hung along the wall. He stopped before the last, depicting the Virgin Mary with seven swords piercing her heart and whispered to it. 'Rejoice, much-sorrowing Mother of God, turn our sorrows into joy and soften the hearts of evil men.' He bowed his head and ushered Leroux past a gilded pulpit to a small door and produced an iron key, worn and flecked with rust. The door creaked open, and the bishop descended, brushing against dusty brickwork.

'We keep the church silver down here. The crypt dates back over a thousand years and there are manuscripts from the old times.'

The bishop set his lamp on a table covered with plates, candle holders and chalices, the silver pieces more tarnished than the gold. The flame flickered in the stale and musty air, and the bishop squinted as he ran his finger along a cobwebbed shelf laden with books.

'Make a space on the table.'

176

The bishop gently set a manuscript down, opened the leather cover and turned the parchment pages. 'Nestor Iskander was a Russian monk. He was captured by the Ottomans as a young novice on a pilgrimage to Constantinople. He was enslaved and forced to convert. But he remained a Christian in his heart, and during the great siege he escaped the Turks' camp and reached the city, hoping to help them with his knowledge of their strategy. He was too late to make a difference. It had been foretold that Constantinople would be lost under the rule of an Emperor called Constantine, son of Helen. It was the last days of the battle, and the people feared every sign they saw in the sky. Their Emperor, Constantine XI, son of Helena Dragaš, strapped on his armour, but his Genoese ally, the great general Giustiniani, was grievously wounded and his troops fled. Iskander watched in horror as the walls fell to the Turks and the emperor died under their swords. The city was sacked, but Iskander escaped and returned to Russia.' The bishop leaned closer to the text. 'Here we are. "The Rusii Rod will defeat the Ishmaelites," by which he means the Muslims, "and their king will become the basileus in the City of Seven Hills."'

'Basileus?'

'It means king.'

'And who are the Rusii Rod?'

'Blond people. And the City of Seven Hills is Constantinople, like Rome before it.'

The bishop turned the page and his finger hovered just above the faded ink. 'He tells the Tsar:

"Heresy caused the downfall of old Rome. The Turks used their axes to shatter the doors of all the churches of the Second Rome, the city of Constantinople. Now in Moscow, the new Third Rome, the Holy Church of your sovereign shines brighter than the sun in the Christian faith throughout the world. Pious Tsar! Let the people know that all states of the Orthodox faith have now merged into one, your state. You are the only true Christian ruler under the sky! Two Romes have fallen, the third will stand, and there will be no fourth. No one shall replace your Christian Tsardom.""

The bishop raised his head.

'That is the prophecy of Nestor Iskander. The Tsar will defeat the Muslims and retake Constantinople and the San Sophia. He will rule over all the kingdoms of the true Christian Church.'

'The Orthodox Church?' Leroux asked.

'That is what Iskander writes. All the Slavs, under one church, under one King. No doubt,' the bishop added bitterly, 'the Armenian Apostolic Church will be considered a heresy ...'

'Maximoff believes this?'

'I am told the Tsar believes it. He sees himself as the true heir to the Roman Emperors. The very word Tsar comes from Caesar. Vladimir the Great of the Kievan Rus married Anna, sister to a Byzantium Emperor. And Ivan III of Russia married Sophia Paleologue, a niece to Constantine XI, the last Byzantine emperor. The Holy Roman Empire is their rightful inheritance. The bloodline has been broken since then, but the Caesars never worried too much about that.'

'And Saint Sophia,' Leroux said, 'was the crowning majesty of the Orthodox Church for nearly a thousand years, where Olga, the Grand Princess of Kiev came to convert to Christianity and spread it among the Rus.'

'You know your history,' the bishop said and rubbed his furrowed brow. 'Saint Sophia holds special power for the Orthodox Church.'

'And if the Tsar seized Constantinople and fulfilled the prophecy,' Leroux said, 'he would gain enormous influence over all Slavs.'

'This is my fear. The Tsar's lust for power will drive him to this. He sees the Slavs as branches of the Russian trunk. As Maximoff says, the Linden tree is blossoming, and it will be the time of the Slavs. The oak of the Teutons bloomed long ago.' The archbishop sank into a chair. 'And we Armenians may simply be trading one tyrant for another.' The bishop picked up one of the gold goblets and turned it by the flame. 'Under the Sultan many of us have prospered. Along with the Greeks, we control much of the trade and worship as we please. Our difficulties are not caused by the Sultan, but by the games your government and the Tsar play, trying to use us to control the Sultan.'

'I thought you were friends with Maximoff?'

'I have no choice but to maintain friendly relations with the Tsar's representative. Many of us live in his lands.'

'You wouldn't support a Russian invasion?'

'Our cousins in Russia suffer heavily under the new Tsar. He despises our culture and our different ways. If he succeeds in uniting the Slavs, we will never be given independence, and the Tsar will see us as a threat, not an ally.'

The bishop rubbed his eyes. 'There. I have been waiting to tell someone of my fears. And you came. Perhaps it is a sign.'

Leroux stared into the flame. Is that what Maximoff was plotting?

'The British stopped the Tsar taking Constantinople before. What has changed? They still fear him having access to the Mediterranean and threatening Suez.'

'Nevertheless,' the bishop said, 'I do not think he will stop trying. Maybe the Tsar has a plan for your Navy. And he will encourage the revolutionaries to rise and help his army. If we betray the Ottoman Empire again, there will be no mercy.'

Maximoff's diplomacy had left Constantinople vulnerable to the Russian fleet, but the Sultan would welcome the assistance of Royal Navy, as he had last time. There must be more to it. Did Currie or Beaumont have any inkling that Russia might be encouraging the Armenians to rise again and unknowingly help them take Constantinople? Had they considered the possibility of the Tsar uniting the Slavs? What evidence could he show them, apart from some prophecies? Currie's dismissive attitude to the End of Times dossier and his condemnation still rang in Leroux's ears. He would need more than the writings of a medieval monk.

'Do you have any proof that Russia is planning this? If I can provide the Ambassador with some evidence, he may be able to act before any blood is shed. But I need more than a prophecy.'

The bishop rocked forward, his eyes closed, as though seeking inspiration. His thumb nervously rubbed the cross and he pressed it back into Leroux's hands.

'This is yours. Thank you for risking your life to learn about Akrag. You have done us a great service.'

'I have seen some things that God should put an end to. I will help, if I can, but I need something more than prophecies. Where has Maximoff gone?'

The bishop closed the manuscript and lifted it carefully back to its place. Leroux hung his head, massaging his temples, trying to process the events of the past week. Was this Maximoff's plan? Did Maximoff fear a British agent travelling to Armenia and discovering it? Only a few days ago, Maximoff was protecting him from the captain. When he looked up, the bishop stared at him, his dark eyes glistening.

'There is a meeting of the revolutionaries tonight in the town, it is where Maximoff has gone. I do not know what they are planning, but there is a man you can talk to called Armen Garo. Tell him you came from me and to be wary of anything Maximoff is suggesting. Tell him what you saw at Akrag – he will know of the rumours. Persuade the revolutionaries not to sacrifice our people. They may listen to you.'

Leroux followed the bishop up the narrow staircase. 'What time?'

'Midnight. I will arrange a distraction for the guard, but make sure you are not followed. They will kill the revolutionaries and anybody they find with them. And do not tell Maximoff what I told you.'

'You have my word.'

The bishop gave him directions to a side street where Leroux would be met by a man who would guide him to the revolutionaries' safe house. He panted as he locked the crypt door, but turned suddenly and tugged at Leroux's arm, pulling him to the altar.

'Let us say a prayer for the girl.'

The bishop clasped his hands, knelt, and began a liturgy in Armenian. Leroux copied and felt a cool draft on the back of his neck, and then footsteps on the paving at the far end, quickening and now deeper in tone on the wooden floor near the altar.

'I trust you have concluded your interview,' the captain said, looking from one to the other.

'Yes, thank you,' Leroux said.

'Then we leave in the morning.'

'Godspeed,' the bishop said.

/

Leroux propped himself up in bed. The guard had just changed and would be alert. Leroux's eyelids drooped, but he had to be ready for whatever diversion the bishop planned. He read over his report, considering whether to add a reference to Iskander's writings and the bishop's concerns. They seemed far-fetched and Leroux did not have the proof or the credibility with Currie to raise them. Leroux doubted Maximoff believed in the prophecy. Of course, you didn't need to believe in the soothsaying for it to help your cause. You could use the story to gain support from the faithful for your plans. Isn't that why the Romans converted to Christianity? An incredible plan. To conquer the city that the Tsars claimed as their inheritance. To command the strategic Turkish Straits. To re-establish Saint Sophia as the head of the Church. To enable the Tsar to claim suzerainty over all Orthodox Slavs. The Balkans and half of Austro-Hungary owing allegiance to the Tsar. That would certainly tip the balance of power on the continent that the British had worked so assiduously to maintain. A strategy that allowed them to concentrate on their worldwide empire while their European rivals fretted about their neighbours. But was there any substance to it? And even then, how would the Tsar manage it in the face of certain British opposition?

Leroux added nothing and slid the report into an envelope without sealing it. Tonight's meeting could shed more light. The revolutionaries may even know who annihilated the village and why. He wound his timepiece and a girl giggled in the passage as he dropped the letter into the desk drawer. He pressed his ear to the door. The guard was talking with a girl and laughing. The stool rattled on the stone floor as he stood, his voice lower and thicker, and the girl squealed in delight. The voices trailed off and Leroux tested the door. It was still bolted from the outside. He went to the window. A guard stood under the bell tower porch facing Leroux, his head lifting a fraction at Leroux's silhouette. Leroux pulled his shirt off, stretched, sat down on the bed, and doused the lamp. He fumbled in the dark, redressing and gathering his slouch hat. A light knock and the slow scrape of the bolt sliding brought Leroux to the door. He eased it ajar to see the bishop's serving girl, her eyes fierce with pride behind a flickering candle. Leroux slipped around the door, blocking as much of the candlelight from the window as he could and pushed the bolt home again. The girl ushered Leroux through the kitchens and mimed knocking on the door three times for when he returned, before letting him out into the night.

A guard stamped his feet in front of the church, shifting his rifle on his shoulder, as he glanced up at the dark window and then across the cemetery, before walking around the porch and back to his post. Leroux crouched at the corner of the bishop's house. A wall surrounded the parkland, but once he was across the drive and past the gravestones he would be at the gate to the avenue. He was at home, like stalking in the long grass of the veld. The guard took another turn around the porch, long enough for Leroux to get across the drive. The dirt softened the sound of his footsteps.

When the guard set off again, Leroux took measured steps, bending low at the knees, placing his heel down first and rolling through the balls of his feet, putting his next foot down close in front and transferring his weight smoothly onto it, matching the cadence of the guard. He faced slightly side-on, crossing his legs over to prevent his trousers rubbing. The guard's lantern announced his reappearance from the back of the porch as Leroux crouched behind a gravestone. The graveyard was uneven and unlit. Slowly he put a foot out, feeling with the outer edge as it rolled down. The guard continued his routine, the features of his face fading as Leroux inched further away. A twig snapped. Leroux froze, one eye watching the reaction of the guard. He'd heard it. He stopped, unslung his rifle, and brandished it in front of him, the muzzle traversing the cemetery until it paused near Leroux. He took a step forward and then turned to take the lantern from the wall. Leroux stole to the side, putting some distance between himself and the source of the sound. The guard ventured to the edge of the driveway casting the lantern beam across the cemetery, long shadows reaching to the outer walls. Leroux waited with his back to a headstone. The light swung away, and a voice called out. Leroux risked a look. The guard was changing. That might do it, somebody else's problem now. He crept further away. The new guard started his round and Leroux was almost at the gate. Where had the first guard gone?

As the new guard slipped from view behind the porch, Leroux flitted through the gate, and a bird scared up from inside the wall and alighted in the tree above him, its head cocked sideways. He kept to the side of the avenue, moving quickly from tree to tree, pausing in cover like a deer to listen. Occasionally he would freeze suddenly, halfway between trees, to catch the footfall of an unseen follower. Was that a footstep? He checked his watch and held his breath to listen. If someone was following, they were good. He reassured himself that once in the deserted streets any pursuer would stand out.

Leroux followed the mental map that the bishop had described. The cobbles under his boots were dry and the slightest scuff of his leather soles on grit carried along the narrow lanes. He approached a crossroads and sunk into a doorway as the staccato sound of marching approached. No one behind. Ahead, a patrol of four men in the dark grey tunics of the gendarmerie crossed over the street and carried on. It seemed an unusually heavy presence for such a quiet city at night, but their direction suggested they weren't looking for him. Maybe they were aware that the revolutionaries planned to meet? The gendarmerie passed from view and Leroux carried on straight ahead. He slipped along the side of the street from house to house until he reached the turning.

Only a sliver of moon lit the road, and that didn't reach into the narrow alley. He felt his way down and stopped at the third door. There was no recess and Leroux flattened himself against the wall as the footfall

185

of the gendarmerie returned along the main road and passed away again. A few minutes later, a shape appeared at the top of the alley and moved silently towards Leroux. It was a short and swarthy man in an oversized coat with his eyes shielded by the brim of a hat. He passed Leroux, barely glancing at him, and stopped after another five doorways before walking back.

'The bishop said I wouldn't have any trouble recognizing you,' the man said pointing at Leroux's hat. 'Follow me.' They went further into the alley, zigzagging through side streets, until just as Leroux lost his sense of orientation, the man rapped on a door. Before it could be answered he hurried on and darted down the next turning. A dog barked at the top of the street, summoning a chorus of replies before an uneasy silence settled again. All the windows were dark. The door cracked open and the wizened face of a woman, wrapped in a shawl, greeted him. She moved aside, softly closing the door on the dark hallway. Leroux had no words to communicate and reached for the tiny silver cross in the gloom. The old lady put her finger to her lips as the stamp of a patrol surged up to the door. They looked at each other, holding their breath, but he saw no fear in her eyes. The clack of iron nails on stone quickly diminished. The lady smiled, touched the cross and felt her way slowly down the passage. Behind a curtain, a young man, similar in age to Leroux, shielded a candle. He introduced himself in French as Khacho.

'The bishop said you would come. Thank you, Mother. The bastard Turks have not caught her once in sixty years. Don't worry, she cannot speak French.'

The old lady's eyes twinkled, suggesting she understood the odd word and she shuffled away. Khacho led Leroux out through the back of the stone cottage and a small yard to a gate. This led into the walled grounds of a larger property. A smudge of light filtered out from a coal hatch. Khacho opened it for Leroux to descend towards muffled voices. Khacho squeezed past and pulled aside a heavy drape, revealing a cavernous cellar. Oil lamps hung from the walls and provided a dim yellow light alongside rusty pitchforks, hoes, and scythes. Sacks of grain were heaped in one corner and about thirty people, mostly men perched on bales and stools arranged in a rough semicircle focused on a low platform at the end of the room with a table and chairs.

They were rats in a trap if the guards came upon the entrance. Curtains hung down to cloak any openings that might emit light. Leroux searched for another exit and to the right of the table a ladder rose up to a trapdoor. Not many would make it out that way. A light flared as a man on a front row bale lit a pipe and briefly illuminated the dark curls and jutting jawline of Maximoff. Leroux instinctively stepped behind Khacho. Maximoff was in discussion with the pipe-smoker and had not reacted to the new arrivals. Khacho ushered Leroux to a seat next to a man with the gentle complexion of a student who looked up, extended his hand, and murmured,

'Armen Garo, I've been expecting you.'

He had a handlebar moustache, and his hair was parted and brushed back with a jaunty curl. His eyes brimmed with optimism and hope that Leroux had not noticed before in Erzurum.

Leroux hunched down on the straw and bowed his head to keep another man in Maximoff's line of sight. Better to watch Maximoff unobserved. Would he still see the charismatic, helpful Maximoff of the voyage to Trebizond and the ride to Erzurum, offering friendship and alliance? Or the picture painted by the bishop?

'Welcome to the meeting,' Garo said. 'The problem we face is not just the Turk. We cannot even agree amongst ourselves.' Leroux coughed as he scanned the room, the air thick with smoke. A low hubbub awaited a presence on the raised platform and Leroux worried whether the noise and scent of the meeting were adequately contained. A loud rap from behind one of the curtains stunned the audience into silence. Leroux instinctively looked at the exits, but no one had moved for them. Armen sat back and rolled his eyes. 'Do not be alarmed. It is Avetis Nazarbekian, one of the founders of the Social Democratic Hunchakian Party. He likes to make an entrance.'

The moth-eaten curtain swept back, and a rakish figure strode on to the dais. His fine Persian features and suit accompanied by an oversized bowtie and a long scarf draped around his neck gave him the air of an intellectual as he cleaned his pince-nez. Garo fidgeted in quiet annoyance. Avetis perched on the end of the table and a babble of anticipation raced around. He banged the handle of a dagger on the table, hushing the audience.

'The Hunchakians were behind the rebellion in Sasun last year,' whispered Garo. 'Tens of thousands died. What do you expect from a poet who follows Lenin?' Armen Garo shook his head, darkly muttering some foreign oaths under his breath.

'Comrades. I have grim news,' Avetis began. 'Last month the heroes of Van rose up against the Bloody Sultan. They fought valiantly and the Sultan was forced to negotiate. Our comrades agreed to leave, and the Sultan promised them a safe escort to Persia. I have just heard that on the way they were ambushed. 1,000 of our brothers were slaughtered by Kurdish tribesmen.'

Moans and gasps spread across the room and Avetis thrust his hands up to command silence. As the murmuring subsided, he drew his hands down and tossed one end of his scarf extravagantly over his shoulder. Armen hung his head. 'Such senseless slaughter. Do they get the attention of the Great Powers? Staging revolts in the hills where no one can see or hear. We must take the fight to the Sultan. We must do something the Great Powers cannot ignore.'

'We all share the grief, but we must not be disheartened,' Avetis continued. 'We must redouble our efforts and remember that we have friends.' Avetis turned pointedly to Maximoff. 'Friends who will step in and help us. We must prepare. The Sultan is fragile. He relies on Kurds to oppress us, and who would rely on Kurds?' Nervous laughter spread out. 'The next time we will sweep all before us!' A swelling of ascent grew, 'Freedom will be ours!'

Avetis stepped down, satisfied with the acclamation while at the same time gesturing at the gathering to quieten down. He joined Maximoff's group and was swallowed in congratulations.

Another man rose to address the gathering. Armen perked up. 'This is Papken Siuni, of the Armenian Revolutionary Federation. Proper fighters,

189

not the children of rich families who are happy to throw away the lives of others. Listen.' He craned forward.

Papken extended his arms. 'I do not want to diminish the sacrifices our countrymen have made. But to what end? Where is the response from the Great Powers? Will they ever raise a hand to save Armenians? They are too busy draining the Sultan of money and protecting their trade routes. And what of the Tsar? What has he done? How many times must we rise before he joins us? Has he done anything to earn our trust?' Papken glanced at Maximoff, who sat stiffly, his countenance revealing nothing.

'I tell you; we must fight cleverly. Not simply rebel and wait for the Sultan to send his soldiers to kill us, hoping that a river of blood will somehow reach the shores of the Great Powers. The ARF has a plan. A plan that does not put the ordinary man in the Sultan's gunsights. A plan that will grab the attention of the Great Powers in a way they cannot ignore. We will seize their wallet! I cannot tell you more, for we only require a small team and secrecy for success. I beg you, do not heed the Hunchakians. Do not flock like lambs to the slaughter. Keep your powder dry and wait, at least for a few weeks. We will deliver.'

The bale sighed as Papken returned to his seat. The gathering sat in silence, perhaps in disbelief or confusion or lack of a concrete plan to rally behind. Avetis cleared his throat and clapped slowly, insolently. 'Well, I for one am not going to stand by and do nothing. It seems to me that having a secret plan is a way of hiding the fact that you have no plan at all!' The meeting descended into rancour and the noise grew alarmingly. Leroux shifted in his seat, checking the exits again. Maximoff must have had the same idea, and he made his farewells, smothering Avetis in his embrace.

Armen spat on the floor. 'Avetis is naïve. If you invite a bear to dance, it's not you who decides when the dance is over. It's the bear.'

Maximoff pulled on his coat and glanced around the room, but Leroux saw no flicker of recognition or acknowledgement. The Russian backed along the wall and out through the curtain.

'We should go,' Leroux said, but Armen handed him a glass, reached for a flask behind him and poured a caramel liquid. A pungent fruity odour cut through the haze. Leroux sized up the spirit and drained the glass. It was surprisingly good and strong. A kind of brandy.

'Not bad.'

Armen refilled the glasses. 'Not bad! This is kanyak, grapes from the slopes of Mount Ararat. We have a proverb. Every guest is a gift from God.'

Leroux sipped the next one.

'So Maximoff supports the Hunchakian Party?' Leroux said.

'Does it not strike you as odd?' Armen said, 'That a Tsarist agent would support men who follow Lenin? Who provoke the Sultan as recklessly as they do, when the Tsar competes with the British for his favour?'

'There is a certain logic,' Leroux said. 'The Tsar publicly claims the right to protect Armenians. And if he wants to have a foot in the resistance he must pick a horse, wisely or not. And all the horses I can see are revolutionaries. You are socialists too, aren't you?'

Armen muttered darkly, 'I didn't say I wanted his backing. The Tsar does not have our interests at heart. The Hunchakians choose to work with him, but what does Maximoff want from them?'

Leroux offered his glass as Armen tipped the flask.

'The bishop fears he wants to use them,' Leroux said. 'To increase his leverage with the Sultan and perhaps secure more protection for Christians or failing that, to help overthrow the Sultan.'

'I know what the bishop thinks. What does England think?'

'I'm not sure. The Ambassador is yet to hear the details of the latest massacre. I saw it for myself and will report back to him. The British public support your cause, but the government will always balance it against their desire to protect Suez.'

'How true. Let us hope a bit more pressure in the right place might persuade them.' Armen smiled. Was he thinking of Papken's secret plan?

'The Tsar only wants to expand his power,' Armen added. 'I will not help him. Why would I put my head in the lion's mouth?'

'What are you planning to do instead?' Leroux asked.

'I didn't say I trusted you either. You English offer nothing but empty promises. The Sultan has only to toss a scrap and you go running.'

'The government's attitude might change now.'

Armen raised an eyebrow.

'My report goes back tomorrow. Even if the government does nothing, The Times at least might publish it.'

'The Times has had no lack of reports over the years. From missionaries, us, your Ambassador must know. Maximoff certainly does. But nothing happens. The Sultan denies it. There is always someone writing an article that disputes the events or downplays them, paid for by the Sultan. The waters are muddied. People in their ignorance give the two arguments equal weighting. There is no distinction between truth and falsehood and the uncertainty leads to inaction. And the Sultan plays you all off against each other.'

Armen was no fool. Leroux swirled the brandy in his glass, fighting the frustration he felt. He could offer Armen no guarantees. The newspaper proprietors and the government would follow their own interests unless he provided clear proof.

'Do you know who was responsible for the massacre?' Leroux said.

'There were no witnesses, but everyone assumes it was the Hamidiye.'

Leroux had already told the bishop about the girl. Armen's network could make contact with her and find out if she knew anything. He had to trust him.

'There was a survivor, a girl.'

Armen didn't react. Just waited for Leroux to continue. Had the bishop already told him? Was he being tested? 'I found her at Akrag and sent her with a missionary to Bayburt. I hope she will find her people, somewhere safe.'

'I will send word. Perhaps she saw who was responsible.'

'She is mute.'

'God willing, she will recover. My money is still on the Hamidiye.'

'Under the command of Zeki Pasha?'

Armen concurred. 'He has a reputation for harsh reprisals.'

'This was more than harsh.'

'They must be trying to send a message, to break our will to resist. But the people have had enough. Word is spreading, and it will be hard to hold them back. Especially with Avetis stirring them up, dangling the promise of Russian protection.'

'Protection? You don't think it's more than that?'

'If the Sultan goes too far, the Tsar will threaten him, make him back down,' Armen said.

'Not invade?'

'Not if you British have any say in the matter. That's where Avetis is wrong. He believes the Russians will deliver on whatever they have promised him. But there will always be some more important consideration that comes up at the last moment, just like the last time.'

'Somebody has been trying to stop me since I began the journey here. They've discredited me and tried to kill me. I don't know who or why. Maybe the Sultan, maybe Maximoff, or someone else. But I'm sure it's something to do with the massacre. Somebody is trying to keep something quiet, and my guess is that it's something that's bad for both of us. Any information about what Maximoff plans could be invaluable.'

If there was any substance to the bishop's suspicions about the Tsar and his pursuit of Iskander's prophecy, then Maximoff may be using the Armenians to help attack the Sultan. Any evidence of that would be useful to Beaumont. Armen looked glumly around the room. Nearly everyone had stayed, gathering around Avetis, jostling to listen and offer their allegiance.

'The bishop will vouch for me,' Leroux added.

'He has, otherwise we wouldn't be talking. Let's go.'

Leroux let the rough drape fall behind them as they climbed the steps to the hatch. 'I head back to Constantinople tomorrow. How shall I contact you?'

'I'm heading there myself,' Armen said.

'You can leave a message for me at the Pera Palace Hotel or with Randolph Simpkins at the embassy. No other, only Simpkins. Any information about Maximoff's intentions would be useful. And I will let you know what I find out. How can I—'

'I will contact you.'

The old lady opened the street door for them and hobbled out, emptying a reeking pail in the gutter. She looked both ways and showed her gums. Her hand reached up and caressed Leroux's cheek and then her fingers slipped under the chain and lifted the cross out. She said something to Armen and let it drop.

'She says you have been sent to help us,' Armen said as they walked to the end of the street, the cobblestones glistening from a recent shower. Leroux's thoughts turned to getting back into the bishop's house unnoticed. He had tested the captain's patience too many times and the guard outside his room may already have noticed his absence. And he hadn't even thought about how he would get back in unobserved. Perhaps the serving girl would have an answer for that too.

Armen thrust his arm out as they reached the junction and listened. Fast footsteps faded in the distance and set off a brief chorus of barking. Armen glanced around the corner.

'What's that?' he whispered.

Something or somebody was slumped in a doorway on the other side of the main street. They crossed over and the shape turned into a uniformed body lying on its side. It was the first guard from outside the church. Eldar, he thought his name was, and if he hadn't gone off duty before, he certainly was now. A puddle of blood pooled under his neck and rivulets spread out between the cobblestones, like spidery veins, black in the moonlight. His throat had been cut.

'Who is it?' Armen said.

'It's one of the guards from my party, not a patrol.' Leroux held his finger to the cold neck more in hope than expectation. 'He's dead.'

'What's he doing here?'

Leroux kicked himself. He was sure he hadn't seen anyone. Eldar must have followed at a distance and lost him when the guide detoured through the streets. Then he would have waited where he last saw Leroux, expecting him to come back the same way. He turned to Armen.

'I'm sorry—,' Leroux flinched as a bullet ricocheted off the stonework by his head. Armen jumped back into the doorway and Leroux crouched behind the body. 'Are you hit?'

'No, it just nicked my jacket,' said Armen brushing his sleeve, 'Where did it come from?'

The gunshot had come from near the crossroads. No movement, but he was sure he heard some footfall, gone now.

'I didn't see the flash. I heard someone, maybe whoever killed the guard,' Leroux said and pointed ahead. He padded the guard's body, unclipped his holster and drew the revolver. Leroux spun the cylinder. Eldar hadn't fired. Armen pulled an ancient pistol from his waistband and braced himself against the door jamb. A shout came from the crossroads where the shot had come from and then more shouts followed by heavy footsteps, in time, double quick, growing louder.

'They're coming this way. It sounds like a patrol.'

Armen would be arrested if he was caught. Interrogated, probably killed. Where had Eldar's killer gone? The body was still warm. He was up there somewhere. The patrol should come upon him before they reached here.

'Do you think the gunman knew who we were?' Armen said hesitantly.

'If it was Eldar's killer, he might have thought we were more guards.'

Armen peered in the direction of the footsteps and then searched for an escape route.

'You go back that way,' Leroux said, 'You can't be caught near here. They'll throw away the key.'

'If I'm lucky,' Armen laughed nervously. 'This is a set up. They've been after me for a long time.'

Leroux nudged Armen. 'Go! I'll lead them off.'

'What if they catch you?'

'It won't be as bad as if they catch you. Get going.'

Armen hesitated. 'Thank you. I won't forget this. I'll contact you in Constantinople.'

'Is that where your plan is?'

Armen looked at him fiercely. 'Yes. And it will save my people. I won't tell you the details, in case…' He looked up the street again. 'But it will be soon, and hopefully forestall the bloodshed that Avetis plans. Bon courage!' He grasped Leroux's hand and hugged him before disappearing into the shadows. Leroux waited until Armen was well out of sight. He had a bad feeling that the shooter was after him. There had been too many coincidences. The patrol was getting closer. Why hadn't they come across the shooter? Had he escaped? Or was he still lurking there?

If Leroux could make it to the crossroads, he could lead the patrol away, then loop around and get back to the bishop's house. He started forward, but the footsteps came on, louder still, and the first soldier appeared at the crossing. The killer must have slipped away. The soldier aimed at Leroux.

'Dur!'

Leroux had picked up enough Turkish to know that meant "stop." It was too late to get to the crossroads. He fired at the ground in front of the patrol, hoping to slow them down while Armen made good his escape. The guard ducked behind the corner, but more appeared and a smattering of fire fizzed inaccurately about him.

Leroux fired again over their heads, retreating to the next doorway. The guards split into two groups hugging each side of the street, darting from cover to cover, their fire getting more accurate. Leroux tried the door, but it wouldn't budge. He looked back where Armen had gone. He should be well away now, and they hadn't seen him, only firing at Leroux. He would make a dash for the next side street. He broke cover, firing twice, but a hail of bullets struck the ground in front of him. He skidded to a halt on the damp road and slowly raised his hands. At least it looked as though they wanted to take him alive. He would have to take his chances with whatever protection his status as a foreigner might provide. His revolver clattered to the ground, and he turned to face the approaching gendarmerie who prodded the air with their pistols, until two ran forward and grabbed an arm each, forcing him to the ground, shouting at him. "Who are you?" was the only bit that Leroux understood.

Tuesday, 11th August, Erzurum

Leroux tested the rope that chafed his wrists. A foul stench permeated from a corner of the cell, and he hunched against the wall, chill air sinking from an opening over his head where a faint smudge of grey heralded the dawn. He had struggled to communicate with his captors and the patrol had not known what to make of him. They squabbled amongst themselves, before tossing him in the cell. Hours dragged by, with just a table and the stinking bucket for company, until footsteps passed outside the window and keys rattled in the cell door. The captain burst into the room followed by Ali, one of his three remaining guards, who launched himself across the short space to land a hefty boot into Leroux's ribs. The same ribs that bore the bruises from the landslide. Leroux fell to his side choking as the captain hauled Ali off. Leroux had slipped his watchful eye again. Another of his guards was dead. He had been roused from bed with the bad news and now prowled the cell, scratching at the stubble on his neck. The gendarmerie officer entered with a folder and a sack of possessions, which he dropped on the table. Captain Emre snatched the folder and shook it open, his head twitching as he read the report.

'I couldn't prove it in the mountains, but you have been caught red-handed now. Why are you here?'

Leroux had spent the sleepless hours running over the events of the last few days again and again. And one name kept coming up. There were too many coincidences with Maximoff. He had been at the mountain pass when Emin was killed, and Leroux barely survived the landslide. Maximoff had left the meeting ahead of them when Eldar died, and Leroux was shot at. That didn't explain the Hamidiye soldiers, but Maximoff was there. Each time Leroux nearly killed and Maximoff smelling of roses. And there was his late decision to join their party just after Leroux was drugged in Theodora's. Maximoff had laid on the charm, offering to set aside their professional rivalry in the face of the greater threat of the Sultan and his punishment of the Armenians. But every coincidence cast a deeper suspicion. And the bishop's recounting of Iskander's tale painted a motive.

Leroux cursed. Maximoff had even had the cheek to claim a favour. Did Maximoff see Leroux's mission to meet the bishop as a sign that the British government was suspicious of Russia's plans? Had Maximoff been stringing him along the whole time, befriending him, watching him, assessing how much he knew, and trying to kill him? Maybe Armen wasn't the target last night. Maximoff had left the meeting ahead of them. If the guard had spotted him, Maximoff would not want it reported back, especially if Eldar knew he had been at the meeting of revolutionaries. Occam's razor. Maximoff had been there. They had seen no one else until the patrol came upon them. He was the simplest explanation. If Maximoff planned an uprising, he couldn't be seen with the revolutionaries. And the rockslide? Leroux only had Maximoff's word that it was set off by the guard. Maybe the guard had caught Maximoff in the act? But why would he be worried that Leroux had been to the village? He seemed to know nothing of the girl. Perhaps he just wanted Leroux out of the way and saw an opportunity. Had he seen another opportunity tonight?

The captain slapped Leroux. 'I asked you a question.'

'I didn't kill your guards, either here or in the mountains.'

The captain nodded at Ali, who grabbed Leroux by the lapels and hauled him to his feet. Pins and needles fired through his muscles as Ali passed a rope through Leroux's hand binds and strung him up to an iron ring fixed in the ceiling. Ali leant back, putting his weight into the rope and Leroux toppled forward onto his tiptoes, his shoulder joints screaming as they took the strain and his hands rose behind his back.

'I gave you the benefit of the doubt the first time.'

The captain closed in, lining up a punch and then rocked forward and smashed his fist into Leroux's solar plexus. Time stopped. His mouth hung open, no breath coming. The captain's fury hadn't clouded his judgement. No damage to his hand. No mark on Leroux. Maximum effect. The captain stepped back.

Leroux's body convulsed trying to generate some breath, any movement to draw oxygen in. His eyes felt as if they were about to burst as he stared at the stone floor. Come on, breathe. Finally, his body relaxed, exhaling, then air flooding in. A trickle of drool leaked from the corner of Leroux's mouth as he panted.

'I'm not the killer. Yes, I shot at the patrol. Someone shot at me first and I fired back. The guard was already dead, killed with a knife. Did you find a knife?'

The captain muttered at the gendarme who shook his head.

'You surrendered rather easily. Why?'

'I hadn't done anything wrong.'

'You fired at my men.'

'I told you, someone fired at me first. Did your men hear that shot?'

The captain paused, flexing his hand. He took the file again and flipped back and forth over the pages. A hint of uncertainty crossed his eyes.

'How long before you fired were you shot at?'

'Not long, maybe twenty seconds. The first shot sounded different. I can't really explain it, but your men and the gendarmes use Reichsrevolvers. The first shot was louder, maybe a shorter muzzle.'

The captain made a note on the file and handed it back to the captain, scowling at him.

'Were you with anyone else?'

'No.'

The captain paused. Leroux concentrated on the end of the captain's nose, just averting his gaze, refusing to fill the silence.

'I ordered you not to leave my sight. Why did you escape the guard and go into town?'

'The guard went away. I wanted to look around as we were planning to leave this morning. No one stopped me.'

'Eldar told the others he saw you creeping out and was going after you.'

So, he had been followed. Leroux hung his head, avoiding the captain's glare.

'Surprised? You are very predictable. We were waiting to follow you.'

Leroux racked his brains. He had had all night to think about this, but the excuse he had prepared had been cut off. Thank God the guide seemed to have shaken off Eldar in the back streets before they arrived.

'Who were you going to see?'

'No one.'

'We know there was a meeting of the revolutionaries last night.'

A bead of perspiration dripped from Leroux's nose.

'Who did you meet?'

'I was on my way there. I didn't have a name.'

The captain slammed his fist down on the table. 'I am not playing games. One of my guards died in the mountains when you disappeared. Now you go missing again, just when there is a meeting of revolutionaries, and are found with another of my soldiers, dead. The Sultan promised you safe passage to report on the malicious rumours spread by the Armenians, but you broke the conditions of your permit and went to Akrag and forfeited any protection that it provided.'

The captain waited for Leroux to respond, then nodded at Ali, who punched Leroux flat on the nose. His eyes smarted, blood trickled over his lips. Ali seemed less interested in keeping Leroux undamaged and the captain admonished him, but it only drew a look from Ali that promised further retribution.

Leroux had to conceal Armen's identity. He could say he was going to meet Maximoff. He was at the meeting. They may even know that. Should he accuse Maximoff? Or would that just be destroying the best hope he had of getting out of here? Was Maximoff really plotting to take Constantinople for the Tsar? It would be an outrageous accusation without a shred of evidence to back it. The Russians would protest, and if he could present no proof, Currie would be incandescent, and Beaumont further embarrassed. And Leroux would have compounded his troubles with a false accusation. He had nothing but prophecies and coincidences and no idea how Maximoff planned to do it. Was it as simple as persuading the Armenians to rise like a fifth column in the rear, and use that as a pretext to invade? The Russians had attempted something similar twenty years before and failed. Currie would not believe that the Tsar would dare to try again. There must be more to it. But he was out of options. If there was any chance of the captain believing him, he needed to make him earn the information, and hope that it might at least make the Sultan suspicious of Maximoff.

'Did they hear a scream?' Leroux croaked through bloody lips.

'What?'

'The patrol. Did they hear a scream? Did Eldar scream?'

The captain consulted the notes again and barked at the gendarme, who shook his head.

'No, why?'

'I didn't hear one either. And I wasn't far behind the killer, the body was still warm when I got there.'

'So?'

'I think Eldar knew the killer. He managed to get close enough without arousing Eldar's suspicion and then took him by surprise. When I found him, his gun was still holstered.'

'Eldar knew you.'

'But he was looking for me, you said so yourself. He wouldn't have let me take him by surprise.'

The captain lifted Leroux's chin with the folder.

'So, who did it?'

Leroux's shoulders screamed as his limp body sagged between them in defeat, his arms raised at an unnatural angle. Earn it. He looked up at the captain, pain seared into his eyes, and drew in a breath to speak.

Someone hammered at the iron door and the captain spun in a rage. 'What now?'

Maximoff ducked into the room, freshly bathed, his long hair neatly combed and his frock coat newly brushed.

'What is the meaning of this?' he bawled. 'Mr. Leroux is a British subject. It is an outrage that he is treated like this! Captain, you should know better. This will not be tolerated by the embassies, nor I suspect by the Sultan. You exceed your authority!'

The captain looked from Maximoff to Leroux.

'He was caught red-handed,' the captain said, his voice quivering with anger, 'leaving a meeting of revolutionaries and killed one of my men.'

'Is that true?' Maximoff asked Leroux.

'No.'

Maximoff's eyebrow arched, and his eye seemed to dance a little jig over Leroux's face. If Leroux had lied about where he was, he could not have betrayed Maximoff.

'He must be afforded the proper protections and process.'

The captain nodded grudgingly at Ali who grunted and let go of the rope suddenly, plunging Leroux to the floor. Leroux wriggled to his knees, the tang of blood wetting his lips.

'Release his hands! And bring some water and soap,' Maximoff said and stalked up and down the cell while Ali scurried away to fetch the items. 'I will see to the prisoner alone, to ensure that he can speak freely.'

The captain began to protest, but Maximoff cut him off. 'Do not make this worse for yourself than it already is. You risk the Sultan's relations with the British Empire, all for the sake of a crude interrogation over the murder of a nobody. I will make sure the Sultan hears of it if you challenge me!'

'Very well.' The captain freed Leroux's hands and ushered the gendarme out. Maximoff followed them and returned with a chair which he straddled as the door clanged shut.

'Well, well, well. What have you been up to?' Maximoff said, eyeing the door.

Leroux slumped back against the wall. He massaged his shoulders and wiped the blood from his face.

'You already know.'

Maximoff ignored the comment and pulled a letter from his jacket. It was Leroux's report on the village. He lowered his voice. 'I took the liberty of searching your room when I heard of your arrest. Never wise to leave incriminating evidence lying about. Luckily, I found it first.'

Leroux was tired. Too tired for these games. 'What do you want?'

'Nothing, yet. Let's say you owe me another favour. Now, this looks urgent,' Maximoff said tapping the letter in his palm. 'Who would you like me to send it to?'

'Can you get me out of here?'

'I can insist that you are transferred to Constantinople. But you will still be in custody.'

That was surely no more than the captain had already planned.

'Thank you.'

'But I don't think I should leave this with you.' Maximoff smiled, half turning to the cell door. 'The news is important. I am sending a telegram to my embassy. I could ask them to pass the news to Ambassador Currie?'

Leroux's mind raced. Did he have a choice?

'Or I can deliver it to someone else at the embassy?' Maximoff tapped the letter again. 'I'm asking because I thought Currie had dismissed you.'

How did Maximoff know that? Did Maximoff want the British to have news of the massacre confirmed by one of their own, to reduce support for the Sultan? He could send it anyway. But it would be better if Beaumont got it. Currie might quash it to prevent damaging relations with the Sultan, say that Leroux was an unreliable source trying to vindicate his actions. 'Please send it to Randolph Simpkins at the embassy.'

'Rand ... I don't know him,' Maximoff stifled a grin and took a pen from his pocket. 'Here just write his name down at the top and I'll see to it.'

Maximoff took the paper back and blew on it.

'Randolph Simpkins it is. Such a shame you're not in Currie's favour. You could tell him how well we work together. Perhaps our countries could learn from that? Is there anything you would like me to add to the report?'

'I saw you at the meeting.'

Maximoff eyes betrayed no flicker of fear, or even of surprise.

'And I saw you. The less said about that the better, don't you agree?'

Leroux's eyes rose to the iron ring on the ceiling, and he probed the swelling around his nose. Maximoff had seen him, which made it all the more likely that he had killed Eldar and shot at Leroux. 'I might not be able to stop myself.'

Maximoff turned to check the door. 'I'll see what I can do. The captain will not risk angering the Sultan, but that may only delay your fate. When the Sultan hears of your actions, I won't be able to help you, and his interrogators are … notorious. It will be up to your own people to help you then.' Maximoff tapped the letter again. 'I will let them know your predicament and deliver this, which might help.'

'Thank you,' Leroux said, torn between suspicion and gratitude.

Maximoff squeezed Leroux's shoulder, a little too hard, and walked to the door, raising his hand to knock, then pausing.

'You know, the situation with the Armenians is very delicate. The revolutionaries are excitable and prone to rash moves. It is all I can do to restrain the Hunchakians from doing something foolish. What are the ARF up to? I saw you talking to Armen Garo.'

'I don't know.'

Maximoff looked as unimpressed with the lack of wit as with the lack of honesty, as if a child had lied blatantly.

'When do you think that this thing you don't know about will happen? I ask because Mr Garo may need to know that you are being interrogated. Will I be able to warn him in time?'

'I really don't know.'

'I'll see you back in Constantinople,' Maximoff said and banged on the door.

Ali watched Maximoff depart and stepped into the room, flexing his fingers, unconcerned at remaining alone with Leroux, unbound, on his feet, a couple of doors away from freedom. The captain's two other soldiers came in behind and locked the door. Everyone unarmed. Leroux grabbed the chair, raising it, ready to crash it down on the first assailant. The soldiers spread out either side of Ali, encroaching slowly, backing Leroux into a corner, feinting, taunting him to play his only card. Leroux ran out of space - any further back, and he couldn't even throw a punch. Ali came first, and took the blow of the chair, but only on his back, he was too quick diving under Leroux's arms, burying his head in Leroux's chest. The others piled on. Leroux drew everything in, protecting his head, curling. Let them have the arms, the legs. They rained blows upon him but struggled to land decent hits, crowded in together, and ended up lashing out with boots. Leroux gasped, fighting to keep his guard up, but they suddenly stopped. Leroux's hands shook as he peered between them. The captain stood in the doorway with a pail and a rag. 'Clean yourself up. We leave for Constantinople. Don't get your hopes up. The Sultan will have you questioned properly. Everyone talks then.'

The ride back to Trebizond felt like an eternity. Maximoff had gone his own way, taking the guide and remounts, including Khalila. Just the captain and his three soldiers accompanied Leroux. He didn't resent the beating. The soldiers were mutinous after the death of Eldar, and the captain had let them work their anger off and probably saved Leroux from a knife in the ribs one evening when he slept manacled on a thin straw bed.

Leroux's horse had an awkward gait and an ill-fitting saddle on a curved back, probably from carrying large loads in its youth. With his hands bound behind his back, the soldiers took turns to lead him as they jolted along, retracing their steps to the sea. Past the turning to Akrag and the road to Bayburt. Would there be any news of the girl awaiting him in Constantinople? Would he even get it if there was? They were delayed for a couple of days when two horses went lame, and they struggled to find replacements. Maximoff would be well ahead of them now.

On the voyage, he was imprisoned below the waterline. The air was putrid, the bilges ripe with burnt tallow and mingled with the rotting flesh of poisoned rats. Leroux made his first acquaintance with seasickness, retching into a half-full bucket. He wiped the bile from his mouth and dwelled on his hopes. Could he trust Maximoff to alert the embassy? Had Simpkins discovered anything? Leroux was sure Nevlinski held a piece of the puzzle. He needed a visit, preferably in a dark alley, but that felt a remote prospect now.

Tuesday, 25th August, Constantinople

Leroux blinked in the early morning sun as gulls crying overhead. His legs were unsteady and with a hard shove in the back he lost his footing on the gangway. One of the soldiers caught him, contempt in his eyes. They bundled him in a covered carriage, which thundered across the Galata Bridge, the colour and noise of people going freely about their business flashing by, up the hill to Pera, past the buildings that felt almost familiar. The balcony of his hotel room faded into the distance. The Bosporus Straits sparkled on his right, a fresh breeze blowing in, which disappeared as they turned through the walls of Yildiz Palace, a city in itself, with its sprawl of factories and pavilions. The carriage came to a rest by the Çadır barracks, and they dragged Leroux down to a dungeon.

The stone floor was swept and washed, but scratches on the walls spoke of the deeds they had witnessed. The thick oak door with wrought iron hinges housed a viewing panel which snapped open. A pair of dark eyes looked in. Leroux turned to the door, desperate for news, but the chains of his manacles snapped taut. His wounds from the landslide were now just a memory, his ribs merely aching. The cut on his back had scarred over and his nose felt like it had returned to something like its original shape. Even the bruises from the beating had reduced to a sallow tinge. But it was the waiting that preyed on his mind. Did anyone know of his plight? Had Maximoff told Simpkins? Would the bishop or Armen

212

have guessed what happened or found out? And would the Sultan admit to having him in custody if a brutal interrogation awaited?

When he helped Armen escape, he had felt on the verge of a breakthrough. He had an insight into Maximoff's motive and a friend in the revolutionaries who might be able to shed light on Maximoff's plans. But that was nearly two weeks past and no news. The accusations against him would have solidified unchallenged. The confinement and isolation ate at his confidence, and the only thing that he could cling to was the memory of the girl. She knew what happened at Akrag. Why hadn't Simpkins come? Was Currie leaving him to rot as a sacrifice? Maximoff must have been days ahead, what had happened to him? Leroux was a pawn and he had been played.

The dark eyes blinked again, the hatch snapped shut, and the door squealed on its hinges. The captain strutted in, followed by a huge man with biceps wider than the span of Leroux's hand. His bald head glistened above one long thick eyebrow that dipped between cruel eyes. A smile spread beneath his hooked nose as he assessed his prey. He unravelled a cloth bundle on the table to display a set of medical instruments and folded his arms over a bare stomach that spilled over billowing trousers. His eyes ran over a scalpel, a pair of tweezers and a hook, before settling on a small hammer and some little metal wedges.

The captain stood close in front of Leroux, confident that the chains would not yield an inch. There was sadness in his eyes. For all their differences, Leroux felt a bond with the captain. He cared for his men, was loyal to his Sultan and had stood up for Leroux, when it would have been easier to let Zeki Pasha's men have their way. He was capable of brutality but not gratuitous cruelty. They were just on different sides, and Leroux had transgressed. The captain took no joy in it. The rage he had shown in Erzurum had subsided. Now it was just unpleasant work.

'You have had time to think. The times you escaped my guards and we found them murdered – admit the truth. What were you doing? And who were you with?'

'Did you find the knife?'

'No. But it was dark. You could have hidden it. Or given it to someone else.'

'I didn't.'

'Don't make this harder than it needs to be.' The captain looked to the tools and pursed his lips. 'You don't even know how these are used, do you?' He stroked his hand along the implements. 'You would look more scared if you did. They seem too delicate for a lump like Osman here, but he is quite skilled.'

Leroux swallowed as the captain's finger drew down the length of the hammer. 'Removing fingernails and toenails with pliers is painful,' the captain said turning one of the small metal wedges over, 'but Osman tells me that it is far worse and takes much longer, if you simply insert a wedge under the nail and tap away at it.'

Leroux's stomach turned and he clenched his buttocks.

'Why are you so stubborn? You hardly defend yourself. Who are you protecting?'

Turkish voices rose in the corridor, one, urgent but halting, sounded oddly familiar. The captain raised his hand bunched up in a fist and spun away in frustration. A moment later Simpkins's flushed face appeared in the doorway, waving a piece of paper, and switching to French.

'You must let me see Leroux. I have permission from the Sultan. You have imprisoned one of our subjects without notifying us, it's an outrage!'

The captain's neck bulged at the collar. 'He is accused of murder! Two guards dead. Both times he is the only suspect.'

Simpkins thrust himself into the room, his hand shaking as he held a paper up for inspection.

'I am entitled to check on his well-being. He has obviously suffered in your custody, and I demand to speak to him.'

The captain's nostrils flared as he snatched the order and studied it.

'You have ten minutes!' he snarled and marched out. Osman looked ruefully at his instruments and joined him, slamming the cell door. Questions raced through Leroux's mind, his spirits rising, as Simpkins slumped into a chair, seemingly shocked by his own behaviour, and composed himself.

'I didn't like the look of that big chap,' Simpkins said at last, his voice wavering.

Leroux nodded at the roll of instruments. 'His tools. You arrived just in time. How did you know I was here?'

'A fellow called Armen Garo came to see me this morning. Said he had heard you were arrested in Erzurum and been sent to Constantinople. I had no idea who he was, but he described you well.'

'What day is it?'

'Monday. The 24th. Just after eleven. What on earth have you been up to?'

215

Simpkins didn't know. Leroux's cheeks burnt and his heartbeat hammered in his ears. He braced his hands on the table to calm himself.

'You look like you've seen a ghost. Are you all right, Leroux? Have they been feeding you properly?'

Nausea washed over him, the dawning realization of an awful mistake.

'A lot's happened since you left,' Simpkins said.

Leroux's heart raced. 'Go on.'

'After you mentioned Madame de Novikoff to Beaumont, he had her followed. Years ago, she manipulated the Liberal Party and their foreign policy, to weaken their resolve to stand up to Russian empire building. She's active again. She's been making the case that only the Tsar can control the Sultan and that Britain and France should leave him to it. By interfering, we are just enabling the Sultan to play us off against one another while he continues to persecute Christians.'

'Maximoff makes the same case. Have you seen him?'

'No. Why would I hear from Maximoff?'

'Is he back in Constantinople?' Leroux already knew the answer.

'Currie mentioned seeing him three days ago. He went to complain to the Grand Vizier about the forts again, and Maximoff breezed in like he owned the place.'

Leroux cupped his forehead, rocking back and forth. The bastard.

'And Beaumont telegrammed me again today. Wanted to know if you had any news. In the last few days, de Novikoff has been spreading a story that atrocities in Armenia are far worse than have been reported and that Russia must be allowed to deal with it.'

'We've got a problem.'

'We have?'

'Have you heard from a missionary called Mrs Willis?'

'Yes. She said to let you know the girl was well, but mute. She is back with her people. And she apologised that she couldn't be of more help.'

She had saved the girl's life, thought Leroux. She had done more than enough.

'It's all true,' Leroux said. 'The massacre of Armenians. I saw it. I went to the village, Akrag. Utterly wiped out apart from one survivor, that girl. I left her with Mrs Willis. I wrote a report. Maximoff took it after I was arrested. He promised he would get it to you. He was going to telegram a summary to the Russian embassy to forward to you. That must have been nearly two weeks ago.'

Simpkins shook his head. 'I've heard nothing.'

Leroux's gut twisted. There was no doubt. 'This is all my fault.'

'What are you talking about? We can send in your report now. What's changed?'

'Everything.'

Leroux pushed his hair back rubbing his scalp. 'This is going to sound crazy but hear me out. You told me about the eagle and the snake, that it meant Christians would one day retake Constantinople.'

Simpkins frowned in concentration. 'Yes, but it's just a story.'

'I told the bishop. He knew it well and said there was more, much more and showed me a book called "The Tale of the Taking of Tsargrad," written by a Russian monk called Nestor Iskander four hundred years ago.'

'Never heard of it.'

'Iskander tells the Tsar it is his destiny to recapture Constantinople, as he is the heir to the old Emperors and the Holy Roman Empire. And that all Orthodox Christians will be united under him, the one true Christian ruler under the sky. That Moscow is the Third Rome and there will be no fourth. That none will replace his Christian Tsardom.'

Simpkins pulled at the hem of his waistcoat, shifting in his chair. 'I don't understand. You're not the sort of chap to get hot under the collar about prophecies.'

'Trust me. This is beginning to make sense now. Maximoff joined our expedition, saying that he was investigating the rumours as well. But I began to suspect something was wrong. I have been attacked three times since I discovered the village. Maximoff always had an excuse, but there were too many coincidences. Now that he hasn't delivered that report, I'm sure.'

'Sure of what?'

Leroux pounded a fist into his palm. 'The connection. He knew I would get word out eventually, he just needed to delay me until his plan was in motion.'

'What plan?'

'The Tsar plans to invade the Ottoman Empire and capture Constantinople and Saint Sophia. Any day now.'

Simpkins stammered. 'That's preposterous!'

'You've just told me about Olga. They are preparing the ground in the press, reminding the public that Russia has the right to protect Orthodox Christians, that their persecution continues and that the British and French competition with Russia in the Sublime Porte only prevents Russia from properly protecting them. There will be a dramatic revelation of the most shocking atrocity yet in the European papers very soon, based on my report. Madame de Novikoff will be placing stories, stoking public outrage, demanding that Russia be allowed a free hand. At the same time there will be a rising in the Armenian provinces, diverting many of the Sultan's forces. The Armenians are champing at the bit, and Maximoff is encouraging them. I saw it at a meeting of revolutionaries, where I met Armen Garo. The rebellion will vindicate the Tsar's claims and give him a further pretext to intervene, to prevent their slaughter as well. The Black Sea fleet will pass the dilapidated forts of the Bosporus and anchor in the Golden Horn. The Tsar's troops will march. In the face of public outrage at home, it will be nigh on impossible for the government to back the Sultan. The public will want the Russians to punish him. The British and French will be faced with a fait accompli. Even if they do try to act, the Russians would probably have seized the Dardanelles forts before they arrived, and the Royal Navy would be helpless.'

'My God. If it's true …'

'Russia will have secured her trade routes and access to the Mediterranean, even threaten Suez. And then it will dawn on Currie and Salisbury that that is not the worst of it. The return of Saint Sophia will electrify the Orthodox Church, with the Tsar at its head, and with the Balkans free from the Sultan. All the Slavs, including nearly half of the Austro-Hungarian Empire, will owe allegiance to the Tsar. With the Slavs united, the balance of power on the Continent will change, perhaps irreversibly, in Russia's favour.'

219

'And he is a tyrant.' Simpkins rubbed the back of his neck. 'What proof do you have?'

'That's the problem.'

'Nothing?'

'Nothing but a prophecy and speculation. And Maximoff has set me up for murder twice over, completely discrediting me.'

'What are we going to do?'

'I'm not sure yet,' Leroux said.

'We should tell Currie and Beaumont to start with, and your editor, Miss Shaw. Warn them about Maximoff's plans. And get them to pre-empt the story of Akrag and make it clear that responsibility for it has not been determined.'

'Based on what? I was disgraced in Currie's eyes before, let alone now.'

'And Currie will rubbish the idea that the Tsar is guided by prophecies,' Simpkins said, his cheeks sinking into his hands.

'The Tsar doesn't need to believe in it, he's just using it. The prophecy is well known by Orthodox holy men. If the Tsar reclaims Saint Sophia, the church bells will ring, the priests will preach. The people will follow. The prophecy will fulfill itself. They will have everybody sleepwalking the way they want.'

'Got to admit, it's brilliant,' Simpkins said.

'Tell Currie and Beaumont. They won't believe us now, but when it starts to happen, they may change their minds. But don't put your neck on the line. I need you here, not on the next boat home.'

Simpkins looked aside, chewing his lip. 'Currie doesn't know I'm here and he'll be furious when he finds out you're in prison. I went straight to see the Grand Vizier after meeting Armen Garo. I made a bit of a stink about your incarceration. The Grand Vizier said the charges were very serious.'

'They only have circumstantial evidence against me. No witnesses.'

'If Currie doesn't stand up for you, that won't matter. I'll do what I can to get you out. But I'm not—'

'They're going to question me again. I'll accuse Maximoff. It might hit a nerve, even if I can't prove anything.'

Simpkins looked over the instruments. 'They'll want more than that. What the Armenians are planning, who you were in contact with.'

'I know.'

'What will you say?'

'I'll tell them the truth. But I'll try and keep the bishop and Armen Garo out of it.'

'Do you think they'll believe you, about Maximoff?'

'Not yet. But I can plant a seed in their minds.'

Simpkins looked over his shoulder at the cell door. 'That large man. He looked like one of the Sultan's interrogators.'

'He is.'

'Armen Garo left a message for you. How to contact him. Do you … want to know …now, I mean before …' He looked back over his shoulder, his collar damp with sweat. Leroux looked at the evil little wedges and doubted whether he could hold out to a professional like Osman.

'No. I know where to find you. We may have only days or hours to foil Maximoff. Armen holds the key to this. He has a plan to get all the

Great Powers to protect the Armenians. I don't know what it is, but if it happens soon, it could forestall Maximoff's uprising.'

Simpkins perked up. 'That's something.'

'Let him know the urgency. He may be able to move quicker. And Nevlinski. Somehow, he's involved in this. He might know something useful. He was staying at the Pera Palace. Can you find out if he's still there? Did you warn Herzl about him?'

'Yes. He seemed a bit frustrated. Still no audience with the Sultan, but Nevlinski was working on the Grand Vizier and sounded hopeful. That was about a week ago.'

Simpkins checked his watch again, putting his jacket on.

'One other thing,' Leroux said. 'The internal opposition to the Sultan – the Young Ottomans – how serious is it?'

'Hard to say. Those in court, that haven't been eliminated by the Sultan's spies, keep a very low profile. And the religious fundamentalists are unhappy too. Why do you ask?'

'Two Hamidiye soldiers attacked me, and it caused a big disagreement between the captain and the local commander, Zeki Pasha.' A guard hammered on the door. 'Get me out of here.'

Simpkins gripped Leroux's arm. 'I will.'

The door swung open, and a guard ushered Simpkins out, staring at his red hair. The captain prowled in and stood at Leroux's side. The interrogator padded him down, removed Leroux's shirt and inspected his wounds. Dread gnawed in the pit of Leroux's stomach. The brutish man returned to his instruments.

'Start with that,' the captain said.

222

Osman's nostrils flared as he went to pick up a long pin-shaped device and a delicate hammer.

'You've had enough time to think,' the captain said.

Leroux twisted to catch sight of the interrogator, who tapped the instruments together in his hand. A gold tooth smirked at him. A great forearm curled around his forehead and inserted the pin into his ear, his head clamped into place against Osman's sweaty stomach. The first tap penetrated his eardrum, like a thunderclap, but not especially painfull. Osman worked the pin carefully in. Leroux bucked against Osman's grip, his face taut with strain, but his burly arm just squeezed harder.

'I'm told the inner ear is quite sensitive,' the captain said. Leroux's eyeballs wrenched in their sockets, straining to warn of any movement of the hammer. The lightest of taps sent an exquisite tremor of pain ricocheting across his head. This was what vulnerability felt like. He lost all composure, his mouth flapping, his eyes pleading.

'You can imagine,' the captain whispered into the ear, 'that Osman can do better than that.'

Perspiration streamed down Leroux's face. The captain would get his confession now and believe it.

'Maximoff.'

'Maximoff? What about him?'

'He killed the guard in Erzurum.'

'Maximoff has been the Tsar's top dragoman at the Sublime Porte for ten years. He is highly regarded by the Sultan. Of course, you would say that. Trying to sully his name and plant seeds in the Sultan's mind. You have been caught red-handed, but you accuse another? Have you no shame? I want a full confession and the names of the revolutionaries.'

'Maximoff was at the meeting of the revolutionaries. There will be a rebellion, like Sasun and Van. I saw him there.'

The sour note of the interrogator's breath encroached as he made a tiny agonising adjustment to the pin. For such a brutish looking man he had extraordinary deftness of touch.

'You admit you were there?' the captain said.

'Yes.'

He smacked his lips. 'And?'

'Maximoff was meeting with the Hunchakians—,' Leroux said, and the captain cursed reflexively, something about dogs in Turkish, '—He left before the meeting ended. I followed shortly after and found Eldar. There was no light in the street, bar the moon, but I heard someone ahead by the crossroads. They shot at me. It was a pistol shot, but not from your men. They must have heard that.'

Leroux studied the captain's eyes for some recognition that the patrol had heard a shot.

'It could have been you firing the guard's pistol.'

'It sounded different to a Reichsrevolver. And check the magazine. I fired two shots, both at the patrol. Your men confirmed that, I'm sure. Eldar's pistol was fully loaded, I checked it. If there are only two rounds missing, then I couldn't have fired that first shot.'

The captain stroked his chin and looked to the side. He made a note and pointed the pen, inviting Leroux to continue.

'A few moments later I heard a shout, a challenge. But not at me, at someone else. Then a man appeared at the corner of the crossroads. I fired, thinking it was the person who had fired at me, but then I saw that it was the patrol.'

'What makes you think it was Maximoff?'

'Suppose he came upon Eldar when he left the meeting. He would have suspected that Eldar had followed him or me and couldn't risk Eldar having seen him go to the meeting place. He could have taken Eldar by surprise, I could not. As you say he is trusted, you have not had him guarded. I took Eldar's gun, but when I found him, it was still buttoned up in its holster. Eldar knew and trusted the person who killed him. He was too able a soldier to be caught from behind with a knife.'

'Eldar was a good man,' the captain said evenly and leant back on the table.

'I was a good few minutes behind Maximoff. They may even have been talking before he slit his throat. The body was still warm when I got there.' Leroux closed his eyes, remembering Eldar's blood still seeping between the cobblestones.

'Maximoff must have seen me approaching and knew that I could place him at the meeting and perhaps also had seen him kill the guard. He fired at me. When he reached the crossroads, he turned away from the patrol. One of the gendarmes shouted a challenge. But he disappeared in the shadows and by the time they got to the crossroads he was gone. I fired and they saw me, and thought I was the person they challenged.'

'That's quite a story.'

Leroux shrugged, he had no more to add.

225

'Maximoff could not have recognised you at that distance in the dark.'

The captain was right. Leroux blinked, thought back. Maximoff could have guessed, though. He had seen Leroux at the meeting, probably as he walked out. And Leroux would have naturally walked back the same way.

'Maybe not. But he may have suspected. Or heard the patrol coming and wanted to get whoever was following him and the patrol to start shooting at each other, while he made his escape.'

The captain looked behind Leroux at the interrogator. A bead of sweat ran down Leroux's temple, tickling his ear.

'No, I do not believe you. You killed the guard in the mountains when he caught you and you did the same here. Your story hangs on Maximoff being at the meeting. Where is the proof of that?'

Leroux gritted his teeth. Damn it. He kept getting caught out because he hadn't recognised Maximoff as a threat early enough. And he had even covered for him. The captain closed the folder. The interrogator tensed in expectation and a tiny tremor of the pin screeched inside Leroux's head. The captain drew his head back, pursing his lips. Leroux felt Osman's belly swell in anticipation.

'You, however, have just admitted to being there. And your story has changed.' The captain checked his notes. 'You said you were on the way to the meeting earlier.'

Leroux nodded, his heart sinking. He knew what was coming.

'How did you know where the meeting was?'

He had risked this by trying to accuse Maximoff. If he managed one thing, he would protect Armen. His only real chance of foiling Maximoff's plan.

'We went to the hospital together, more than two weeks ago, do you remember? You said all the patients were Muslims. One grabbed my hand and gave me that cross. He told me the name of the village, Akrag. He begged me with his last breaths to go there and take news of what I saw to the resistance.'

The captain put his fist to his mouth and coughed. 'Convenient.' But his voice had moderated, probably embarrassed at being caught in a lie about the patients.

'The old man said if I waited in the third doorway of that street after sunset a man would approach me. If I showed him the cross, he would take me to the revolutionaries' hideout.' It was a feeble explanation, full of holes, but the captain reached for a sack that contained Leroux's few possessions and tipped them out. His slouch hat, the map, wallet, pocketwatch and as he stretched up to tug the bottom of the bag higher, the cross plinked on the table. The captain turned it in his fingers, examining the intricate engraving.

'Where did he take you?'

'It was at night. We turned left and right many times, and I lost my bearings.'

'And Eldar.'

'He must have followed me, but I didn't see him.'

The captain rubbed his eyelid and made a note in the file. And Osman's arm was getting tired. Leroux winced as he sensed the interrogator tensing his hand.

'And when you departed?'

227

'They took me through a courtyard to the street. They pointed in the direction of the church, and I had only gone a few minutes when I saw Eldar.'

'Is that it?' the captain said. 'Not a single piece of proof.' He picked up the folder and turned a page. You could have surprised Eldar, just as you surprised Emin in the mountains. The first shot could have been fired by an accomplice. I don't believe you were alone.'

Leroux sensed that the captain had been wavering on the edge of believing him, but now he felt he was losing him, and accusing Maximoff of killing Emin as well risked infuriating him.

'How do you explain the Hamidiye soldiers attacking me? You know they were not friends of Emin. Somebody is out to get me. To stop me finding something. And I believe that same person killed Emin and Eldar.'

'And what is it they are trying to hide?'

'A plot against the Sultan.'

'It is you that is plotting against the Sultan.' The captain's eyes narrowed, and he turned to Osman.

Leroux braced himself, flexing his arms hard against the restraints, welcoming the metal cutting into his sores, diverting his attention. He drew a deep breath, eyes screwed shut, ready to roar against the pain. The door creaked on its hinges. He opened an eye, as the captain closed it behind him. Osman withdrew the needle with infinite care, wiping it down, sliding it into its pocket and carefully rolling his bundle of tools and knotting the tie around it. Wordlessly he left the room. What had happened? Leroux sagged. His mouth was so tacky he struggled to swallow, but as the minutes passed a seed of hope grew in him. He lived to fight another day and Simpkins would find a way to get him out of here.

He could not reach the table or chair set near to the door, but even if he could the opening high in the wall above him was too small, not a window but a kind of chimney for ventilation. He could not wriggle up it, even when he was a child. Below that, at waist-height the ring that secured the manacles was set deep into the stonework. Leroux draped the chains over his shoulders and clasped them to take the strain away from his wrists, walking his feet up the wall and driving with his legs and his weight, the links clinking as they took the pressure. The fixing yielded not an iota. Brown eyes stared through the door hatch again and brought in a plate of rice and thin lentil gruel. The soldier looked at the chains and smiled. He must have heard that sound plenty.

Time was not his friend. Maximoff's plan was in action. Tomorrow? The next day? The papers would scream with the news of the massacre. The Armenians would rise in the east. The Black Sea fleet probably already at sea, just over the horizon, and the Tsar would declare that he was coming to the Christians' aid. Currie would not listen to Leroux. No one believed in prophecies anymore. And when the Tsar took charge in Constantinople, Leroux would disappear – Maximoff would make sure of that. Memories of his childhood rolled across his mind. His mother teaching in the mission school. He had been a reasonable student, but easily led astray. His friend Tom had only to mention an adventure and

229

they were off, running over the hill, crawling on their bellies in the long grass, fighting with sticks by the stream. The shock of the recoil, the first time he had fired a gun, stolen from his mother's cupboard. At least it had scared the lion. He had never been able to say no, but he had always been able to get out of trouble just a little quicker than he got into it. Now it felt like trouble was finally catching up with him. As it had with Tom. As it had with his father.

The door lock squealed with the turn of a key Leroux's pulse quickened, but a young girl glided in, the hem of her voluminous cloak skimming the floor. A thin white muslin headscarf covered her head, revealing only her startling green eyes, edged with kohl. A soldier followed with a neatly folded pile of fresh clothes, towels, soap, and a bucket and sponge. As the soldier unshackled Leroux and left, the captain looked in. 'Clean up. The Sultan wishes to speak to you. And if he is not satisfied with your answers, remember what awaits you here.'

The girl stood with her hands folded in front of her until the captain withdrew, when she wet the sponge and washed Leroux's back. The water was warm, and the suds were soft and smelled of roses. She worked around the scar where Leroux had been shot in the back, back on the veld, running for the safety of the circled wagons. That was a close shave. He was the only survivor from their patrol. The wounded officer he had carried back did not last the day. And then Chief Malaboch's men had charged the wagons. They fell like skittles, but it was no game and he tried to push the memory from his mind. The girl's scarf brushed against his cheek. The curve of her jaw pressed against the muslin and Leroux caught glimpses of her lustrous hair which was wound and bunched on top of her head and smelled of jasmine. She touched a painted nail to the fabric which moulded to her lips. 'Say nothing,' she whispered in French.

She stood with her back to the door and opened her cloak a fraction, revealing a yellow satin dress and ran a finger under the collar, flicking out a necklace. An Armenian cross hung down, just like the one that lay on the table. She briefly removed her veil. 'You will see me again. When you do, follow without hesitation. Au revoir.' Leroux reached up to touch the cross, but the girl had turned and tapped lightly on the door. He wrung the sponge out and finished washing himself. Who was she? Had Simpkins seen Armen already?

Leroux was clean for the first time in weeks and was relieved that his ear didn't trouble him. How long had Simpkins been gone? An hour? Two? Time left no mark in the bare windowless cell but slowly whittled away his hopes. Footsteps approached at last, but it was the captain. He prowled around Leroux, inspecting him from head to foot.

'Bring him,' he barked, and a guard exchanged his manacles for iron bracelets, locked with a simple screw key and joined by a short chain in front of him.

They marched out and up onto the driveway, the fresh air, the clear sky, the sounds of horses and wheels and birdsong, and even the scent of vanilla. Leroux rolled his shoulders. They strode up the hill, four soldiers tramping behind him and the back of his neck prickling in the afternoon sun.

'The Sultan enjoys questioning people,' the captain said in an unexpectedly cheery manner.

'More than Osman?'

'Oh yes. He is an admirer of Sherlock Holmes. You have read him?'

'Some.'

'He has the latest books translated for him. And he loves Sarah Bernhardt. Have you heard of her?'

'Of course.'

'I have met her! She came here two years ago to perform especially for the Sultan.'

'Do you mind if I smoke?' Leroux said, recalling Oscar Wilde's famous question to her.

'I don't mind if you burn!' the captain replied as Bernhardt had done, a little too enthusiastically for Leroux's liking. They crossed the courtyard, past the soothing splashes of a fountain in a playful rococo style and two doormen swept open the doors to an Italianate pavilion. They proceeded through rooms of increasing opulence. Every detail was gilded, the fireplaces porcelain, the bannisters red crystal. Leroux caught himself in an ornately framed mirror. He had not shaven, and his hair was more dirty than blond. Two huge soldiers in dark blue uniforms with gold cross belts and red fezzes guarded the final set of doors and saluted. The captain inspected Leroux and the soldiers behind him, adjusting a buckle here and a collar there. Satisfied, he nodded to the doormen, who opened the doors with precision and announced their entrance.

All eyes turned to Leroux, on the threshold of the Sultan's personal reception room. The Ambassador, furious. Maximoff, dismissive. The

Grand Vizier and Zeki Pasha, baleful. The Sultan, furthest away, unreadable, sat on an ornate high-backed chair. The captain led Leroux forward and to the centre of the room. Maximoff and Currie to his right. The Grand Vizier and Zeki Pasha to his left. Four soldiers behind him. The captain approached the Sultan, kissed the tasselled banner, and snapped to attention to the side in front of a carpenter's table, complete with chisels, saws, and planes. The beginnings of a small box basked awaited the Sultan's attention. The Sultan stroked his trim black beard and rolled a silver topped cane in his hand until it tilted in the direction of the Grand Vizier. Leroux imagined that in different circumstances, they could have a conversation about canes and knobkerries.

'Begin.'

Ambassador Currie adjusted his tie and smoothed his hair. The Grand Vizier, tall and bald in a scholarly way, cleared his throat. 'The Sultan granted you permission to travel to Erzurum to interview the bishop. You broke the conditions. You visited forbidden areas. They are restricted for a reason - for your own protection - bandits operate there. Two of our soldiers are dead. And you conspired with revolutionaries. Is this not true?'

'All those things are true,' Leroux said. 'But there is more.'

The Sultan leaned forward. 'More truths or mere accusations?'

'I did travel to a see a village, Akrag. I was told about it by a man in the Kum Kapu hospital that you allowed me to visit. The village had burnt to the ground. I found a survivor.'

Maximoff's jaw muscles tensed as he glanced between the Grand Vizier and the Sultan. It must have been the first he had heard of a survivor.

'I have read nothing of an incident like this in the reports,' the Sultan said. 'If it were true, my informers would have told me.'

'I saw it with my own eyes. And on my way back, I was ambushed. Somebody wants to keep it quiet.'

The captain bent by the Sultan and whispered.

'Someone set off a landslide and I was lucky to escape with my life. The guard, Emin, was not so lucky. I think I was attacked because I had seen the village. Emin, perhaps, because he had seen the real killer.'

The captain murmured and the Sultan's hooded eyes slid over to Zeki Pasha.

'Go on.'

'Two nights later I was attacked by Hamidiye soldiers. I do not know why, perhaps for the same reason.'

Zeki Pasha interjected. 'I have questioned them. They were exacting revenge for the soldier Emin, their comrade.'

The Sultan looked up at the captain, who shrugged.

'At Erzurum, I told the bishop about the village.' Leroux considered relating the Tale of the Taking of Tsargrad, but his story lacked hard evidence as it was. Introducing a prophecy would invite derision. 'Then I distracted the guard and went to the revolutionaries' meeting.'

Leroux turned to the Russian. 'Maximoff was there. I wrote a report about Akrag, but Maximoff stole it after I was arrested.'

234

Maximoff rolled his eyes 'Your Majesty!' But the Sultan held up his cane, stern-faced behind the glint of its polished silver top. 'Your turn will come.'

'Maximoff left the meeting before me. I found the soldier, who I knew to be Eldar, dead. And then I believe Maximoff shot at me. He murdered Eldar as well as Emin.'

'Why would Maximoff do this?' the Sultan said.

This was his chance, slim though it felt. Almost doesn't fill a bowl.

'The Russians plan to conquer Constantinople and Armenian revolutionaries will support them with a rebellion. Maximoff realised I had uncovered his plans.'

'Leroux, really!' gasped Currie.

'Must I listen to these ridiculous accusations?' Maximoff said.

The Grand Vizier sighed in exasperation. 'This man was caught red handed. The reports are clear. He is simply making up stories to cover his guilt and incriminate his rival.'

The Sultan struck his cane on the marble floor and the Grand Vizier smartly bowed his head.

'So, you say there will be an uprising in Armenia. The Tsar will invade. And you think neither I nor the British will be able to do anything about it?'

'This is ridiculous,' Currie shouted at Leroux. 'What on earth do you think you are doing? Preposterous. Ignore him, your Majesty, he does not speak for Britain. In the unlikely event that the Tsar would take such a rash action, the Royal Navy will act, as it has before.'

'Continue,' the Sultan said to Leroux.

'The massacre goes beyond previous attacks on the Armenians and demands a response. Knowledge of it is spreading and the people are ripe for rebellion. The British press is being told to expect proof of the massacre imminently and when they publish the story, public outrage will make it impossible for the British government to come to your defence.'

'Ah yes,' the Grand Vizier said, 'the report you wrote. You say Maximoff has it?'

Maximoff shrugged his shoulders and splayed his hands. 'Haven't we heard enough of this nonsense? I'm accused of stealing a report that doesn't exist. It's about a massacre, you say?'

The Sultan beckoned the captain. 'Did you see anything of this report?'

'No, my Sultan.'

'Or the massacre?'

'No, my Sultan.' The captain looked uncomfortable. 'There are... there are rumours.'

'Rumours? Have you seen? With your eyes?'

'No, my Sultan.'

'Or this survivor?'

'No, my Sultan.'

Leroux was caught again in a trap of his own making. All the time he had been concealing his actions from the captain, thinking it was the Sultan who hid the truth. Currie was right, his accusations sounded preposterous. He knew Maximoff was lying about the report, but he couldn't even prove that. And Currie seemed happy enough to leave him to his fate.

'And did you alert your embassy, send a message or telegram? This was the real reason for your journey, wasn't it? To see the bishop as a cover for investigating the Armenian rumours?'

'No, I did not send a telegram. I was arrested before I had the opportunity. Yes, that was the purpose.'

'Instead, you went to a meeting of revolutionaries with Maximoff?'

'I didn't go with him—'

'He certainly didn't. I wasn't there at all!' Maximoff bellowed. The Turkish courtiers looked sharply at Maximoff, who lowered his gaze.

The Sultan struck the floor with his cane, harder this time. 'Maximoff! Reply to these accusations.'

Maximoff strode forward, his powerful shoulders back and the barrel of his chest forward. He looked almost sad as he stretched a hand towards Leroux.

'Even his own Ambassador does not support his desperate attempt to besmirch me. This is wrong on all counts. Not one shred of evidence has been presented. Captain Emre can confirm that I had nothing to do with the death of the soldier in the mountains, or the attack on Mr Leroux by the Hamidiye soldiers. I was in my quarters in Erzurum when this supposed meeting happened, and the guard was killed. This is a blatant attempt to smear me by the British. Their paranoia over Suez knows no limits, and they are jealous of our mutual interest - the trade that flourishes through the Turkish straits.'

'There is no evidence against the Dragoman,' the captain said.

'Is there evidence that he was not involved?' the Sultan asked.

'Maximoff was not under guard. I cannot confirm his whereabouts on any of the occasions.'

'This is easily solved,' Maximoff said. 'Catch one of the revolutionaries and interrogate him. Leroux says he was there. He can give us the names, places.'

The Sultans eyes darted to Leroux. 'Well?'

'Questioning the revolutionaries, the bishop, the Hamidiye soldiers or the witness would all help my case. But there is no time! The rebellion will happen any day now. The news of the massacre will break in the papers and the Tsar's fleet will anchor out there!' Leroux jabbed his finger at the floor to ceiling window that overlooked the Straits.

The Sultan turned to Zeki Pasha.

'Have you found them yet?'

'Not yet. But we are searching every house. A few days. A location and names would help.' The Sultan addressed Captain Emre. 'Will the prisoner provide any names?'

'No.'

Leroux stared at the ground. He thought of Avetis, the Hunchakian leader. But it would be too late, and Maximoff would warn him anyway. He felt the Sultan's eyes on him.

'Zeki Pasha. This village is under your Governorship. Is there anything to these rumours?'

'There have been punishments, my Sultan,' Zeki Pasha said. 'of course. Reprisals, certainly. And the Kurds traditionally take their share from the Armenians. But nothing that rises to the stories I have heard today. I saw Mr Leroux in the provinces, and he said nothing of it then.'

'It does seem,' the Grand Vizier said, 'that someone may be spreading exaggerated rumours. Our agents in London say that there is talk of bad news from Armenia.'

'There is always false news,' the Sultan said. 'Make sure favourable stories are published by our friends.'

The Grand Vizier bowed. 'As you command.'

'If it is as bad as the rumours suggest,' the Sultan said, 'Why would I do that? I have Armenians working for me, some of our best administrators. My minister of the privy treasury is Pasha Portakalyan and before him Pasha Kazazian. Each Armenian pays more tax than three Muslims. And here they may worship as they please and are free from conscription, unlike in Russia.'

'I do not accuse you,' Leroux said. 'It was done precisely to cause outrage and provoke a rebellion against you.'

'You make it sound like the work of the Young Ottomans,' the Sultan said, his prayer beads clicking in his right hand. 'Treacherous snakes trying to undermine me.'

Zeki Pasha stepped forward, one hand clasped to the medal at his breast, the other on the hilt of his sword. 'Show me where those dogs are, and I will be the first to strike them down!' He cleared his throat, and in a higher pitched tone said to Leroux, 'This witness – we must question him.'

The Sultan concurred. That was something. None of them knew who the girl was. She was safe for now.

'I don't know the name or how to contact the witness,' Leroux said. There was a dark cunning in Zeki Pasha's eyes. Leroux had to keep her out of his hands. He swallowed at the thought of Osman's fat fingers on his tools.

'How convenient,' Zeki Pasha sneered.

The Sultan beckoned the Ambassador. Currie stepped forward, his neck raging red against his starched wing collar.

'If your man will not defend himself, he cannot expect clemency. What is he doing?'

'He has his own misguided sense of purpose. He thinks he can protect the Armenians on his own and acts without thought for the consequences. However, Her Majesty's government understands that this is a complicated issue that must be treated with tact and delicacy.'

'Isn't it obvious?' Maximoff said, 'This is a British trick. Their people support the Christians and are growing restless with all the rumours. The British government will have to insist on more protections for the Armenians to appease their voters. But they do not want to anger you or encourage our friendship, so they come up with this farcical plot to sow division between us.'

The Sultan slumped into his sofa. The questioning was fruitless and circular. He looked weary and haunted, like prey that had finally been cornered, exhausted, knowing the end would come. The Sultan could not provoke the Tsar too much and give them the excuse for war, a war they had fought ten times over the past two centuries. The Sultan's army was not strong enough, nor could he afford it. He could not provoke the British either. If they lost confidence in him, they would stop financing his debts and attempt to replace him. There was no shortage of willing candidates. When all your choices are bad you can only hope that time and tide will serve you. He was hanging on, just as trapped as Leroux.

The Sultan's brow furrowed, and his eyelids drooped in thought. He sighed and spoke to no one in particular. 'My Balkan territories have been stripped from me. Algeria and Egypt too. And I have endured it. They were my arms and legs. If you strip me of the eastern provinces, you will disembowel me! You think Armenia can be independent? Nowhere do they outnumber Turks. I am not punishing Christians - I am punishing traitors.' The Sultan looked between the Ambassador and Maximoff, as if deciding which card to play, how best to finesse some advantage that could be cashed in when he needed it.

'Ambassador, if you admit that this is part of an English plot, I will be merciful. Mr. Leroux will be handed over to you for punishment. If you do not, then he will be tried here as a common criminal.'

If Currie admitted to a plot, the Sultan would parlay that into an advantage or concession elsewhere. Leroux ears burned. Currie would not save him.

'Your Majesty,' Currie said. 'It is true that Mr Leroux arrived here on government business. But after some regrettable behaviour, I ordered him home when he was last in Constantinople. His continued presence here is as a private citizen. I am appalled to learn of these accusations against him. At each turn, he seems to have dug himself deeper and deeper into trouble in a vain attempt to redeem himself.'

The Sultan's voice rose now, tremulous.

'Even your own countrymen disown you. I will give you one last chance to tell the truth.'

241

Leroux sensed the soldiers edging closer to him, fearful he might try some desperate act.

'I stand by my claims.' All he could do was keep Armen safe. His plan to get the Great Powers to intervene together, whatever it was, was his last hope for foiling Maximoff. Perhaps then the truth would come out.

The Sultan raised his cane. He beckoned a courtier who advanced with a large cedar box and lifted the lid. Another with white gloved hands took a sheet of paper from within and held it up for all to see. It was blank except for the most exquisite calligraphy in gold leaf at the top, three vertical lines with swirls and flourishes entwined with an intricate design of stacked Arabic letters. Sultan Abdul Hamid's tughra, the seal that gave legitimacy to imperial letters. The first courtier closed the box and held it steady, while the Grand Vizier took the paper, laid it on the lid and began to write. Leroux stared blankly. The Sultan's mouth moved. In his wisdom he made a decision that pleased everyone. Leroux's ears rang, not hearing any more. Maximoff's piratical beard twitched, and he suppressed a grin even as Leroux noticed grey hairs amongst the dark curls. The treacherous eyes of the gregarious man from the steamer, pouring vodka in the stable, visiting him in prison, gleamed in triumph. The Grand Vizier stopped writing.

Once back in the dungeon in the Çadır barracks, there would be little prospect of escape. The interrogator would extract the names he sought. And if he survived that, the trial would be a formality. It would only be a question of who killed him first, the Sultan's executioner or Maximoff. He would hold out as long as he could. Time and tide … Someone, Simpkins, or Armen perhaps, had sent that girl. He would play for whatever time he could. And if they didn't come, at least he knew that Armen Garo was only a nom de guerre.

Leroux resolved to make a break for it somewhere in the outer gardens between the palace and the barracks. The grounds were vast and wooded, and he would have a chance, however small. The cuffs were tight, but he could still run fast with them. Maybe he could escape his pursuers in the trees if he wasn't shot. He might find a tool in one of the workshops they had passed on the way up the hill, break the cuffs and then scale a remote part of the wall. It wasn't much of a plan.

'Take him.'

The captain backed away from the Sultan and signalled to the soldiers. They grabbed an arm each and dragged Leroux, withdrawing, heads bowed, never turning their back on their sovereign. The Sultan and his courtiers disappeared as the great arched doors clunked shut. Leroux felt the familiar prod of a muzzle in his back. Click.

The captain nudged Leroux along a different passage from the one they had arrived down.

'Slowly.'

Two guards marched ahead. Two more followed Leroux with the captain.

'When we get to the jail,' the captain said, 'make it easy on yourself. You will talk in the end. Everyone does. There is no heroism in prolonging torture. No one will hear your screams.'

They passed through the next room and into a dazzling corridor. The panels were inlaid with mother of pearl and threw dizzying reflections of silver, green and pink. A scream halted the soldiers. It came from behind the double doors ahead. One door opened and a woman in a yellow silk floor length dress and hijab ran out. The dress was the same, but it wasn't the girl from the prison cell. A teacup followed her, flying over her head and smashed against the wall. A second woman ran out, similarly attired, and lunged at the first, shrieking. That wasn't the girl either. The two guards ahead of Leroux looked questioningly at the captain, who barked an order. They jogged forward as the first woman ripped the hijab off the second, grabbed a handful of hair and wrestled her to the ground. The first soldier tried to step between them, but they both turned on him, the first woman biting his arm. The second grabbed a crystal lamp and swung it, losing her grip. It smashed on the marble. The captain cursed and ran forward shouting, calling one of the other soldiers with him. Leroux turned slightly, just enough to get the remaining guard in his peripheral vision. He carried his rifle across his chest. The first two soldiers were hesitant to put hands on women from the Sultan's harem and hopped about helplessly. The captain's protestations had no effect, and he holstered his pistol and tried to pull them apart. The reflection next to Leroux moved. The panel had shifted. The soldier behind him was captivated by the brawling women. The panel opened like a door. And there were those eyes. Black edged, brilliant green, and a hand bidding him to come. Leroux turned side on to the soldier, took one skip towards him, cocking his knee across his body and thrust his heel hard into the guard's groin. The soldier gasped as he doubled over, and Leroux ducked through the doorway. The woman closed it, sliding top and bottom bolts across before her hands brushed over Leroux's, leading him down the narrow passage.

'This is the secret entrance to the Sultan's harem,' she said over the hammering on the panel. For now, the soldier only used his hand, perhaps unwilling to smash the precious décor with the butt of his rifle or fire inside the palace. The passage turned and widened, and the sound of pummelling diminished, and the scent of sandalwood wafted from incense burners. The woman held her arm out to stop Leroux under an arch. 'Chut!'

Leroux hushed and peeked around the opening. A huge palace eunuch had his back to him. Bare from the torso up, a woman in a gossamer dress caressed him, tempting him towards an alcove and a bed draped in a muslin veil embroidered with flowers.

'Who are you?' Leroux whispered.

'No names,' the woman said and produced a key and Leroux unscrewed his cuffs. He thought he heard a splintering sound from the passage, but the eunuch did not want to be disturbed. The woman had slid the eunuch's pantaloons down and Leroux took a second take. His rescuer suppressed a giggle and raised an eyebrow. 'Some of them still work, but no babies.' The eunuch let himself be tugged by his member into the boudoir. Leroux slipped the cuffs off and followed the woman as they tiptoed past and through a room of sofas covered in silk cushions and carpets that stretched the width of the floor with patterns so intricate, they must have taken a village a year to weave. Women, some naked, lounged, drinking sherbets and coffees, and braiding each other's hair.

None seemed alarmed that a man had entered their sanctuary. Sunlight flooded the next room, facing south with high glazed doors opening out onto a walled garden.

'Who sent you?'

'Va vite!'

Leroux took one last look into the green eyes and saw no fear. Who was she? Dressed in the clothes of the Sultan's harem, astonishingly beautiful, Armenian by her necklace. She shooed him out the door and pointed at the garden. 'Va!'

Leroux charged over the lawn directly away from the building, but a body of water, stretching hundreds of yards each side, blocked his path and as he got closer his heart sunk as he realised it was nearly a hundred yards across too. Guards appeared around both corners of the building, angling towards him. There was a bridge to a small, wooded island in the middle of the water. He couldn't go round the ends of the pond, which was shaped like a long wide S, as the soldiers would intercept him. He barrelled onto the bridge. The first shot splintered the handrail five yards in front of him. That was a terrible shot at this range, not what he expected of the captain's men like Eldar, who had tracked Leroux unnoticed through a maze of streets. Maybe that's what happened if you were a palace guard for too long. The second shot plucked the water below him. Now he was on the island, plunging into the undergrowth, an odd mixture of sycamore, judas and apple trees. He swerved around a magnolia bush. Behind him two soldiers jogged over the bridge, flushing him onwards. The others had turned for the ends of the lake.

There was no going back. Leroux crashed out of the copse, and ahead another bridge led to the far side of the water and a wall a few hundred yards beyond. Leroux put his head down and pumped his legs over the span. He ran straight for the wall, putting as much distance as he could between him the guards. He would be a sitting duck as he scaled it. The limited cover at least let him scan for a place to climb and he made a beeline for a creeper and leapt at it, scrambling up. Over his shoulder the two soldiers were just ambling over the second bridge. Leroux squatted on the top of the stone wall. They were trying to take him alive, fully able to answer questions. The others had turned back, but he could hear hooves over flagstones in the distance. The two soldiers following seemed content for him to get over the wall into the outer gardens. For all he knew the Sultan had royal tigers prowling the grounds. Maybe they didn't care if he lived.

The woods sloped steeply away to the outer wall and beyond that the Bosporus. To the right he could see the pink second story of the Çadır barracks peeking through the trees. The driveway from the palace to the main gate ran past it. He jumped and headed diagonally left down through the heady scent of pine, the soft springy ground easing his way. He wiped the sweat from his brow and rubbed his hands in dirt as he faced the outer wall looking for a handhold. Up he went, sideways now for a good grip and then up another few feet. His fingers curled over the top and felt the rumble of cavalry. Leroux hung still listening, four maybe five horses, getting closer, no way they could see him. They passed. Leroux pulled himself up, his nose hovering over the guano that covered the cap stones. The backs of the soldiers jounced around the curve of the shore. Leroux

247

waited for a cart to pass, heading out to the countryside, and hit the ground, rolled up and scampered over the road.

The sea glimmered through a short brake of trees and Leroux dropped down behind a spruce. The fast clopping of horses approached again and faded away just as quickly. Leroux followed them towards town, bending low, moving from tree to tree and soon losing sight of them. Maybe his luck was turning. The guards had made a complete muddle of their chase. Overconfident or too used to palace duties and policing the harem. Leroux's thoughts turned to his next steps. He had to find Simpkins. The embassy was the first port of call, on the way into the city before the Galata Bridge Then Nevlinski or Armen Garo.

He overtook tradesmen hauling their handcarts until finally he saw what he wanted, a carriage catching up with him on the way to the city. Smart enough that the driver might have some French. Leroux dusted himself down, tucked his shirt in and strolled onto the road, waving the cab down. The driver could not resist fleecing a lost European, however suspicious the circumstances, and he tugged on the reins pulling the four-wheeler Landau over. The two horses snorted and shook their heads. From the side of his turban a strip of cloth hung over the driver's shoulder, his teeth crooked through a bushy beard.

'British embassy.'

The driver reached back from his perch and opened the door and Leroux slumped back into the black leather, grateful for the shade and the privacy.

'A lot of soldiers about,' the driver said through the hatch.

'Why is that?'

'No idea, but I've passed four patrols just going past the palace walls,' the driver said and turned to peer at Leroux again.

'Is their trouble in the city?'

'Not when I left. What are you doing out here?'

'Riding. My horse went lame at the last village, so I started to walk back.'

A patrol thundered up behind them. There was no use in keeping up the pretence.

'Double fare if you haven't seen me.'

'Seen who?' The driver squinted hard at Leroux's pockets and closed the hatch. Leroux slid down onto the floor and the troop cantered past. One of the soldiers cast a glance inside the carriage but didn't seem to register the odd shape on the floor and didn't bother the driver.

They turned inland and up the slope to Pera and the embassies.

'I have a request. I'll double the fare again.'

The driver's face appeared in the hatch, the eyes sharp and clear.

'Do you even have any money?'

'No. But my friend at the embassy does.'

'If you trick me, I will call the soldiers.'

The guards at the embassy gates waved them through.

'I can't go inside. Tell the doorman that the cab for attaché Randolph Simpkins has arrived from Beaumont's man.'

Was Simpkins even there? Had Currie got wind of his visit to the Sultan and his efforts to help Leroux? He scratched at the coachwork, tapping impatiently. A few minutes later, Simpkins stumbled through the door, still pulling his jacket on, flushed in the face, and grasping a sheet of paper.

Leroux pushed the door open. 'Glad to see me?'

'How the? Currie was just telling me that you dug your own grave and would be executed in the morning. Are we on the run?'

'I'm afraid so. You didn't send the lady?'

'What lady?'

'The Armenian from the Sultan's harem.'

Simpkins looked blank as he counted coins into the outstretched hand of the driver. 'Head towards Galata Bridge,' Simpkins said, wanting to get away from the embassy before anyone recognised Leroux.

'Did you tell anyone that I was imprisoned at the Palace?'

'I sent a message to Garo straightaway saying I'd seen you and stressing the urgency of his plan...' Simpkins hands dropped. 'But I haven't had a reply. What is the plan?'

'I don't know,' Leroux admitted. 'And Nevlinski?'

'No one has seen him the last few days. Suddenly gone dark. Even Herzl was puzzled.'

Leroux slid the hatch open. 'The harbour, Theodora's!'

Simpkins looked shocked. 'Look, I know you've been in prison, but we're in a bit of a –'

'Nevlinski may be keeping a low profile, but I doubt he will forego his peccadillos. If anyone knows where to find him, they will.'

'There's something else,' Simpkins said, proffering the piece of paper, a telegram. 'This just arrived from Beaumont. Olga de Novikoff is telling the papers that proof of an atrocity in Armenia is imminent. And she is hinting there will be a scandal, that the highest levels of the British government are complicit in covering up the Sultan's murdering ways. She will provide the evidence any day. What do you think it could be?'

Leroux slammed the side of the cab. 'I'm sorry, this is my fault. We're about to be made scapegoats, blamed for this whole mess.'

'We are?'

'That devious bastard. I was arrested after leaving the revolutionaries' meeting. Someone shot a soldier. I'm sure now it was Maximoff, but I was arrested for it. The Turks interrogated me. He came to visit me, made sure they treated me properly. He searched my room and found my report. Said it was to remove any incriminating evidence and offered to get it out. He tricked me into writing your name on it, I thought so he would know who to send it to. I'm sorry, he completely fooled me.'

'But why will we be blamed?'

'Maximoff saw an opportunity. A cherry on the cake. And he improvised his plan. He had in his hands signed and dated proof that the British Government was aware of the massacre. And now he will present it, saying that while Russia strives to protect the Armenians from persecution, the British Government has done nothing, perhaps even covered it up. He will drop my name, the mysterious government agent mixed up in the notorious Jameson affair. Miss Shaw told Olga de Novikoff that I was about to meet Beaumont. They know my connection to the Ambassador. They have your name on the document, nephew of the head of British Naval Intelligence and attaché at the embassy. They will say we all knew but kept it quiet. Weeks have gone by. This must be the scandal that Madame de Novikoff is teasing. It could bring down the government. And then Russia would be faced with a Liberal administration, weak in their support of the Sultan and opposed to foreign wars. Even less likely to order the Royal Navy to sail against the Tsar. It'll be a re-run of '78, but with nothing to stop him this time.'

Leroux kicked the floor in frustration and looked back at the embassy. Four of the Sultan's cavalrymen cantered into the courtyard.

'Ambassador Currie is going to have a sense of humour failure,' Leroux said.

'Oh, hang Currie,' Simpkins said, 'and don't blame yourself. How else could you have got the report out? It's not as though you had much choice.'

That was the way Maximoff had set it up. How had he not seen it. He could have fought Maximoff then and there. The guards would have come in and seized the report. He had already told the captain that he had been to Akrag.

'That was nearly two weeks ago. Olga de Novikoff could have the report in London by now.'

Simpkins closed his eyes and groaned. 'I can see the headlines now.'

Leroux looked at his watch. Nearly 3 o'clock. He didn't care for the forts or Suez. He cared even less for the young Tsar who had a reputation for repression. Now it seemed he wanted to make a name for himself and use war and religion to dominate Europe. And Leroux would be just one of many casualties along the way. And Maximoff had made a fool of him. Leroux smiled. It wasn't just escaping jail that gave Leroux a feeling of freedom. He had nothing left to lose.

'I need to see Armen Garo,' Leroux said, 'you said you know how to contact him?'

'He's staying at a house in Pera, belonging to an Armenian, Hratch Tiryakian.'

'And Herzl?'

'He's lodging with the Grun family near the Pera Palace Hotel.'

'How is he?'

'Guarded. He has been in to see the Grand Vizier several times, but I haven't heard of any progress.'

'I'm going to look for Nevlinski. Can you update your uncle. We can't prove any of it yet, but it tallies with de Novikoff's actions. There's plenty we're in the dark about. Who was Nevlinski working with when he drugged me? Was it Maximoff or someone else? Was he behind the theft of the dossier? And who helped me escape from the palace and why?'

Simpkins pushed a purse into Leroux's palm and jumped out. 'Good luck. I'll be at the embassy.'

The carriage rattled down the hill to Theodora's. What would Maximoff be doing right now? He knew Leroux was onto him, even if no one believed the accusations. Did he know that Leroux had escaped? Would he speed up his plan? How much time did Leroux have?

The carriage pulled over and the driver nodded over the road at the cracked mortar of Theodora's. The wooden door had chips and the place looked cheap and unloved in the daylight. Leroux rapped on the door.

'Fermée,' a reedy voice called from inside.

Leroux rapped again harder.

'Who is it?'

'I need to speak to the manager. Urgent.'

The door opened a crack and a beady eye looked up at him, the black tassel of his fez hanging down the front.

'C'est moi. What do you want?'

'Count Nevlinski. He's a regular of yours.'

The manager's eye twitched and Leroux shoved his foot in the door just as the man tried to press it shut. Leroux added his shoulder and shoved him back into the bar.

'Where is he?'

'He's not here.'

'I can see that. Where would he be at this time of day?'

'How would I know?'

Leroux vaulted behind the bar. If the manager had a weapon, it would be here.

'Because you know him well enough to help him drug me.'

The man swallowed. 'It was you?'

Leroux rummaged under the counter, keeping one eye on the manager. 'The way I see it, you owe me.'

He found the weapon, a British Bull Dog revolver. A pocket gun with a short barrel, but deadly enough at this range.

'He stays at the Pera Palace Hotel.'

Leroux shook his head. 'Hasn't been seen there for days.'

The manager spread his hands.

'Mon ami …'

'Where else would he stay if he didn't want to be found?'

254

Leroux opened the cash register. The manager's eyes darted to the float as Leroux lifted it out.

'I don't know...,' the man wrung his hands torn between the money and running. 'Please, the owner will make me pay.'

'The Count was very friendly with one of your girls.'

The manager's eye flicked to the door and Leroux jumped back over the bar and waggled the gun.

'Name.'

'Hasnija.'

'And where does Hasnija stay? Leroux counted cash onto the sticky bar.

'She has a room, by the harbour, next door to the Café Parisiana, one of the upper floors.'

'I'll keep this for the trouble.' Leroux stuck the little gun in his pocket and left the takings. He ran over to the docks, slowing as he reached the quay and saw the awning of the Parisiana. Leroux slipped into the wake of a sailor, stopping when he saw Nevlinski, right there on his own - his back to the wall, reading a newspaper, sipping a coffee, facing the pavement, empty tables on both sides. Not a care in the world. Leroux drew up a chair, the unmistakable outline of a muzzle pressing against the cloth of his pocket.

'Don't make a fuss. You must know I haven't got much to lose. I'll happily shoot you right here.'

Nevlinski shook his newspaper extravagantly and set it down, hoping he had attracted some glances.

'Keep it quiet.' Leroux drew the gun under the table, poking Nevlinski in the leg. 'What's the news on Armenia?'

'Not much today.'

'You were very interested in my journey there. Why?'

Nevlinski checked about him. A waiter hovered and Leroux dismissed him.

'You were interfering in my affairs.'

'You drugged me.'

'I did no such—'

Leroux cocked the gun. Nevlinski licked his lips.

'I had no choice.'

'Who was with you?'

'You don't understand. He will—'

'Was it Maximoff?'

Nevlinski inclined his head, pushing chins over his collar. His hands curled on the tabletop, and he fidgeted out a cigarette. The waiter swooped in with a lit spill, and the Count took a draw, the end of the cigarette trembling in the flame.

'Why was he so interested in my relationship with Herzl and what's the connection to my journey to Armenia?'

Nevlinski smoothed his thinning hair down and his lip quivered.

'I don't know. He thought you knew more than you did.'

Over the road, stevedores and porters tossed cargo between them, lashing the larger items to pulleys, gathering smaller ones in nets, or just humping sacks on their shoulders. Merchants haggled with ships' captains while knots of seamen disappeared into the alleyways. Leroux pressed the muzzle into Nevlinski's flesh.

'What is his involvement with Herzl?'

'He's never met Herzl,' Nevlinski stammered, his eyes searching the street. Leroux checked again for policeman. The Count looked ready to shout out, probably doubting whether Leroux would fire. Probably right.

'That's not what I asked.'

Nevlinski sucked on the cigarette, his eyes narrowing against the smoke but questing along the dock. Leroux slid two coins on the table for the bill and prodded Nevlinski.

'Where are we going?'

Leroux ushered Nevlinski over the road, one arm over his shoulder, the gun back in his pocket.

'Why is Maximoff interested in my connection to Herzl?'

Nevlinski stopped and took a final drag on the cigarette. Over his shoulder Leroux spotted the dark blue tunic and scarlet fez of a policeman, about a hundred yards aways.

'It was his idea,' Nevlinski said.

'What?'

The policeman calmly parted a jostle of porters and traders, swinging a baton in front of him, getting closer. Behind Nevlinski, two hamals bought a trunk down from a ship moored alongside and set it next to a cart stacked with a jumble of ornaments. They opened the empty trunk and the driver jumped down and began to untie his belongings.

'Maximoff knew that I was close to Herzl,' Nevlinski said. 'He came to me and suggested a deal that the Sultan would be interested in.'

Leroux curled his arm around Nevlinski's neck, hugging him close.

'What deal?' A trader in a long red kaftan talked to the hamals and they started unloading the cart.

'Paying off the Sultan's debt in return for Palestine.'

'Does Herzl know it wasn't your idea?'

'No.'

The policeman, close now, called out to a stevedore lugging a rolled carpet, not looking where he was going. Nevlinski craned his neck, but Leroux grabbed his collar before he could turn and pressed the muzzle into his gut.

'Did you arrange the theft of my case on the train?'

'No. That wasn't me. I was as surprised as anyone.'

Leroux cocked the gun.

Nevlinski sniffed. 'Honestly. Why would I want it? I already knew what Herzl had given you.'

Leroux hadn't expected that. Nevlinski sounded sincere and he made sense. Leroux slid behind Nevlinski and wedged his forearm firmly under Nevlinski's chin. He bought his left arm up, gripping the top of Nevlinski head, while threading his right hand inside the fold of his left elbow and squeezed. His forearm and bicep constricted both sides of Nevlinski's neck. Leroux pressed the Count's head forward.

'I can't...' Nevlinski gasped. His fingers scrabbled at Leroux's arm, as Leroux shoved his hip into the small of Nevlinski's back and gently lowered him. By the time he was halfway down, the Count sagged, a dead weight in Leroux's arms. Leroux hauled him over to the trunk and sat him up against the side, bending down to block the policeman's view, who was only a dozen yards away. Nevlinski could regain consciousness any moment. The hamals gathered around and the trader waddled over to see what was disrupting his porters.

'Are you the owner of this trunk?' Leroux shoved his hand in his pocket and pulled out half the money Simpkins had given him.

'Oh yes, I am being the owner. Definitely.' The trader nodded vigorously, rubbing his palms together. The policeman's shadow glided over Nevlinski. Leroux cupped the Count's cheek.

'What's wrong?' the policeman asked peering down his long nose.

'Just the heat. He'll be better in a minute.'

The policeman's sense for trouble had been aroused and he could smell money, but an argument broke out just ahead of them over a dropped hogshead of wine. The trader didn't miss a beat and protested about the interruption to his business and the policeman turned his attention to the dispute.

Leroux looked at the boat.

'Is the trunk going on that?'

'Oh yes. You want to ship something?' The merchant prised his eyes away from the wad of cash.

Leroux pointed at Nevlinski. 'Where is the boat going?'

The merchant said something unintelligible under his breath.

'Is that far?'

'Two days.'

'That's far enough.'

'But it is being very expensive.'

'Is this enough?'

The merchant shook his head. 'No, no. Not quite.' The merchant focused on Leroux's pocket and the faint outline of the remaining funds. Leroux took the pouch out.

'Let me see,' the trader said, cupping it in his hand as though to measure its worth, but also to get a hand on it. 'Maybe this is just sufficing. Only just. For very special man like you.'

They tipped Nevlinski into the trunk and closed it. The hamals lifted the weight deftly and Leroux could just hear the muffled cries of Nevlinski as he was carried up the gangway. Leroux needed him out of the way for a few days, and it was no more than the double-dealing rogue deserved. He couldn't risk Nevlinski alerting Maximoff.

It came as no surprise that Maximoff had been the mystery man at Theodora's. He was interested in the British government's involvement with Herzl. He had proposed a solution for Herzl's ambitions in Palestine to Nevlinski, who passed it off as his own. Why? Was Maximoff trying to scupper Herzl's plan by proposing a solution that he knew the Sultan could never accept? Did he want to stop the British from helping Herzl? Was he worried that if Herzl succeeded, Christians across Europe would latch on to the prophecy of the End of Times, perhaps overshadowing the Tsar's fulfilment of the Iskander prophecy? That still left the mystery of the dossier. If the thief wasn't with Nevlinski, then who was behind it? Leroux could hear Beaumont's voice. Spies spying on spies. At least with Nevlinski out of the picture, Maximoff would lose a pair of ears. Hopefully he didn't know that Leroux had escaped. Leroux took a cab to Pera. It was time to catch up with Armen. They had a lot to discuss.

The walls of the city of seven hills bathed in a honey glow as the cab strained up towards Pera through lengthening shadows. The domes and minarets set about a perfect harbour gave the city a fairytale look. Leroux squinted into the sunset at the carriages that followed, but none caught his attention. He hopped down at the top of the road that led to Armen's hideout. The other cabs trundled past without pause. The muezzin began the call to prayer, and Leroux wondered why anyone had ever thought of using a bell. The lyrical mystical song had grown on him, along with the intoxicating fragrances of spices and flowers, and the wild variety of colours and clothes that abounded in the city. Leroux walked down the side of the street which afforded him a better view of the safe house. He passed it and reached the end of the street where two young men in the typical modern attire of white shirt, waistcoat and black trousers smoked on the corner, laughing, not partaking in the Maghrib prayer. Leroux looped around the next street and when he returned only smouldering cigarette butts remained. It was dark now, with no streetlights in the side roads, and Leroux knocked on the door as the chorus of dog howls warmed up.

A stolid middle-aged woman filled the sliver of an opening. Her neutral expression told Leroux he was at the right place.

'Peter Leroux for Armen Garo.'

She stared blankly at him. 'There is no such person here, this is the house of Iskuhi.'

'Please let the master of the house know that Peter Leroux is back from Erzurum.'

The door clunked shut. An overweight Turk in a brown jacket crossed over the street, hands in pockets. A little out of shape for a porter. He sneezed and his moustache twitched in a familiar way. Leroux looked to his feet but kept the man in his peripheral vision. To a casual observer he looked no different from the typical middle-aged men who went about unnoticed, but Leroux felt uneasy and tugged his cuffs down over his chafed wrists.

The woman returned, cautiously looked down the street and admitted Leroux. He followed her gesture, ascending narrow flights of stairs, his steps hollow on the wooden treads. As he neared the top, he heard voices. A door opened onto a roof terrace looking out over the Golden Horn, now a dark crescent through the lights of the city. A murmur of appreciation spread around the circle of a dozen revolutionaries, mostly young men with a few women, seated on an assortment of stools and chairs around a low table. Armen was already on his feet and embraced Leroux. 'Comrades, this is the man who saved my life in Erzurum.'

The fresh-faced demeanour of the students and youthful teachers, no older than Leroux, jarred with the table loaded with small bombs in varying stages of manufacture. What did they know of war? And then he felt the rush of elation. A ray of hope bursting in his chest. Was that the girl? Her hazel eyes glistened behind the sweep of her hair, now shiny. The dirt and tear-streaked skin of his memory, now radiant. But the fierce expression, just the same. A tear rolled down her cheek, now one of joy. She wiped it away with the edge of a yellow scarf and hid behind her long locks that tumbled down the front of a simple white dress.

262

Leroux stumbled through the introductions. One of the other leaders was Hratch Tiryakian, who Leroux recognised as one of the revolutionaries at the meeting with a walrus moustache and large almond eyes that seemed far away when not staring at Miss Iskuhi, a fetching woman with strong angular features, the owner of the house. Papken Siuni was the third musketeer, who had spoken at the meeting, with close cropped hair, small shrewd eyes, and a narrow long face that lent an air of melancholy. Finally, Armen gestured to the girl from Akrag.

'And of course, you must remember our new friend. The life you saved. The missionary took her to Bayburt as you said, and we found her there. We have named her Eva.'

She understood the gist of the conversation, if not Armen's French, and bowed her head, embarrassed by the attention. 'She still hasn't spoken.'

Leroux smiled at Eva, but she kept her head down, discreetly brushing her cheeks with her hand.

'She cannot write either, and when we try to ask her about the village, she becomes distressed.'

'She must have seen some terrible things. What I saw was bad enough.'

Armen pulled Leroux aside while the revolutionaries continued to make bombs. More hollow cannon balls appeared from a sack which were delicately filled with a brown mixture that Leroux knew to be dynamite. The last step was to plug the hole in the ball with a fuse, although the dynamite could explode just from the shock of falling from a height. Some had percussion caps containing mercury fulminate, which would ignite with minimal pressure, detonating the bomb, and hurling iron fragments at bystanders. Others had simple wooden plugs with a thin hole drilled in the middle and crammed with gunpowder. Leroux watched until he was satisfied that they knew how to handle and pack the devices. They had been well taught, but some had evidently been at it too long and they risked being poisoned. Their eyes were already red-rimmed, and their hands stained yellow.

'What happened?' Armen said. 'I heard you were arrested, and then your friend Simpkins told me you were being held at Yildiz.'

'You don't know?'

Armen looked blank.

'I thought it was you that sent the Armenian girl from the Sultan's harem?'

Armen shook his head. 'What girl?'

'She helped me escape earlier today. Then Simpkins told me where to find you.'

Armen glanced down at Leroux's wrists.

'It wasn't us. Were you questioned?'

Who else could have sent help? The bishop?

'Briefly. I escaped before the torture began. But I told them I was at the meeting and Maximoff was there. I said he killed the soldier and fired at us.'

'Maximoff? Why?'

Leroux recounted his theory, admitting the paucity of his evidence. The only accusation he could make for sure was that Maximoff took his report and failed to deliver it.

'And I doubt Maximoff's plans are good for you,' Leroux added.

'I told Avetis not to trust Maximoff,' Armen said.

'When is their uprising?' Leroux asked.

'I don't know, but soon. The bishop here in Constantinople received a warning today - to be wary of reprisals.'

'You have to move first.'

'Simpkins said. I agreed. We've brought it forward.'

'When?'

'Tomorrow!'

The gathering had fallen silent. All ears were on them. A cannon ball rolled towards the edge of the table. Eva stretched out her hand and stopped it. Leroux tore his eyes away from her. 'What are you planning?'

Armen smiled broadly. 'You will like this, my friend. You know the Ottoman Bank?'

Leroux nodded. 'Full to the brim with British and French deposits.'

'Exactly. And their employees. We're going to hit them where it hurts – their wallet and their pride. We will storm the bank and hold the employees hostage, until Britain and France force the Sultan to agree to protect the Armenian people. There are over a hundred Europeans working there and millions and millions of francs. All the taxes which are collected to repay the Sultan's loans.'

'How many of you are there?'

'Seventy. All with guns. At least two hundred bombs between us, and extra dynamite. We can hold the bank for as long as it takes.'

'And if the Sultan sends the army in?'

'We will dynamite the building.'

'With you and the hostages inside?'

'Yes. We will not surrender. Will you join us?'

It would certainly get Britain's attention. The British Empire's gold and citizens held to ransom by a small band of Armenians. They would be called terrorists. The Sultan detested the bank, a stain on his sovereignty. He would jump at the opportunity to raise it to the ground. The Ottomans would line a few canons up across the street. A couple of salvos to reduce the entrance to matchwood. Volley fire from the soldiers to clear the entrance hall with a hail of lead, followed by a bayonet charge. He looked across the table at the callow idealists. They wouldn't stand against a forest of sharpened steel. Somebody had to stop it reaching that point.

'How could I refuse?'

Armen hugged Leroux. 'You will see! The Great Powers will come to our rescue at last. All we will ask for is protection.'

'And Avetis' rebellion will be unnecessary,' Leroux said.

'We will save much Armenian blood.'

But not the flesh and blood here, Leroux thought. But it should put a spanner in Maximoff's plan. Without a rebellion, Maximoff's pretext for an invasion would be up in smoke.

Armen grabbed Leroux's hand. 'Let us drink a toast! We go tomorrow!'

Leroux saw a path forward. If they took the bank, Britain had to respond. The money was bad. The hostages worse. But the loss of face, completely unacceptable. HMS Dryad lay at anchor, at the mouth of the Golden Horn. She would send a party of marines ashore. Officially to protect British nationals in Constantinople. It would make the Sultan think twice about storming the bank. But it would also be a problem for the Tsar if he planned to take Constantinople. And if it helped the Armen negotiate with the Sultan that would blunt the impact of any news stories that Maximoff and de Novikoff had planned.

What then? Maximoff would react to keep his plan on track. And that might expose his guilt. If it worked, Currie could not complain if Russia's relations with the Sultan were damaged, and the Sultan might even pardon Leroux. If it failed? He didn't need to imagine Currie's face. It was a chance, however slim, and Armen needed all the help he could get. Leroux raised his glass. When you have nothing to lose, double down. They could only kill him once.

Even up on the roof they heard the sharp rap on the street door. Miss Iskuhi clutched at Hratch's arm. The bomb makers froze. A man known as Shorty Hovannes quietly reached for a revolver. Miss Iskuhi tightened her scarf and went down the stairs.

'Were you followed?' Armen said.

'I didn't think so.'

'That's what you said last time.'

Heavy footsteps clumped on the stairs. Miss Iskuhi tumbled through the door, flush of face, her arms laden with parcels.

'It was just,' she panted, 'Mr Stein's delivery man.'

Hratch untied the strings and shook out four smart European style suits in the current fashion. Pinstripe, four buttons, high cut lapels. 'Here we go gentleman, our attire for the bank.'

He passed one each to Papken, Armen and Shorty to try on for size. Miss Iskuhi produced a small wicker basket and some rags. 'Don't try to stop me,' she said to Hratch as he hoisted his new trousers up one leg, hopping on the other. She loaded the basket with half a dozen bombs, padded the contents with rags and lay a gingham cloth on top, tying a red ribbon around the handle. It creaked when she lifted it in the crook of her arm, and she leaned to balance it on her hip like a baby. Hratch hitched his braces and filled a dentist's bag with more bombs. He picked it up tentatively, testing the handles. The stitching looked sound and held firm and Hratch straightened up. Together the lovers tip-toed down the stairs.

'This evening,' Armen said, 'We take the bombs to safe houses near the bank. Keep a sharp lookout. There are secret police everywhere.'

Shorty and Papken packed two old Gladstone bags with more explosives and departed into the night. Leroux offered to help, but Armen refused. Too risky. The police were looking for him and he didn't know the back streets. A final sack of cannonballs arrived from the Armenian's secret smeltery, and Leroux sat where Eva had made a space for him. Leroux let her demonstrate how she made the devices and followed her example precisely, although he knew well what to do. One of the revolutionaries cast a protective look at Eva and introduced himself as Sarkis, almost knocking over a small pyramid of bombs as he briskly shook Leroux's hand, trying and failing to wring the life out of it. Frustrated he sat back down, and the quiet, careful work continued. They finished just before Hratch, Miss Iskuhi, Papken and Shorty returned, flushed with success. Sarkis volunteered to deliver the remining bombs with Eva.

'Take Levon with you,' Armen said. 'Eva stays here. If you get separated, she won't know her way back or be able to speak to anyone.'

Levon sprang up, delighted to be named, and began to pack a sack, dressed as a hamal porter, his disguise for the bank raid. Sarkis looked bitterly at Armen but went ahead and filled a carpet bag. With the table clear of explosives, it was now piled high with cheese pastries, vine leaf parcels stuffed with mince and spiced rice, chickpea dumplings, flat breads, lamb kebabs and bulgur wheat. A feast worthy of a last supper, but some of the young comrades could not eat, managing only a little wine and fruit, nauseous from over exposure to the chemicals or simply anxiety. The young revolutionaries melted away, exhaustion etched into their faces, some simply wrapped in a blanket under the stars. Leroux felt the press of Eva's back where she had curled up against his thigh and the soft rise of her breathing. He propped himself up with some cushions and gazed at the stars that bore witness to everything beneath them. Armen produced a bottle of kanyak.

'What's on your mind?' he said.

'Do you think the Sultan's spies have any inkling of what's about to happen?'

The man in the brown jacket with the twitch of the moustache in the street earlier had been bothering Leroux. He had seen that man before but couldn't place him.

'The police are everywhere. I have even seen them at the end of this road. But,' and Armen crossed himself, 'we have not been stopped with anything incriminating.'

'There is someone I need to see before I go to the bank,' Leroux said.

'Simpkins? It would be good to have him arguing our case with your Ambassador when we are on the inside.'

'Him too, although it would be better if Currie didn't know of my involvement. It's Theodor Herzl. I need to warn him. Somehow Maximoff is using him.'

Armen looked doubtful but didn't object. 'We assemble at the English School at eleven o'clock, to make the final preparations. We take the bank at noon, don't be late.' He picked up the empty bottle and looked down at Eva.

'Is she coming?' Leroux said.

'She has nightmares, but never screams. She needs to go, to fight her demons. Get them out.'

Leroux knew that feeling well enough and focussed on the night sky and the gentle rhythm of Eva's breathing. And then it came to him. The moustache. The twitch. When he first arrived at Sirkeci train station, that man had been watching Simpkins, dressed more smartly, yes, but Leroux was sure it was him. Had he failed to recognise Leroux in the street? Possible. Dishevelled and without his distinctive slouch hat. And he had been speaking French to the lady at the door. Armen had seen policemen at the end of the street before, so it didn't mean that Leroux had been followed. And nothing had happened since, even with bags full of bombs leaving the house. Leroux drew his blanket in around his neck and closed his eyes, leaving just the soft press of Eva on his senses. For all that had gone wrong over the last few weeks, Eva was one thing that had gone right. He had not a possession, bar the clothes he lay in. And a plan. A hope. He felt calm and as free as he had ever been.

Leroux drifted in a half-sleep, the afterburn of brandy still in his throat, and remembered the last time he had seen his childhood friend Tom. They had been eighteen, drinking moonshine in Johannesburg. Leroux about to go to college, Tom seeking his fortune in the mines. Tom had taught him a Zulu war dance and the rhythm of it came back to him. The moonshine and the hangover had been terrible. Leroux had left for college and never saw Tom again, killed in a mining accident the next day. He tossed in his sleep. Now he was back on the veld with the Commando. Kneeling behind the wheel of the wagon, firing his rifle as fast as he could, the pain of the wound in his shoulder as he cycled the bolt. The acrid sting of cordite, the rat-tat-tat-tat of the Maxim gun scything down Chief Malaboch's warriors. Now he saw the pile of bones by the church door. So much death. He woke in a sweat. Eva did not stir. Tomorrow he would have the chance to make things better.

Wednesday, 26th August, Constantinople

Leroux rubbed his eyes. It must have been the aroma of freshly baked flatbreads that had woken him. Eva brushed by, setting the table with figs, yoghurt, and honey. The revolutionaries gathered with muted greetings and silent clenches. Armen adjusted Shorty's tie. Papken and Hratch joined him and admired each other's outfits. The suits ran through the plan and assigned tasks. Comrade Misakian would bomb the barracks next to the bank with two men. A young man called Edward and his friend would lay in wait on the Galata Bridge and demolish Prime Minister Sadrazam's carriage as it passed. And just after the raid started, yet another group would drop bombs on soldiers as they marched to the bank along Pera Street. Someone else would plant the biggest bomb at the Galata Saray government building, detonating it just as troops emerged. The Turks would be blown away. The bank would be stormed, and British troops would land to protect the bank and the hostages from destruction and prevent reprisals against the Armenian population. The revolutionaries would receive an amnesty and march out as heroes.

Their eyes believed. Leroux felt a gnawing in the pit of his stomach. Could such an inexperienced group pull off such an ambitious plan? The destruction promised by the diversions would infuriate the Turks. They were playing with fire, but now was not the time to dampen their spirits. When the firing started, they would need all the brio they could muster.

The Albanian guards might dress like pantomime villains, but they were hardened fighters who would gut you without hesitation.

Hratch detailed the bank assault. Armen would go in with Leroux to change money and check that no additional guards lurked inside. On Armen's signal the assault group would storm the entrance, taking the Albanians by surprise. Once the raid started, Armen and Leroux would prevent the employees escaping in the chaos, gathering them as hostages. The assault group included Hratch and Papken as well as Shorty. They had all volunteered, the most experienced with firearms and wanting to lead from the front. But if it went wrong, all the leadership, with Armen stuck inside, would be wiped out. Taking the bank by surprise wasn't the hard part. Defending it and making a success of the negotiations was the real challenge.

Then Miss Iskuhi left the room in tears, after Hratch forbade her participation. The feeling in Leroux's stomach wouldn't go away. The planning was too optimistic, there was no contingency, so any mistake threatened the whole venture. But they were past the point of making changes. The plan was already in motion. At least Armen had agreed to let him help with the hostages, where he would be best positioned to ensure their safety and reduced the chances of his having to fire at the Sultan's troops. He did not welcome the thought of finding Captain Emre in his sights. The captain had treated him fairly, kindly even, in the circumstances. It was a desperately fine line that Leroux trod. He risked alienating everyone.

Leroux slipped out to find Herzl. He strode without hurrying and checked for a tail without looking. The podgy man with the twitching moustache was nowhere to be seen. Leroux turned on to Pera Street, where iron shrapnel would tear through soldiers later, and reached the road where Herzl stayed with the Grüns. Grand stone houses built around courtyards were interspersed with modest wooden dwellings. A French gentleman in a silk top hat batted away a dog with his cane, and the mutt returned to his pack, milling around a shack. The lady owner tossed them a disc shaped flatbread which they tore into. Herzl's lodgings were just beyond the shack. When Leroux reached the tussling dogs, a gendarme walked out of Herz's front door, turned to say something, and walked away.

The dogs returned to the shade, except the pack leader who investigated Leroux, its cool snout nuzzling his hand, smelling the honey from breakfast. Leroux scratched the dog's chin as he waited for the gendarme to disappear, and a troubling thought came to him. Had Herzl organised Leroux's escape and now the police were on to him?

Leroux stepped up to the arched wooden door and tentatively tapped the knocker. A boy with the merest wisp of a beard under a fez appeared, his weight shifting from foot to foot.

'Is Theodor Herzl at home?'

The boy swallowed, his bleary eyes sliding sideways. 'Um…'

Something was wrong. 'I'm a friend of his.' Leroux edged forward to see into the hall. 'Are there more police here?'

The boy nodded vigorously.

'I'm going to wait over there, by the lady with dogs. Please quietly tell Mr Herzl, and only Mr Herzl, that Mr Leroux is waiting with an urgent message. It is very important that we speak. Can you do that?'

The boy sucked his top lip, blinked, and pushed the door gently shut. Leroux waited with the dogs in the shadow of the shack and gave the woman a coin for one of her flatbreads. If the police came charging out, he would run for it and toss the bread behind him, so that the dogs might at least trip them up.

The long dark figure of Herzl shuffled out, carrying a sack. He looked dreadful. His stoop was more pronounced and his face greyer. He leaned heavily on a cane but smiled as he recognised Leroux.

'Simpkins bought this last night,' Herzl said, handing over the sack. They walked arm-in-arm to the end of the street.

'Apparently you escaped prison. Simpkins went there to request your things. Is that true?'

'I'm afraid it is,' Leroux said and hailed a cab. Herzl's breath rasped as Leroux asked the driver to take them around the cemetery behind the British embassy, where the traffic was quiet, and they could talk undisturbed.

'Oy vey, what a night!' Herzl said, slumping into the back of the carriage.

'What happened?'

Herzl wiped his brow and patted Leroux on the leg. 'Could have done with you being there. Some men broke in while we were asleep. Young Samuel, who you spoke to, woke up and interrupted them. Thankfully, they ran off and didn't hurt him. He was quite shaken.'

'Did they take anything?'

'I don't think so. There were some valuable ornaments in the house, but the only things that were disturbed were papers. My briefcase was emptied, my files strewn all over the floor and old Grün's desk was forced open and searched. Quite strange.'

'No idea who did it or why?'

Herzl smoothed his beard down. 'None. And things have been going very well since I last saw you. Look at this.' Herzl produced a silver star from his pocket attached to a red silk ribbon. 'The Commander's Cross of the Order of the Medjidie. The Grand Vizier presented me with it. An award from the Sultan to demonstrate the seriousness of our negotiations. So, tell me. What have you been up to?'

And Leroux did, leaving nothing out, up to the point of his escape.

'So, the rumours were true?'

'All too true.'

Herzl's eyes clouded over. 'This is terrible. And the Sultan was responsible?'

'That's what everyone assumes. But there is no proof.'

Herzl shook his head slowly, the circles around his eyes darker than Leroux remembered. 'What will you do?'

'Somehow, this is all connected. From the beginning. The village, your negotiation, the prophecies, my investigation. All connected to the senior Russian diplomat at the Sublime Porte, Dragoman Maximoff. Nevlinski has been working for him all along.'

'For Maximoff?'

'I'm sure.'

'Why? And what's happened to Nevlinski? I haven't seen him for days. Normally, I can't get rid of him.'

'He drugged me and set me up as a fool to discredit me with Ambassador Currie.'

Herzl bit a nail. 'I got your message not to trust him, but he's a persistent man, and he has delivered.'

'He's been lying low since I returned to Constantinople,' Leroux said, 'but I caught up with him yesterday. He confessed to working for Maximoff. Nevlinski's proposal was Maximoff's suggestion.'

'What? Why would he get involved? It has no bearing on Russia's interests.'

'You agreed to repay the Sultan's debts in return for the right to settle in Palestine?'

'Yes.'

'And it was Nevlinski's idea?'

'Yes, he was very pleased with himself. I never thought the Sultan would agree, but desperate times…'

'I'm sorry. I think we are both being used by Maximoff. Both parts of a plan to overthrow the Sultan and take Constantinople for the Tsar …'

'That's preposterous. Are you sure?'

'As sure as I can be.'

Herzl bent forward, clutching a hand to his chest. 'But, why?'

'Doesn't it seem strange that the Caliph of all Muslims would negotiate over the sovereignty of Jerusalem? It is a holy city for Islam too, where the Prophet Muhammad ascended to Heaven. It would cause uproar amongst his most devout followers.'

'True. But it is also true that the Sultan is drowning in debt. The Grand Vizier made a great show of how the Sultan was unable to pay the soldiers and it would not be long before they took matters into their own hands. We have thrown him a lifeline. He must have no other because he has grabbed it. Nevlinski is a chancer, but he was right.'

'The agreement has been accepted?'

'Nevlinski and I saw the Grand Vizier three days ago to receive the decree. I have arranged for the transfer of the first payment, but for such a sum, it will take a week a least.'

'His supporters will be infuriated just when he needs them …'

'The Grand Vizier highlighted that exact problem. He stressed that the agreement would not be unveiled until an opportune moment for the Sultan arose and the funds are confirmed. He gave us the decree as a sign of good faith so that we may arrange the finances.'

'But you haven't seen the Sultan personally…'

'No,' admitted Herzl. 'But the decree bears his seal, it is valid. I understood that he avoided meeting in person to reduce the risk of any unwanted rumours spreading prematurely.'

'Who has seen this agreement?'

'The Grand Vizier, Nevlinski and I assume the Sultan.'

'No one else even knew of it?'

Herzl shook his head.

'You said the burglars took nothing last night. You're sure they haven't taken the agreement?'

'There are only two copies, mine, and the Grand Vizier's. And mine is not at home. Nevlinski sent me a note this morning wanting to read it again to check something.'

'That's impossible.'

'What do you mean?'

'I put him on a cargo ship yesterday. There's no way he could have sent a message this morning. Did you reply?'

'Yes. I'm meeting him this afternoon at 3 o'clock.'

Maximoff was beginning to make mistakes. He couldn't know where Nevlinski was. He was blind and bluffing.

'The burglary last night. It must have been Maximoff's men looking for the agreement. Now they are posing as Nevlinski to try and discover where it is. Where did you send the message?'

'The Pera Palace Hotel. Why does Maximoff want the agreement?'

'I'll get to that.'

Maximoff would already have the message. The cab turned a corner of the graveyard, and the driver opened the hatch for instructions. 'Go around again,' Leroux said. 'Do you have the agreement?'

'In my safe deposit box. I was going to pick it up before meeting Nevlinski.'

An idea began to form in Leroux's mind. Was this the final piece of the jigsaw. The piece that Maximoff was waiting on?

'Which bank?'

'The Ottoman Bank, of course. The only place that's safe around here.'

'You can't go there. It's a long story, but I believe Maximoff is using us all. I told you that Maximoff plans to overthrow the Sultan and for the Tsar to conquer Constantinople. In doing so, he hopes to fulfill a prophecy, the prophecy of Nestor Iskander. That Christians will reclaim the Saint Sophia and all Christians, all Slavs will unite under the one true king – The Tsar. Maximoff is using the Armenians, encouraging them to rebel, to divert the Sultan's forces and give the Tsar a reason to invade. He has used me. I was sent to confirm rumours of the massacre. But Maximoff found out, stole my report and had me imprisoned. Now he will release the report, claiming the British knew of the persecution and covered it up. Public sympathy for the Armenians and anger at the government will prevent Britain from supporting the Sultan. And I think he is using you - to turn the Sultan's most faithful supporters against him. If Maximoff gets the copy of your agreement and publishes it, Muslims everywhere will be outraged. There will be no one to stop the Tsar's armies.'

Herzl stared ashen faced out of the window.

'Maximoff has no interest in helping you settle Palestine and far less in fulfilling the prophecy of Zion. And if the Slavs are united and the Tsar rules from Budapest to Constantinople, I doubt that will be good news for you.'

'You don't have to tell me,' Herzl said bitterly. 'I remember the pogroms. It's why a state of our own is the only way. Our dream of Palestine will be mere ashes in the wind…'

Leroux rummaged in the sack and pulled out his timepiece. Twenty past eleven. 'There's something else.'

'What?'

Leroux dreaded telling Herzl the truth. But if he knew now, he might be able to salvage something from the mess.

'Your agreement is worthless, even if the Sultan survives.'

'You doubt his word?'

'If I'm right, the Sultan doesn't even know about the agreement. It makes no sense. I think the Grand Vizier is also plotting to overthrow the Sultan and restore their parliament. Maximoff has used him too. Probably told him that the Tsar supports them. That if they concoct this agreement and publish it, the Sultan will be weakened, ripe for a coup. But Maximoff has double-crossed him too.'

'But the agreement has the Sultan's seal. Approval for our settlement in Palestine. I've seen it,' Herzl protested.

'I've seen a decree authorising my own execution. It was written by the Grand Vizier in front of the Sultan, but the Sultan never touched it. The paper already had the seal inscribed, and there was a box full of that paper. It's done so that decrees can still be issued when the Sultan is somewhere else in his vast empire. All the Grand Vizier would need to do is acquire some of those pre-inscribed papers.'

'He would be risking his life to do that,' Herzl said.

'As does any traitor.'

'It was just smoke and mirrors all along?'

'The Sultan has played his enemies off against each other for a long time. And Maximoff found a way to use them all against him.'

'You think Nevlinski knew?'

'I doubt it. He didn't need to know. I think Maximoff used him too.'

'Do you have any proof of all this?'

'None.'

'What will you do?'

'I need you to trust me. Tell me the number of the safe deposit box and how to access it.'

Herzl blanched. Moments ago, he must have felt on the cusp of achieving his dreams, but now he was being asked to offer up the instrument of his destiny.

'Any minute now, Armenian revolutionaries are going to raid the Ottoman Bank and hold it hostage to force the Sultan to meet their demands. I don't know how it will turn out, but I am going into the bank with them. It may derail the Tsar's plan, forestall the rebellion in the east, and bring the British and French into Constantinople to maintain order. Or it may further weaken the Sultan. But I will make sure that your agreement stays secret and that Maximoff cannot use it to discredit the Sultan.'

Herzl looked blankly at the vast cemetery and the sun-bleached gravestones packed together on the hill. Was that all that awaited him? 'Perhaps one day, if the Sultan survives, we will be able to come to an agreement...' His voice trailed off. The cab had stopped again. Herzl pulled the window down, blinking as warm air wafted into the carriage. 'A part of me knew it was too good to be true. The box number is 274.' He fetched a chain with a small key on it from his inside pocket and handed it to Leroux. 'Make sure Maximoff doesn't get it.'

Leroux draped the key around his neck and added the Armenian cross from the sack. He clutched his old slouch hat and told the driver to head for the English School in Galata. They crested the hill and Herzl looked back over the shimmering waters of the Golden Horn and the gleaming dome of the Hagia Sophia. 'So, in the end, it was all about a prophecy. Just not the one I thought. You say that Christians will be united under the Tsar?'

'According to Nestor Iskander. He survived the fall of Byzantium and foretold that Moscow was the Third Rome and that there would be no fourth. All Christendom would unite under the Tsar's holy rule.'

'God help us! Try telling that to the Reverend!'

Leroux took his hand to say goodbye, Herzl's grip slacker than before.

'I nearly forgot. Do you know anything about an Armenian girl from the Sultan's harem helping me?'

Herzl shook his head slowly, lost in thought. Leroux closed the door.

'Keep away from anywhere Maximoff might look for you.'

Herzl opened one eye. 'You are a good mensch. Shall I tell Simpkins what you're up to?'

Leroux nodded and waved as the cab rolled away. He fingered the key around his neck. He had been made a fool of the first time he had met Herzl and lost the dossier. This time he would make it right. He turned to the small gathering huddled around the school gates. They were arguing and staring at him. Where were the rest of them?

Armen raised his hands to calm the group, perhaps a dozen in total.

'Papken and Hratch have gone to find the others,' he said.

Leroux stepped inside the wrought iron gates. The faculty had dispersed for the summer vacation. The front door opened a crack, and the bald head of the caretaker beckoned them. Half of the Armenians filed inside and gingerly carried sacks out of the doorway, suitably dressed as halals in brown jackets over homespun tops with loose baggy trousers cinched at the calf. They gently lifted them onto their shoulders, the awkward way they carried their loads at odds with their disguise. The rest were smartly dressed in bow ties as professors, which looked equally odd during the holidays. As they finished collecting the bombs, Hratch and Papken returned in their fitted pin striped suits with another dozen men and the arguing started again.

'Where are the rest? There's supposed to be seventy of us!'

Leroux checked his watch. Two minutes before noon. A few more stragglers arrived.

'We are thirty-one now,' Armen said, 'That is enough. Hand out the weapons.'

Hratch distributed a motley assortment of pistols. Some Reichsrevolvers, no doubt pilfered from the Ottoman military, and a few aging Colts. Each came with a hundred cartridges. Leroux needed more than the tiny British Bulldog in his pocket and stepped forward to take a Colt. He selected one he was familiar with, the cavalry model with the longer barrel. He weighed it in his hand, checking the action, and tucked it under his belt in the small of his back. Of the twenty-eight men and three women few appeared familiar with the weapons. One of the women was Eva, standing last in the line for a gun. Leroux pressed the British Bulldog into her hand and showed her the mechanics of firing and reloading.

The revolutionaries talked nervously, the anticipation building. They had no real idea what to expect. As the moment neared, they turned to prayer. Leroux wiped his hands in the grit and swayed from one foot to the other. With the rhythm of Tom's war dance in his head, he calmed his breathing, focusing on what needed to be done. He pushed the thought of the captain appearing in his sights from his thoughts, hoping it wouldn't come to that. Now Hratch gave a speech, in plain sight, with thirty armed revolutionaries loitering with bags full of bombs. Eva guarded a basket of them like a mother hen.

'Fellows,' Hratch said, 'today we shall fulfill our duty. We attack the Ottoman Bank, to hold it hostage until our demands are met by the European powers. Take care that no harm comes to the bank officers. Fire only on the army. Our password is freedom! The best shots will lead the assault. Save the last bullet for yourself!'

Leroux checked his watch again. They were running late, but there was no sign of any of the diversions. Perhaps they knew to wait until they heard firing.

Armen adjusted his bow tie and tugged Leroux's arm. 'Let's go.'

They walked briskly, confidently, and turned onto the financial street, Bankalar Cadesi, expecting the usual heavy police presence. The Ottoman Bank building stood head and shoulders above its neighbours, sixteen windows across and five stories high of classical stonework. Half the building was occupied by REGIE, the tobacco monopoly run by the French, but the main entrance facing onto the street was the bank's, a huge pair of plate glass doors at the top of a short flight of steps with wooden shutters splayed back behind a pair of giant Albanian guards. Armen and Leroux weaved through the pedestrians. The twitching moustache! Leroux swerved to the other side of Armen to avoid bumping into the Sultan's agent. Leroux pulled his hat down. The agent was looking to his left, dressed in a casual suit now, paper under his arm. Somehow, the man had not seen him. Leroux searched for Simpkins, perhaps he was here and being followed, but Armen steered him towards the steps and the agent disappeared in the crowd.

The Albanians stood to attention, rifle butts grounded, resplendent in white triple pleated skirts that skimmed their knees, matching red waistcoats and leggings, gold sash cummerbunds and slippers with upturned toes. But there was no doubting their steely stares. Two Ottoman soldiers in dark tunics and trousers approached from either side, about faced, and continued pacing along the street façade.

Armen turned to Leroux and placed a hand on Leroux's shoulder, gripping hard as much for support as encouragement. They nodded to each other, pushed their chests out and mounted the steps. The Albanians ignored them, and two doormen pulled the glass doors open from inside. They hit the cool air of the marble hall and their footsteps echoed between the pillars. Perspiration chilled on Leroux's neck as the bank murmured with hushed conversations and the discreet counting of bills during the lull of the European lunch hour.

Armen approached a bald Italian teller, to exchange money, while Leroux waited in an adjacent queue to make a deposit. Gold Napoleons clinked loudly on the counter as Armen placed them and requested French currency. All appeared normal to Leroux. No sign of extra security and only a dozen customers to worry about. The teller dealt out francs methodically. Armen scooped up the money and turned, forgetting to thank the Italian. Leroux caught his eye, slowly lowering his gaze. Be calm. Armen paused, patted his pockets, and slowly swaggered out through the main doors and raised a hand to his eyes. Nothing happened. Leroux was one customer from the counter, ready to deter any heroes among the staff. Armen descended a few steps and waved as if hailing a cab, shielding his eyes from the sun again, and then reached inside his coat.

Six brothers-in-arms broke from the stream of passers-by, hands going to their waistbands. Three in pin stripe suits and three dressed as professors. Their job was to deal with the guards and hold the doors until the others joined them with the bombs, dynamite, and ammunition. The first, Shorty Hohvannes, squat and strong, drew quickly, too quickly and hastily fired twice at the nearest Albanian. He missed. Shorty panicked, or his gun jammed. The guard recovered his poise, looked almost indignant at dealing with someone who couldn't hit him at point blank range and levelled his rifle. Shorty collapsed on the pavement. Armen shot the guard, but the second Albanian dashed inside and up the main flight of stairs. Leroux let him go to avoid starting a gunfight just as the customers and staff sought safety.

The small group of Armenians bunched in the entrance, shouting to their comrades. The first Albanian was dead, and the two other soldiers had fled. Shop doors slammed, iron shutters rattled down and carriages careened away as people scampered every which way, clutching their hats and newspapers. The rest of the raiders, almost two dozen, ran with their sacks of ammunition to the steps just as ten gendarmes came out of a side entrance, rifles in hand. They looked up and down the street, unsure what was going on. The last of the pedestrians swirled past them, clearing the field of fire. The officer glanced at the entrance, the fallen soldiers, the gaggle of bandits brandishing weapons in the doorway, the ragtag group of people rushing to join them and bellowed an order. The soldiers lined up and took aim. The Armenians sprinted pell-mell to the steps firing wildly with their handguns.

'Fire!' Smoke puffs erupted along the line and then the crash of the volley echoed in the street. Six men sprawled on the ground, plucked by the hail of bullets that riddled the stonework. The rest bundled between the pillars flanking the entrance as Papken Siuni bought up the rear with a sack full of bombs. A second volley rippled out, less disciplined than the first, firing virtually blind behind the smoke that hung in the still air. Only one bullet hit home. A bright flash filled the doorway, and the blast knocked Leroux off his feet. A hail of shrapnel peppered the pillar in front of him, his ears ringing as his cheek pressed on the cold marble floor. He blinked against the choking dust. There was no sign of Papken. The glass doors were shattered, and scraps of clothing floated down amidst the smoke outside. Two contorted bodies crowned the steps, at the edge of safety. Those merely wounded by the first volley were surely finished. The bullet had hit Papken's bag of explosives.

Leroux stumbled to his feet as sixteen shaken Armenians staggered into the deserted hall, slack-jawed and ashen-faced. The customers and cashiers had fled up the main staircase after the Albanian. Armen crouched behind a column, ten paces back from the entrance, and Leroux scrambled over to him. A soldier ran across the street and down a side road, drawing a smattering of inaccurate fire from two revolutionaries who had maintained their composure and manned the entrance.

Armen stared after him, glassy eyed, his face smeared in grime, visibly shaken by Papken's fate.

'Armen,' Leroux said. No response.

Leroux shook his arm and shouted into his ear. 'Armen! You're in charge now.'

Armen snapped out of his nightmare and cast about him.

'There's only a twenty of us left...' He pulled out a hipflask and took a swig, passing it to Leroux, who tilted it to the ceiling and gulped some of the firewater.

'To Armenian spirit!' Armen said. He took another gulp. 'Let's get on with it.'

Only two of the men assigned to shut the doors and barricade the entrance lived. The heavy plate glass had gone, and the wooden shutters lay flat against the outside wall. Two attempts to sortie out and close them were met with a shower of lead, and they couldn't afford to lose any more men. Leroux had not heard one of the planned diversions take effect, and it was all they could do to fire out from behind the door jams and pillars to keep the soldiers at bay. Volley fire hammered the entrance, ricocheting off the pillars, raining plaster down from the ceiling. At least it stopped the floor becoming slick with blood.

'Those soldiers appeared quickly,' Leroux said.

'It's cost us some good comrades,' Armen said more confident now, 'But we can still hold the bastards off.'

'Did the men detailed to secure the roof make it? One of the guards ran up there.'

Armen looked over his shoulder. 'I don't know. I need to stay here, will you look?'

Leroux dashed for the stairs. Five fighters positioned themselves at first floor windows and lined their bombs up by their feet. That should

289

give the soldiers plenty to think about for now. Down in the hall many of the Armenians struggled to aim correctly and fumbled as they reloaded. Their fire was enough to deter the score or so of soldiers outside, but it wouldn't be long before reinforcements arrived.

Hratch conferred with Armen and then took the stairs two at a time with a comrade called Eki. 'Where are the bank officers?'

Leroux pointed to the other side of the internal balcony overlooking the atrium where numerous doors led to offices. A head timorously peeked out of the nearest one. Hratch strode over but it slammed shut.

He hammered on the door. 'We do not want to hurt you. We are only here to demand protection for the Armenian people, to request that the European powers intervene. If you help us no harm will come to you. But if we are attacked, we will blow the bank up rather than surrender.'

A tall red-haired man edged out of the next office. 'I'll help you,' he said calmly.

Leroux left them to it and bounded up the next flight as hurried footsteps fled up the building ahead of him. Where was the other Albanian guard? He edged around the half landing, checking the next staircase, revolver first. Still the footsteps went up. The roof?

Up he went and a door banged still higher. Another floor and he was there. He tested the handle – not locked – and eased it open. Through the crack he saw the back of the distinctive Albanian uniform walking carefully along the parapet. Leroux stepped out. Behind the Albanian was a distinguished looking man with snow white hair and beard in a morning coat. The Albanian turned, brandishing his rifle, but not aiming it at Leroux, his fingers flexing on the stock, hovering above the trigger.

Leroux kept his revolver pointing down, moving calmly. They eyed one another, each at the other's mercy, neither making a sudden movement. Killing should be a deliberate act, not an unnecessary or careless reaction. There might be a shoot-out going on, but nobody needed to do anything foolish. The banker about-faced like a Coldstream guard.

'Who are you?'

'Peter Leroux. I'm in Constantinople for Rear Admiral Beaumont, Director of Naval of Intelligence –'

'Yes, I know who Lewis is.' He kept a sharp eye on the door over Leroux's shoulder. 'I am Sir Edgar Vincent, the governor of the bank. What the deuce is going on?'

The Albanian held his rifle steady, eyes fixed on Leroux.

'That's a longer story than we have time for. The revolutionaries will be up here any minute – do you have a way out?'

'Yes, there's another door at the end of the roof. Leads down into the other half of the building, the part occupied by the Tobacco concession. We can get out on to a side street from there.'

Leroux cocked his head. 'Someone's coming. The raiders are Armenians. They don't want to harm anyone. They just want assurances from the Sultan. Go quickly. I'll make sure the others are looked after.'

The guard looked from Leroux to Sir Edgar without comprehending, and Sir Edgar looked puzzled, but self-preservation won over curiosity, and he summoned the Albanian. They hurried along the remainder of the roof and disappeared down the far staircase. Leroux barricaded the door shut after them with some loose planks and bricks as a studious looking lad named Setrak appeared with a bag of bombs and an old Colt pistol.

'You know how to fire that?'

He grinned, shot his arm up in the air and pulled the trigger. There was no time for details, point and shoot was good enough to cover the roof. 'Stay here and stop anyone who tries to come through that door.' The lad nodded and made himself comfortable, sitting back against the casement, gun pointed between his knees at the door. A street away an Armenian called Levon waved from the top of the English School. Leroux signalled back and Levon scurried off to alert the embassies.

Over the harbour, past the entrance to the Golden Horn, the steel warships of the Great Powers rode at anchor. A white ensign fluttered from the stern of one, two tall masts bracketing dormant double smokestacks in the middle. Her deadly guns pointed forward flush with the deck, towards the strange, inverted bow, which raked backwards and was believed to increase speed. Armen would be disappointed that the governor had escaped. He was a high value hostage, but Leroux had been at a stand-off with the guard and the governor would argue hard for anything that would save his staff. Hopefully he could persuade Currie to land a contingent of British marines before the Ottomans could respond in force and overwhelm the paltry Armenian force. Leroux returned to where Hratch and Eki had gathered the bank staff and customers into the first-floor dining room. There were well over a hundred of them, shepherded by just two. The red-haired man spoke, an Irishman by the sound of it, calming the skittish staff. Leroux turned to the windows. A fighter flattened himself against the wall next to one, occasionally taking a squint outside. More soldiers gathered in the street, forming up, preparing for an assault. The Armenians were hopelessly outnumbered. Leroux pounded down the steps to the entrance hall. Armen flitted from comrade to comrade, geeing them up but warning them to conserve ammunition. Eva followed handing out cartridges from a leather satchel slung over her slender shoulder.

'Only fire when they threaten the doorway,' Armen called out. They had given up trying to close the shutters and had pushed some tables, chairs and a cabinet into the breach and reinforced them with a second row of heavy desks.

'We've got the bombs,' Armen said hopefully, looking at the woefully inadequate barrier. Leroux weighed one of the rudimentary devices in his hand. So far, the bombs had killed more of the raiders than anyone else.

'They're coming!' one of the lads upstairs called.

'Where?' Armen said.

'From the sides, along the wall,' the young man called Misak said, who guarded one of the windows above the atrium.

'Drop bombs on them.'

The first one fell. A shriek outside and a scrambling of boots on cobblestones. Leroux turned a table over in front of the staircase facing the entrance and cocked his gun, praying he wouldn't have to use it. The bomb exploded and one of the soldiers had not run away quickly enough, his stomach-churning shrieks drowning out the chaos. The firing stopped and the screams shrunk to a whimper as the patter of footsteps receded.

'That should make them pause for a while,' Armen said, peering down the street. The Turks positioned men to fire at the windows to cover their next attack.

Misak called out another warning.

'Get ready and don't show yourself at the windows!' Armen shouted.

Misak struck a match and edged to the opening. He lit the fuse and stretched out his arm to drop it and was met with a burst of gunfire, splintering the window frame. He fumbled the bomb, cursing. It hadn't exploded but rolled at his feet, the fuse smoking. Misak scrabbled, picked it up and heaved it out, but was raked by gunfire. He staggered back, and toppled over the balcony, landing in the middle of the marble hall with a sickening thud just as the bomb detonated outside. One of his friends screamed and leapt out from behind a pillar, firing angry shots over the barricade, yelling obscenities. He was met by another fusillade, splintering the chairs and desks, and one bullet ripped through his gut. His hands clutched at his belly, and he stumbled, toppling towards two comrades manning the entrance. Leroux watched in horror, grabbed Armen, and rolled him behind a pillar. The man had a bomb attached to his belt, and it detonated as he fell. The blast shook the hall, gore splattering against the columns. Leroux felt a searing pain in his calf, steeled himself and glanced around the pillar. The young man's body was unrecognisable, and the two others lay prostrate on the floor, their legs shattered.

The first had lost one leg below the knee, his other leg a bloody pulp. He hauled himself over the debris, trailing a crimson smear, and propped himself up by the door, his face ghostly white. His arm shook as he raised it, grunting through gritted teeth, aiming it between a gap in the defences. He pulled the trigger, and the recoil knocked his arm against the wall. Panting he struggled to lift his arm again, tears streaming down his face. He fired again just as his body was shredded by rifle fire. His mop of curly dark hair fell forward, and he slumped to the floor, stone dead. His companion sat in the middle of the floor on ruined legs begging for mercy, clutching the stump of an arm, which pulsed blood. Eva crawled towards him and tore a strip of her green dress to use as a tourniquet, but the young lad's eyes bulged with pain and he suddenly put his revolver to his mouth and fired, jerking his body backwards.

'No, oh God, no,' Armen said. Eva scrambled over the floor towards them, wiping blood from her face, but still in control, focused. She pointed at Leroux's leg, tore another strip from her dress and opened her water bottle. Her eyes blazed with determination as she cleaned the wound, a ragged tear in his calf. Leroux gritted his teeth as she dug out a piece of shrapnel with a knife, rinsed the laceration and bound it. Outside, orders echoed down the street. The bomb had destroyed the middle of the barricade, and the soldiers were alert to the chaos in the bank and prepared to take advantage. Shouts rang out as men bulled themselves up, and through the smoke soldiers zig zagged, forming into groups. A row of soldiers fired constantly at the windows, and some had positioned themselves in the buildings opposite where rifles poked out of the first-floor windows, firing straight across at the bank. Others fired into the barricade, forcing the defenders away from it. The Armenians regrouped behind the hall pillars, shooting back incessantly, if ineffectively. Armen reloaded, checking his bandolier. 'I've used fifty already!' The return fire grew hotter through the dust and smoke. Anything exposed in the hall was swept with lead. The commands of the Turkish officers grew louder and closer.

'Inside, men!' one officer shouted, his sword whirling above his head before pointing straight at the entrance.

Armen grabbed Leroux's arm. 'Here they come.'

Bayonets bristled through the smoke as they climbed the steps, but none of the Turkish fire hit home. The revolutionaries fired desperately, a last-ditch attempt to defend the doorway. If the bayonets charged, they would surely be overrun. Armen shot the leading Turk pushing through the wreckage of the barricade just as two bombs dropped outside. A second Turk fell dead, and with a shout of alarm the bayonet tips backed down the steps, despite the cursing of the officers. A flash, the floor shook, and a thunderous crash followed by screams. The barricade was matchwood now, but the Turks had retreated. Only one of the Armenians, Sarkis, had been injured in the thrust, and Eva scampered over. A bullet had torn through the bicep of his shooting arm. The revolutionaries had no medicine, so she tipped a hip flask over the seeping hole and wound a cloth around it. And then picked up the gun herself.

There were perilously few of the raiders left. One on the roof. Hratch and Eki with the staff. Just fourteen to man the windows and door, four of whom were injured. The Armenians, elated that the soldiers had retreated, still poured fire out the door.

'Get rid of some of the bombs,' Leroux said, 'save the bullets.'

Armen and Leroux lobbed a couple of bombs over the wreckage and the last soldiers ran out of view.

'Cease fire!' Amen called out hoarsely. The bombs exploded, a powerful reminder to the Turks of what awaited, and the din of their gunfire subsided. The soldiers withdrew to each end of the street, and they settled into an eerie informal truce. A haze of blue smoke and white dust hung in the hall, masking the movements of the revolutionaries. Armen knelt by each fighter whispering words of encouragement. Even those that had shown they could shoot looked bewildered by the intensity of the battle. Armen collected bombs from those that carried them in their belts. They could not afford any more accidents and he stored them safely out of the field of fire ready for their last stand. Leroux raised his canteen and let the water tumble into his mouth, but his tongue still felt as dry as the summer dirt of the Great Karoo desert back home. He wondered if he would ever see it again and coughed, the sulphureous fumes sharp in his nose. Leroux cocked his head. The street was unnaturally quiet, but in the distance a faint though raucous noise grew.

'Armen!' Ashot called down from the balcony.

Everyone looked up. What was that sound?

'Armen! There's smoke rising from the Armenian quarter!'

Leroux ran up the stairs and joined Ashot. He was right and the noise grew, drums banging, shouting, breaking glass, axes splintering wood. Riots had broken out. And at the end of their street young Turks gathered pointing towards the bank.

'There's fighting in the city,' Ashot said. 'A mob is heading this way.'

Leroux sprinted up to the roof. Setrak looked out over the city to where flames scorched the sky, tears in his eyes.

'My parents live there. What have we done?'

'Keep alert,' Leroux said, an arm around Setrak's shoulder. 'The sooner negotiations begin the better it will be for everybody.' Setrak bit his lip and nodded as a gust of wind carried the bedlam of the mob. Armen joined them. On the bridge and at the crossroads beyond the police watched idly as roughnecks set about passers-by and swarmed towards the Armenian district, and at the end of their street the mob grew.

'The Sultan is letting this happen,' Armen said. 'He'd rather they vented their frustration on us than have it linger and fester. They're ransacking our quarter. The soldiers are just standing by, doing nothing.'

'Did you have the feeling you were being followed recently?' Leroux said.

'I always have that feeling, but we took extra precautions in recent weeks.'

'Do you think the Sultan knew about this raid?'

'It's possible, his spies are everywhere. He probably knew we were planning something, but not the precise target.'

A dark thought crossed Leroux's mind. Had he led them to Armen's hideout? Had that agent with the twitching moustache been following him all the time?

'I may have led the police to you,' Leroux said, 'there's a man I've seen a few times today and yesterday who works for the Sultan.'

Armen shook his head. 'There were supposed to be seventy-five of us today. Where are the rest? Any one of them could have been picked up by the police and talked.'

'Doesn't it feel like they were expecting us?'

'No. Why?'

'The speed with which they responded. The way the police are allowing the rioters free reign, as though they wanted you to do this – to give them an excuse to stand aside and let the mob take out their grievances.'

'Constantinople must be getting to you. If they really knew how few we are, it would be over already.'

'What do you think they're waiting for?'

Armen looked over the ledge. 'Disagreeing about how to proceed. The Sultan probably wants to crush us. But the French and British won't want the bank destroyed or the lives of their employees risked.'

At the end of the street a squad of artillerymen unlimbered a field gun and led the horses away. Riflemen appeared on the neighbouring roofs and Leroux pointed them out to Setrak.

'Keep your head down, they'll pick you off if they can see you. If they try to force the door, drop a bomb. We'll hear that.'

The young lad's hand trembled as he took some matches. Armen and Leroux went back down to check on the hostages and asked the red-haired Irishman to address them again.

'Do not be afraid. These men are not bandits. They are revolutionaries. They have no wish to hurt you.'

Nearly one hundred and fifty bodies crammed together, more a prisoner of their own ignorance than the guards. Hratch kept his gun on the Irishman and said: 'If you cooperate you will not be harmed. But we have dynamited the building and if you try and escape, we will not hesitate to blow it up.'

A gasp swept through the room, and a few began to sob. 'Do not be concerned,' Hratch said, 'the Great Powers will negotiate. It is in your interest to encourage them. When they come, you will send a representative to plead our case.'

'What makes you think they will bargain with you?' a timourous voice said.

'Be patient,' Hratch said, as confidently as he could. An assured middle-aged man stepped forward. He smoothed his thinning dark hair over to the side and introduced himself. 'I am Mr Aubineau. I have dealt with the Ambassadors before. I will speak for us when the time comes. What are your demands?'

Leroux ushered Armen aside, while Hratch spoke with Mr Aubineau. 'When the representatives arrive, they will want to see that nothing has been taken from the vault. Has it been secured?'

Armen shrugged his shoulders. 'No one was assigned to that, and I doubt anyone's had the time.'

'I'll see to it.'

'I'll send someone down to help you,' Armen said.

Leroux took the main staircase to the ground floor where Eva tended to the wounded and Sarkis dozed peacefully nearby. The others huddled in small groups whispering as though they feared that raising their voice would draw gunfire. They didn't have enough ammunition to trade bullet for bullet and needed to better block the entrance. Leroux roused up the unwounded and started with the filing cabinets. He left them to it and retreated to the vault, past the counters and down a couple of steps at the back of the building.

The steel door hung ajar and inside a table was covered by bundles of banknotes and heaps of coins either side of two open ledgers, pens abandoned in the centrefolds. The tellers had fled, and nothing had been touched. Deposit boxes lined the walls, orderly and peaceful, little rectangular metal drawers with a keyhole. The right-hand corner of the room was caged off protecting a squat stack of bullion. Leroux tested the door. Locked. Next to that a cast iron safe lay bare, its door wide open, the contents presumably being audited on the table. Leroux ran his hand along the deposit boxes, until his finger rested on number two seven four. He pulled the key over his neck just as footsteps clattered down the steps. The key fitted and he slid out the box which contained a single piece of thick parchment, foolscap size, folded in three. He slipped it into his jacket pocket and pushed the box in, but the key wouldn't turn. Leroux left it, continued around the wall, and tested the iron cage again just as Armen entered with Mr Aubineau and two secretaries carrying sheaves of paper.

'As you can see, we are not bandits,' Armen said. 'Everything is in order, not one gold coin has been touched. These are our demands, write six copies.' The secretaries cleared a space and sat at the table.

Armen began: 'We, the Armenian Revolutionary Federation are in control of the Ottoman Bank and shall not leave until the following conditions are met:

1.   Stop the massacre now occurring in Constantinople.

2.   Stop the armed attack on the bank, or else we will blow up the building when our ammunition is exhausted.

3.   Give written guarantees concerning the enactment of reforms for the protection of the Armenian population as delivered in a communication to the embassies today.

4.   Set free all Armenian revolutionaries detained because of current events.

Armen Garo

On behalf of, The Central Committee, Armenian Revolutionary Federation.

Armen flicked through one of the ledgers as the secretaries' pens scratched out the copies. Four hours had passed since they had taken control. Levon must have contacted all the embassies by now. The Ambassadors would be discussing what to do with the Sultan. That probably explained why the soldiers were holding off, but the mob gathering at the end of the street was ominous. They were easier to fight than the soldiers, but the Armenians were low on ammunition and the situation could spiral out of control. The last thing anyone wanted was for them to have their hand forced and dynamite the bank.

The secretaries finished their work and Hratch and Armen signed the papers and instructed the tellers to complete the audit of the safe contents and verify nothing had been taken. One secretary would take a copy of the terms to the Sultan at Yildiz and Mr Aubineau and the other secretary would go to the embassies.

The key chain hung conspicuously from the deposit box, but the tellers paid it no notice and focused on the banknotes, coins, and bullion.

Armen left them to it and took a white tablecloth from the dining room and waved it from a window. The Turks had crept forward unmolested to drag away their fallen and one of them called up.

'Are you surrendering?'

'No. We want to send two negotiators out. They are employees of the bank.'

The soldier withdrew a few paces and called out to an officer.

'Send them.'

They dared not risk dismantling the barricade at the door, so Hratch rummaged up a ladder from the storeroom and lowered it from a first-floor window. The two secretaries needed no encouragement to leave, clinging grimly to the rungs and hurrying down the street with the soldier, one mopping his brow with a handkerchief.

Armen and Hratch turned to more mundane matters. The rooms away from the street overlooking the Golden Horn were designated as sleeping quarters, although the continuing din from the riots would make sleep impossible. The mangled bodies wrecked by their own bombs were covered in sheets. They had attempted to hide their lack of numbers from the secretaries by rotating every different fighter past them. During the negotiations they would keep the staff upstairs in the dining room to prevent any communication. They took stock of their ammunition - just over twenty cartridges each and eighteen bombs.

The mob edged down the street and the soldiers moved to block the path, but without conviction and backed away before any clash. This apparent triumph spurred the crowd and their chants and pace picked up.

'The mob's coming!' Leroux shouted down to the hall. There were hundreds of them but armed only with sticks and axes. They howled up at the windows and tore at the barricade.

Leroux took careful aim at a tall burly man with extravagant whiskers and a fez who seemed to be one of the leaders. He knocked his hat off, but it only seemed to inspire him, and he dragged a table from the entrance. Those with axes hacked at the barricade, undeterred by the pistol shots that knocked their neighbours down, as each one was replaced by two more, clawing at the obstacles. One man, in a cream kaftan struggled to the top of the heap with a cudgel and screamed 'Allahu Akbar!' He leapt down into the hall but was hit by a shot from Sarkis and fell at the base of the first column. Eva stretched forward and pulled the club from the man's limp hands. The horde, sensing a breakthrough was imminent, surged and the barrier began to buckle under the strain. Ashot, and three others called Ruben, Mkhitar and Arakel rushed to brace themselves against it.

'We can't waste any more bullets,' Hratch shouted above the bedlam. 'Drop the bombs.'

Three fighters at the window lit fuses. Leroux leaned out, searching for someone in command. A Turkish officer leant against a doorway opposite. Leroux fired at the door jamb above his head to get his attention and shouted. 'Bombs!' Tell them to run!'

But it was too late. Three cannonballs dropped into the throng, fuses smoking. Those close enough to notice the danger desperately tried to run away, but only stumbled into their neighbours. Some fell and were trampled. The panic spread like wildfire, and the mob stampeded, but not fast enough. The detonations ripped through the crowd, leaving a swathe of bloodied bodies, many still alive, writhing in agony. As the last of the mob streamed away the soldiers closed the street. An officer strode calmly forward over the broken bodies and looked up at the windows. The injured begged for help. No one fired. He bent to lift one of the injured under the arms and waved at his men to help him. In ones and twos, the soldiers came forward to take the wounded first, and then the dead, away.

Armen and Hratch looked out over the carnage. The din of the rioting across the Armenian quarter began to rise again.

'Just ten rounds each and fifteen bombs left,' Armen said.

'And the explosives,' Hratch said. They had always said they would dynamite the bank rather than surrender. It was their ace card. The move the Turks couldn't beat. And easy to say. But now they paused, looking at each other, waiting for a better suggestion. Finally, Armen said: 'We'd better prepare them before they attack again.'

Hratch checked on the men and women that remained of their force. Nearly half had died and five more were injured. The only medicine they had was brandy. On the steps outside, their dead comrades from the initial assault had been left by the Turks and were now bathed in a yellow glow as the streetlights fired up. One of the bank managers came out of the dining hall to show Armen how to turn the bank's lights on and to ask for food.

Leroux adjusted the torn rag that dressed his wound. Eva appeared, her thin hand pressing his hard as she applied a little of the spirit from her hipflask. She had found a cane in one of the offices and gave it to Leroux. It had a nice weight, good quality hardwood with a carved horn handle.

No match for his old knobkerrie, a king among fighting sticks, but good enough to walk on. He had not dwelt on the loss of his stick at the beginning of this journey. When his bad luck had started. Tom had given it to him, a beautiful stick fashioned from blackwood, the hardest he knew. The bulb at the end had given it balance and clout without being too conspicuous. Now it was gone, as was Tom. And Lara, and his father. If there was an afterlife, perhaps they weren't so far away.

What were the embassies waiting for? The pillaging in the city showed no sign of abating, and the soldiers showed no interest in stopping it. At least they seemed in no hurry to storm the bank. Hratch assigned Mkhitar and Arakel to rebuild the barricade again while Ruben and Ashot went to find cooks among the hostages and returned triumphant as an amiable Greek in an apron bought cold meat, macaroni, and cans of sardines while his assistant distributed bottles of beer.

'Listen,' Armen said. 'The city is quieter. The rioting is stopping.'

Hratch put his plate down. 'You're right. Do you think they are trying to meet our demands. Do you think they will negotiate now?'

'When they come,' Leroux said, 'Make sure they see the dynamite strapped to the pillars. It may be the only deterrent when they see how few we are.'

Ashok appeared with a satchel and a glum face. 'We only have one bag of dynamite left. Papken must have been carrying the others.'

'Then fill bags with anything we can find,' Leroux said. 'Strap them to the pillars and the outside of the dining hall. No-one will know the difference. Put the real explosives by the entrance. That might give them second thoughts if they try to storm the barricade again.'

Thursday, 27th August, Constantinople

A whistle blew outside, and the bank clock struck midnight.

'They've bought up two more cannons,' Armen said.

Troops funnelled into both ends of the street and arranged themselves in ranks four deep.

'Get ready.' Armen shouted. The men at the windows darted quick looks out. The informal truce had held, but no one knew the rules. The Turks posted in the building opposite hadn't fired for hours but leaned behind their sights aiming at the bank's windows. The Armenians lined up their few remaining bombs. Armen came to Leroux and handed him a box of matches. 'If they breach the barricade, detonate the explosives.'

Leroux turned the matches over in his hand. At least the staff in the dining room should be safe, even if the fighters in the hall would be buried when the roof above the hall collapsed. A death sentence was all that awaited Leroux outside of the bank, twice over – murder and terrorism. He clutched his chest and felt the reassuring crinkle of the agreement. He would destroy that too, stuffing it in the bag of explosives as he set the fuse, rather than risk Maximoff making use of it. The bastard.

What a fool Leroux had been. Beaumont had warned him of the dangers of Constantinople. How many times had he been deceived by Maximoff, right under his nose? He reloaded his Colt. A trusty gun he was familiar with. The face of the man he had killed with one flashed before him. The man who killed his father. He had caught up with him and taken his revenge in cold blood. Now things were catching up with Leroux. He opened the cylinder. Six bullets. He touched the last one. It looked like all the rest. Nothing special. Would he use it? He finished fixing the yellow leather bag of explosives to the pillar just above his head and crouched, covering the entrance.

Across the hall, Eva bought a glass of water to Sarkis's lips, as he drifted in and out of consciousness, the dressing on his arm sodden, the stain seeping over his chest, his brow glistening and the dark stubble on his cheek only emphasising his pallour. Eva clutched his pistol in her tiny hand and caught Leroux's eye. She would not hesitate to use it or the last bullet. He told himself she would not have to. When the time came, he would send her to the roof. The lad up there knew the door out and they might be able to slip away. Something good had to come of all this.

It was Christmas when he had fallen in love with Lara, under the tree that looked over the river at home. Just whispering her name snatched at his heart. She had died helping Leroux, at the hands of a vengeful German agent. He could not bear to lose someone else. Lara was why he was here, why he had stayed in the service of the British Empire. He had sworn revenge, but their paths had not crossed again, and now he was cornered, surrounded by destruction. The misshapen lumps covered by tablecloths, the debris, the barricade, all stirred the memories of his time with the Boer commando, defending the wagons. The heap of bodies that piled up before them. Perhaps it was fitting that he would die here. Leroux crept forward to look out. Three cannons were sited along the street with just enough angle to blast the barricade. It wouldn't last one volley. Rows of troops waited, just out of throwing range of the bombs. The fighters manning the windows crossed themselves and mumbled last prayers. Armen knelt next to him.

'We won't hold against the cannon,' Leroux said.

'Remember the dynamite.'

Eva looked over, a sadness in her eyes, sadder even than the night he had found her under the altar. What had happened to Simpkins? He was a good man. He would be urging Currie to insist on negotiations.

'Somethings happening,' Ashot shouted from above. The formation of soldiers shuffled forward and then split into two creating a passage between them. An officer emerged from the gap, striding forward. Leroux recognised the gait, and now the moustache. It was Captain Emre, the Sultan's most trusted soldier, leading from the front. Behind him, a hulking figure with a curly mane of dark hair, Maximoff. Leroux sighted down the long barrel of his Colt. He could drop him now, get it over with. But that would destroy any hope Armen had and would give Russia even more justification for attacking. And Leroux would die in disgrace, no one knowing the truth about Maximoff. Was the Russian so desperate to get the agreement that he would go in with the first wave of the assault? Come and get it.

'Hold your fire,' Armen commanded.

'They want to talk!' Ashot cried out.

Leroux blinked. He stared down his gun's sight at the captain, his breath leaking out as the captain unfurled a white flag, swaying it from side to side. Armen scrabbled to his feet and dashed upstairs to join Hratch at the window. Mr Aubineau appeared alongside the captain,

309

hopping from foot to foot, his lantern swaying, almost shaking, still in his pinstripe trousers and waistcoat.

'I know the soldier,' Leroux called up to Armen, 'he can be trusted.'

'The Ambassadors are here to speak to you,' Mr Aubineau called out.

'It might be a trick,' Ashok said. 'Why are they coming so late at night?'

'Steady lads,' Armen said, 'this is the moment we came for.'

Armen stood square in the window. 'Come forward.'

Behind the captain, Maximoff, Ambassador Currie and the Grand Vizier emerged from the shadows and marched behind the captain. All appeared unarmed except Maximoff who rested a hand on a cavalry sword slung low from his belt.

'Leroux,' Hratch called down, 'make a passage with Ruben to let them in.' The two of them opened one end of the barricade while Hratch arranged every spare fighter around the balcony overlooking the hall.

The captain approached the barricade alone, the flag of truce held forward, and his gleaming boots crunched on broken glass as he entered the hall, his military eye taking in the positions of the fighters and the explosives.

'Where are the employees?' the captain said, showing no surprise at seeing Leroux.

'They're all safe. Upstairs.' Leroux said.

Armen and Hratch descended the main staircase together, pistols tucked into their belts, and Leroux melted into the background. He knew what he had to do and hurried back to the vault. The last copy of the revolutionaries' list of demands lay on the counting table, inscribed on thick Ottoman Bank notepaper. Leroux folded it and pocketed it with Herzl's agreement. The key still hung conspicuously from the deposit box. It could work. He crept back into the hall to join Eva.

The captain called to the diplomats to bring them in. Maximoff abruptly shoved part of the barrier, as though he was too big to fit through the gap and strode past Mr Aubineau to the centre of the hall, Ambassador Currie and the Grand Vizier following stiffly behind.

'You rabble have our attention,' Maximoff said. 'Do not waste it.'

Armen turned to the captain. 'Who are we negotiating with?'

'The Grand Vizier is here on behalf of the Sultan. Dragoman Maximoff is here as the representative of the Tsar, protector of Armenians in Ottoman Lands. Ambassador Currie is here as the representative of Britain and France, the owners of the Ottoman Bank. Each has an interest in the outcome.'

Maximoff towered over Hratch and Armen, his dress shirt unbuttoned at the neck and his frockcoat hung open displaying his sword. Leroux slipped behind the pillar next to Eva, but Ambassador Currie caught sight of him, his eyes full of disdain. Had Herzl not managed to find Simpkins? Did Currie not suspect the Russian at all?

Maximoff turned to the balcony and the windows and laughed derisively. 'So few? Listen! I am authorised to take you to a steamship in the harbour. Your safety will be guaranteed, and you will leave Constantinople tomorrow. I suggest you agree quickly before anyone changes their mind.'

'Our safety is the least of our concerns,' Armen replied evenly. 'What about our other demands?'

311

Maximoff coloured and his hand clenched on the hilt of his sword.

'The riots have already stopped, as have the soldiers attempts to take the bank. Is this not true your excellency?' Maximoff turned to the Grand Vizier who nodded in agreement. 'As to the reforms for the protection of Armenians, you have our word that we will reach a satisfactory solution.' The Grand Vizier nodded again, as did Currie.

It was a more than fair offer. To get the signatures of the Great Powers to such a sensitive agreement in the middle of the night was impractical and the word of the Grand Vizier and Currie, if not Maximoff, could be relied on. And waiting until dawn risked the riots starting again. Leroux knew it was a good offer, one that Armen ought to accept. But Maximoff wasn't interested in the Armenians' demands, he needed them out of the way, the British and French subjects unthreatened, and Herzl's agreement in his hands so that he could press on with his plan. Leroux stepped out from the pillar. Currie glowered. It was late and no doubt he had been torn away from an agreeable dinner. Maximoff followed the Ambassador's gaze and a look of alarm flashed across his face.

'There is no massacre now,' Armen said, 'but what guarantee do we have that the riots won't resume again tomorrow after we have departed?'

Maximoff returned his attention to Armen. 'What guarantee do you want?'

'The landing of British and French sailors.'

'Out of the question,' Maximoff said, 'Russia is absolutely opposed to any armed intervention in the internal affairs of the Ottoman Empire. That is non-negotiable.'

The captain took a copy of the list of demands from Mr Aubineau and shook it at Armen. 'Everything you asked for has been agreed. You have the word of the Ambassadors.'

'There is sympathy for your plight,' Ambassador Currie said. 'But if you refuse this offer and the hostages are harmed, public opinion will swiftly turn against you. It is a good offer, accept it.'

Armen and Hratch whispered to each other as their comrades looked on anxiously. Surely, they would accept. They had the word of the Ambassadors on all their demands. But Maximoff could not be trusted. Leroux imagined the Tsar's fleet steaming across the Black Sea. What Maximoff needed right now was to prevent French and British soldiers landing, and if possible, get his hands on Herzl's document. When news of the massacre broke, he would say the Sultan had broken the agreement and proceed with his invasion. But if Leroux could expose Maximoff as a liar and the Ambassador and the Sultan believed Leroux's accusations, there was a chance that they could forestall the rebellion, stand by the Sultan, and spike Maximoff's plans.

'Ambassador, what is the news from London tonight?' Leroux said.

Currie chuntered. 'The Times is leading with the Armenian massacre at Akrag, accusing the Sultan, and demanding he faces consequences. I hope you're pleased with yourself. Ignoring orders, gallivanting around. This is the result!'

'I also have some demands,' Maximoff said imperiously, 'I must verify that certain items in the custody of the bank have not been violated.'

'The bank tellers can attest that not a single piastre is missing,' Armen said.

'I will be the judge of that,' Maximoff said.

Leroux tested his leg. The bandage was wet, and a trickle of blood ran down his ankle, but he could put weight on it and run if he had to. Maximoff was after the agreement. Did he know the number of the box? Had he found some reference to it at Herzl's house? The key was there waiting, pointing the way.

'And that man,' Maximoff continued, jabbing a finger at Leroux, 'is a wanted criminal under sentence of death. He has nothing to do with our negotiations and must surrender to the authorities.'

'He is one of us,' Armen said.

Leroux hobbled to Armen leaning on his cane. 'Trust me,' he said under his breath and handed Armen his gun. 'It's not worth jeopardising these negotiations for one person,' Leroux said aloud. 'I will submit to the Sultan's justice after I have recovered what is mine.'

Leroux gritted his teeth and ran past the counters. Maximoff bellowed. Leroux launched himself down the steps and into the vault. Maximoff's boots pounded behind him. Leroux reached Herzl's deposit box and turned as Maximoff filled the entrance to the vault and assessed the situation. No other exits, he had Leroux cornered. A key protruding from the deposit box next to Leroux. Triumph glittered in his eyes as the others crowded behind him, bewildered. Eva's hands clutched at her breast, her eyes like a startled deer, her mouth trying to form words.

Maximoff snarled at Leroux and edged towards him, the key dangling, tantalisingly close. Leroux limped away, keeping his distance, his cane raised, pitifully slender against a heavy sword. Maximoff tested the key and slid the box open as Leroux fumbled out his matches, backed away

314

towards the bullion cage and lit one. Maximoff glanced up from the box and then pulled it all the way out, tipping it over, letting it clatter to the floor, empty.

'A murderer and a thief! You falsely accused me. Now you have stolen from me. You shall have my justice.'

Leroux pulled out the folded sheet of weighty Bank Ottoman notepaper. 'Looking for this?'

'Give it to me!'

Leroux set the match to it.

Maximoff roared, and his long blade rasped out of its scabbard. An intricate engraving of a running wolf stretched down the weapon, glinting under the electric lights. A guttural keening startled him. Eva convulsed, her face ashen, pointing at the Russian, her gaze fixed on the blade. She was saying something, speaking, but Leroux only understood the horror in her voice.

Maximoff hesitated, glancing at the captain and the Ambassador and then brought his sword back over his head and lunged at Leroux. The weapon swept down. Leroux dropped the paper through the bars of the cage and dived forward, to get inside the arc of the blade, swiping his cane at Maximoff's wrist. They met in the middle. Maximoff's arm was deflected just enough to crash down on Leroux's back, the tip of the blade sparking on the vault floor. Maximoff's sheer bulk drove Leroux back against the bullion cage. Maximoff snarled in his face, huge fingers digging into his windpipe. The paper burned, almost half gone now. What had Eva said? She recognised Maximoff. Had she seen him at the pass that night? Leroux managed to get a hand under Maximoff's chin and pushed back. No, Eva's reaction was too visceral. Had Maximoff been at the village during the massacre? Had he been involved? Maximoff snarled and slammed his knee into Leroux's groin. Maximoff's grip tightened on his throat, but he was looking down into the cage, his foot reaching through the cage to try and reach the paper. Leroux wrenched his head around. What was Eva saying? Armen passed his gun to the captain. Was the massacre part of Maximoff's plan to whip up the fury of the Armenians as well as to tarnish the Sultan? Maximoff foot scraped and stamped on the floor, the paper burned, curling, blackening, almost gone. Nobody else moved, watching in stunned silence. Maximoff twisted his sword hand free and clubbed the hilt into Leroux's temple. His head smashed against the cage, the captain's face blurring as Leroux's strength ebbed, his throat surrendering. Maximoff drew his blade back. Leroux's vision dimmed. Click. The hammer of a pistol cocked.

'Stop!' the captain shouted. Maximoff's fingers released. Leroux's senses flooded back. Armen was there too, Eva clutching his arm, shaking with terror. Maximoff twisted, panting, his sword hanging in the air.

'The Englishman is to face the Sultan's justice,' the captain said. The last wisps of smoke rose from the bullion cage. Leroux put a hand to his heart and the agreement under his jacket. Who was to say what had been burnt? Maximoff's sword slammed into its scabbard, a primal fear in his eyes like a cornered wolf. Whatever Eva had said, Maximoff understood. However lowly a witness she was, his cover was beginning to unravel.

Leroux slid down the bars, woozy from the blow but seeing clearly for the first time. That was why Maximoff was so concerned about Leroux's trip to Armenia. He feared that Leroux might discover Maximoff's connection to the village, that he was involved in the massacre. Maybe even uncover the purpose of the massacre, to infuriate the Armenians, to help overthrow the Sultan and fulfill the Tsar's dream. Had Maximoff heard from Nevlinski that the British Government had an interest in prophecies as well as the Armenian situation. Was he worried that British Intelligence knew about his plans and lured Leroux to Theodora's?

'Why are you protecting this criminal?' Maximoff demanded.

'The revolutionaries have accepted the terms,' the captain said, 'and there will be no more bloodshed. Leroux is my prisoner as you demanded.'

Maximoff turned to the bullion cage and the charred scraps of paper resting on the gold. As far as the world was concerned the contents of the deposit box had gone up in smoke, but his demeanour was one of grim determination, not defeat. One small part of his plot was in ashes, but as every commander knew, no plan survived contact with the enemy.

'I must inform my embassy of this development at once.' The Russian glared at Leroux and stalked out of the bank without a backward glance. Why did no one stop him? There was no time to lose.

'Armen told me,' Captain Emre said.

'About the girl?'

'Yes. She witnessed the massacre. Seeing Maximoff draw the sword unblocked her memory, bringing everything back, including her voice.

Leroux took Herzl's agreement from his jacket and showed it to the captain. 'This is what Maximoff was looking for. It purports to be an agreement between Theodor Herzl and the Sultan for Jewish settlement in Palestine.'

'This cannot be true! Jerusalem is sacred!'

'Herzl will confirm that this is the agreement that was kept in that box, the agreement that Maximoff risked his life to get.'

'The Sultan would never agree to this …' the captain stammered, inspecting the seal.

'I don't think he did. I think the Grand Vizier was tricked by Maximoff.'

The captain looked over his shoulder. The Grand Vizier had left. 'Why?'

'I believe the Grand Vizier and Zeki Pasha support the Young Ottomans and were looking for an opportunity to overthrow the Sultan. They thought Maximoff was on their side and that Russia would back the new regime. They both hope the Sultan will be fatally weakened by the blame for the massacre and for making this agreement. But Maximoff intends to move first, on his own. Russia is about to invade.'

The captain's eyes widened in alarm, and he concealed the agreement in his tunic. 'In the mountains and in Erzurum… this is what Maximoff was trying to conceal?'

Leroux nodded. 'He thought I would discover his plans.'

'You truly believe the Tsar's forces intend to attack?'

'Any moment. Everything points towards it. Ambassador Currie said that the London papers will lead with reports of the massacre tomorrow, blaming the Sultan. The Prime Minister will not be able to stand up for you then. The Armenians may rise any moment in the East unless Armen can get word to them about the success of these negotiations. The Tsar will use that as the pretext to invade. At least he will not be able to undermine the Sultan with that agreement.'

The captain summoned an aide, instructing him to send news of the negotiations by telegraph to the eastern provinces. Bank workers filed down from the dining room, shirts untucked, sweat stained, holding one another, some crying, some praising God. Leroux turned to a commotion at the barricade as Simpkins arrived in a fluster, waving a telegram.

'Ambassador!'

Currie straightened from signing the copies of Armenian proposals. 'What is it?'

'The late edition of the Times is running with a story. Not just that the Sultan was responsible, but the British Government has known for weeks and covered it up to try to protect the Sultan.' Simpkins put his hands on his knees, recovering his breath.

'We have the evidence to refute it,' Leroux said. 'Eva, here, witnessed the massacre. She can tell you Maximoff was there. The Times is being used. Olga de Novikoff is planting the story. Maximoff instigated the massacre to incite a rebellion and discredit the Sultan. He followed me to Armenia because he suspected I knew his plans. Then he stole my report and had me imprisoned so that I couldn't send it. Now he has made it look like we were covering it up.'

'Leroux is right,' the captain said. 'Maximoff fooled me too.'

'And, so it seems, me,' Currie said, reading the telegram while loosening his wing collar. He dropped the telegram onto the desk and ran a hand though his hair. 'Simpkins send this message to the editor at The Times immediately, copied to Salisbury and Beaumont. Matter of state

319

security. Olga de Novikoff planting false information to discredit the Sultan. The Sultan not responsible for the massacre. Recall the last edition. Agreement reached with Sultan and Armenians over protections. Ambassador Currie.'

Simpkins's pen stopped scratching. 'Another for Salisbury, sir?'

'Yes. Explain Maximoff's plan. Suggest he summons the Russian Ambassador at once.'

Armen approached Simpkins with a hand-written message. 'Send this to the Bishop at Erzurum. It must get to him as soon as possible. He will be able to contact the revolutionaries and tell them of our negotiations. There is now no reason for them to rebel, and God-willing, they will find out in time.'

Captain Emre joined them. 'Inshallah, we will be in time.'

Simpkins ran past the soldiers that lined the street, tired and confused faces in the glow of the streetlamps, awaiting orders. The revolutionaries gathered in the hall between the pock marked pillars and smears of blood.

'Where are the rest?' The captain said.

'The rest are dead,' Leroux said.

'If Maximoff had known how few you were, he would have insisted on storming the bank. He was reluctant to negotiate.' The captain gestured at a squad of men who double-timed over. He handed Leroux back his gun. 'You must go with the Armenians. And I will visit the Russian embassy with my men to make sure they understand the situation.'

'There's something in this that I haven't figured out,' Leroux said. 'The woman from the harem. Who helped me to get out of Yildiz?'

'Dangerous to suggest that a member of the royal harem would be loyal to anyone other than the Sultan.' The captain grinned. 'The attack on you by the Hamidiye made no sense. The Sultan knew someone was lying, so he secretly let you escape and had you followed, hoping the real attacker would come after you and expose himself.'

The revolutionaries filed out bearing their arms and Leroux joined them. They lacked the training to march but walked tall, escorted to the harbour by the Sultan's soldiers to board Sir Edgar Vincent's steamship, Gulnare.

Leroux had hardly slept. The oily calm of the Bosporus lapped against the gleaming white hull, and he could just pick out the gold lettering of the yacht's name. The rioting in Constantinople had started again at dawn and the politicians did nothing. Armen joined him and watched helpless and betrayed, but a message came from the captain saying the rioting would stop at sunset, after the population had sated their anger.

'Thank you, Leroux,' Armen said, 'We must go now. We will continue our work in exile.'

'Where will you go?'

'Our ship sails for Marseilles. But I fancy New York. And you?'

Leroux shrugged. He had no idea, but it was enough to part as comrades. Armen waved from the yacht's gig as it pushed off with the first party of revolutionaries and rowed to the French warship, La Flèche. They were to be taken to a new life away from the Ottoman Empire. Eva was with her people, under the protective arm of Sarkis. They looked good together, both on the mend.

HMS Dryad rode at anchor, near La Fléche, canvas covers over the muzzles of her guns. A word from the Ambassador and the long barrels would traverse to the palace and put an end to the riots. But no word would come. A deal had been done and the blood price would be paid.

'The Times recalled most of the late edition,' Simpkins said, 'and printed a special late one. "Sultan peace deal with the Armenians. Britain supports," are the headlines. Olga de Novikoff has gone to ground, and Salisbury hauled the Russian Ambassador in. The Black Sea fleet is returning to Sevastopol. He sent a congratulatory message to Currie. Beaumont knows your part in it, but… you understand … feathers need to be smoothed.'

'At least that should keep Currie off my back. Any word on Maximoff?'

Simpkins grimaced and his eyes darted behind Leroux. The Ambassador sidled up.

'I have a delicate matter to discuss,' Currie said, his tone clipped. 'Dragoman Maximoff is demanding your head.'

'Surely he has been arrested?'

Currie stood ramrod straight. 'We have only the word of a young Armenian girl. A peasant and a terrorist to boot. Zeki Pasha and the Grand Vizier deny everything.'

'But…'

'The threat of the invasion has passed.' The Ambassador smoothed his hair. 'The Sultan must keep his friends close, and his enemies closer. You will leave on the next boat.' He excused himself to return to Yildiz, saying as he left: 'And remember - you were never here.'

A kayik arrowed towards them, four banks of oars pulling in unison. Sparkling drops of water ran off the dipping blades. The captain and Herzl sat in the stern thwarts chatting animatedly.

'An unlikely couple,' Simpkins said.

The captain helped Herzl onto the gangway and followed him slowly up. Herzl wheezed as he took a seat on the stern deck.

'I wanted to thank you,' Herzl said. 'For your discretion. I understand from the captain that the Sultan would not have agreed to the terms. No one is embarrassed, and perhaps in the future, who knows?'

'Your help in exposing Maximoff's plot will be known when I report back,' Leroux said. 'You have supporters in Britain. Your dream is still alive.'

'I fear I will not see it in my lifetime,' Herzl coughed, rheumy and loose. 'But in my mind's eye, it is a beautiful place.'

Herzl leant back and turned his face to the sun, closing his eyes. The pallour had gone for the moment, perhaps from the exertion of boarding the yacht, and tranquillity settled over his features.

Captain Emre beckoned an aide. 'The Sultan wanted me to express his gratitude.' The aide approached and presented Leroux with his knobkerrie.

'How on earth…?'

'Who did you think took it? The Sultan watches everyone. Even so, the Young Ottomans surprised him. But he has ways to control them.'

The thought of what those might be sent a shudder down Leroux's spine. Captain Emre laughed. 'Not only that! Although it is true that the neck of a servant is but a hair's breadth.'

Leroux tapped his foot against the stanchion, peering down into the murky depths of the harbour. The Armenians would have peace, at least for now. For better or worse the Sultan survived to fight another day. But it was not Leroux's fight, and Leroux still had a score of his own to settle. Captain Emre escorted him down the gangway to the kayik. He stepped into the boat and doffed his slouch hat in farewell. To where he didn't know. He had no forwarding address.

Historical Note

Constantinople

After Nestor Iskander wrote "The Tale on the Taking of Tsargrad" there were ten Russo-Turkish wars between 1568 and 1878, in addition to the Crimean War. Catherine the Great's 'Greek Plan' would have seen her grandson, Constantine, become the first emperor of a restored Byzantium. In 1878, the Royal Navy intervened as Russian forces reached the approaches to Constantinople.

During World War One, a secret exchange of diplomatic correspondence between Great Britain, France, and Russia, known as The Constantinople Agreement, promised to hand Constantinople and the Dardanelles to Russia after the war. However, when the Bolshevik Revolution ended the Russian Empire and the Tsar's life, the British and French did not implement the agreement. Turkey joined NATO in 1952 despite strong Soviet opposition.

Sultan Abdul Hamid II

In his early progressive years, he instituted the Ottoman Empire's first constitution in consultation with the Young Ottoman modernisers, but after disagreements he suspended the Parliament in 1877 and ruled as an autocrat for the next thirty years. He was known in Europe as the 'Red Sultan' or 'Bloody Sultan' for the persecution of Armenians. As the Ottoman Empire slowly disintegrated, swamped in debt, the Sultan resisted Armenian demands for reforms. The 'Hamidian massacres' peaked between 1894 and 1896, with an estimated 300,000 Armenians dying, as the Sultan gave semi-official status to the Kurdish bandits who were already mistreating Armenians in the provinces. There is considerable historical debate about the extent to which the Sultan personally orchestrated the 'Hamidian massacres' or whether they were initiatives of local officials and paramilitaries. What is not a matter of debate is that the 1915-23 Armenian Genocide was far worse.

In 1905 the Armenian Revolutionary Federation attempted to assassinate the Sultan. In 1908 the Young Turks (a subsequent and similar group to the Young Ottomans) forced the Sultan to recall Parliament. When the Sultan attempted a counter-revolution in 1909, he was dethroned and replaced by his half-brother Sultan Mehmed V. Sultan Abdul Hamid II spent the rest of his life in captivity, dying in 1918.

Theodor Herzl

Herzl was an Austro-Hungarian Jewish lawyer, journalist, playwright, and political activist. He wrote Der Judenstaat (The State of the Jews) and founded the Zionist Organisation to promote Jewish immigration to Palestine and form a Jewish State. With introductions provided by Reverend William Hechler and Count Nevlinski, Herzl negotiated with the Grand Vizier in 1896, even receiving the Commander's Cross of the Order of the Medjidie as a public relations affirmation for Herzl and the Jewish world of the seriousness of the negotiations. The Sultan turned down the proposals, but the Zionist Congress committed itself to a homeland in Palestine after rejecting a British offer of land in modern day Kenya in 1903. Herzl never lived to see the founding of a Jewish homeland, dying in 1904 aged only 44, from overwork, stress and pre-existing medical conditions. However, the Israeli declaration of independence was held beneath his portrait, and Herzl is today remembered by a national holiday.

Armen Garo

A leading member of the Armenian Revolutionary Federation for two decades, Garo was one of the masterminds behind the 1896 Ottoman Bank raid, leading it after Papken Siuni was killed. He became very depressed when the Armenian Genocide broke out in 1915 but lived to see Armenian independence 1918 and was elected Ambassador to the United States for the short-lived First Republic of Armenia. His sickness worsened when Armenia lost her independence in 1920, and he died in Geneva in 1923 aged 51.

Zeki Pasha

Zeki Pasha was decorated for his participation in the Sassoun massacre of Armenians in 1894 and was quoted as saying "not finding any rebellion we cleared the country so none should occur in the future." He rose to the rank of Field Marshal and led the Ottoman delegation that signed the Armistice with Russia in 1917.

Nestor Iskander

Author of The Tale on the Taking of Tsargrad in the late 15th century, Iskander claimed to have been captured by the Ottomans in his youth and forced to convert to Islam, before escaping the camp laying siege to Constantinople and then witnessing the city's fall. He was probably a monk who ingratiated himself to the Tsar with the prophecy that Constantinople would be retaken, and that the Tsar would be the one true king.

Reverend William Hechler

Born in Benares, India to a German father, Hechler became an Anglican clergyman. Wounded and decorated in the Franco-Prussian war, he later became a tutor to the children of the Grand Duke of Baden. During this time, he became acquainted with the young Kaiser Wilhelm II. In 1884 Hechler wrote his own treatise, "The Restoration of the Jews to Palestine." He called for the Jews to return to Palestine as a precondition for the return of Jesus. He later became chaplain to the British embassy in Vienna and first met Theodor Herzl in March 1896. He used his connections to support Herzl, notably arranging a brief meeting with the Kaiser in Palestine in 1898, the first public recognition of Herzl as the leader of the Zionist movement by a major European power.

Madame Olga de Novikoff

Olga de Novikoff (1838-1903) was a Russian socialite and propagandist. In dozens of letters to Prime Minister Gladstone in the 1870s she nurtured Gladstone's disgust at the Ottoman Empire and encouraged him to doubt rumours of Russian atrocities in Central Asia. She was a Pan-Slavist (promoting the unification of the Slavic peoples) and earned the soubriquet of 'M.P. for Russia' from Disraeli, such was her role in spreading pro-Russian views across the British elite.

Dragoman Maximoff

Little is known about Maximoff, the senior Russian diplomat in Constantinople at the time. Armen Garo's memoir 'Bank Ottoman' relates that Maximoff convinced the Sultan not to bombard the Ottoman Bank to prevent the landing of European sailors. Maximoff then persuaded Garo to leave the bank, having promised that he would deliver a letter the next day signed by all the Ambassadors guaranteeing the safety of Armenians in the city and the implementation of reforms for the protection of Armenians across the Ottoman Empire within six months. The rioting did not stop, and the letter never came.

Count Philipp Michael Nevlinski

The Count was a mysterious figure, an impoverished aristocrat from Poland, then part of Russia. He worked as a journalist and for the Austro-Hungarian embassy in Constantinople. He became an advisor to Theodor Herzl and helped his negotiations with the Sultan. He died in 1899 after returning from another visit to Constantinople on Herzl's behalf.

Flora Shaw

A highly regarded and influential journalist, she was the Colonial Editor for the Times, the highest paid woman journalist at the time. She was required to testify before The House of Commons Select Committee investigating the Jameson Raid as she had frequent correspondence with the main protagonists Cecil Rhodes, Leander Starr Jameson, and the Colonial Secretary Joseph Chamberlain. She was exonerated on all charges and became Lady Lugard.

ACKNOWLEDGMENTS

The Iskander Prophecy is a work of fiction weaved into the historical events surrounding the Hamidian massacres and the raid on the Ottoman Bank. I owe thanks to the London Library, for their wonderful resources, the Wilbur & Niso Smith Foundation for their generous prize of a year's membership of the London Library, and to Henry Buxton for proofreading the draft manuscript. And most of all, to my family and friends for all their help and support.

Printed in Great Britain
by Amazon

38432954R00189